I0628434

MILKING A STONE

by Michael Owens

This is a work of fiction. All characters, organizations, and events portrayed in this novel are either products of the author's imagination or are used fictitiously.

Copyright © 2020 by Michael Owens

All rights reserved. No part of this publication may be reproduced in whole or in part, or stored in a retrieval system, or transmitted in any form or by any means, electronic, mechanical, photocopying, recording, or otherwise, without written permission of the author, except for the inclusion of brief quotations in a review.

For information regarding permission, please write to:
info@barringerpublishing.com
Barringer Publishing, Naples, Florida
www.barringerpublishing.com

Cover, graphics, and layout by Linda S. Duider
Cape Coral, Florida

ISBN: 978-1-7352525-4-4
Library of Congress Cataloging-in-Publication
Data *Milking A Stone* / Michael Owens

Printed in U.S.A.

To my wife, Helena,
  And our children,
    Cecilia and Alexandra

"Only those who travel shall see the obscure roads which guide them."

—Unknown

"The heroes of finance are like pearls on a string—
when one falls off,
the rest follow."

—Henrik Ibsen

PREFACE

This book is a novel. The story is based on actual events and facts from sources deemed to be reliable. It is a mixture of reality, fiction, and truthful facts. Non-existent individuals have been fabricated who are a mixture of several people involved in the story. Actual events have been relocated in time and location for the benefit of the reader but are nonetheless truthful in fact. The author's intent is that nothing described in this book shall be knowingly false or misleading. It shall be truthful in its content and historical depiction. Several individuals are fabricated, as well as their respective characteristics. Names of living individuals who may recognize themselves or events in which they were involved have been altered for discretion unless facts were public at the time.

PART ONE

Disaster Strikes

MICHAEL OWENS

CHAPTER ONE

Boca Raton, FL · June 1985

Charlie was as usual the last person to arrive at the office this hot, Monday morning. The short walk from the white bungalow-style house to his white Cadillac had made him sticky. His irritation grew as he pulled into the semicircle at the front doors of his company and saw a Lincoln parked in the no parking zone. That was Charlie's space, and it was now occupied.

He had long ago abandoned the thought of simply having his own sign marked *President* due to the annoying circumstance that mail delivery vans and other less disciplined individuals often conveniently blocked the entrance in spite of signs. The space even had a white cross painted on it, to no avail. It was just in front of the entrance and everybody wanted to park there. He was used to this problem and could take it in stride, but having it taken by *that* car on this morning would surely mean a difficult day.

It was already hot, and Charlie wore his customary white, short-sleeved shirt without tie (unlike the *bean counters* who couldn't seem to function without one) and light grey, cotton pants, with customary black loafers. On this particular morning, he had a seventy-two hour, reddish-grey shade of a beard, having spent most of the weekend trolling off his *Merlin* boat and therefore had mental tranquility sufficient to skip the procedure of shaving. He swung around past the entrance and made his way from the guest parking area nearby to the shade beyond the smoked-glass doors marking the entrance.

From somewhere past the doors, the ordinarily friendly voice of the receptionist was heard in a state of animation speaking on the phone with someone obviously well known. Her name was Gail. She had married at twenty-five to a crab fisherman and moved with him to Nome, Alaska. The untold story: relocating to permafrost in an eternally dark wintertime may have contributed to her appearing back in Florida some twelve months thereafter, unmarried. She had been working as a receptionist for about one year and was well-liked by both Charlie and staff for her integrity and jolly manner. Animation in her was rare unless someone chided her about sensitive matters like environmental or racial issues. In all likelihood, the crab fisherman was on the other end of the line and was put on hold when she spotted Charlie. She gave her Monday morning welcome smile and said, "good morning," followed immediately by a strained "two gentlemen are waiting for you." Charlie expected as much.

Laurel and Hardy, he had said to himself when he spotted their car outside. Hardy was big even when seated in a Lincoln and typically indulged in eating breakfast, in the car, en route to one of *VenCap's* affiliates. During a trip to the bank in May, Hardy had picked up Charlie at the office and proceeded to *Arby's* where he had ordered a ham and turkey sandwich, extra mustard, two donuts, and coffee. Charlie had settled for coffee.

Laurel was Hardy's opposite—tall, skinny, and always well-dressed. Laurel was never to be trusted. In fact, he was a walking disaster. Not dangerous physically—just vicious in every other sense. He had his own agenda, which rarely was made public. Charlie hated him. Both were around forty, some ten years junior to Charlie. Charlie had been around long enough to stay balanced when necessary, and very few situations could ruffle him. Banks, and these two visitors, however, could.

"I know—I saw their car."

"They are waiting in your office."

Gail could tell by looking at Charlie that this was a bad morning. He had not said his usual *good morning* to her, and she knew to proceed with caution when Charlie's lips narrowed, as they now did.

"I gave them coffee."

"Thanks Gail," he said, and walked past the reception to the left by the mail counter where he picked up his brown manila folder marked *President*, took another left turn and entered his personal suite.

The suite had three rooms: a small lobby where visitors could wait to be admitted, a large office with wooden paneling all around with large smoke colored windows overlooking the delivery parking lot and further out Main street, and a small conference room adjoining the office. The conference room also had a separate entrance, so visitors could enter without disturbing Charlie.

Laurel and Hardy were in fact named Jay and Gary, and were waiting in Charlie's office, comfortably seated in his guest sofa. Charlie despised the fact that these two vultures always insisted on entering his office unannounced, and, even worse, entered his office unbeknownst to him. It was in Charlie's mind a deliberate method to spite him.

"We have waited for half an hour," Gary blurted.

"Good morning to you too" said Charlie and continued: "If you had announced your visit you probably wouldn't have had to wait at all. By the way, use the visitor's parking from now on—parking in front of the entrance is forbidden."

"We're not staying all day," said Jay.

The problems with Laurel and Hardy had begun about the same time, two years earlier. Charlie had then been in the automobile business nearly two decades and had "Long Cadillac" dealerships all the way up to Pensacola. His desire to buy three large dealerships, one in Fort Lauderdale and two in Miami, prompted him to discuss financing with a venture capital company, after being advised to do so by his bank. For many years, his bank had found financing difficult. It was what they referred to as *rapid expansion,* since banks were going bankrupt in Texas, due to declining oil production and declining real estate prices. This, in turn, was due to the population flight caused by lower oil production. To Charlie, this was simply the whitewashing of a situation where the bank was unwilling to play ball. The situation in Florida was quite the reverse—people were moving in and prices were going up—not down. Charlie had pondered on this issue and had concluded that commercial bankers could turn on you at any time, regardless of past performance.

He thought to himself: *it's just a matter of how the wind blows— they're just in it for the money, siphoning your assets in good times and even more so in bad times, and you as client are like a fallen leaf in the wind—it just depends on where it happens to be blowing.*

Charlie didn't know much about automobiles. He was having lunch at a diner in Boca Raton, in 1964, having just returned from Australia to the U.S.A. with a slight but distinctive Australian accent, and was by chance asked by a car dealer at the counter if he had any selling capabilities.

"I can sell sand to the Bedouins in the Sahara Desert, Mate" was his response, and was hired on the spot as car salesman for Ford of Boca Raton, Florida. His timing could not have been better. Lee Iacocca was head of Ford Motor Company and had forced through a daring decision—to make an affordable, sporty vehicle named

Mustang. It was introduced just as Charlie entered the automobile business and it was to be one of Ford's greatest success stories, and at the same time a kick start for Charles Long Jr.'s career. He was perfect for the job: mid-thirties, foreign accent, tall, light red hair, somewhat square features, with a build that lacked any ounce of fat. The weather called for Hawaii-style shirts, sunglasses, combined with the not-so-great difficulty of selling light blue Ford Mustang Convertibles. This made for a pleasant period in Charlie's life. He was dramatically contributing to the success of Ford in Boca Raton.

One morning when on his way to show a Mustang for a presumptive buyer, a lady stopped him in the street with a big smile meant to say: *here I am—look at me!*

She had blond, almost white short hair, was probably Charlie's age, and lived at the bottom of the only little hill in Boca Raton. She told Charlie that her ten-year-old son, Scott, had pestered her about buying a car just like the one Charlie was sitting in. Her name was Muriel, and Charlie being a professional, introduced himself as the Ford salesman he was and offered her a ride. The situation was picture perfect: Charlie in his wildly colored shirt and sunglasses, a cute blonde by his side, top down, and the Beach Boys on the Mustang's built-in radio.

Approximately fifteen minutes later, Charlie had sold an identical vehicle to Muriel—even the same light blue paint job. Charlie's natural talent for selling, combined with being a little exotic, made him a successful salesman and he loved it. He was selling something that almost sold itself, and he liked the attention that it gave him, not to mention the element of showing off to housewives.

Charlie's popularity had unavoidably been noticed by the sales manager, who openly displayed his resentment of the brash newcomer, whom he feared may someday replace him. He had the attributes of a sourpuss, intolerance formed by years of effortless selling, along with arrogance probably inherited from his parents—chewing gum and all. He was probably ten years older than Charlie and was never seen with any friends.

One evening as Charlie was locking the rear entrance to the service shop, the sales manager and two unfamiliar less-than-friendly goon types jumped out from a big Ford LTD.

"Get in" said one of them.

Charlie tried to run back into the shop but to no avail. They grabbed him by his arms and placed him in the middle in the back seat. "What is all this about, then?" said Charlie. No reply. The sales manager drove out of town a short distance before stopping on the dirt road by a swampy area. They scrambled out of the car.

The sales manager said, "You don't belong here. I'll give you the chance to leave, but if you don't, we'll be back for you and next time you won't get off easy." Charlie had spent years of hustling cattle at Hammond Station, as well as tossing sheep for shearing and swam like a Seal after years of diving off the Great Barrier Reef near Cairns. He was more fit that the three rednecks put together, even if that thought never entered his mind. The motor was still running. Charlie was overcome by rage, and never planned his course of action. What happened next could be read on the first page in the following day's *Boca Daily News*:

Kidnapping ended in near death for assailant

Mr. Charles Long Jr. was abducted from the facilities of his employment by three assailants yesterday evening at 6:15 p.m. Having forcefully brought Mr. Long to the outskirts of town, the assailants claim to have had their vehicle stolen by Mr. Long, after the ensuing roadside brawl. According to Mr. Long, he acted without thinking in rage under threat, in self-defense. He described bending into the groin of the driver, tossing him over his back onto the other assailants, jumping into the vehicle, and gunning it for a safe getaway. What happened next is based on the assailant's statements. During the commotion, there was a slight splash behind the trio, who were getting up as the car sprayed gravel onto them. This disguised what apparently was a sizeable alligator, which clamped down on one assailant's leg. Shocked and stunned by the event, the remaining two picked up some branches and started pounding on the gator, which then let go of the leg and slid back into the water. The leg was badly injured, and life was saved by tying belts around the upper parts of it to stop the blood loss. The trio were picked up by a passing truck and rushed to the county hospital. Police soon made arrests as physicians reported the injuries and Police put the incident in connection with Mr. Long's report.

Charlie was in no mood to return to Ford after the incident. Despite pleas from the branch manager, Charlie resigned without having a new job offer, and left Boca Ford the following day, with excellent recommendations.

Charlie was the talk of the town. His picture had been on the front page in the Boca Daily News and the *man from the outback*, as he was called, was a hero. Some said it was too bad that the gator didn't finish the job. Well-known as he was, he paid a visit to Boca Cadillac and asked the owner if there might be a position for him, after explaining that Ford at that point gave him some discomfort, having been abducted and all. They knew very well about Charlie and were indeed interested. But Cadillac was a prestige brand and that would require experience from the service department selling spare parts, where there just might be an opening available to him.

"Then I'll go somewhere else" was Charlie's response. He was then offered the position of assistant sales manager, which he promptly accepted. Their sales manager was in his early fifties, and very much different from Charlie. He had an unnatural, aloof way of dealing with people, as if he were an old schoolteacher and the potential customer a grade school pupil. Then, in closing a transaction, he would suck up to the client in every imaginable way, particularly the wives. It was just a short while before customers asked for Charlie, having been recommended by happy clients, and he was soon bumped up to first assistant sales manager—which he could live with.

Boca Cadillac was one of some two dozen independent dealerships in Florida at the time. The owner was in his early sixties and as he liked Charlie, he had confided in him plans to sell his dealership and to sail around the world, or at least, sail the Caribbean. Charlie was still a partner in the sponge factory near Cairns along with the Danish owner, who could neither read nor write and his longtime friend Ritch from California, as he enjoyed annual dividend distributions from the factory. He let the owner know that he would be interested if the price was affordable. The owner came from Louisiana and was named Bob Cloutier. Charlie had explained that his name, Long, was short for Longchamps and that his ancestry was also southern. That together with Charlie's history appealed to Mr. Cloutier, and a deal was consummated by a handshake. Thereafter, the price and financing arrangements were negotiated. A fair price, which included the large property which housed the dealership along the northern section of Boca on Dixie Highway would be four hundred twenty thousand dollars, which was an exceptionally large sum indeed. For comparison, it was nearly identical to the sum paid in foreign aid to Pakistan the same year by USAID, in Washington.

Charlie would cough up one third, and Mr. Cloutier would provide a loan for one third, provided Charlie financed the balance through a loan agreement with the bank. The dividends from the sponge factory amounted to ten thousand dollars annually, which was sufficient to cover the interest to the bank, and FSB (First State Bank) agreed to finance one third for a mortgage on the property.

The contract was drawn up by the attorney at the bank, signed by the Notary Public (another bank employee) on June 30, 1967. Charlie's savings were gone, and he was the owner of an automobile dealership.

The migration into Florida was increasing as the economic boom continued during the 1960's, and Boca Cadillac was successfully increasing its market share. The property itself was rapidly increasing in value. This provided Charlie with the basis for buying several dealerships by mortgaging his property and paying relatively low interest. He renamed the company to the more appropriate *Long Cadillac*. Charlie was an entrepreneur at heart. His natural talents led him to see opportunities where others might not. Commerce was as natural to him as breathing. His pleasant smile and positive attitude also contributed to his success.

The value of his various properties kept increasing, and he kept buying dealerships all over Florida. His reasoning was that this would continue, and he would keep adding properties and dealerships as long as the wind kept blowing in a favorable direction. At the time his bank advised him to talk to a venture capital outfit, for the financing of further expansion, he owned a majority of the Cadillac dealerships in Florida. They added up to twenty-one, and he was Mr. Cadillac in the State.

A *venture capital company's* objective is to invest in other companies to make money—thus the name *venture*. They may provide managerial expertise, and seek to enrich the business, meaning generally the target company's shareholders and affiliations, and specifically, the shareholders of the venture capital company. Their role may be beneficial for all concerned but can also develop into an adventure, as they invest their own as well as other investors money, in known companies. The thought comes to mind that the term itself is short for *Adventure Capital*. Charlie knew next to nothing about such companies, and in all fairness, they were generally unknown to the general public in the early 1980s.

Banks liked the notion of sharing risks with others. It would appear to the layman as a desire among bankers to be acknowledged by a third party—to have someone else make the same decision would justify their own. Long Cadillac was a large operation, and profitable. It was family run, and FSB had advised Charlie to put third party representation on the Board of Directors. This, thought Charlie, would contribute less to his business and more to the pockets of such persons, supposedly to be plucked from the ranks of the Bank.

Charlie was neither opposed to venture capitalists, or for them, knowing what little he did about such companies. The only known company was *KKR*, a constellation of investors named Kohlberg, Kravis and Roberts, whose interest they may tempt only after they owned all other existing companies.

Yet, there were others, lesser players as one could say, and FSB cooperated with several. Their cooperation could be direct, or via the large, investment banks like Merrill Lynch. These would then cooperate (swap clients) informally with the smaller venture capitalists to obtain target companies as the clients were called. These could be financed for a portion of their shares, and a corresponding seat on the board was par for the course. Charlie agreed to meet with representatives of VenCap at the bank.

Typical of such meetings, the target company was never made aware of the goals of VenCap, nor any other aspect of what was going to be suggested. Things were tossed about in favorable terms, and just like selling an automobile, the sales rep spoke well of his proposal. Surely Long Cadillac would like to expand, and along with the clout of robust partners, the sky was the limit.

The trick for the bank was, of course to, disguise their own ambition into something desirable for Charlie and Long Cadillac, in that order. In the mind of any banker or other employee of an obscure entity, the person running another company always sits on a flood of money. Envy is inherent. For that reason, they believe that the ultimate goal of the head of a target company is to have *more* money. Bank goals, envy, greed and a little persuasion tossed in was made in the proposal by FSB along with VenCap to Charlie: In his best personal interests, capital ought to be generated by divesting the properties. This could be done by a fad procedure called 'sale and lease back,' in which Long Cadillac would sell all properties to VenCap and enter into a lease agreement lasting forever. Charlie instinctively rejected the idea. The increase in values were the main reason he had been able to finance the expansion so far. Letting future increases pass on to VenCap was nothing less than stupid, Charlie had told them in more diplomatic phrasing.

The rejection had called for plan B. To provide financing, FSB proposed to sell a portion of Long Cadillac shares (by way of emitting new shares) to VenCap, which would provide capital to pay off loans and to expand the business. Thus, Charlie would not only reduce risks, he would benefit from dividends which would be available to all shareholders. As an added bonus, he would have access to new board members, which in all probability would be beneficial for the company and ultimately for himself. This proposal struck a chord. It was, after all, the dividends paid by Aussie Sponges that had enabled Charlie to buy Boca Cadillac to begin with, and it seemed logical to agree to the financing arrangement proposed by his long-time banker and the smiling cobra representing VenCap. Charlie accepted the offer.

The end result was that the share capital grew, and everybody was happy. For a while. Charlie's good faith along with sloppy representation by his attorney would prove otherwise. Charlie had placed reliance on his attorney rather than to scrutinize the agreement. As he was a businessman, he naturally highlighted the sections regarding costs, i.e. banker's fees, rather than considering any long-term effects the agreement may have on Long Cadillac, or ultimately, himself.

One paragraph stipulated:

Of net income, fifty percent shall be distributed within three months subsequent to fiscal year end to VenCap.

His only concern with this particular phrase was that he too would benefit from dividends, made possible by the capital injection, after emitting the new shares.

Another paragraph:

Capital injected shall solely be used for investments in expansion, whatever that meant.

VenCap abided by the agreement to the letter. It was their money, or so they reasoned, ant they wanted it back. Fast. Any company dishing out profits realized will run out of cash, without adding by borrowing or otherwise. The strain becomes even worse if the company is growing, as it will then be financing customers by increasing receivables, building up inventory to produce more product, and so on.

The net effect these measures had on Long Cadillac were harshly noted within two years after the share emission and corresponding cash injection, resulting in VenCap owning fifty-one percent of the stock. Long Cadillac operated five more distributorships, cash dividends had stripped the remaining cash available, and the company was in a tighter spot than it had been before Charlie ever heard of VenCap.

Laurel and Hardy were now comfortably seated in Charlie's guest sofa.

"You have a situation here that needs fixing," said Jay.

"A predicament brought upon us by your stupid agreement and sorry board representation," Charlie shot back. Charlie was always very much inclined to skip all small talk, and when pushed had a sharp tongue.

"It can be solved," continued Jay, "by the following: You need capital:" was all he managed to say before Charlie cut him off . . .

"*We* need capital," he said.

"Correct," said Jay, "and that is just what we propose to furnish," Jay mildly continued.

"Something tells me I'm not going to like it," Charlie replied as his lips grew tight.

"Here's what we'll do," said Jay.

His colleague was searching the room noticed Charlie glancing over his way, *probably expecting something to eat*. Jay continued: "we will buy your shares at a reasonable price." Charlie couldn't believe his own ears, thinking that they must be playing tricks on him as he was becoming increasingly irritated by these lollipop gophers.

"Excuse me?" Charlie hissed.

"You remain president, and can keep nine percent of voting stock, and all cash problems are solved" was the sweetener tossed in by Jay.

Whatever mental state Charlie was in when he drove to work was now long gone. He spoke sharply without raising his voice:

"I let you through the door because of trust. This is my reward—you plan a takeover. Well, it's not gonna happen, Mate. Now, please leave."

Gary finally managed to say something remotely intelligent: "We expect your answer by the end of the week."

Charlie beeped Gail to show the gentlemen out. No farewells were exchanged. It was over in just a matter of minutes, but Charlie felt drained. It took however only seconds before he cleared his mind of the conversation just concluded and he reached for the phone. The first action point was to reach his attorney to see what could be done about the agreement, if anything. He was in court and would be gone for the day. Charlie then had the unpleasant sensation of being caught in a bind. In situations like this, he was his best. He once more beeped Gail, now for some coffee, something he rarely asked others to bring to him. She was a keen observer, and said upon entering his office, brew in hand:

"Forget your shave this morning?" That brought out his first smile of the day since getting into his car.

"Left it on purpose to show off my beautiful weekend" came the somewhat lame reply.

Charlie liked Gail and he appreciated her company. For those reasons, and her integrity, he often told her a little more than he ought to he realized, but it did help to let out some steam.

"Try to get hold of Bob Haskins for me, please," he continued. "Pronto!"

Gail gave him a smile and simply said: "Sure!"

A few minutes later the beeper buzzed, and Charlie was informed that Mr. Haskins was in a meeting and couldn't be disturbed. Gail had Mr. Haskin's secretary on hold, and Charlie could speak to her if he wanted to.

"Put me through" he said politely.

"Nora, this is Charlie."

"Good morning" said Mrs. Stevens.

"I need to talk to Bob, and I hear he's in a meeting."

"Yes, he has company and does not wish to be disturbed," said Nora.

"Nora, this is urgent, I really need to speak to him."

He had known both Nora Stevens and her boss, Mr. Haskins, for over a decade, and they were on a first name basis—at least he was with her.

He continued:

"Mrs. Stevens, put me through to Bob or I'm coming over there myself!"

She heard the urgency in Charlie's tone of voice and replied calmly: "Charlie, Jay and Gary are here along with Mr. McKinley."

Charlie was dumbfounded. What in the world were they doing together, with Jim McKinley—Charlie's first acquaintance in Boca Raton and very close friend, as well as customer. James McKinley owned a sizeable company that operated pneumatic drilling equipment and serviced installations for frost protection of Orange groves in Florida and California. His largest client was Apache Corporation of Minneapolis, which owned large Orange plantations and had hundreds of oil wells in California. Charlie knew very well that Jim was not doing business with Bob Haskins of FSB.

"Nora, I know all of them, so please put me through," he said.

"Haskins" said Bob on the other end of the line.

"Good morning to you too," said Charlie. "I realize that you are in a meeting, but I have to get your opinion on something."

"Such as?"

"Our financing needs."

"That is a delicate situation, as you well know."

Bob Haskins was President of FSB, and Charlie could sense the strain in his voice. Mr. Haskins continued after a brief pause: "... in light of the amortization plan, we are at this time unable to extend further credit" was what Charlie heard the emotionless voice say.

By this time, Charlie had put two and two together. In all probability, VenCap was closing a deal with Haskins and McKinley & Co. It was more than likely that VenCap had pressured Bob Haskins to squeeze credit extended to Long Cadillac so they could take over the company—Haskins reward being the sizeable new client named McKinley.

"Bob, we have cooperated for twenty years and we've never missed our amortizations. Is this really the best you can do?" said Charlie with irritation.

"The Board of the Bank have specifically ordered us to reduce risks and that applies to Long Cadillac" came a monotone reply.

Charlie then knew that all present with Bob knew that Charlie was on the other end of the line.

"And when was I to be informed?"

"Within the next few days."

"Does this have anything to do with your visitors?"

"I don't understand," said Bob.

"Never mind. What do you propose I should do about financing then?" asked Charlie.

"As far as the bank is concerned you can take your loans and ride towards the sunset," was Bob's reply.

It was now clear that VenCap had Bob Haskins in their pocket.

"Bank policy," Bob continued.

He went on to say that Charlie had an agreement with VenCap that he had entered into voluntarily and that the bank was simply abiding to policy.

"Well, you know where you can shove your policy!" Charlie yelled, and hung up.

Charlie's coffee was untouched. He could feel the law of gravity now. Approaching another bank with zero liquidity and a lousy agreement with VenCap was not an option. Selling the properties in a sale-and-lease-back transaction would be time consuming, even if possible. Other options would be to perhaps sue VenCap for the unfair and unreasonable agreement, but that would imply that Long Cadillac was being unwise. Putting up personal assets for the benefit of the company would be unwise for all the reasons considered.

The office was air-conditioned, but Charlie's shirt was glued to his back with sweat. It was obvious that the Bank and VenCap had cooperated from the beginning as the attorney at the bank had drafted the agreement. *Why should I rely on my own attorney if he couldn't foresee the consequences from the agreement—had he even bothered to read it?*

Charlie beeped Gail again and asked her to call Jim Walther, a real estate company in Tampa. Minutes later she beeped Charlie back and said that the Manager was a Mr. Mike Burns, and he was out for lunch. Charlie asked Gail to bring him a Subway sandwich when she came back from lunch, and then he waited for Mike Burn's call. The call came at one thirty.

"How would you like to buy the properties of twenty-six car dealerships all over Florida," was Charlie's question.

"As much as I would like another hole in my head," came the reply.

He indicated that they would be interested in land for building condominiums for migrating *snowbirds*—people who live in Florida from Christmas to April. Charlie thanked Mike and that was that.

Nine percent would make me a sleeping partner. Without me they wouldn't have anything at all, he thought. The untouched Subway was on his desk. Charlie looked at it, threw it into the wastepaper basket, swiveled around in his chair and looked out the smoked glass windows thinking: *How could I? The company is profitable, yet the cash is gone. And it's my fault.*

Selling the distributorships to Cadillac was not an option as their policy is not to own them. *In my next business, I won't have any policies.*

He beeped Gail for a cab. He then placed his keys to the office and car keys on his desk. He picked up the Subway and put it in his trouser pocket where the keys had been moments earlier, rose, and left his office. Passing Gail, he said he would be gone for the rest of the day and unavailable. He promised to call the following day. The next day was June 30, 1985.

PART TWO

The Making of a Person

MICHAEL OWENS

CHAPTER TWO

Corona, CA · 1935

Charles and Anna Long had a son who would be named Charles Long Jr. and called Charlie. The surname was an abbreviated version of Charles' grandfather's name, which was Longchamps, but was shortened by a commander when Fredèrick Longchamps had fought for the southern states during the American Civil War.

Charles father owned a substantial hog farm on a ranch between the Cleveland National Forest and Lake Matthews, just southeast of Los Angeles. Charles' duties at the ranch had been, since boyhood, to shed dung from the enclosures, shovel out the corn mixture the pigs fed on into the ditches, along the fences that surrounded the pigs, and watering. Watering the pigs took the most time. If the pigs became too hot, it led to unnecessary weight loss, which Charles' father was keen to prevent.

The ranch had 5,000 pigs and it took about two hours to walk around it. Charles enjoyed the freedom of the farm with free expanse and free vision as far as the eye could see. The food truck was a 1923 Ford pickup that Charles had been allowed to drive out to the pigs, after school every day.

Those who had the heaviest jobs, moving the pigs back and forth between the stables on muddy grounds, past the feeding ditches and finally up the trucks for their final trip, were mainly Mexicans. They could withstand the heat and were cheap to operate.

Charles was eighteen and he had met Anna two years before. Anna was equally old and was the daughter of an Irishman, in the newspaper business. Her father had a local newspaper called "Whittier Daily News."

Charles was often seen in Whittier in his black Ford pickup and soon Anna was pregnant. Anna's father was a man not to play with and Charles realized that it was probably safest to ask for Anna's hand in marriage, as soon as pregnancy was a fact. Given that Charles' father had a ranch and that Charles had aspirations to become a pilot and to apply to the US Naval Academy, in Annapolis, Maryland, to get his wings there, Charles and Anna got consent for a wedding.

The wedding was in a small parish hall in Whittier pastorate, with few invited. It was a Catholic wedding, and no one ever mentioned anything about pregnancy. Newly married, Charles and Anna moved out to the farm where they were allowed the use of two rooms, in a small adjacent building.

Anna managed the vegetable plantation that belonged to the farm and immediately became a family member for real. Charles learned to handle simple veterinary duties in addition to his other farm work and life was for a time laborious but enjoyable.

Charles had been fascinated by airplanes since he was a little boy. The neighboring farms were sprayed with all kinds of pesticides from the air and Charles could both see and hear the airplanes from a distance.

His application to the Navy had been preceded by three days of physical and mental testing at the "El Toro" air base outside Los Angeles, as well as a written test that lasted for a full day. In addition to his personal data, Anna's father had written an article on hog breeding and therein described in detail the discipline that is involved in handling so many animals and the work effort required by both the owner and the farm staff. Although Anna had refused to allow Charles to apply, he had submitted his application, with his father's total support. Charles' loyalty to his father was greater than to Anna. Charles father was boundlessly proud of his son, whom he adored. Now, it remained only to wait.

Naval flight was really a young phenomenon. Military flight in the United States was originally part of the US Army. Their first plane had been purchased from the Wright Brothers in 1909. The US Navy designed a platform for the "Birmingham" cruiser from which a civilian pilot took off, on November 14, 1910, and received its first three planes, in July 1911. Naval flight was then a fact.

The basic idea of separating flight between the Army and the Navy was that the pilots of the Navy would fly from water and the army from land. This soon proved to be impractical as the Navy had remote land bases, so in 1915, Navy pilots began training to fly planes with wheels instead of pontoons. It was simply so that only the uniforms separated the pilots, and Charles wanted to become a Marine Corps pilot.

In 1922, seventeen new pilots were certified as Marine Corps pilots, nine of whom died in air crashes. You could be recruited as a pilot with a three, four, or five-year contract. During a conversation with an applicant, the general received a question from an applicant as to what the death toll was and received the response of 25%. "Set me up for five years" the applicant had said, "I will be 125% dead when I return."

During the 1920s, the Marines were active against Charlemagne Peralte and his successor Benoit Batraville, in Haiti, and against the constant unease in Nicaragua, where they stayed until December

1932, after which they left the control there to the *Guardia Nacional*.

In 1932, Marine Corps Aviation had one hundred thirty-two pilots. This was the smallest group of all who flew and had the reputation of being the most effective of all, even though, as they themselves put it: "We fly what others have discarded." This attitude attracted both Charles and others to Marine Corps Aviation.

During the depression and the early 1930s, the budget for all branches of aviation was at starvation level. At the time of Charles's application as a pilot, the number of certified Marine Corps pilots was one hundred thirty-eight which would only increase to two hundred twenty-seven at the outbreak of World War II, in 1939. Charles would be one of them.

In December 1933, the role of Marine Corps Aviation had been defined to: ".". . fortify bases for the Navy's operations," as opposed to the previous expedition-like, simple, ready for action gang that would fight "Banana Wars." In the end, they had eliminated the risk of always coming in second and the risk of never being assigned other than guard duty. It was into this small corps of pilots that Charles was adopted, in the fall of 1935, with orders to begin his training as a pilot at the US Naval Academy, in Annapolis, Maryland. He had signed on for five years and was stationed there when Charles Jr. was born on October 4, popularly called "ten-four day" which in pilot language means "understood." Little Charles Jr. grew up on the ranch with mommy, Anna, and Grandpa and Grandma, but daddy, Charles, was only home on weekends once a month, during the first two years of his training as a flight officer.

During this time, Anna showed signs of depression and delusions and became increasingly tired and gaudy. Little Charlie was exuberantly active, and Anna was barely able to meet the boy's needs. During Charles' third year of education in Annapolis, which was the last before he would receive flight training in Pensacola, Florida, Anna became gravely ill and was found dead outside, in the vegetable field.

Charles took it hard but realized that he had no choice but to continue with his education as it was contractual. Grandmother was happy, with Charles Jr. on the farm, and had help from the foreman's wife, Imelda, taking care of him. However, Grandpa could not devote himself entirely to the grandchild.

In the spring of 1938, Charles graduated from the US Naval Academy and threw his white hat in the air along with the forty officers who had been his mates (out of a total of sixty-eight accepted), with the degree of "Second Lieutenant."

After four weeks off, Charles would report to the Naval Air Station, in Pensacola, and he wanted to make up for lost time with little Charles Jr., now almost three years old. They were almost daily at Lake Matthews swimming and it didn't seem like Charles Jr. missed his mother. But, sometimes, he would burst out crying and said "Mommy" suddenly and could be inconsolable for a little while. Charles said that "Mommy is gone my little friend—you have grandma and Imelda."

Four weeks at the farm passed quickly. When it was time to take the train to Florida, it was hard to say goodbye to Charles Jr., as he stood there on the platform between Grandma and Imelda and cried for his father.

Charles spent the three days on the train reading the book *The Guerilla and How to Fight Him*. Pilots' dilemma, if they survive being shot down, is to end up in water or enemy territory and run the risk of being captured. All Marine Corps pilots have gone through "Boot Camp" where they have been trained in close combat and therefore have the possibility of managing one or a few enemies on their own.

Their equipment is a revolver and a bayonet with dark steel so as not to shine and thereby reveal their presence. The book had been recommended as part of the flight training that would take a year. Another factor that the book clarified was how vulnerable the pilots on remote island bases were, or at least could be. They occupied stamp-sized islands and would always be vulnerable to ground attacks and air bombings, which is why ground defense was an important part of a pilot's training.

Although Charles was an officer, the entire group from Annapolis shared a large barrack, with stacked bunkbeds. Pensacola was hotter and more humid than California, but the eternal snoring in the barracks was the worst.

Theory was interspersed with physical training, during the initial period. Physically, it was extremely demanding to jog around the base with packing and lift logs in four-man teams, until you almost fainted.

It took a whole month for the rookies to get up in the air, in the US Navy school airplane. Although the students themselves had only performed exercises on the ground, they were allowed to handle the controls once they were in the air, during the first flight out over the Gulf of Mexico. It soon became clear that Charles had the ability to handle aircraft, and he loved every second of the US Naval Air Station.

Each flight would be documented in report form, after the briefing, by the flight instructor. In this way, mistakes would be documented and eliminated.

As an aviation student, Charles was able to fly in transporters to Los Angeles from the nearby Eglin Air Base when he was on leave and used the opportunity constantly, during the training year. Charles Jr. liked to go with Grandpa and Charles in the pick-up and feed the pigs when he got the opportunity.

In the spring of 1939, Charles, as one of thirty-three officers, got his wings. Charles now had four weeks off, before he would be assigned to serve, and he flew to the farm, with a transport flight from Eglin. The summer of 1939 was the happiest in Charles' life. He knew he was going to fly a lot and he spent all his time on the Ranch with Charles Jr., now almost four years old.

Imelda was like a mother to little Charles Jr. and the boy enjoyed his grandparents in the yard. For the first time, Charles took little Charlie to the coast where they stayed at a small motel, in Santa Monica. Every day, they swam in the calm water with their fine swells and kicked a ball on the beach. Charles Jr. went to the cinema for the first time in Santa Monica. It was a matinee with a cartoon that came two years earlier—*Snow White and the Seven Dwarfs*, and Charles Jr. did not leave until they had seen the movie again. He didn't talk about anything else when they got back to the Ranch and Grandpa promised they would see it again soon.

The weeks went by quickly. A telegram arrived at the ranch from Naval Air Station, San Diego, addressed to Charles. Marine Corps Aviation had its operations designated, in January of that year to: "The naval aircraft shall be equipped, organized and trained primarily in support of the Fleet Marine Force, in landing operations and support of troop activities in the field; and secondary, as replacement squadrons for aircraft carrier-based naval aircraft." It was the latter that Charles had hoped for in his own duty. His heart began to beat faster when he read "San Diego" because it was the largest naval base in the United States and there was the chance for ship service, or at least Charles thought so.

On July 1, Charles would report for service in San Diego. That was the content of the telegram. It took four hours by bus and Charles could come to the ranch more often now which was good for Charles Jr.

He was allocated a real bed in the officers' dorm, together with three others from his class in Pensacola and, during his first briefing, was told that unrest was extensive in Europe and that leave was not granted without special reason.

For the rest of the summer, Charles flew two to three passes a day training on "Grasshoppers;" a small, single-engine aircraft that would be used to transport commanders, with gold stars in battle between islands, and the one-seater, fighter aircraft F4F-3. The grasshopper was standard training for all pilots, so that it would be possible for any pilot to transport a commander. The fighter plane was another beast. It was clumsy even in comparison to the trainer planes, in Pensacola, which, by the way, there were a number of in San Diego, but it could take off and land from aircraft carriers, which contributed to Charles's enthusiasm.

He got a good feel for the plane and tested angles in the air that exceeded the permissible, with the impression that the plane behaved well in all positions, for which he was reprimanded in briefings, after making a steep descent at maximum speed and pulling up at low altitude over the beach in Santa Monica, where he and Charles Jr. had been swimming just a few months earlier.

On the way home, he and three others in the same squad had come overland and had flown over Hollywood at such a low altitude that they saw the letters "HOLLYWOOD," on the mountain above the cockpit, which was too much to pass unnoticed. However, since Charles had been spotless before, the matter only warranted a reprimand.

Routinely, they started to build on flight training with bombing exercises over San Clemente Island, just northwest of San Diego. The F4F-3 was able to take two 250 kilo bombs and pilots practiced dropping them on targets on the island at different angles and speeds.

Charles had a nack for it, and he passed with flying colors.

The exercises had always been prepared with weather reports that were provided to the pilots, before each session. One afternoon in September, two groups of four planes would bomb targets at San Clemente, and at the last pass, the island was surrounded by fog, so the bombings could not be carried out. Routinely, a squad would be scattered at poor visibility, and thus all eight planes split by increasing or decreasing height and changing course so as not to collide. The fighter plane was not approved for night flying and had no lamps in the instruments or cockpit.

Charles was number two after Major Hicks in the lead. The major stayed on course and Charles veered east in the dense fog. Two of the planes were forced to land in the sea and they were picked up by a destroyer. Charles was never heard from again, and the other four were able to return to base.

It was September 2, the day after Hitler's invasion of Poland, and to the day, six years before General Douglas MacArthur would receive Japan's capitulation on the battleship Missouri, on September 2, 1945. For Charles, the war ended before it had even begun, but for Charles Jr., it would just start.

The next day, a large, dark green, Dodge military car swung into the Long driveway to the ranch, in Corona. Two officers, in dress blue USMC uniforms, with white caps, stood in the entrance when Imelda opened the door. Little Charles Jr. thought his dad had come home but was disappointed when he did not recognize the faces of the gentlemen who held their caps in their hands and asked to speak to Mr. and Mrs. Long.

Imelda sent Charles Jr. to pick up his grandmother while Imelda asked the gentlemen to step into the library. She would pick up the gentleman from somewhere out in the yard. He was worried when

Imelda told him that two soldiers were waiting in the library and rushed to the big house with a leap. When he entered the house, it was completely silent.

Mrs. Long, Charles Jr. and the officers sat quietly waiting for Mr. Long. Major Clark, who had been Charles's closest commander and a colonel named Mitchell had been greeted by Mrs. Long and Charles Jr. and asked to wait, until Mr. Long had arrived. They greeted Mr. Long politely and the Colonel spoke:

"Mr. and Mrs. Long—we have the painful duty to state that your son, Charles, died in a plane crash, during a bombing exercise over San Clemente Island yesterday. We deeply regret it."

The first to be heard in the otherwise silent room was Charles Jr. who just said, "Daddy." Then there were snorts from Imelda and a shout from Mrs. Long. "Lord Jesus" was all that was heard from Mr. Long. Then he said: "The kid is orphaned," commenting in a monotonous tone.

"Charles will receive the highest military honors," added the colonel, whom Charles had looked up to as his role model. The Colonel had been Commander in Nicaragua, in 1931 and was highly respected at the base.

"Just tell us if there's anything we can do," added Major Clark. By then, Mrs. Long had to go to bed and Imelda took little Charles from the library. He didn't understand what had happened and wondered if dad would come home. Mr. Long asked about the circumstances of the accident, but the officers did not yet know in detail, other than that it was foggy, and several planes had disappeared. Charles' vector, the course he took as second in the squad, caused him to crash into the mountain at Aguora Hills, north of Santa Monica, the Major said. He added that in the short time he had the honor of knowing and training Charles, they had had great mutual respect for each other and that, in addition to being a very promising pilot, Charles was also an honorable man in every way.

Major Clark had two boxes with him. In the one, which was white and oblong, there were Charles gold wings (which were taken from the uniform in the officers' dorm) and in the other which was square and dark blue, lay The Navy Cross, the finest medal the Navy can give for honorable service. "We pass these on to you as a next of kin," Major Clark said. "The Navy will take care of all formalities, in connection with the funeral. The only thing that is required is that you choose the location," he added.

The funeral took place in the small village of Corona on the Saturday of the following week. In addition to the family and ranch employees, almost the entire village was gathered at the cemetery. In addition, an honor guard in parade uniforms was lined up next to Charles' coffin, which was covered by the American flag. Major Clark and Colonel Mitchell were there, along with a trumpeter.

When the priest had expressed his honors to the hero of the area and Anna's father had said a few words about the accidents that had hit the family, the trumpeter, in Marine Corps dress blue uniform, played taps. Those who until then managed to hold back tears surrendered. Charlie wondered where his dad was, and when Grandma couldn't answer, Imelda told him that he was under the flag and would not come back.

"May I stay with you then?" Charlie wondered.

"Certainly, you may little friend," Imelda replied, though she knew it would not be so.

After the taps, the Honor Guard fired four shots into the air, then took the flag and carried it in the air in front of the coffin to Major Clark, who folded it into a triangular shape, with only the stars visible. He carried it respectfully to Mrs. Long and gave it to her, saluting her.

Charlie saluted back.

After the ceremony, those closest were invited to the ranch for coffee. Mr. and Mrs. Long sat in the back seat with Charlie between them and Imelda and her husband sat in the front of the light yellow, Buick convertible, with exterior fenders and spare wheels on each side.

The priest and Anna's father and mother, Major Clark and Colonel Mitchell and some friends also came out to the ranch. On the way home, Charlie wondered:

"Why can't Dad come home?"

"Mom and dad are in heaven and can't come home. You have Grandma, me and Imelda and we will take care of you," said Mr. Long.

"Can we go and swim then?" Charlie wondered.

"Of course, we can," replied Mr. Long.

They were soon at the ranch and the guests stepped into the large, quiet, dark lounge. It was warm, so the windows were open but the thick curtains to keep the heat out were halfway drawn, and it was dark. The room was entirely in wood, with thick wooden beams across the ceiling, and there were several sitting groups, with heavy armchairs. Charlie had rarely been to the salon because Grandpa was there mostly, and he liked to read undisturbed. During the coffee, Colonel Mitchell took Mr. Long aside and asked carefully if there were any plans for Charlie's near future and schooling, which were relevant in the short term. "He is fine here with us and Imelda," replied Mr. Long, "and he meets friends at Sunday school, in Corona," he added. The Colonel explained that the Navy had a program to take care of military orphans. It worked much like a scout camp or boarding school said the Colonel and for the youngest, the closest possible home was in Santa Barbara, just north of Los Angeles.

There were eighty children there of all ages up to ten and the home was adjacent to "The Mission," an old, Spanish church erected in the early 1800's and more like a monastery, with a large courtyard of flowers and herbs surrounded by a wide-paved walkway with stone pillars all around. "It's very beautiful there and it might be good for Charlie to have friends more regularly," the Colonel suggested.

"Thank you for mentioning it," replied Mr. Long, adding, "I shall discuss the matter with Mrs. Long and notify you."

"You know where we are," replied the Colonel. "Just tell us if there's anything we can do," he added.

When the priest said goodbye to the mourners and Major Clark and Colonel Mitchell stood to say goodbye, Charlie stood on the stairs and saluted them. They were not in the habit of saluting private individuals in such situations but made an immediate exception: they stood in front of the green car, put on their white caps with gold emblems at the front and saluted back at Charlie.

When they had left, Charlie wondered if he would ever get a uniform.

"Maybe," replied Mr. Long, "Maybe."

CHAPTER THREE

Santa Barbara, CA · September 1940

The war in Europe had engulfed both England and France and even Norway, and the United States helped England with military equipment when it was in their security interest that England defend itself. The build-up of war resources was accelerated even though the United States was not at war yet. During the summer, the US Navy had been granted congressional approval to build 10,000 planes.

When Charlie started preschool as a new student at "Mission Elementary" he would soon turn five and the Battle of Britain was at its height. The number of pupils now amounted to just over one hundred and there were half-a-dozen five-year-olds. The best thing about the school in Santa Barbara was that the students, in the afternoons, could walk to the beach and swim in the sea, something that Charlie really loved.

He soon found himself at home and got a bestie named Mark who was just as old. They were protected by a ten-year-old named "Tim," with whom no student wanted to fight. If Tim saw that someone was stupid or mean to Charlie, Tim would be there and then others would leave.

One weekend, Tim and Mark were invited to the ranch which was the beginning of a long friendship. They were shoveling out the corn mesh to the pigs and they were swimming down by the lake, with Imelda, who missed Charlie.

Mr. Long had carefully explained to the boys that firearms were something that you should never, never, touch other than in the company of adults. At the ranch, most weapons were necessary for both hunting and emergency slaughter. In addition, there were "BB guns" and regular guns. BB guns are air rifles that shoot small, round pellets.

Mr. Long brought a BB gun and a semi-automatic rifle to a booth where they practiced target practice. First, he showed how to load a BB gun and then he tried several rounds. Then he showed Tim who was allowed the first shot. He did well. "I want to," Charlie said, but was told that Mark would shoot first. Mark was too short for the gun, so Mr. Long had to hold it at the same time. He hit nothing but was lyrical about the effect the weapon had in his hands.

Then it was Charlie's turn to shoot with a rifle, for the first time in his short life. Grandpa held it and Charlie hit the board on the first try. His pride was evident, and the others were very impressed. After a few misses and hits, Grandpa showed them how a semi-automatic rifle works. Five cartridges could be loaded and fired in succession with the trigger pressed. However, he only loaded it, with one round. The reason was that as a beginner, you risked holding your finger on the trigger and then you might fire again unintentionally, which could be fatal.

He fired the rifle once and it had a powerful sound. Then he reloaded the rifle and showed Tim carefully how to shoot. Tim trembled a little but pressed slowly on the trigger. It was more sensitive than a BB gun, so the shot went directly low, under the target. At the next shot, Charlie and Mark held their ears. Things went better and Tim hit the target.

Full of stories, the trio returned to Santa Barbara on Sunday and were then almost inseparable. There were no others who had fired weapons and they became heroes in the eyes of their friends. It became Charlie's best memory of his grandfather. Others were significantly harsher and bordered on tyranny.

At graduation from school the semi-final year, there was a contest to push off, with a stick, an opponent as they were balancing on bowl-shaped plates, and Charlie made the finals. He was prepared for the competition and wanted sneakers.

"You don't wear sneakers at school," Grandfather had said, and Charlie was forced to wear shoes, with a smooth leather sole—good looking to look at, but Charlie slipped off the plate and lost in the finals. He didn't show it, but he was inconsolable. At that very moment, he hated his grandfather. It was a loathing that would endure, and be reinforced by, more important events for the boy. The result of the loss on the bowl was something that he would be characterized by for the rest of his life. Use the right tool for the purpose. Ignore "protocol" and what it looks like, if you want to achieve a certain result—form must be subordinate to reason. Life at Mission Elementary was strictly structured. They lived four and four in the same age group. Different age groups had various lights-out times. Those who were older helped the dorm staff in looking after the younger ones. The war years at Mission Elementary made Charlie a very independent boy but passed rather peacefully. The biggest change during these years was the increase in the number of pupils which forced Charlie to have five roommates instead of three when he started. He had seen five graduation classes at school, and, with the absence of Tim, needed to defend himself against both schoolmates and Grandpa.

His grandfather seemed to take out missing his son Charles, on Charlie. Grandfather's temper had become increasingly intolerant of Charlie. That's how Charlie experienced his grandfather. What he did not know was that the grandfather was constantly reminded of his lost son, by the sight of Charlie, which was almost unbearable. Conversely, Charlie didn't want to remind him of the loss of his father by confiding in him. But, of course, Charlie knew nothing about it, and so he felt unwanted. Although Mission Elementary taught him how to eat in orderly form, it was with children that milk was sometimes spilled, legs kicked continuously under the table, the fork was dropped on the floor repeatedly, and it was more than Grandpa could put up with.

Charlie was jettisoned to the kitchen.

The era ended in a test of endurance when Charlie was seven years old and had a loose, canine tooth that refused to come out. Thoughtlessly, Charlie mentioned the problem to his grandfather, who pulled out a big, dark pair of gray pliers from a box in the kitchen, raised Charlie in a kitchen chair, and, during a minor eternity, twisted and pulled out the tooth with the pliers. The tooth turned out to have an unnaturally long root, which must have been the reason it did not want to come out. Charlie did not show with tears what he felt, and he was proud of himself. However, another red card was added to the collection against Grandpa. This upbringing characterized the wiry, ruddy, almost ten-year-old Charlie.

He remained at Mission Elementary, until the summer before he was ten, autumn of 1945.

CHAPTER FOUR

September 1945

When Japan's capitulation was signed on the Battleship Missouri on September 2, 1945, totally, including the Jewish extermination, somewhere around 35 to 45 million people had lost their lives, during the war. The joy and sense of freedom that everyone felt after Japan's capitulation was enormous, something that Charlie would be characterized by for the rest of his life. He had no memories of the Depression at all when he was small in the '30s, and his family always had food, as they had their ranch with pigs and their vegetable farms. They had fared better than most. Even Anna's father had managed the depression period well, with the daily newspaper in Whittier. Many other magazines either went under when editions almost remained unsold, or were bought for a song by William Randolph Hearst, who owned eighty miles off the coast of San Simeon, just south of San Francisco. He owned twenty-eight newspapers at the end of the war and was probably the richest individual on the US west coast. An example of the newspaper king's ability to suck up newspapers was an unconfirmed reputation: on one trip he had met an editor-in-chief of a newspaper at a bar over lunch who knew who W.R. Hearst was and had told him that "you can take over my newspaper, if you pay the salaries on Saturday." Said and done, W.R. paid wages to the staff and thus took over yet another daily newspaper.

It is often the case that money is drawn to money and the war had been a gold mine for Hearst. The editions had vastly increased and the profitability was in line with the increase in circulation.

W.R.'s father's name was George, who had participated in the gold rush in 1849, but did not make his fortune on gold in California but on silver in Nevada. He had bought the land along the coast which was 300 square miles to the surface. W.R. inherited the land at the age of fifty-six and was tired of camping and tenting on the hills of San Simeon and is said to have told architect Julia Morgan: "I would like to build something on the hill in San Simeon, further: "I would like something a little more comfortable." This was in the early 1910s, and by the end of the 1940s, he had spent the astronomical sum of $5 million on the building that reflected Spanish colonial style, or early Hollywood style, with forty-two guest rooms, fourteen living rooms, library, cinema where Walt Disney premiered the movie *Snow White and the Seven Dwarfs*, pool room, and two Roman-style pools with Olympic format. An additional $3 million was spent on furnishings and antiques, mainly purchased in Europe at auctions, such as the several thousand-year-old Egyptian statue in the park at the main guest house where Bob Hope and his wife reportedly spent their honeymoon.

Many great celebrities were often seen at "Hearst Castle" such as Sir Winston Churchill, Charlie Chaplin, Orson Wells who based the story of "Citizen Cane" there, and many others, e.g. the banker J.P. Morgan.

Hundreds of wild animals roamed freely around the castle, most of them imported from Africa. It was and is a rather bizarre place. W.R. Hearst donated what he called "The Ranch" later to the state of California, and it is now a national park open to the public.

During the summer of 1945, Charlie had been working on watering and feeding the pigs, swimming, and routinely attending Sunday School in Corona. He found his first favorite girl there, a peer named Judy.

Charlie longed for the Sundays when he would meet her. She lived and attended school in Corona, which was cycling distance from the ranch. He sometimes borrowed one of the ranch hands' bikes and rode the dirt roads that led into the city. Judy lived on a street close to a park where there were tennis courts and a clubhouse with a small forest area towards the residential area.

It was there in the forest he kissed Judy the first time. His heart pounded so that it probably sounded out of the woods and he was king for a day. From the clubhouse was heard Glenn Miller, who had disappeared during the war, in a plane over the English Channel. He was immensely popular. Judy was elated when Charlie returned home for dinner.

When Charlie came home, he was met by Imelda who announced that he was late, and that Grandpa was waiting for him along with Grandma. Once inside the dark lounge, Charlie felt some tension in the air as he greeted his relatives.

"I hear you often cycle to the city," said Grandpa.

"There are friends there," Charlie replied. They didn't know about Charlie's liking for Judy and so it would remain.

"We have discussed your near future," said Grandpa, and continued, "we agree that the best thing for you, now that you have become older, is to go to a boarding school," Grandpa said. It was as if the world had collapsed; Charlie began to sob.

"But," he sobbed, "I can live here and go to school in Corona," he added. Grandma filled in that it would be harder for them to help Charlie given their age and that he would naturally have more friends at a boarding school to hang out with than at the ranch. Charlie looked at Grandfather who was sitting and rubbing his hands without saying anything and who was only slowly nodding in agreement with what Grandma was saying. It was the first time in his life that Charlie felt himself against the wall, with the feeling that the battle was lost.

"I don't want to," Charlie said. Grandpa was used to dealing with staff who spoke Mexican and he was not a person to object to. He just said, "*Vamos!*" which meant Charlie was allowed to leave the room.

Charlie, sobbing, told Imelda what was wrong, and she did what she could to comfort the boy. This would mark the onset of Charlie's rootlessness in life. He would not meet Judy except maybe in Sunday school once a month and he was in despair. Furthermore, the idea of brand, new friends was not very appealing either. After all, Charlie and everyone in his class had to leave Mission Elementary, because the school had no higher grades than fifth grade. The students came from all over the state and were therefore scattered around California. At the dinner that followed, Grandma talked most about the school they had chosen. They would go and look the coming weekend, a few weeks before school started. Grandfather said it cost a lot of money to go there, so Charlie should appreciate the chance he had to go. That argument was not something that impressed Charlie. The fact that the Navy paid for some of it did not improve the matter either.

It's all the Navy's fault, Charlie thought. He missed his father. He missed Tim and Mark and just wanted to go back to Corona to meet Judy. In a few weeks, it would be too late, he thought. "You can come and help out at the paper on the breaks," said mom's dad. That was the best Charlie had heard that day. Then he didn't have to be at the dusty farm, although Whittier was further away from Corona than the ranch was. Then, at least, he could avoid Grandfather who was now the main cause of his problems.

"I would like that" Charlie replied.

"That's it," mom's dad replied. "Who knows?" he said and continued: "You may become an editor one beautiful day and take over the newspaper."

"If he doesn't want to take over the Ranch, of course," Grandpa said.

That kind of adult talk was nothing for Charlie who thought that if there was something he wanted to take over, it was Judy. It was a miserable dinner. Charlie felt that his fate was sealed and wondered if he might shoot himself, with Grandpa's semi-automatic. Then he would never see Judy again, of course, and it was an even worse proposal than just seeing her on certain Sundays. Imelda brought in a hot apple pie for dessert and Charlie smiled for the first time during the dinner. Imelda smiled back. There, at least, he had a real friend, he thought.

The world was facing a new era. In the US, purchasing power was strong and the restrictions that the population had lived under, since the outbreak of war, would disappear quickly. War gives birth to new industries and some then exist for a long time. Existing industries such as the automotive industry had been transformed into the manufacture of military equipment i.e. jeeps, trucks and aircraft. During the war, the textile industry had expanded with the production of hundreds of thousands of uniforms. Some businesses such as the media and consumer goods (pig breeding) had survived without difficulty.

The wartime had brought a number of restrictions and the purchasing needs were great. Some goods such as import goods (tobacco, oil, alcohol, coffee, etc.) were rationed. In order to track the consumer's right to fill their rations, a young entrepreneur in

Minneapolis named Curtis Carlson, a Swedish descendant, introduced coupons that showed the quantity and item. These were printed in the millions and became a success for the company he founded which was then called the "Global Bond Trading Stamp Company."

The coupons came to survive wartime and then in the form of discount coupons which were purchased by producers of e.g. foods and chemicals. These were introduced as inserts in newspapers and have been successful ever since. Curtis Carlson's company expanded into the hotel and travel industry. Through corporate acquisitions over the years, it has become one of the world's largest travel companies. Following a merger in 1994, with French "Wagon Lit," the company is now called "Carlson Wagonlit," with 10,000 employees.

Development had largely been at a standstill in the automobile industry. Cars that were manufactured in 1945 were actually 1939 models, although they were made in 1945. It would take a couple of years before completely new models were introduced.

Prices in the US had been frozen on everything by a special war regulation called "OPA," equivalent to price control. Congress wanted to completely eliminate price controls. After all, a free market would regulate itself, many argued. Others believed that there would be sharp price increases on the order of 20-50% and thus sharp inflation. The Washington administration tried a formula where wages and prices were correlated. If production and consumption increased, rising profitability could pay rising wage costs. What happened was the reverse: wage increases led to price increases, and everyone had the same purchasing power as before.

In June 1946, the Senate voted by a large majority to remove virtually all price controls. It was thought that six months later the industry would be back to normal production volume and that the market would be able to regulate prices. If some goods were relatively priced higher, all other things being equal, some goods should become cheaper since consumers must consider purchases with respect to their own financial restrictions.

Prices were thus released from control, after four and a half years of price restrictions. The public was concerned that prices would rise. Many therefore wanted to strike for higher wages.

How high is a price? The price is actually so high it can be without the consumer declining a purchase. In a market economy, things are regulated by supply and demand. If a manufacturer raises prices (the car industry was concerned about not being the first to raise prices), they will be at a disadvantage compared to competitors.

The decision was really about the desire to get as much goods and products as higher prices would help to create. Earlier, Henry Ford thought that an economy should be based on abundance and not scarcity. As early as 1914, he offered the car workers five dollars an hour, for an eight-hour day, when competitors paid $2.40 an hour for a nine-hour day. The motivation was that his running belts were so effective that they were still more profitable than the competitors' production. He wanted everyone to be able to afford to buy his cars. This has been called the "production miracle" which has contributed to the high standard of living of the United States.

In fact, after the war there was a shortage of many basic commodities such as steel and glass and the producers adopted a wait and see attitude. Once the accumulated consumption needs were satisfied, declining price pressures would probably be the result. The number of employed persons increased sharply after the end of the war. Housing construction, appliances and cars increased as well. The market succeeded in balancing the situation and it was not at all the price increases some had feared. Afterwards, many believed that the OPA control, in 1946, contributed to the success, which resulted in an economic boom that would last for many years.

What contributed to the economic upturn was savings. During the years of rationing, total savings in the United States had increased from $40 billion before the outbreak of war to $130 billion, in 1945. The hope for the future was great and was characterized by the events of the time.

In 1946, a young man named John F. Kennedy, popularly known as "Jack," was elected to Congress. During the war, his older brother and brother-in-law had perished. Mothers who lost a son in the war were awarded a gold star and were called "Gold Star Mom's." Jack's mother was a Gold Star Mom.

Jack himself was injured when the Japanese destroyer, *Amagiri*, split his torpedo boat "PT-109," in August 1943, in the Solomon Islands when he was on patrol in areas controlled by Japan to disrupt their operations.

He promised in a speech that began with: "As ships sank and young Americans died . . . I decided to serve my country in peacetime as honestly as I tried to serve it in war." He was a Democrat from Massachusetts. He argued that security in the United States and peace in the world depended on the determination and endurance of the United States.

Kennedy won the election in 1946, after 450 speeches, and became the Massachusetts Representative to Congress at the age of twenty-nine. At the same time, the build-up of Germany and the opening of lockups in international trade were underway.

The primary need in Europe's war-torn countries was food. Many still lived on a calorie intake below 1,550, which was considered the number one goal.

Companies in Europe with operations in the United States had their assets frozen, during the war. International companies such as Dutch Unilever (with more than 400 companies in different continents, under holding companies in London, which controlled subsidiaries in the British dominions, and in Rotterdam which controlled all other subsidiaries) helped to keep profits out of Nazi hands.

In addition, Unilever had four layers of holding companies in between those who controlled the companies. American "Liver Bros." could send profits to "Overseas Holdings Co." in Durban, South Africa. Unilever claimed that the holding companies were separate, which they were under civil law, but in practice all were one. The boards were identical. Policies were common, as well as joint merchandise purchases, profit transfers and dividends.

Now, Unilever was able to pay frozen dividends amounting to 29.6% of the profits. A total of $80 million accumulated in the United States during the war was sent to Rotterdam to rebuild damaged factories. They had big expansion plans. After buying "Pepsodent" for $15 million, in 1944, they wanted to acquire the remains of Germany's soap company and invest 100 million in global expansion. In 1945, Unilever had sales of $1.2 billion. The company's head in the United States was named Charles "Chuck" Luckman and at the age of thirty-seven was the head of the second largest company in the soap industry, after Procter & Gamble. He looked like and was sometimes mistaken for Bing Crosby and lived on a Cattle Ranch of 22,000 acres called "Lucky Five," near Julian, California. He gave the following three attributes for his success: luck, courage and ability. Contributing to the sales success was the company's radio advertising. They had a contract with Bob Hope, which was then one of the biggest celebrity names in the entire United States. Companies such as Unilever contributed strongly to the reconstruction of Europe and its structure remains to this day. This company group was a clear example of the functioning of the market economy and was the result of a peculiar ability to draw the longest straw and get to the top.

With Mr. Long at the wheel of the yellow Buick, Charlie in the passenger seat and Mrs. Long in the back seat, the suitcase and the rest of the back seat full of Charlie's personal belongings, the trio traveled east toward the boarding school. In addition to bedding and clothes, there would be several items itemized by the school on a special list. All owned clothing would have the name embroidered on a small strip of fabric. Boys would also wear black trousers and a gray blazer for dinners on Sundays, at church and on solemn occasions. Beginners were not allowed to wear buttons on their sleeves. After a year at school, you got a button on the sleeve, etc. However, everyone would have the school badge embroidered on the chest pocket. It was round with a black frame and with a small eagle in the middle with the letters "CBS" in a triangle around the eagle.

It stood for "Coachella Boarding School" (once TV made its entry into human life, the same letter combination would represent the largest television production company in America).

CBS was a three-hour drive, just east of Coachella, located between Palm Springs and Indio. Palm Springs is a celebrity retreat, with its beautiful palm trees, a large mountain right next to the city and its many golf courses. Often Hollywood celebrities traveled there on weekends to hang out.

Bob Hope was one of the most famous and he settled there. Subsequently, he had the main street named after him: "Bob Hope Drive." The farther east from the coast, the drier and clearer the climate became. Around the school, there are only deserts and mountains except items planted and built by man. The nearest water is a huge lake called "Salton Sea," an hour's drive south.

Charlie was solemn during the long haul. Grandfather confirmed that it was good for Charlie to make new friends and Grandma quietly agreed. However, it was a selling point that did not bite on Charlie. He thought of Judy and was worried about not being able to meet her for a month. In addition, he was worried that he probably wouldn't know anyone at school.

He had heard that many from Santa Barbara were going to boarding school as the Navy was sponsoring some of the costs, but he did not know if someone his age would start there. There are many boarding schools in California and why would he be so lucky that someone he knew started at his school?

You were allowed to bring your own things to the room, such as photographs and paintings, books, writing materials and such, as well as sports equipment. Charlie, like many others, had a baseball bat, mittens and some baseballs. Swimsuits were mandatory as the school had a pool.

They had visited the school during the summer, looking at the school building, the student dorms and the sports halls. They had also talked to the school's principal. Much was recognizable from the time at the Santa Barbara Mission, but two things differed markedly.

One was that the student dorms were a sad sight to see and even worse to imagine living in, and the other was that the sports halls were really nice. If Charlie had been given the choice, it would have been the other way around.

It is warmest during the period July to September and now it had cooled to about 40 degrees Celcius in the shade. They were thirsty and hungry and pulled into a roadside cantina for lunch. Here, Charlie chose his favorite food—hamburger steak, with French fries, lots of ketchup and two Cokes. It would be his last good dish, until he left school again a month later.

It was said that the food in the school (which was served in the student dorms) was good. As any advertisement in general, the product did not really meet the quality promised. Once out on the road again, Charlie felt ill at ease. He was about ten years old. Grandpa and Grandma would return home to freedom and he would be left out there in no man's land, with lots of completely foreign people. Even Imelda was silent, and Charlie started to cry.

Grandfather said, "We must not show that we are miserable when we arrive" and continued: "wipe the tears and be a man." Charlie couldn't talk but just sniffed for a while to Grandpas annoyance.

"It will be fine once you get to know some, you'll see," continued Grandma. "We will be visiting in two weeks," she added.

Parents were not welcome for the first two weeks. It was thought to reinforce homesickness, if family and friends visited the students early in the semester. Students were not informed of such issues.

Charlie wondered, "Can't you come next weekend?"

Grandfather replied: "You go to school on Saturdays and you go to church on Sunday; the weekend after that fits better"

"You don't want to" Charlie exclaimed.

Grandma tried to soothe the situation by talking about something else and it was quite frosty the last bit up to Charlie's new home, or "Dorm." It was a home for boys only. Charlie had so much to think about that he never thought about why boys and girls lived in different dorms. His dorm was called "Chapel Hill," as it was just above the school's chapel which was halfway up a hill. There were many student dorms that all had different names. This led to immediate local patriotism in favor of one's own dorm; or so it was believed. In addition, it was an advantage for the school to know where the students lived. Charlie was used to going to Sunday school but writing to Judy and telling her that he lived on Chapel Hill felt a little embarrassing, he thought. Anything would have been better. The home had about forty students and two principals. There was a couple in their sixties who ran the home named Mr. and Mrs. Fuller. The dorm was large, Charlie thought. On the gravel in front of the home, there were lots of cars and people when Grandpa Long swung into the parking area. It felt like everyone was staring at just them, Charlie thought. It was pure chaos. Mrs. Fuller came forward and introduced herself and Charlie greeted her for the first time. She welcomed him and asked him to come along to meet his roommate. He was a student who was a year older and he had attended CBS the year before. They wanted it so that the older one could show the new pupil the right procedures, to relieve the managers. The boy Charlie was supposed to live with was Peter but was called "Petey" and he came from La Jolla, just outside San Diego. They got to meet each other in the yard and to Charlie's disappointment he did not recognize Petey from the Mission.

Petey said, "Come on, I'll show you our room," and Charlie chuckled reluctantly. Petey told Charlie that the younger ones lived two and two while those in their final year had single rooms and were like kings at the school. "Just do as they say and everything will be fine," Petey said. It was not in Charlie's nature to do things as told. When Grandpa says one thing, you have no choice, Charlie thought. When others say things, it's just the beginning of a debate. But he didn't worry about that for now. He was curious about the room. The youngest lived on the ground floor. Inside a large entrance there was a large hall. It resembled a waiting room outside a doctor's office, with a few chairs and a telephone booth. To the right was a shower room and toilets in a row. To the left was a short corridor, with three student rooms, of which Charlie's was the furthest away. It was in the corner of the house and had windows in two directions, with a desk in front of each. At the sides were two beds that resembled something that had been discarded by a prison—gray steel pipes with steel wire mesh bottom and mattress. If there was any paint on the walls at all, it had faded and worn away much earlier. The room was completely colorless and had a circular ceiling lamp that hung in a metal bar that resembled a full moon when lit.

"I don't want to live in this dump," Charlie said loudly to Petey. Petey replied that you get used to it quickly.

"We can cover the walls with sheets if you like," he added. Then they went out to the car and picked up all the things Charlie had with him while Grandpa and Grandma talked to the managers. It was hard to say goodbye to them, but it made it easier for Charlie to get to know Petey. Charlie arranged his things in the room and was amazed at the ruckus throughout the house when everyone was running around like chirping chickens. Dinner was at 6 p.m., sharp. The managers sat at the end of each of their long tables. The elders sat next to them and then in order, which meant that Charlie was sitting farthest away from them. At the other end, sat the orderly, who was in the highest grade, and next year's orderly sat in the corresponding place at the second table. Charlies place was next to him.

Everyone would stand by the benches, until it was quiet, and Mr. Fuller told the congregation to sit down. Then it would be quiet again and he blessed the meal. Then the food was sent from the end towards the center. Mr. Fuller tapped his glass, stood, and then welcomed everyone to a new semester at CBS.

After dinner, there was a gathering in the main room where the elders drank coffee and the others got nothing. Mr. Fuller explained the lights-out times that applied and described the school's procedures.

He said that all pupils have an obligation to help, supervise and correct younger pupils. He quoted H.G. Wells who had stated: "Civilization is a competition between education and disaster." He added: "Your time at school is short. Use it well."

Between 18:00 and 19:30, it was silent time and the students were not allowed to leave the rooms except to go to the toilet. Dinner was usually at 5 p.m. Charlie was among the younger students and their lights-out time was 21:00. For the older students, it was 22:00. If one was not in his bed at this time, the orderly would impose various penalties depending on his mood. The most common was to clear the tables after dinner. The worst was to wake the students because then you had to get up first, a quarter hour before everyone else. After the gathering, Petey showed Charlie around and they greeted several students in other rooms. A common topic of discussion, among the new students, was the question of where they came from and what their parents did. Charlie was immediately accepted even by the elders when he told him that his mother died when he was little and that his father had been a pilot and died during the war.

He learned during the evening that new students were secretly inaugurated. Not even the managers knew what was going to happen. It was hard to fall asleep the first evening. The next morning everyone was awakened at 06:30. The walk to school only took five minutes and Charlie got to meet his classmates who mostly came from other dorms. After school, you could go to a kiosk and buy candy and Coca Cola.

Then new students had to gather at the school pool. There were rubber boots and raincoats waiting for them. Then you had to swim from one side to the other, one dorm at a time. The dorm that came last was named the term "Turkey" corresponding to last, which Charlie's home dorm managed to avoid.

After dinner, the silent period was relaxed as everyone was

allowed to arrange things in their rooms. Petey was a good roommate and he was well-liked. He and Charlie also got along well. Petey said that on Saturdays there was a movie in the school auditorium, which cost money. All students had weekly allowance, the size of which depended on the grade they attended. It was not much, and you really had to save to afford the cinema. The students were encouraged to have a safety box.

As money was tight, barter developed. Charlie exchanged one of the many different knives he had brought with him without Grandpa seeing it, for a box with a broken lid. Charlie loved his knives.

Petey said that the older students were allowed to shoot, with the school's rifles, on the shooting range. Charlie thought it was unfair that he couldn't take part, but such were the rules. At CBS, it was almost impossible to change rules.

This meant that the students developed refined systems to avoid or circumvent the rules. They learned to be discreet. Reading after lights-out was done, under the cover, with a flashlight. If you were going to mess with someone, like for example bag-bedding, by folding up the bottom sheet and making it look like a normal bed, it was all about not being detected. To be in other people's rooms when they were not there was forbidden. You needed to have a companion close by that could signal if the housewife or anyone else was approaching. If you got caught, any punishment could be exchanged for knives and other desirable things, in the barter system.

The third day was the first time Charlie wrote to Judy. There was a lot to tell and he filled both the front and back of the page. The fourth day was the first fight. It was in the main hall between two older guys. The orderly handed out punishments to both to awaken even the "intestines" for one week each. The intestines were the students in the lowest classes. It was this group that in many different ways had to cater to the older students. An example was going to the kiosk and buying candy for them. If messages were to be sent to someone, they simply sent it with a messenger, i.e. an intestine.

Some days, Charlie started an hour later than usual which soon proved to be of no use as there was such running in the stairs that you couldn't sleep anyway. After a week, the orderly came in when Petey and Charlie had gone to bed and he asked Charlie:

"When did you last shower?"

"None of your business," Charlie replied. It was the first time Charlie got slapped at school, and more was to come.

"I told you to just do as they say and everything will be fine," Petey said.

"He shouldn't mind when I shower," Charlie replied.

The next day, Petey and a few others got caught smoking behind the gym. Petey got an hour's early bedtime, for a week.

Over time, however, Charlie adapted and became friends with many students at the school. However, it was difficult to take orders from guys who were only a few years older, which Charlie could never accept. They learned to cope with finesse at CBS. Salt was exchanged for sugar in the dining room. The lids were unscrewed so they were loose, which was effective.

The beds had to be made neatly. This was important. If you wanted to mess with a certain person, you checked that the room was empty and simply tore off someone's bedding, who then had to make his own bed. This was standard procedure.

Sometimes, they went too far. Certain things were harassment. One trick that was on the borderline was to tear many newspapers into tiny pieces and store them in a suitcase. When you wanted to mess with someone, you emptied out the contents in their room. The result was that pieces of paper were everywhere in the room, for a long time.

Worse was to sneak in when someone slept and pour a bucket of water on him. If you got caught, it was early bedtime for a week.

What the new intestines were most worried about was the inauguration. It was to take place during the third week, which was after visiting weekend. All new intestines were ordered to appear at the pool one evening. They should wear gym clothes. All the students crowded around the large pool and wanted to watch. The new students would once again have a swimming competition, with their clothes on. It turned out that some could not swim and then others had to help them. After struggling frantically for two laps, they were exhausted and were told that they were now inaugurated at CBS. What no one had said was that they did not select a winner. Life was easier after that evening, Charlie felt. Over time, visits from Grandpa and Grandma were less frequent. Charlie felt better at school as he moved up in classes and his former tormentors gradually quit. Communication with Judy ceased completely. There were others at school who were of greater interest to him. The only problem was that the boy girl ratio was five to one, which meant that boys were like flies around hot food. It was about approaching many girls to have a chance. Charlie was lucky enough to have a "date" for the graduation party.

On weekends, there was not much to do that interested him at school, but they spent time in the main room, with cards and chess games and the like. Charlie developed collecting as his hobby, like many others at the school. He collected both coins and stamps. The school was a perfect marketplace, for the exchange of duplicates, and Charlie's collections grew as the knife collection shrank. He constantly believed that one day the collections would be valuable, which stimulated savings. When it was time to graduate, he had been a mediocre student, but the tenure at CBS had trained him in diplomacy and made him friends for life. After the graduation with parents in attendance, all belongings were packed into a newer Buick, along with diplomas and grades, farewells exchanged with the teachers, managers and all the schoolmates. Then it was off to the ranch. It was May 31, 1953, and Charlie was seventeen years old.

MICHAEL OWENS

PART THREE

A New Continent

MICHAEL OWENS

CHAPTER FIVE

The school years at CBS had given Charlie a strong longing to get away, from the world he knew. He had not been outside California and even less abroad. The environment at school had been separate from the rest of life. To be back on the ranch was admittedly freedom in itself, but watering the pigs was something Charlie had had enough of. Grandfather assumed that Charlie would take over the farm one beautiful day, because there were no other possible candidates as Charlie had no siblings.

Charlie got a salary like everyone else now when he worked at the ranch. With filled pockets, he went to Corona on Saturdays and met friends at the cinema and in the diners. Judy had moved and he never saw her again. There were new times now and the music in cafes and bars was characterized by Frank Sinatra and something jazz-like which was fun to experience, unlike cinema at school.

Certainly, events in the country had been closely followed, but the outside world was little mentioned. Politically, it was the hot topic of communism that frightened ordinary people. In Cuba, which is only ninety miles south of Florida, communism had a strong hold and in Indochina people were on the rise. A congressman named McCarthy spread terror in the United States through accusations against known and unknown citizens that they were communist sympathizers. Charlie knew very little about communism and cared even less.

For him, it was excitement that drew interest. On weekends, there was besides baseball and other sports, which Charlie couldn't care less about, stock car racing, which he appreciated. It is reminiscent of the rodeo but with cars. You compete with scrap-ready cars on a large, dirt track and it is allowed to push another off the track. However, an immobilized car is protected. It was at these competitions, on the outskirts of Corona, that Charlie became friends with a wild brain named Richard but who was called "Ritch" who competed. Ritch was a couple of years older than Charlie and worked in the workshop of a gas station. He lived carefree and was generally quite popular in town.

They used to joke about just leaving town, but they had no money. By the way, where would they go? You could lift around the state and work on farms during the trip, for example, harvest pumpkins further north. They both thought it would be fun to see San Francisco where neither Charlie nor Ritch had been. One day on the ranch when Charlie read the Whittier Daily news that the family subscribed to, Charlie saw a notice under "Messages." It was a list of arriving and departing vessels to and from San Diego, with their respective departure and destination locations. A freighter would arrive from Panama the following week and depart three days later towards Sydney, Australia! *Wow*, Charlie thought. He cycled to the station in Corona to tell Ritch. Charlie took Ritch with him across the street to a Coke machine and they each inserted a dime, and each got his Coca Cola.

"Maybe we can get a job on the boat and go with it!" said Charlie.

"You're nuts," Ritch replied. "We have no money," he added.

"We bring some stuff to trade with and then we work our way up," Charlie replied.

"You may never go," Ritch said.

"Not if I ask," Charlie replied, adding, "and I'm not going to. They probably wouldn't miss me either," he continued. "We can always take the bus to San Diego when the boat has arrived and ask the captain," Ritch replied.

"Yes, yes, yes!" exclaimed Charlie.

"I've had enough of both the workmen and Corona," Ritch said, and continued: "we can always try."

They took the bus one day when the ship would be in port. San Diego's harbor was lined with cargo ships and there was a lot of life and movement there despite it being Saturday. Out in the bay, lots of ships lay waiting for their turn to enter the quay. The boat they were looking for had the flag of Panama and was called *Quantas*.

They inquired and found her soon. It was no beauty but looked like being among the bigger ones in the harbor. To get on board, you walked up a long staircase with railings on the sides. They found a sailor and asked for the captain. They were told he was doing paperwork and was in his cabin. The sailor showed them there. Somewhat nervous, they knocked on the cabin door and heard a harsh, "Enter!" They stepped into a fairly large cabin that had no bed. It looked like a simple office and the captain was sitting at his desk with round windows behind, looking down, with a cigarette in his mouth. He looked up and asked, "Who are you?"

Ritch was used to handling people from the workshop and he replied:

"We come from Corona and read that you are going to Sydney."

"That's right," replied the captain.

"We want to go," Charlie said without further ado.

"We will not take any passengers," replied the captain.

"We do not want to be passengers" Ritch continued, adding, "we wonder if there is work on the boat?"

The captain continued: "On such a long journey there is always extra need for crew, especially when it is hottest in the Pacific."

Ritch told him that he worked in a car repair shop, which the captain considered a good background. Charlie said he was used to heat from the Ranch and used to dealing with both people and animals.

"I can take you for payment," said the captain. "I can pay ten dollars a day and free food," he added, "if you sign up for the whole trip."

Charlie and Ritch accepted, and the signing papers were prepared.

"Be back in the morning," said the captain. "We put out Monday morning."

"Aye, aye, sir!" the two friends answered and almost ran down the stairs back to the quay. "We did it!" exclaimed Charlie.

They now made plans for the following day. Charlie wouldn't tell anyone where he was going. Then Ritch wouldn't either, he promised. Ritch was the son of an Irishman who was an unemployed drunkard and he would not miss Ritch either. He had a slogan: "God created Whiskey to keep the Irish from ruling the world." His mother had left his father, for another a few years earlier and moved north.

After Sunday's breakfast, Charlie helped out and when he was alone with Imelda, in the kitchen, he told her:

"If I should be gone one day, you should not worry about me. I will leave and cannot talk about where to. I will not announce where I am. Know that I won't go alone but will have a friend with me." Imelda looked sadly at Charlie and gave him a hug.

"You are probably doing the right thing," she replied, adding, "but I will miss you."

"And I you," Charlie replied.

On Sundays, Charlie was free from the watering of the pigs and no one took special notice of the cloth bag he carried with him to the bike. He had his total savings, a few different knives, an envelope with stamp duplicates and a few silver dollars in the bag, in addition to some toiletries, swimming trunks, two shirts and some underwear.

They met at the workshop and the bike was parked inside the gates. Ritch was ready and they didn't look back when they got on the bus to San Diego. No more cars or pigs for a long time they agreed.

Once aboard the *Quantas*, they were assigned their cabin by a sailor. It was small but there were four bunks and a small round window. They could take any bunk they wanted as no one else was living in their cabin. There was a table in the middle of the cabin and four chairs, ceiling lamps and bedside lamps, but nothing else. It smelled murky and the window had to be open in port.

There was dinner at the mess at 18:00. The captain was there, and he introduced his new sailors to the crew, which amounted to a dozen different nationalities. He went on to say that it would take a week to Hawaii where they would be in port for three days. It made the new sailors rejoice. After that, the trip would go through the Marshall Islands, Fiji, New Caledonia, and finally reach Sydney, an estimated four weeks after the boat set sail from San Diego. Charlie thought about his savings. *Four weeks is almost thirty days, times ten dollars—makes 300 dollars! It will make a good start in Australia*, he thought further.

The time of the trip was summer despite the heat when the risk of hurricanes was slight.

"The captain wants to go south of the Devil's Sea" a sailor whispered to Charlie.

"What is that?" Charlie whispered back.

"If you gentlemen have something to share with the crew, feel free now," said the captain.

"No Sir," the sailor replied.

The captain continued: "If anyone wants to sign off, it's time now—otherwise I expect you to be on board at 07:00 tomorrow. We sail at 09:30." After dinner, which was better on Sundays, the sailor told Charlie about the Devil's Sea. North of the Mariana Islands, in the direction of Japan, there were stories that ships just disappeared and waves that were thirty meters high. During the war, a submarine named *Scorpion* had disappeared without a trace without issuing emergency calls. Last fall, in September 1952, a Japanese research vessel named *Kaiyo-Maru* had disappeared without a trace. She had fifteen tons of fuel oil on board but not a trace was seen.

"Good that the captain chooses a southerly route then," replied Charlie, who was not particularly frightened.

Among the crew, Charlie was probably the one who had gone to school the longest, which the sailors quickly became aware of when they would be messing with him. On a ship, you can question anything and everyone except the captain. However, Ritch and Charlie had no problems fending for themselves on board and being rookie sailors. The first night on board there was so much noise in the ship that they had trouble sleeping. When they woke up at 06:00, it felt like they had just fallen asleep, but now they would cast off! Charlie was commanded to the kitchen and Ritch to the engine room. It turned out that kitchen service was the best you could have on board, and that machine room was the worst. The food in "Merchant Marine," or the merchant fleet was good, although the sailors called their meat stew on bread for "SOS," or: "Shit on a Shingle." The most fun, Charlie thought was the dump. He took the barrels to the stern and sent the contents overboard, to the gull's delight. After the first day, he noticed that only a few birds orbited the ship. He realized for the first time that he was at sea. For the first time in his seventeen-year-life, he felt free. Looking over the railing and seeing the white foam, from the otherwise dark, blue water, was a sign that his life had meaning. The strong breeze caused his hair and white kitchen shirt to flutter and he felt real happiness in being on the path to somewhere. Charlie had been institutionalized throughout his upbringing, by being in schools far from the ranch. Being able to feel the sea, with its salty scent, and watch dolphins swim along with the ship gave him a fantastic feeling.

Ritch had it worse in the engine room. They worked to keep oil pressure and temperature as constant as possible and therefore had to monitor the valves at all times, in forty-degree heat. There were no fans down there but simply four, large pipes up to the deck that would supply air to the engine room. That was where you had the shortest shift. When the heat came up to fifty degrees, you worked thirty minutes and then went on deck for as long, and so it went. Ritch was slim before the trip but would lose a few kilos, before it was over.

At sea, it was about twenty-five degrees at night and thirty in the cabin, so all sailors slept on deck in calm weather. The cargo consisted of consumer goods to be unloaded in Pearl Harbor. There they would load sugar and canned pineapple for Sydney.

The Pacific Ocean is bigger than all the other oceans together. The distance between the US west coast and Hawaii, is approximately 2,100 nautical miles. If pilots navigated wrong, during World War II, and missed the islands, they did not have much margin to fly around and look for land, when they were flying on fuel vapors.

Together with Iceland, Hawaii is the youngest landform on earth. The islands were formed by volcanoes over time, with the largest island "Hawaii" last, about 400,000 years ago. Several volcanoes are still active among the islands.

The group of islands extends as a string of beads northwest about 250 miles with Midway and the Kure Atoll furthest west, and these are also the oldest at nearly 28 million years. The volcanoes below Hawaii are active and it boils in two on the island and one below the surface. The latter is called *"Loihi"* whose peak is 1,000 meters below sea level. In just 60,000 years, *Loihi* will reach the surface.

What has happened and is still going on is that the plateau below the islands is slowly shifting westward as on a running belt. Seen from the bottom of the ocean, the islands resemble a saw blade whose youngest islands are the highest and the ones we call Hawaii. At the highest is "Mauna Kea" on the island of Hawaii which from the bottom of the ocean is slightly higher than Mount Everest. Captain James Cook landed on one of the islands for the first time in January 1778. The natives called the island *O'why'he* which became Hawaii in English. In Hawaii, Captain Cook met his fate, in 1779, in a dispute with the natives on the west side of the island in *Hikiau Heiau*, where he was killed. His visit opened the way for ships with missionaries who were on the hunt for souls and whalers for other hunting. The islands had been isolated for over a thousand years and the white man's illnesses decimated the population from Cook's days, until 1853 from 300,000 to 71,000. Through the seclusion, thousands of species of plants and birds had evolved over time that did not exist anywhere else on earth. Today, there are 8,800 species in Hawaii that they are unique on earth, e.g. the *Apeape* plant whose leaves can be two meters in diameter. Since the first Polynesians arrived, in their double hull sailing boats about 1,500 years ago, over 1,000 animal species have been exterminated. The first were about twenty species of birds that could not fly which were an easy prey. On Hawaii's highest mountain, "Mauna Kea," despite the cold at the top, you can find an insect called *Wékiu* that appears to have glycolic-like substance in its blood. It lives on other insects that are brought there by the wind. Mosquitoes were introduced to the islands in the 1820s as free passengers in the whalers' water barrels. These spread malaria among the birds that lacked immune systems to such an extent that the population talked about the birds falling like rain from the trees. The only mammals to travel to these remote islands were Monk seals and a bat. Polynesians from Samoa and the Marquesas Islands had built double hull boats lashed together with coconut fiber rope and sails made of braided leaves. With these, around 400-600 AD, they sailed to Hawaii, with a cargo of the root fruit "Taro," potatoes, bananas, sugarcane, pigs, birds and dogs that could not bark as provisions.

Rats also came with the canoes, and then with European ships. The rats eat bird eggs, and this quickly led to the extinction of bird species. The Europeans and the animals they introduced changed the islands more in 200 years than the Polynesians did in 1,400 years.

The bird that is the state of Hawaii's landmark bird is called "Nene," It is cousin to the Canadian goose and was nearly extinct in the early 1900s when their land areas were converted into sugar cane and pineapple crops. In 1951 there were only thirty living "Nene" birds. Captive breeding has meant that today's population has grown to 800 birds, all closely related to each other.

The islands are undoubtedly among some of the finest examples of paradise on the earth, with their unique bird species and plants and a stable, year-round climate that is sub-tropically pleasant.

The inhabitants are a blissful mix of Polynesians, Micronesians, Japanese, Chinese and many whites. The mix you experience on the islands is everything from chalk white people to café-latte colored "natives," with distinct features of Asia. The relationship was about 60/40 in Asia's favor when Charlie was to land on Oahu.

The mix with Westerners took place in the 19th century when the merchant fleet arrived. Now they were on their way to Pearl Harbor where Japan had bombed the port without warning, on December

7, 1941, twelve years earlier. It was an event that will forever be remembered in infamy in the United States. Japan's diplomats negotiated that peace would continue to be possible with the United States, until the moment of the bombing. However, the US had embargoed oil deliveries to Japan, which depended on imported oil, which was one of the reasons for their attack.

The operation had been called: "Climb Mount *Niitaka* and was well prepared on Oahu, by Japanese spies. These had reported back to Japan exactly which ships were unfortunately in port. It was Sunday. At eight o'clock in the morning, the first wave swept over Pearl Harbor and at 9.45 came the second and last. Eleven battleships and destroyers were sunk or seriously damaged, 188 planes were destroyed, 2,335 soldiers were killed and 1,143 were injured. Japan lost twenty-nine planes and 185 military. At the time of the outbreak of the war, Hawaii was a protectorate of the United States. People of Asian origin were not allowed to become American citizens, until 1952, which led to numerous applications in the near future. Hawaii was to become the fiftieth state of the United States, after Alaska in 1959.

CHAPTER SIX

The first few years, during the 1950s, were marked by poorer times for farmers in the United States. Charlie had heard Grandpa complain that pork prices were falling. However, this was offset in his case by the fact that the corn-mix he bought for the pigs had also fallen in price. For as long as he could remember, he had heard Grandpa talk about the pigs. Whether the prices were good or not, there was always a problem with the pigs. They shrunk during transport to the slaughter, the veterinary costs were too high, the staff was lazy, and so it went on. That was the only thing grandfather seemed to care about. Charlie didn't want to hear about pigs anyway. For the farmers it was a recession. Hawaii was completely dependent on its sugar crops and pineapples. When Charlie arrived, the harvest of pineapple had been greatly reduced by a hitherto unknown nutritional deficiency in the crops. For a long time, the plants had been sprayed against small worms called Nematodes. The same spray had been applied in the spring and the worms were not found on the plants at all. Other answers were sought, and it was concluded that there was a nutrient deficiency in the soil; most lacking was zinc. Although the amount was negligible, the shortage seemed to lead to diseased plants. Chemical agents had led to depletion of the soil. Harvests and therefore exports shrunk significantly that year.

As a ship's boy, Charlie was assigned two duties in addition to kitchen service. They worked in six-hour shifts and there was time for more than peeling potatoes. Painting is constant on ships. Daytime, Charlie would scrape and ground the railing with rustproofing. It was a good job because then you were at peace with the waves as company. After standing on his knees and painting the outside on a few posts, he came up with the brilliant idea that you can lie on your back on the deck and hold on with one hand and paint with the other. The painting itself is silent after all.

When Charlie applied this method behind one of the lifeboats, the chef, or "Highball" as he was called, because he was constantly boozing, searched for Charlie and no one could find him. The captain was close to turning the ship around with the emergency call "man over board" when a crewman found him. The captain was glad to find Charlie, although he was noticeably annoyed.

"Always tell someone else where you are when you work on deck," Charlie was reprimanded by the ships mate.

"Aye, aye, sir," Charlie replied.

"If you go overboard even if the sea is even calm and still and lie in the water and watch the ship steam away to the horizon, you are basically already doomed," the ships mate added. Charlie had learned a lesson. He made a harness, with a loop larger than the steel posts he would paint and tied it around his waist as he painted, and everyone was satisfied.

As rookies, Charlie and Ritch were given responsibility for the "dog watch." The watchman must look out for other vessels that may cross their own route. Other garbage such as barrels or timber and other things that can float around the sea can be ignored. The dog watch was between 02:00 and 08:00.

As the captain did not trust one of the boys to stay awake, they were assigned the watch jointly. Even with company, it is easy to fall asleep at best under starlit, pitch darkness. Charlie and Ritch stood up all the time. Sitting was the same as falling asleep. Leaning comfortably against something was the same as falling asleep. They took turns to be out and about and to look inside at the radar at thirty-minute intervals.

Sometimes the ships mate said in clear weather that he could take the radar observations and the boys could scout outside together. It was during these long nights that they could talk about their thoughts of the journey, women, and the life that would await them in Australia.

An early morning when Charlie got into the rhythm that would be his routine for the next month, he heard gulls around the ship. Far above, he could see the contour of Mauna Kea, which towered up like a gray-white mass over the sea surface. "Land-ho, land-ho!" he shouted, and the message was relayed by the ships mate to the crew via the speaker system. Charlie felt extremely proud to have fulfilled his various commitments and that it was he who had announced that they had sighted land, after seven days at sea.

However, it would take until the afternoon, before they could head into Pearl Harbor on Oahu.

They steered into the Kaiwi Channel which lies between the islands of Oahu and Molokai. At Molokai, people who had contrived leprosy, during the mid-19th century, had been interned. The place is today called Kalaupapa Park and is located on a remote, hard to access peninsula. During leprosy time and even today you can only get there on foot, donkey or by boat.

It was calm and clear weather when *Quantas* rounded the peninsula "Diamond Head" on Oahu. The peninsula got its name after English sailors found calcite crystals there, in 1825, which were mistaken for diamonds. On the mountain is a volcanic crater where King Kamehameha the Great sacrificed people after winning a battle against rival chieftains, in 1795. When Charlie could see the coast with Honolulu, he thought he had come to paradise.

There were numerous boats, beautiful Waikiki Beach, white, wooden houses on the slope above the beach, and deep greenery that seemed to cover the island with moss. The captain had been notified via telex to enter the port of Honolulu as Pearl Harbor was suspended for civilian traffic. Above the starboard side of the harbor entrance, a palace towered, the only one on American soil. It is the Iolani palace where former monarchs had their residence. The palace is a large red-brown stone building that made an impression on the crew.

Entering the harbor, Charlie was filled with pride. The machines were now running at low rpm and the vibrations and the hum were a pleasure to feel, Charlie thought. People were buzzing about the quay. Some had chores and some just wanted to watch as the ship docked.

Ritch was down in the engine room and could not see the interaction that existed between the captain and the crew when they parked 1,000 tons of steel next to the quay, without the slightest scratch on the ship. It's like observing a well-practiced circus number. Charlie had to help a sailor take home the slack on the stern hawser (the rear hawser as seen from the bow) as the propulsive force eased. Nobody says anything. It's like a bunch of speechless people performing a common act in full consensus.

Highball was standing on the deck and he celebrated his arrival in his own way, with a sip from a hip flask. They were lucky not to lie at anchor in the bay. The crew was eager to get ashore but first the ship would be unloaded. Then you had two days leave! Everyone except the captain, the ships mate and Highball helped with unloading which took the rest of the afternoon. Ritch and Charlie could barely wait to step down the gangway and feel solid ground under their feet again.

They put on clean shirts and shorts that they had saved for this occasion and went with several others of the crew to look at the town. Even though the ground was not moving, it felt like it was swinging a little. They really were in paradise.

Lots of different people and scents, narrow streets and restaurants on the right and left. The first stop was a watering hole to celebrate the arrival. It was "Paddy's Bar." an Irish pub, with wonderful atmosphere. In one corner, two men played Irish music and there were a lot of people, including many soldiers in uniform. Ritch could buy beer, but Charlie only bought Coke, as he was under twenty. He got beer from the others and soon became a little looped like most in the pub.

When Charlie and Ritch sat down in a half-moon-shaped sofa, two women sat down with them and asked if they wanted to buy them a drink.

"Certainly" Ritch replied and ordered drinks for them. They were a little older than Ritch and had typical colorful dresses and fluffy hairstyles.

"What is your name then?" the darker of the two asked Ritch. He told them their names and Charlie said:

"And what's your names?"

One was Darlene, but simply called "D," who was the slightly darker one, and "Victoria" who was a little lighter and simply called "V." When Charlie and Ritch woke up in the morning with a hangover, after contributing to the women's rents, they realized that the names must be contrived. How else could you be called "V" and "D" which together become Venereal Disease.

It was Charlie's first close contact with a woman, and he remembered at most half. Overall, none of them could have been particularly successful. The money they earned on the trip over and was received, before going ashore, was now almost completely gone. They had breakfast at a joint near the harbor and wondered what was next. Ritch suggested that they walk off their hangovers and decided to go to Pearl Harbor, a mile from the port of Honolulu.

A few hours later, they could look out over the huge bay, with its many coves. There were many warships in the bay that lay at anchor. It was decided, after Pearl, that aircraft carriers would only be in port to bunker, which was rare as bunkering oil and supplies from supply ships at sea was routine.

They continued their hike until they could see an island in the bay. The remains of a ship tower with twisted and black-burnt steel protruded, from the water on the island. It was the battleship *Arizona* that remained untouched, since that fateful Sunday, in September twelve years earlier.

At the submarine museum, you could take a ferry out to the *Arizona* which they did. During the trip that took ten minutes, the war became a reality for Ritch and Charlie and the others on the ferry. "Those bastards," exclaimed an elderly gentleman from the mainland. The ferry circled around the *Arizona* a full lap—visitors in complete silence. When the engines were turned off, the captain ordered all hands to observe a moment of silence, for the thousands of sailors and soldiers who remained down there.

Charlie saw bubbles of oil creating a blue-purple rainbow-like shimmer on the surface, and he mentioned it to Ritch. A crew member on the ferry heard their observation and he told them it was the ship crying.

Charlie got a tear in his eye at the same time as he thought of his dad. The older passenger noticed it and said, "I feel like you kid."

"My dad was a pilot," Charlie said. "I was four years old when he died," he continued. The older man shook his hand and shed a tear as well.

The ferry returned to the dock, with a noticeably solemn group, of visitors. They walked back towards Honolulu, through the "Moanalua Gardens" which eased their minds. There were flower shows that they had never seen before. Across the canals were small, wooden bridges surrounded by low, crooked trees, with wide crowns, miniature palm trees, various birds, with curved beaks, of different colors and Carp fish in the water. Along the shoreline were Hibiscus plants ten meters high. They are called *Punaluu*. It was simply the most beautiful place they had ever seen.

They ate a burger at a small café, inside the garden, served by a Chinese, with long black braid. The Chinese had experienced an upswing, in the islands, during the war, when all Japanese were interned, whether civilian or not. Charlie had never seen any Chinese before. It suddenly felt like he was far from home.

They continued their walk and came to the "Bishop Museum." They decided to go in and well inside the entrance, they got a look back in time. Here was the world's largest collection of boats, household goods, clothing, huts, stuffed birds and personal items such as barrels and combs from the islands. There was also a 1:10 scale model of the Polynesian double-hulled canoe.

By now, they were once again near the city's bustling nightlife. They did not want to waste their money and chose to sleep on the *Quantas*. It went well—once you got used to a steel room and a sixty cm. wide bed and the engines were silent.

The next day they would be back for loading, in the afternoon, so they took a taxi to Waikiki Beach. Several of the crew did the same and they enjoyed being off a few more hours. They would be at sea for at least a week to Fiji and it was important to use time their well while they had the chance.

After lunch, they returned to *Quantas* and helped load tons of "Dole" pineapple jars and sugar, into jute bags. There was no cooling room or dehumidifier in the hull, so it was important for the sugar to be able to air. Otherwise, molds were often formed in the tropics. The crew was instructed by the ships mate to pay special attention to the weather, during the upcoming trip. Without warning, it can downpour, with fierce winds. All the hatches of the ship were open constantly to ventilate both the cargo and the crew's spaces, in warm areas. If there was risk of rain, the hatches would immediately be closed which was every crewman's duty.

After loading, it was high time for Charlie to help Highball, in the canteen again. When dinner was over, they would cast off. Ritch made preparations in the engine room and the engines were started up. When the captain signaled, the circus act was done in reverse order and they veered out from Honolulu.

Charlie and Ritch had to sleep for a few hours, before it was time for the dog watch again, at 02:00.

At the time they had entered the port of Honolulu, there had been an underground earthquake outside Japan, just over 1900 miles from Hawaii. Charlie had slept just a little while when he was thrown out of his bunk. *Quantas* had steered southwest, past the islands' protective breakwaters, and was hit hard by a flood wave, without warning. The boat was able to straighten up, after a short while that felt like an eternity.

Fortunately, the hatches had been closed. They had been hit by a *tsunami*, waves that can reach up to thirty meters and can easily overturn a ship. No one in the crew slept that night.

During dog watch, Charlie asked the ships mate as he was monitoring the radar, if someone else could take that duty, during the trip to Fiji. The officer was lightly annoyed and replied:

"The captain decides who does what during each sailing. If anything needs to be changed, he will discuss it with me first, and we have not changed any routines regarding tasks, during this trip."

"Ten-four" Charlie replied.

The trip to Fiji was similar to the one they had made to Hawaii from the west coast of the United States, in distance, but the ships mate explained that the first sailing took longer because the currents there go from west to east. Sailing south, one would probably cut three days, for the same distance, because the currents there normally went from east to west.

"As you fulfill your chores to my satisfaction, I will address your duty list with the captain, before the sail from Fiji to Sydney," added the mate.

"Aye, aye, Sir," Charlie replied.

He had gained the utmost respect for the crew, the ships mate in particular, and he knew that discussions were over. The officer resembled Grandpa in manner: focused solely on the ship, cargo and the task they had to perform.

Nobody in the crew ever argued with the ships mate, except possibly Highball when he'd been fortified by whiskey while serving dinner. This was tolerated and the ships mate let him be as his skills as a cook were widely appreciated by the crew.

Drinking was only prohibited for the person who had the watch and the person the ships mate at the time allowed to steer the vessel. Nobody complained about that system. The giant wave was the big topic of conversation on this stretch. It was agreed that should this happen again, the ship would be hit from behind, which had a calming effect on the crew. After all, they had the broad side to the wave when it happened. Everything that was loose on the deck was gone. Barrels of water used during the day, lots of ropes and tools that the crew had left on deck and one of the lifeboats. There were three lifeboats left, which was more than was needed for twelve people.

Some windows on the deck had been pushed in and several hatches had been torn off.

"It was a rather mild Tsunami," the captain said afterwards. "Otherwise we would not have been alive now," he added.

Charlie, after the captain's statement, had even greater respect for the sea and for his watch duty. It was perfectly clear, the second night at sea, when Charlie noticed that the polar star disappeared behind the horizon. He had had plenty of time to study the constellations and the ships mate was happy to explain when he visited the bridge to check the radar, as to how to navigate with constellations. In the past, it was all you had to go on. Already, Columbus knew that the polar star would be parallel to the horizon to keep a constant course westward. Charlie went to the bridge. The ships mate was not there but he told what he had noticed to the helmsman who said:

"You just passed the equator my friend. The captain is going to invite everyone to a glass of Rum tomorrow," he added.

"What should I look for now?" Charlie asked.

"Where we are headed, you are safest keeping track of your scalp," replied the helmsman. "Back to your post now" he continued.

Charlie wasn't very scared, but he became thoughtful by the helmsman's serious tone.

He had never been outside California, before mustering onto the *Quantas,* in San Diego and could not know that there were cannibals on Fiji. After all, they would only take on provisions on Fiji, so what could there be to be afraid of, he wondered.

He had a strange feeling that he was in the wrong place. Oddly enough, the noise from the sea that had previously given Charlie such a sense of freedom, now seemed to make him feel queasy. It felt like he was leaving the world behind. Suddenly, he thought of the deep water he had underneath him and a little, steel plate that made up the hull. They had been dangerously close to becoming a total wreck a day ago and the feeling of desolation churned in his head. He told Ritch what the helmsman had said.

Ritch replied, "If he talks about scalps and where we're going, he probably means they eat people there."

"Surely it's just fairy tales?" Charlie replied.

"It's true," Ritch continued.

"How do you know that?" Charlie asked.

"I heard some in the crew talk about it," Ritch continued, "and they don't even want to go ashore," he added.

"It must be banned?" Charlie wondered.

"Maybe so," Ritch replied, and continued, "what could you do about it? Out here, there is no police who can prevent the natives from doing exactly what they want."

"Then I won't go ashore," Charlie replied sorely.

"Haven't you read *Mutiny on the Bounty*?" Ritch asked his friend.

"Yes," Charlie replied, continuing: "they were hung in England and not eaten."

"Captain Bligh went to Fiji and when he was to leave, he and his crew were pursued by two canoes—they wanted Bligh for lunch!" replied Ritch.

"Obviously he made it," answered Charlie and continued: "And I intend to do that, too."

After breakfast the next morning, Charlie and Ritch were summoned by the crew, had to put on swimming trunks, and marched up on deck. They were forced to stand on a strong net laid out on the deck and which had a heavy rope attached to the four corners. The net was hoisted with a crane and, screaming, the couple were heaved over the railing and into the foamy water. When they were hoisted up on deck again, both had their swimming trunks at their feet, to the satisfaction of the crew. Ritch wanted to pee on them, but Charlie managed to prevent revenge by the expectation that they would probably be thrown overboard again if he did.

"Equator Dip," cried the crew, as they landed on deck.

They passed Samoa, after three days at sea, and would enter the port of Fiji, after another day. There is a string of islands around Fiji which is why the captain chose to go ashore, during daytime.

During the morning hours of day four, Ritch and Charlie could hear the screams of seagulls long before they could see them.

"We're approaching land," Charlie said. Ritch did not answer. He slept. Charlie woke him gently, so no one else would notice what was going on. When he awakened, they could see the first gulls. They were big gulls and had a band of black feathers around their wings and tail feathers like swallows, long and two-edged like in a "V."

"They look different," Ritch said.

"Compared to what?" Charlie wondered.

"To the gulls in Hawaii," Ritch continued.

Shortly thereafter, they heard a strange noise above their heads, in the early, dawn light. It sounded like a puppy dog imitating a bell. Soon, they were able to locate he strange sound. It was a peculiar sight.

An orange bird sat on the railing. It was reminiscent of a pigeon but colored in bright, orange feathers. The head moved like a pigeon as it went, so it must be a pigeon thought the boys. After seeing ten-foot Hibiscus, on Oahu, they had now become accustomed to strange creatures. It turned out later when they told of their discovery that it was a local pigeon called Biib.

The captain chose to pass through the Mamanucas islands, which make up some of the archipelago's more than 300 islands. They appear as dark green, small islands surrounded by green and turquoise coral reefs, with white foam all around. The captain sailed around the main island called Viti Levu and went south from the Kadavu Passage to the capital of Suva. *Quantas* passed large numbers of smaller fishing boats, from the night's and early dawn's fishing, on their way to the harbor.

It was a hot and humid morning, but the crew was happy to approach the shore, although some did not want to leave the ship. The captain had heard the rumor and he reassured the crew that it was known that there was cannibalism but that it became illegal when it became a British colony, in 1874.

"Hope they ate some of them," a crew member said, "for they are everywhere, with colonization in the service of Her Majesty."

Fiji's original population had expanded dramatically, with the English imports of Calcutta Indians. The phenomenon of working for money had not worked with the locals, which is why the English used labor from their largest colony.

The captain had been to Fiji several times before and knew their local chieftain Tatanoa who had sent a message to *Quantas* that the captain and crew were invited to a party in the evening. Because provisioning would take until the next day, the captain chose to respond at once that he and the crew would attend.

Fijians can handle sailboats, hunting, fishing and everything related to agriculture, but loading on order, in a given time, was against their way of life. Just the water refill, took most of the day of arrival. They gladly stretched loads because then they could charge an additional port fee, if the ship was still there the next morning.

The captain managed to convince the entire crew that it was safe to go ashore and take part in the festivities. It was a relief and the crew appreciated having solid ground under their feet for a while. However, he needed two volunteers who would guard the ship. They were promised double pay that day and leave the day after, until the ship sailed. The helmsman who had told Charlie of cannibals and another crew member volunteered and then the matter was settled.

The crew was instructed by the captain to greet both Chief Tatanoa and others with the courtesy phrase "Bula." It was the only word they needed to say.

A messenger brought the crew to what would become a magical ceremony. After half an hour's walk in the humid heat, they arrived at a courtyard surrounded by pink-colored single-story houses of raffia mats and thatched roofs. In the middle of the small square, there was a rock formation that had to be the top of a well and torches were burning all around the yard. Charlie noticed that they were significantly darker than Hawaiians and well-grown. The men had nothing on their upper body. Many of them had sticks through their ears which were some kind of decoration. The women wore thin colorful, cotton dresses and many wore wreaths on their heads.

In a raised, wicker chair, Chief Tatanoa sat. Around his neck, he had a leather strap, with a large tooth and another strap, with a human jawbone. At the sides, stood guards with machetes, in their belts. On their knees, next to them, sat many women who looked really inviting. The chief welcomed the captain with a big smile, and with outstretched arms, he shouted so everyone could hear: "*Bula.*"

"Bula," answered the captain, bowing his head lightly in disguised awe. The chief repeated the word to the crew and received the same answer and the chief looked pleased. The captain handed over a box to the chieftain who immediately called a servant who gave the captain a small pack. These were gifts to the captain personally. The crew was unable to see what the package contained, but the string lined ball of leaves was assumed to hold gold dumplings.

He gave a new order and two other servants went to each crewman and hung a leather strap around the neck of each, from which hung a whale tooth.

"It's called 'Rabuka' and it's a gift of honor," said the captain.

Then you heard "Yaquona!" from the chieftain and a servant came to each crewman, with a coconut mug containing a drink that the English called "Kava." It is not alcoholic but mildly numbing. The chief clapped once and then one would drink from his "Bilo," as the mug was called.

Charlie soon felt that both his lips, cheeks and then his head were mildly numb. The drink is made from crushed paprika roots and tastes much like clay or yesterday's rejected tea.

At that moment, he noticed a pair of eyes staring at him. They belonged to a beautiful woman who stood up beside the chieftain. *Strange that she gets up when everyone else is on their knees*, Charlie thought, and his conclusion was that it must be a wife or daughter. He gave her a weak nod, but she didn't as much as twitch. Her hair was black, and he felt he could return her gaze when she didn't move her eyes.

When everyone had emptied their *Bilos*, the chieftain clapped three times and shouted some instructions, and palm leaves were brought out for the guests to sit on. They sat in a half-moon on each side of the chieftain on the ground. Straight ahead, there was a coal bed that ran about five feet across a short distance from the guests. Traditionally, those who wanted to show their masculinity and claim to be leaders in the clan would walk barefoot over the coal. Half a dozen warriors took the walk while Charlie hoped no one would ask him to do the same.

At the same time, he wondered how it could be that these natives could be controlled by England, on the other side of the globe? He concluded that it must have been weapon power, as the inhabitants were few and their weapons were no match against rifles. That was only half the truth. The islands were and still are extremely isolated. When missionaries were to Christianize the population of the 19th century, it was easy to convince the population that it was better to serve other gods. The English knives were better than the Fijians, so it was logical to think that their gods were better.

He had a sense of harmony as he sat there among friendly-minded Fijians. They seemed so relaxed and safe. After the coal promenade, the chief clapped again and all *Bilos* were refilled. Fruits were presented on palm leaves.

Then a pig was heard protesting wildly. A large pig was brought up to the middle of the pitch, in front of the chieftain. The captain explained that it would be slaughtered and then be dinner. The chief took out a large knife, with a white shaft, and held it in front of the captain. The captain said he had never slaughtered a pig before, but the chief did not understand it.

"I have" Charlie said, and reached out with his hand to the chieftain.

The chief smiled broadly and handed the knife to Charlie. Four warriors held the pig as Charlie went forward and quickly cut off the two main arteries and trachea in what appeared to be a single sweep with the knife.

The chief clapped three times and invited Charlie to sit down next to him. Charlie thought he would be adopted on the spot. The woman with the eyes came up with another *Bilo* to Charlie, who now felt lightly stunned by *Kava* and everyone's cheers over the slaughter.

The pork was cut and grilled over the glow on the palm leaves and everyone ate and drank for hours. When everything was fuzzy, the woman, with the eyes, took Charlie's hand and pulled him away from the glow of the fire. She put one hand on one breast and took Charlie's hand and placed it on the other.

"Bula," said Charlie, as he was told by the captain.

She smiled and pulled Charlie to a small hut some distance away from the others. No one in the crew returned to the ship that night. Charlie had experienced genuine tenderness and was paradisically happy when the woman took him to the beach to swim in the morning. It turned out that she was the chieftain's daughter and she knew English well.

"Stay," she said.

"Australia" replied Charlie. "Must go," he continued.

"Better here," she replied. "All free." "Everything," she added.

"I have a job on the boat," Charlie continued.

"Why?"

"To take me to Australia."

"Why?

"I have to do it."

"Why?"

"I do not know."

"Do you like me?"

"Very much."

Charlie was sweaty from the humidity and her presence. He realized that at that very moment he wanted nothing more than to swim with her again and be seduced into infinity. He kissed her slowly and got up to leave.

"Are you coming back?" the woman asked.

"Maybe," Charlie replied, "maybe."

Charlie was delusional as he walked toward the harbor. Maybe he could stop for a while and take the next boat? He had signed on. It wasn't just jumping off. By the way, he and Ritch were a team. He had told Imelda that he would not be alone.

Imelda, yes. It seemed like everything was so far away. He was, in fact, in another world. Here no one was thinking about falling prices for farmers. They did not think about work. They did what was needed, when needed. Such freedom!

During the day, they managed to get the supplies they needed. The captain wanted to leave the harbor in the afternoon to precisely locate all the islands. Once out on the high seas, it was then clear sailing down to Sydney.

After dinner, the captain called Charlie and Ritch to the captain's mess.

"You did a nice show with the pig yesterday," said the captain.

"I grew up on a pig farm," Charlie replied.

"Ritch has the watch 08:00 – 14:00" said the captain. "You are relieved from watch duty and will paint daytime, with a harness."

"Aye, aye, sir!" Charlie replied.

"What are you going to do in Sydney?" the captain wondered cautiously.

"We don't know," Charlie replied.

"We need people like you and Ritch," the captain continued, adding, "you are welcome to continue with *Quantas* if you wish."

"Thanks Captain, but we have plans on land," Ritch replied, adding, "Maybe we can sign on next time you come there?"

"We'll see, we'll see," replied the captain, pointing to the cabin door.

"It's nice to avoid the engine room for a day," Ritch thought.

"You can help me paint at the same time," Charlie replied.

"Funny," Ritch thought.

"We probably have a couple of three days left for Sydney. "What are we to do?" Charlie asked.

Mostly his thoughts were occupied by the lovely night with Emori.

"We sign off when we arrive and then we can check if there is anything to do in Sydney—otherwise we can hitchhike to another city and look further there," Ritch replied.

"Or else we can sail on a boat back to Fiji," Charlie continued.

"Why not, we are real sailors now," Ritch said. "There are a lot of sheep where we are headed," Ritch continued. "You are used to animals—maybe we can work on a sheep farm," he continued.

"Never!" Charlie replied, adding, "I would have been just as happy watering the pigs at home on the ranch. I want to do something here that you can't do at home," he continued.

"And what would it be then?" Ritch wondered.

"If we rent a boat, we can ferry tourists," Charlie thought.

"Our money won't be enough," Ritch replied, "It is better to take on something that makes money directly without having to spend first."

"Okay," Charlie replied, "as long as we don't become sheep farmers, I'm game for everything."

"Good," Ritch replied.

Two days later, *Quantas* entered Sydney's port. The port entrance is huge. As they rounded North Head and headed to starboard, there were three ports to choose from, in the one-and-a-half-mile long channel that leads through Sydney. They were going to Port Jackson, which is the largest of these three. Charlie was on duty and standing on the deck, with the ships mate at the helm.

"We are on a new continent now," said the ships mate.

"How big it is," Charlie replied.

"You forget quickly," the mate continued. "It is reminiscent of San Francisco Bay," he added.

"Never been there," Charlie replied.

Just then, they saw the back of a whale ahead of the bow near Bradley's Head, on the north side of the inlet.

"It swims under the ship," said the mate, ordering a full stop in the machines. Ritch reacted, with lightning speed and throttled the engines to idle. A ship goes on as if nothing happened for a while, but they slipped over the whale without noticing any contact with it.

They continued portside to Double Bay, on the south side of the inlet, where they would dock a moment later. *There must be a thousand boats in this channel*, Charlie thought. The water was crystal clear and calm. The whale was an experience, he thought further. The sky was clear blue and everything Charlie could see shone beautifully, in the harbor and around the wide inlet. Lots of small houses surrounded the harbor, with its many quays. It was dark green all around the houses. It was low, in contrast to what he saw in Hawaii and Fiji. Those were volcanic islands and they were now on a continent.

He got a sense of grandeur when he looked around. This was a sight he would never forget.

"Go out and keep your eyes open for small boats," the ships mate continued.

"Aye, aye, Sir" Charlie replied and went to his post on the deck.

In all directions, there were ferries that were red and yellow, reminiscent of shortened riverboats on the Mississippi River. They routinely carried out their circus number at the quay and were ordered to unload quickly, only then would they be able to sign off. Unloading took the rest of the day.

In the evening, everyone had leave and Charlie realized that they had nowhere to live ashore. They talked to the captain about signing off the next day which was acceptable. The salary would be paid in connection with sign-off. The crew longed ashore and all but two watchmen were left on *Quantas* to make Sydney unsafe. The captain offered to invite the crew to dinner to celebrate their completed first stage of their journey to Europe and then via the Panama Canal back to San Diego.

They took a couple of taxis to Chinatown bordering Hyde Park and soon found an inviting tavern called "Wang-Li's" where they got a big round table, with a food wheel in the middle. The captain explained that it is hardly possible to find open bars and restaurants, after six o'clock in the evening in Sydney. Therefore, there were plenty of people in the evening in Chinatown. The food wheel was filled to capacity and loads of *Tsingtao*, the Chinese beer, and Fosters, the Australian ditto, were brought in for the crew. Charlie had never eaten Chinese food before, and he really liked the different dishes. One of the crew called the food fish bait but he ate anyway. The captain solemnly told everyone what they already knew, that Charlie and Ritch would stay in Australia. He thanked them for doing their job very well and asked them, "What are your plans now?"

"To earn our living," Ritch replied.

"Any way except working with sheep," Charlie added.

"Then you have excluded the area where you have the best chance of reaching your goal," the captain continued, adding: "You probably do well to leave Sydney, because there are only industries here. Head north along the coast and you will surely find work easier."

"Thank you for your advice," Charlie replied, adding, "and thank you for trusting us and for giving us the opportunity to join the *Quantas*."

"It was a pleasure to have you on board," replied the captain.

After dinner, there was nothing to do on the quiet streets, so they made their way back to the boat. Charlie and Ritch wondered what to do the next day.

"We'll check if we find anything in town in the morn," Charlie said, and continued, "otherwise we try to lift from here."

"Sure," Ritch replied.

When they finished breakfast, it was time to sign-off the *Quantas*.

The captain paid the agreed salary of ten dollars a day with a supplement of two dollars per night when they had the dog watch.

"You did a good job and you can be proud of yourselves," the captain said.

The boys grinned and with a common "Aye, aye, Sir," took their few belongings and bid farewell to the crew. Highball said he would miss his assistant and that he would console himself with a snort from the hip flask. They laughed and then they left the ship.

Sydney was not as inviting in daylight. The quays were rugged and lined with wooden sheds with large gates. People pulled carts with pallets and other debris to take care of fish and it smelled old and like dung everywhere. They did not have much to carry and decided to hike to town. They walked past Rushcutters Bay, through a large park and on towards the city center which was near Hyde Park and facing the water. It was lunchtime so they took in an Italian tavern near a cape called Bennelong Point where there were large hangars for trams.

Sydney had been founded by the English, during the late 1780s when they carried prisoners from their homeland to their new exile. They docked at Circular Quay, a U-shaped harbor at what is today the city center. Next to the harbor, there was a collection of fragile workers' homes on what is called The Rocks. This is where the prisoners had built their sheds in the 19th century. There is a pub on every street corner. This was the view from the restaurant they had chosen to visit.

The menu had mostly British dishes even though it was an Italian tavern. The waiter was called Beppi and they asked why the many British dishes.

"People here do not want anything different from what they know," Beppi replied, continuing: "When I came here last year, there was only one Italian restaurant despite the fact that it has been strong Italian immigration in recent years. I try to sneak in pasta and garlic, but it is not often appreciated."

"We take chicken," Ritch said, adding, "in Italian."

"Pronto," Beppi replied with a big grin.

Beppi served a glass of red wine "on the house."

He said that Americans were popular in Australia. Some had stayed after the Second World War because they liked the climate and just because they were popular. Many Italians and Greeks had also come after the war. It tasted of England's way of life when it came to food, literature and social life which was uneventful, but it gradually changed, through these influential people.

Furthermore, since the gold-digging period in the mid-1800s, many Chinese had come, which was most noticeable in the cities.

"Do you know where we could find jobs in town?" Ritch asked.

"I have several friends working in the state sheep slaughterhouse in Homebush Bay," Beppi replied. "I can ask them to ask their Manager," he added.

"OK," Ritch replied.

Beppi left again and Charlie protested: "That's not what I came here for."

"We have nothing—and anything is better than nothing!" replied Ritch.

"I guess so," Charlie said. They got chicken with pasta and garlic and it tasted better than anything they had eaten since leaving the US.

"Do you know where we could stay a few nights?" Ritch asked his new friend, Beppi. "Sure," Beppi replied, "there are empty houses on the other side of the bay—just occupy

any room there. You can have breakfast in the pubs and there are public showers in the area."

After lunch, the boys wandered off to The Rocks to find a place where it didn't rain and something inhabitable. Beppi had told them to contact him the next day to see if there was any message from the slaughterhouse.

It was not far to walk from the taverna, around the harbor area towards The Rocks. The whole area was littered with old, wooden houses, the highest being four stories high, and all were colorless. They must be at least 100 years old, they thought, as they walked close to half a dozen piers in the water. People seemed to live in most houses. At a small square, they found public toilets and showers separate for men and women, respectively. They asked an elderly gentleman who looked homeless if he knew where there was a vacant house to spend the night. He replied that there were several, just look around. He asked the guys if they were cockeys because they were from America. Charlie thought the guy asked if they were cockey or stubborn and replied that all Americans are not cockey.

"I mean cowboys," replied the old man. "We say cockeys here," he continued.

"We are sailors," Charlie replied, and continued, "and we need somewhere to live."

"I know a lone lady who can rent temporarily," replied the old man. She has a pub nearby and there are a couple of rooms upstairs. "Follow me," he continued.

They walked for a few minutes on a narrow street where the houses reminded the boys of the Mexicans' houses, in California, and resembled the school's student dorm, Charlie thought. They knocked at Mrs. Evans and the guy introduced the sailors.

"You don't look like sailors," said the lady.

"We came here by boat for a fee," replied Ritch, adding, "so we are sailors."

There was a room upstairs that they could rent weekly. It was pure paradise compared to the cabin on *Quantas* and after negotiating a good price the boys accepted their new home. They had to pay in advance, which they gladly did. The house, like all the others in the district, was completely uninsulated, which made it very noisy, even indoors. The houses stood close together and were generally crowded with people.

Mrs. Evans had a private bathroom, but the guest room lacked amenities. There was a sink with running water, and it was enough. Guys can do well with that asset they thought. After the installation at Mrs. Evans, they went to the pub to see if anyone knew anything about work. With American accents, there was no problem getting people to talk—on the contrary. They could only talk to each other and someone wondered where they came from. People in Australia were curious about Americans, especially of California where movies came from. The Korean War had just ended, and it was quickly pointed out what a fine effort the US had made against the communists in the north. Since Charlie had gone to CBS during the war, he hadn't noticed much of it. There was no military service, so Ritch hadn't noticed much of the Korean War either. He had not been attracted to the Air Force seeking civilian mechanics, either. He was satisfied with his life at the Corona station and with his stock-car hobby. They spoke with an older guy who really looked like a cowboy. He said that in the city and around Sydney there were only industries. "Most people from the outside end up here, he said. Much is about fish," the guy continued, "and we have big, brick factories and the state wool mill that employs people all the time."

"May we ask what you do?" Charlie wondered.

"Whalers" replied the man. "You guys seem to be far from home."

"Yup," Ritch replied.

"What are you doing here?"

"We don't know that yet," Charlie replied. "We talked to an Italian who told us that the slaughterhouse always needs people, but we are not keen on it," he continued.

The whaler said: "I know the place. It is at a brick pit at the far end of the harbor. There are 20,000 sheep slaughtered daily and I would not set foot there," and continued, "I come from Papua in New Guinea. The alternatives one had were to live as farmers and hunters there or to travel to Australia. The biggest difference is that the opportunities here are endless, just as the country. I have been at sea for many years and this is my right environment. In the north, there are two types of environment: either scorching heat, which applies ten months a year, or monsoon rain. People are constantly yearning for water, and when it comes, there are often floods in the villages. I was lucky to find a fishing boat in Cairns that needed a helping hand and that became my trait.

We cruised along the coast and, after a while, I jumped on a whaler, in Brisbane. Admittedly, we are out for weeks at a time, but it gives decent pay."

"We got here by boat," Ritch said.

"Paying passengers or as crewmen?" wondered the whaler.

"As crew," Charlie replied.

"I can ask the skipper if anyone on ours or any other vessel is needed."

"We're probably more interested in being on land, but thank you," Ritch said.

"Then you will probably leave Sydney. There are Stations, i.e. ranches and finer areas north, along the coast. People are often needed most everywhere. Remember that the country is huge, and the population is small, along the coasts. Inland, there is only steppe and Aboriginal people."

"What are Aborigines?" Charlie wondered.

"They are like your Indians, our indigenous people," the whaler replied, and continued, "they are black, live on the steppe and do not want contact with whites. By the way, they can't speak English. Twenty years ago, a railway was started between Melbourne, Alice Springs, in the central part and Darwin up north. They went on until, very recently when they put down construction. A hundred years ago, you managed to connect coast to coast with rail. We made a serious effort with the same thing and lost to the elements. Not only did the heat make cabbage of the workmen, heavy rain washed away the rails, termites ate up the crossties; we also had constant feuds with the Aborigines about the hunting grounds. They were simply terrified of both the track and the machines."

"If not so many live in the country, can you do without rail?" Charlie wondered.

"That's probably what we have realized now," continued the whaler, adding, "shipping was pleased with the decision to skip the railroad. Now sea freight thrives, and everyone seems satisfied except the ranch owners who have big problems with transporting sheep and cattle to the coasts for slaughter and export."

"We will probably stay along the coast," Ritch added.

"You will be well received everywhere," said the Whaler. "Americans are very popular here after the war. Many stayed here and you are considered reliable."

"We might stay here too," Charlie said. The moment he said it, he came to think of Imelda and Grandpa and the ranch and home for the first time. They had been away for a month now and it seemed like an eternity. It almost felt as if there was no home. He cleared his thoughts when the whaler stood up to say goodbye, with a "Good luck."

Ritch introduced himself and Charlie did the same. "Chris," replied Whaler, adding, "my father was an Englishman."

Once back at Beppi's tavern, Charlie and Ritch were thinking about an action plan.

"I think we should get out of here and head north," Charlie said.

"The sheep slaughterhouse does not attract me either," said Ritch, "but we do not have much money. Beppi said that Americans could probably easily lift with trucks, on their way back north. They usually went to Melbourne, with iron ore, and from there, with clothes that the large Chinese part of the population in Melbourne sold to buyers.

The Chinese had come by boat, during Australia's great gold rush in the 19th century, and settled there. Melbourne went in the classic, colonial style, heavily influenced by the English.

"We should probably make contact home," Charlie said.

"Do we want them to know we're here?" Ritch wondered.

"Not really, but I think Imelda is really worried about me," Charlie replied.

"You can always send a postcard. After all, we aren't staying here, "Ritch said.

The next day, Charlie mailed the first of few postcards home:

Sydney, September 2nd, 1953

Dear Imelda, Grandma and Grandpa:

Ritch and I came by boat via Hawaii and Fiji. Looking for a job. Will probably stay for a time. Don't look for me.

Charlie.

Some of the sense of freedom he experienced on deck in the Pacific when he felt the wind in his hair and the fluttering clothes, he experienced again when he put the card in the mailbox. Now, he knew there was no need to worry and that everything was OK. It was like cutting the umbilical cord, or the little remaining thread that was left.

The rent was paid in advance for the whole week and the landlady had no objection to Charlie and Ritch wanting to leave. On the contrary, she was really encouraging when they told her that they were going north to do something that they hadn't really figured out.

"You are going to Never Never Land," she said.

"What does it mean?" Charlie wondered.

"It is up in the north that you find land untouched. since the beginning of time, land that the Aborigines say you never, never leave of your own free will."

"I'm all apples!" she exclaimed in a natural delight at their decision.

"We're probably doing the right thing," Charlie thought.

They packed their few belongings and went on foot to the center, to have a final lunch with Beppi. On the way, they passed Circular Quay where the ferries dock and the Botanical Garden held its 7,000 species of vegetation.

They stopped on a park bench and noticed small, small movements up in a tree. Hardly noticeable, you could see a hundred budgies that completely melted into the tree's crown. They agreed it was a good sign for the forthcoming journey. The feeling of freedom was reinforced by being on the road again. Beppi recommended taking the ferry over to North Sydney and then a bus north to Newcastle. There you could choose to stay overnight or try to take a night trip north.

When they were leaving, Beppi made them promise to come back, which they did, said goodbye and wandered to the ferry. During the short trip to the north shore, they noticed the beautiful, green hillside on the other side, with many seemingly newly built white-sided stone houses—"there we will stay when we come back" Charlie said.

"If we come back," Ritch replied.

There was a bus stop, at the ferry site on the north side, and the evening bus to Newcastle would depart at five p.m. Until then, they could do absolutely nothing. They each bought a "Fosters" and soon they were up and running with the bartender, in a lively discussion. It was now clear to the boys that Americans were popular.

The bartender told them that the fine area just next door was called Kirribillie, which according to legend originated from an Englishman in the 19th century, who apparently only drank "Kirin" beer and was named "Billie." He was said to have owned the peninsula and died in poverty.

The big bridge next to the small ferry location had been celebrated the year before when it turned twenty years old. The bridge had radically changed communications between southern and northern Sydney and for a bridge it was immensely popular. Every New Year's Eve, there were torchlight trains across the bridge that attracted most of Sydney's population, the bartender continued. His spontaneous comment on their plans to travel north was, "We'll see you again."

The bus was a joke. Admittedly, it went with typical British punctuality at the appointed time, but it had probably survived the war. Well, the trip would only take a couple of hours. The road to Newcastle stretched a bit inland, so you completely missed contact with the sea. It did not take many minutes before they were on a dusty road and the civilization ended. When they arrived in Newcastle, it was almost dark. There was a diner at the bus station, and it was the next stop. At one table sat four, typical Australians—shirts that had not been washed for a long time, shorts and boots. Ritch and Charlie sat down at the table next to them and soon the plans for the trip north were discussed. One of the four was about to drive north and he invited them to come along. His next stop was Brisbane and he planned to drive for a few hours, sleep in a small village called Coffs Harbor and continue the morning after. The boys were grateful and were carried off in a truck that was as rickety as the bus. The driver was happy with his new company and liked to talk about Australia. He told them that the country had broken apart from Antarctica about 50 million years ago, from a then-supercontinent known as Gondwana. It is these remnants that one sees today along the south coast, cliffs that from above resemble a well-cut puzzle, with smooth, green surface and brown edges that look like cut plywood. Since the breakup, the landscape of Australia did not appear to have changed much. Other continents had ice ages that replaced each other and changed the landscape. Mountains were pushed up by landslides and eroded over time. Valleys like the Grand Canyon were formed by the Colorado River, gradually, six million years ago.

"None of this has happened here," said the driver named Bob and did not seem to live in any particular place. "Australia was and is in a coma," he continued. "Millions of years of rain have leached the nutrients from the earth. Salt from the sea and from dried-up lakes has been deposited by the wind, which has resulted in a harsh and largely unusable landscape. When the first Englishmen were to use the land, they did not realize how long dry periods or rainy periods were, which caused them great problems. The indigenous people, the Aborigines, had for 60,000 years learned to deal with life in the country. They know full well that every five or ten years comes the great river, which floods large parts of the country. Some species are completely dependent on these rivers of water, e.g. The mulaga tree that has been able to survive for fifty years, with very little water interspersed with these rivers. The truck had a small steel ramp at the front, "for the sake of the kangaroos. They sense dry periods and then they do not reproduce. As soon as real rains come, they start having young ones again. When the Aborigines arrived, there were kangaroos larger than today's people and an animal large as a rhino called Diptrodon which resembled a giant dog and soon became extinct. Then, as man depleted the gifts of nature and when gifts came to an end, one had to adapt to reality."

"Of course, there are forests of Eucalyptus trees that we call Karri, but compared to desert and steppe, it is negligible. Then we have the Station—the owners who create pastures through forest harvesting and drain water from the existing river gullies, which means that forest growth does not occur," Bob continued.

"We constantly harvest more than is planted. We have more sheep and kangaroos than trees." Bob rolled a new cigarette.

"What should you do then?" Charlie wondered.

"People think from dry period to the next wet period. You have just enough to get by on a farm and you do not think about the next generation other than the fact that the sons will continue," Bob said.

"It sounds the same way where I come from," Charlie added.

As the scent of burnt straw came rushing through the cabin, Charlie began to realize that even though the world was completely different in other places, humanity had a common trait: "Take what's available—tomorrow is the problem of others."

They continued in the dark, in silence towards Coffs Harbor. All three were affected by the conversation and thoughtful. When they arrived, they went into a cafe at a local gas station and rented two rooms—one for Bob and one for the boys.

Bob wanted to leave at nine o'clock the next day, and after a hearty breakfast of beans, bacon and fried potatoes, the trio pushed further north. At Grafton, a few hours later, Bob stopped to refuel and buy drinking water on High Street.

Charlie and Ritch took a little walk in the village and rested on a concrete bench.

"What are we doing here?" Ritch wondered.

"I wonder," Charlie replied, and continued, "one thing's for sure; I'm not going home again."

They returned to the truck and then continued their journey towards Brisbane. Soon the terrain opened, and the road was bordered by burnt fields that smelled fiercely.

"Has there been a forest fire?" Ritch wondered.

"You can say that," Bob replied, adding, "The landowners burn off the sugar cane at the harvest that was a month ago. It hasn't rained since then. The locals call it "the black snow." In Brisbane, I will be loading up for the return trip to Sydney tomorrow, so you must continue without me. We will surely to find someone to lift with and I can introduce you if you want."

"That would be kind," Ritch said.

"You can go on to Townsville, if suitable. There, the climate is the best in the country and there are always jobs on the coast."

Bob arranged for a ride north with a friend who shipped canned fruit to Cairns, to be exported to Japan. Cairns is our most important export port, the driver explained. It has the safest route through the Solomon Islands and Japan is Australia's largest export market.

On the road again, the driver thought it would take them three to four days to reach Townsville.

"We can squeeze time, if you can drive too," he said.

The driver was named Ron but was called Tolly, and he was not much older than Ritch. At Buderim, the road licked the sea which was appreciated after several days on the road.

Then, as always in Terracotta color, the road went a bit inland

and the environment became increasingly tropical. Tolly told them that they were approaching summer and the north would be getting really hot soon. The boys took turns driving, with Tolly, and, in the afternoon of day two, they entered Rockhampton. The city lies on the meridian Capricorn, Capricorn's tropic, which separates the temperate zone, from the tropics to the north.

Tolly told them that a legendary, sheep farmer named "Big Jackie Howe," in 1892, broke the record as a shearer that still stands today, with 321 sheared sheep in seven hours and forty minutes, with scissors! They get paid per cut sheep and work like demons, Tolly explained.

"You can't leave Australia without trying it," he continued. "But remember—never mess with a shearer—you will surely lose."

"We'll remember that," Charlie replied.

He continued with a story about a cattle thief named, Henry Redford, who, in 1870, stole 1,000 cattle nearby and drove them 160 miles, through unknown desert to the market in the south. The same desert took the lives of two scientists named Burke and Wills ten years earlier. Redford would probably have managed, if the herd had not had a white bull that felled him. Redford had the public on his side. At trial, he was declared innocent by a jury of like-minded adventurers but that he should return the cattle.

The judge became furious and demanded a vote.

Said and done: "Innocent, and he can keep the damned cattle!"

"To be accepted here, you simply have to be a decent person."

At that moment, both Ritch and Charlie felt there was something about this country. After all, they had been good boys thus far, well received everywhere, and they intended to continue the same way.

They said goodbye to Tolly, after becoming accustomed to driving the truck, and without incident. Cairns is a tropical harbor surrounded by mountains, with rainforest. The sea at Cairns is called the Coral Sea and it was flat like a mirror. The temperature was about 40 degrees in the shade and wind was at a standstill.

"Just like home in August," Charlie thought.

They were at a small restaurant by the harbor and pondered on the following day. Inside the restaurant, they asked the waiter if he knew anyone who hired people. He told them that there was a Dane who had a small sponge industry a few kilometers away, who shipped his sponges from the harbor on a weekly basis.

He had mentioned that there were more sponges than he could handle himself, but that he had no money to hire. They could always ask him. They got his name and wondered what to do. They needed money.

CHAPTER SEVEN

The next day, they went to a quay where "Aussie Sponges" was located and searched for a Preben Mortensen, popularly called Preb.

Preb was a short, round, light-haired, middle-aged man who had come to Australia, after World War II. His hobby was diving and, where quite near Cairns there were plenty of natural fungi, which formed part of the great barrier reef's younger vegetation.

"The Japanese and Europeans like them and it's a good business," Preb said. You simply dive down and pick the sponges, put them in nets, hoist them up, wash them in fresh water, and then air dry them. Then they are silky and fully usable as sponges.

He wanted someone to help with the diving and someone to take care of the afterwork, with the sponges.

It was time consuming to manage everything alone and he would welcome Ritch and Charlie, if they could work towards self-sustainability and, after a trial period, shares in the company. There was plenty of room to live in what Preb called the "workshop" and work consisted of fishing while diving. Each time Preb was paid for a shipment, they would share 10 percent of the proceeds. The boys liked Preb and his suggestions and the agreement were sealed by a handshake. They would start the next day.

That day Charlie turned eighteen. Preb happily explained that it was then legal for him to drink alcohol in restaurants and pubs, although one was rarely denied who did not obviously look too young. Although it was morning, it was already hot, when Preb explained the cleaning process in the workshop.

There were about ten, large copper bins with various liquids, in the hall. The first ones usually contained fresh water, where the fresh sponges were allowed to soak for a few days for the salt to leach out. Then they were emptied of water and the contents were allowed to air dry on grids, with drainage into the sea.

Once dry they would go to the next bin which contained a slightly, acidic solution, with vinegar and some powder which was good for the PH level in the sponge. Thereafter, the fungi would again bathe in fresh water, for a few days and then air dry again. To speed up drying, you walked on the sponges, until most of the water was gone. After final drying, they would be packed in boxes airily, ten items per box.

Preb wanted all to be able to dive and do the finishing work, which is why the first day at work meant a diving course, at the nearest reef. Aussie Sponges shared a jetty, with a small number of fishing boats that were all white. Other colors were impossible, Preb thought, as the deck becomes toasty hot even when white. Water was rinsed on the deck to cool it off. As a rule, people went out at dawn to return at lunchtime, to avoid the worst heat. Preb had a white, clinker-built, small boat, with a small cab and a large cargo space in the middle of the boat. In the bow, there was a raised deck from which you could wind up the nets and look for fish. The boat was called Mermaid.

All the other fishermen in the area devoted themselves to fishing Tuna and Snapper, a reddish fish that was the basic food on the coast. Tuna was a good export as a canned product and went to Japan and the United States.

Preb was considered a bit strange with his sponges, but he was respected by the others. After a minimal breakfast consisting of sandwich, coffee and in Preb's case, a small Aquavit, Mermaid was started, and various equipment was carried on board.

"We are in the middle of the big barrier reef," Preb said. "There are many taboos when diving and we will go through them all," he added. "We will stay very close to the reef and at three to five meters depth. A shark can also attack in shallow water and there is one simple basic rule: avoid them. Most often they are curious and just swim by, but if they show interest, you should swim calmly to the reef or to the boat—never up to the surface, if the boat cannot be reached!"

"Understood," Ritch replied, and Charlie nodded in agreement.

"Then we have the fire jellyfish. You see them at some distance. What you must watch out for though, is their tentacles that can be longer than the boat. If you get tangled up in one or more of the tentacles, you can die on the spot. Down in the water, it is taboo to step on the reef. A stonefish completely camouflages itself to resemble the surroundings and can have a myriad of pink, yellow, white, gray and black colors and look just like vegetation. They have thirteen poison needles and treading on one can mean death."

"If we stick to what we are supposed to do, we should avoid trouble?" Charlie suggested.

"Your best friend is your eyes," Preb replied. "I started fishing with a small sailboat on which I built an auto rudder. Then I jumped in, with a rope under my armpits, and with fins and goggles. The others in the harbor said I was crazy, but I learned what is out there. Once, we drifted at two to three knots and I had the spear gun at the ready. I was about five meters behind the boat. It was probably ten meters deep and I didn't look back. Below me, a black shape appeared, slowly, slowly, with majestic wings, passing me at a few meters' depth—a stingray, maybe four meters, from wing tip to wing tip. It probably weighed 300 pounds, at least. It makes you respect the sea. You have to be humble; it's not our natural environment."

Charlie remembered when he learned to swim at home in Lake Matthews ...

It was a day in July and the heat was oppressive. Quite windy, and Charlie had persuaded Imelda to come along to Lake Matthews. What he didn't know was that Judy was there with many other friends. Most people were a bit older and could swim, but Charlie couldn't. Now he had to swim in front of everyone and Judy too. Nothing could be worse. The others didn't know he couldn't swim. No one had taught him. Dad had only been splashing with him, near the beach in Santa Monica when he was four years old and grandfather never had the time or desire either, for that matter.

When Charlie saw Judy, he just wanted to go home, or rather be invisible. In addition, Charlie thought that his Sears & Roebucks swim trunks were ugly. They were made for a much larger person, he thought. That's why he tried to hide his skinny body, with the big towel around his neck.

What was supposed to be a nice day turned out to be something completely different. There must have been one hundred people on the beach and just as many in the water. They threw small American footballs to each other, sunbathed and swam in a blissful mix of activities that all meant one thing: freedom.

Imelda chose a little, secluded place to park the packed lunch bag that held the obligatory apple pie. The beach was much narrower there and people did not pass, which Imelda appreciated. The sunlight shone through the trees and you could partly have shade if you wanted. There was a little slope downhill towards the lake and on the opposite side of the bay, you could see two large cliffs partly submerged.

On one of the rocks, Judy lay sunbathing. That day, as was his habit, looking for small fish on the shoreline was completely impossible.

Judy wore a full length, light blue swimsuit, with white polka dots. Around the rocks, older guys and girls and others were swimming. Some jumped off the rocks and tried to splash the sunbathers.

Charlie stepped into the lukewarm water and tried to act discreetly. He went further and further out, until the water reached him to the armpits. Imelda did not look out to the water but devoted herself to sleeping. Charlie slowly waded a little further out with his arms outstretched, farther than he ever had before. No one took any notice of him. The feeling of being outside the other's lively games was something he clearly remembered as completely suffocating. The last thing he saw, before he disappeared under the water were little rainbows that formed and disappeared, just as quickly by the children's wild splashing. The bottom disappeared. The bubbling sound and muted screams that Charlie heard was a whole new experience. It probably only took a second or two, but Charlie was in another world.

Then came the terror. He started kicking and crawling with his arms frantically while inhaling water that made his entire chest crunch, in trembling rhythmic convulsions. He came to the surface, gasping for air, coughing and screaming: WOW! He was wrestling with the water now. Charlie was moving forward on the surface!

Fear disappeared as soon as it arrived and no one seemed to notice anything about the course of events, not Judy either. Happiness! Instead of turning back, he continued toward the rocks. Now, Judy discovered that Charlie was approaching painfully, and she smiled at him. He reached the cliff and kept kicking with his legs to stay afloat, breathed fiercely and felt like a little hero.

"Hello!" she said. Charlie couldn't reply but smiled back, kicked himself free from the cliff and wrestled back, after doing a small, half-moon in the water. All he thought was "look at me," but he couldn't speak.

He crawled up onto the cliff and sat down next to Judy who seemed moderately impressed. They were the same age and had never been so close to each other before. As he lay down, she thought it looked funny when he was breathing heavily, and he developed a small slope between his chest and stomach.

He wanted nothing more than for the day to last forever, but he had to return to Imelda and the lunch bag, which he, for safety's sake, chose to do on foot. When he came home, he told everyone who wanted to hear that he had been swimming that day. That night he fell asleep a true winner.

He got the feeling that this would be something completely different—seriously different. Admittedly, he had a freedom he had never known before, even though they had work to do. It became real when you could see the equipment that was being carried aboard and he heard Preb talk about deadly animals in the sea. However, sponges were peaceful creatures.

Preb told them that they belonged to the oldest living beings on earth. They have been around for six hundred million years, he said. They reproduce by releasing a bud which then becomes a new fungus and so it goes on indefinitely. He had met a Japanese who announced that their bathing habits were a science and an important part of their culture. It created *Wa*, or harmony in the home, he had said.

His name was Masaharu Otani and he had said that natural sponges were expensive in his home country. If Preb could deliver, he would buy and resell the sponges, through a Japanese trading house.

"This is the way things go," Preb continued. They had agreed on the jetty and celebrated with what Preb called Aquavit, until the Japanese buyer fell asleep on a bench outside the workshop. Preb had thus gained a loyal customer.

In addition, it was good to have your own business that was not in direct competition, with the locals. Fishing was completely dependent on a composite crew and lots of equipment. The nets would also be dried on land and there was a lot of afterwork. It sometimes happened that there were disputes out at sea with fishing trawlers from other countries, even boats from Japan, regarding the right to trawl in a certain area. Outside Australia's territorial boundaries, the law of the jungle prevailed—anyone could fish for anything.

Modern sonar technology had meant that the vessels sometimes pursued the same fish schools, which could cause serious ramming. Preb was completely satisfied staying on the land side of the reef. Each day's work began with the fact that the *Mermaid* would be provided with enough diesel to handle at least two-day trips. You can drift far out, if the currents are strong, so never, ever, run dry on diesel. Diesel was purchased from a manual pump on the dock that was operated by the fishing team. Payment was put into a metal box, then adding a small sheet of paper, with a form, and you simply filled in the number of gallons and who paid what.

At this time of the day, late in the morning, all the fishing boats were still out or on their way home. However, a fishing boat was left at the dock, Preb had noted. It belonged to a skipper who was called "Sandy," but who also bore the nickname "Jolly Roger." The nick name Sandy was said to be because, during the Second World War, he was the skipper of a transport ship, under the command of the Australian Navy up in what was called "The Slot," in the Solomon Islands. It was a strip along the islands, partially occupied by Japan, but where American airbases needed supplies in huge quantities. Sandy became his name when he insisted on ignoring the docking procedures if there was no jetty. He steered the ship onto the sandbanks, unloaded by hoisting the goods overboard to those waiting on the receiving side, and then pulling away, with full reverse of the engines.

He had been called Jolly Roger, by the Americans, as it really stood for a skipper who, two hundred years ago, swapped the career of skipper, in the service of Her Majesty, to private practice as a pirate. Sandy had, of course, followed orders, but executed them in a way that was somewhat unconventional. Thus, it was without exception that, if the recipients were to receive full delivery, he always demanded something in exchange—usually alcohol, the most valuable asset in the island system. What he charged this way was later sold, with good profit, to other islands. As the war against Japan would largely be decided by the Allies entering the Solomon Islands, their efforts there were enormous.

The Americans flew their own transports, during the war, along "The Slot," which the "New Georgia" strait, north of the Guadalcanal, was called, corresponding to 340 times around the earth, Sandy had said. Kennedy's PT 109 had been demolished northwest of New Georgia near Kolombanga island.

Now Sandy came walking on the jetty and looked generally sour.

"Have you found volunteers?" Sandy called to Preb.

"Not just volunteers but partners," Preb replied.

"No shit," Sandy thought.

"What are you doing on land?" Preb wondered.

"I've had problems for some time now that the engine has been weak. It has not revved up and this morning it refused to start," Sandy continued.

"My name is Ritch and I can look at the engine if you want."

"Charlie" Charlie said, nodding to Sandy.

"Do you know anything about boat engines?" Sandy asked.

"I was born in a workshop," Ritch replied.

"We'll practice diving today," Preb added, continuing, "Ritch can service your boat this afternoon."

"If you are going to dive, I can be skipper today. I still can't do anything sensible with a broken boat," replied Sandy.

"You are welcome to come along," Preb said.

Sandy knew the reef like his own back yard. However, he was not a diver. Preb warmed the engines while the equipment was being carried on board.

"If I can borrow the spear gun, we can toss anchor and go fishing," Sandy said.

"We can, of course," replied Preb. "I can't fish and keep track of these two land crabs at the same time."

Charlie and Ritch looked at each other and rolled their eyes at the comment, but they realized that they were wise to hush up. Preb flung everyone a cap and asked the crew to loosen the hawsers. When Preb veered away from the dock, Sandy commented, "You seem to be used to handling ropes. How did you get that experience?"

"We've been working on a freighter," Charlie said, continuing, "that's how we got here from America."

No shit, Sandy thought again, with a distinct look that radiated appreciation. The water was crystal clear and changed from light green to dark blue and back to light green depending on the depth.

Preb told them that most reefs are further out, but right near Cairns, there were many reefs near land and there you could practice diving. They went out at full throttle and Preb asked Sandy to take the helm and steer southeast, toward a peninsula where there were reefs suitable for diving. During the trip he gave a lesson in snorkeling, which was the form of diving that would apply in the beginning.

Preb himself used oxygen tanks and announced that it will only be relevant if they are able to become sponge pickers with goggles and fins.

"There are no shortcuts," he said. "The sea is treacherous in shallow water, and a thousand times worse at depth."

Preb took a pair of goggles and showed the breathing method to be practiced by his new students. Inhale, dive, swim to the bottom, pick sponges, if there are any (without touching the reef), look around, blow out some air in short bursts, swim, pick, swim, pick, and then rise up and at the same time slowly blow out the air, during the ascent.

He showed how to spit in the goggles, so that they would not get foggy and how to soak the flippers before putting on them, to make it easier.

"When we then go into the water, we always have a knife with us. In worst case, it is used as self-defense," Preb told them. He continued, "Today we will only think about security. Looking around should be as natural as breathing. If the skipper wants you to come up, he blows a whistle. It is heard several meters under water, and then you release everything you have and ascend to the boat like a shot out of a cannon—understand?

"Aye, aye, Skipper," the boys answered in unison.

After an hour or so, they tossed anchor at a spot where you could see the bottom. Preb was now observing his apprentices and demonstrating the process he had mentioned, during the trip out to the reef. Then he flipped himself in the water backwards on the ladder, after instructing Sandy and giving him the whistle.

Sandy would be vigilant, with respect to the surroundings, so he could alert them to unexpected company, weather changes or other danger. Charlie and Ritch followed.

"Start by orienting yourself," Preb said, continuing, "You should always know where you are in relation to the boat. Just swim in one direction and then swim back without having to think about the direction."

They spit in their goggles and put them on. When Charlie looked down into the water, he couldn't believe his eyes. The painting that spread out below and to the sides was undoubtedly the most beautiful he had ever experienced!

Here were colors he did not know existed—yellow, white and pink corals, in all imaginable and unthinkable forms, and fish. Fish in every direction. Schools of Sweetlips swam by. Preb explained what they were called and pointed at the same time. They are reminiscent of a mackerel, with pink, powerful "lips" framed in yellow, with yellow fins.

The bottom was probably four or five meters down and Preb made signs of diving. They inhaled and dived. When Charlie was on his way to the bottom, he did not remember any of his previous instructions. He didn't know where the boat was, he didn't look around. He just marveled at what he saw all around him. A few meters down, he instantly had pain in his ears and rose again to the surface.

Preb and Ritch also ascended when they saw Charlie making for the surface. They gasped a little and Charlie just screamed, "Great!"

"I thought you might like this. Welcome to the Barrier Reef," Preb said.

Charlie explained why he interrupted the dive and got a response from Preb, "If your ears hurt, during the dive, hold your nose and do pressure equalization; blow, until it pops in your ears, and then continue diving."

They tried again. Charlie equalized without problems. He forgot the other procedures again, mesmerized by this huge aquarium. The fins helped him to quickly get down to the bottom and back quickly. This time things went better, with the blowout.

The next dive was preceded by reminders from Preb regarding what he had said on the boat, and now it was starting to work. After four dives to the bottom, Preb commanded ascent onto the boat. A break, coffee, biscuits and a review of their first dive followed.

Sandy took the speargun and asked Preb to keep an eye on the surroundings, which everyone agreed they would. The boys were quite busy with their own review of their experiences in the sea.

"I didn't know there were so many different fish," Charlie said.

"Nobody knows how many varieties there are," Preb replied, "but probably at least a couple of thousand." Charlie sat with his legs hanging out over the rail and tried to see the dark fish swimming along the bottom. When he looked up, he saw brown Boobies flying over the boat and realized that it was their shadows he saw on the bottom. After the review, Preb talked about the sharks.

"They hunt in small groups. Two to three meters long, bronze whale sharks, gray reef sharks and silver tips. They come right towards you and are happy to touch you. Swim calmly towards the reef if it happens. Never swim to the surface."

Preb instructed them to make two more dives and then the boys would follow Preb up to the surface, as he showed sponge picking. Sandy came back empty-handed and kept a lookout while the others were diving. The next two dives went much better. They began to jettison discipline and enjoyed the surroundings when Sandy frantically blew the whistle. He saw dark shadows from the boat and took no chances.

It was not easy to get up, with fins on the steps, especially when in a hurry. Sandy grabbed the first man and pulled him aboard to make room for the next. When all three were on board, Preb wanted Ritch and Charlie to try and see what it was, for their own training.

Whatever Sandy had seen, it was gone now, but the boys would realize, from that moment, that diving wasn't to play with.

"Enough for today," Preb said. At that moment, a fly fish landed on deck. "You can take it," Preb told Sandy, "so you don't come home empty-handed."

"Funny," Sandy replied. "I'd rather take a little sip of your Aquavit," he continued.

"By all means," Preb replied.

On the return journey, the boys tried to take in everything that had happened this first working day.

"It's probably going to be tough work this," Charlie thought.

"Preb managed this alone," Ritch replied.

"True."

During the return, Preb told them that the sponges do not look like the sponges in the workshop.

"In the sea they have a purple color, and tower up like high-rise buildings with leprosy," he said. "Small sponges are avoided as they do not sell for a good price. Then I usually cut them with a knife so as not to foul the water and destroy visibility."

"You must have had eyes in your neck to do this alone," Charlie said.

"I stay in shallow water and look more out in the water than look for sponges. A glance is enough to know if there are any sharks nearby, and the rest of the attention is directed at the ocean."

When they were approaching the dock, Charlie and Ritch showed how well-oiled machinery works: Before Preb had a chance to even ask to take the hawsers, the boys had fixed the hawsers so fast that even Sandy couldn't hide his appreciation.

"Now we must have a beer to celebrate this, and for our crewman becoming eighteen today," Preb said.

"Then we check your boat," Ritch told Sandy.

The equipment was rinsed so that the salt would not remain on everything and Fosters was brought to the dock.

"Cheers to Charlie," Preb said, and everyone agreed. Never before had Charlie felt so appreciated.

"To our new friends," Charlie replied, lifting the bottle in the air.

Ritch told Sandy that there were probably two out of three possible failures with his engine. The lack of energy can be due to poor compression, which could be due to worn pistons and crankcase. The fact that it did not even want to start was a bad sign and was probably because the cylinder head gasket was broken, and probably it was both the first and second problem. The third possible error was dry tanks, which was dismissed Sandy, but they agreed on one and two.

"Can you fix that?" Sandy wondered.

"Surely," replied Ritch, "but we need spare parts."

"Say what you need, and I'll order it directly from Cairns," Sandy replied. Ritch made a list of parts and the Perkins diesel engine number to identify the model, and Sandy went to order the stuff.

"Find out the delivery time," Ritch called after him.

After a shower in the outdoor shower, behind the workshop, the new friends gathered in the pub tavern, next to the harbor, to celebrate Charlie. It soon spread that these two Americans would be permanent in the area and they were welcomed with acclamation. Everyone would also drink to Charlie's birthday and soon the pub would be bustling. Sandy told them that they also had a motor man in Ritch which was good news.

"Just what we have been missing," said a bunch of fishing colleagues.

"If we rearrange the workshop, we can make room for a workbench, drills and other appliances and Ritch can have his machine operations there," Preb suggested.

"I would like that," Ritch replied.

"Settled," answered Preb and they toasted to celebrate the newly started business. Charlie and Ritch were soon involved in the community and felt that they could actually add something with their own skills.

Sandy told them it would take a week for the parts to arrive at the Cairns store. So it is. Everything took time to arrive.

Sandy thought it might be a good idea to take the land crabs, on a trip along the reef, when he still couldn't fish. Preb thought it was an excellent proposal.

The next morning, Preb took his apprentices around the workshop, to change sponges in their baths. Those who had been immersed in the acid bath for a few days would now be moved to the freshwater tank, and those who lay there would be moved out for drying, to be dry when they got home. Preb taught the boys to use time to their advantage. This meant doing such things before doing anything else, such as making them ready for packing when returning home.

"Ten-four" Charlie replied, and Ritch agreed.

When the work with the sponges was completed, Preb said that basic provisions such as coffee, biscuits, bread, fruit, water, Fosters, and the obligatory Aquavit would be arranged for the journey, which could take five days. Extra provisions would be included, if the trip was unexpectedly long. Basic food, fish, would be arranged, during the trip.

At lunchtime, the preparations were ready, and the *Mermaid* was fully fueled. The sea was calm, which was the usual, and it was hot. Preb let Sandy steer the boat on a direct northern course. The goal for first leg was Hastings Reef.

"It's a dive-friendly area," Preb said. The reefs in the Cairns area are relatively close to the coast—only approximately forty kilometers out. In the middle of the afternoon, they tossed anchor, at a safe distance from Hastings Reef. Preb said that the *Mermaid* had several anchors and anchor lines, as it was often necessary to cut the line, if the anchor was stuck. With a crew on board, it was easier to retrieve the anchor, by allowing Preb to dive down to dislodge it.

Preb suggested diving training, which was resumed, after a rehearsal of the exercises. He specifically reminded them not to trample or touch anything on the bottom. The diving went much better that day. At the bottom, Preb noticed that Charlie was swimming very close to what looked like a jagged starfish lying on a white coral. Preb indicated immediate ascent, with his hand.

On the boat, with a coffee cup in his hand, he explained that Charlie was far too close to a starfish—a poisonous one.

"Perspectives and proportions are different with goggles underwater," he explained. "And you were too close for comfort. Currents may push you against the reef, and it's not fun" Preb added.

"Must remember that," Charlie replied slightly embarrassed. Sandy threw out a line with some corks so it wouldn't get stuck at the bottom.

"We'll get fish for dinner," he said. An hour later, Sandy had picked up three fish he could keep: one that resembled a lizard, a sweet lip big as a human foot, and an orange—blueberry colored one that no one knew what kind of fish it was.

After a Fosters and some Aquavit (which Charlie thought smelled of diesel, but which warmed well), Preb got the grill started and dinner was on the aft deck. The remains were thrown overboard and soon Terns and lots of small fish came to the boat.

"You will soon learn how to behave by the reef," said Preb.

"Do you ever become fully educated?" Charlie wondered.

"Never, never," Preb replied.

"Never Never Land" Charlie thought.

Early the next morning, the bell clapper hit the clock itself, without anyone touching it.

"Wake up signal," Preb said.

The waves were big enough to cause *Mermaid* to roll so much that the bell rang and then it was time to move. Sandy looked at the horizon and thought it was OK to move on. Should the weather deteriorate dramatically, they could take shelter in the lee further north. Breakfast had to wait.

Preb started the engines and warmed them up before steering towards the wind to tow the anchor with the boat. The anchor came off as planned and the *Mermaid* headed north while the boys arranged for coffee and biscuits for breakfast. To avoid the risk of grounding against the reefs, Preb kept the boat far from the protective bank of reefs. The waves were larger there but did not bother him or Sandy. However, Ritch and Charlie had some feeling of nausea, which was temporarily relieved by the coffee.

Preb told them to do some good, so they would have something else to think about. Ritch had to stay in the wheelhouse and keep an eye on the sonar, while Charlie was a scout on the front deck. The latter he was grateful for as the boat rolled least, at the bow. The sun was already strong, and it was very dangerous to be on deck, for a long time without a long-sleeved shirt, cap and sunglasses. Charlie thought it was impossible to see anything special. Breakers were also difficult to see among the white foaming wave crests.

The reefs were largely unexplored and there were no charts available. The skipper had to rely on his and the crew's eyes. Charlie slowly began to realize the greatness of the Barrier Reef. It seemed endless. It was blowing from the northeast and he calculated that they would get a comfortable breeze, during the return home, which was encouraging. Soon, Charlie saw in the backlight, in the direction of the reef, a small vessel beached on the reef. It was deprived of bridge and other things that may have been on the deck before. It had been there for a long time, he thought. Later, Preb told them that there were stranded ships almost everywhere on the Barrier Reef.

Sometimes dolphins came out of the water quite close to the bow and Charlie thought of the first time he saw them when he emptied the garbage on the *Quantas*. He felt that they had to be man's best friends, along with the dog. Preb noticed a shift in the waves ahead but said nothing to anyone. The sonar was not of great use on the reef, as it was either deep or shallow. Coral pyramids can extend for several hundred meters almost vertically from the bottom, and it is important to notice changes in the behavior of the surface.

What Preb saw was that the waves were shorter, the white caps smaller and that they also moved faster than nearby waves. He wanted to test if the land crabs would notice anything. Ritch noticed nothing when he had his eyes on the screen and saw indications that ranged from 60 to 120 meters deep.

Charlie peeked northeast into the backlight and had a hard time seeing anything at all. He thought there was less movement in the boat and wondered why. Then he saw what Preb had already seen.

"Hell," he thought, waving his left arm frantically.

Preb immediately steered west. Now the wind was blowing hard, and the bow went down into the waves, so Charlie got soaked. He turned to the bridge and got a thumbs-up from Preb.

"Nice," Ritch thought.

They continued west for a while and then took a northern route again. They now had the opportunity to look back and see the large plateau of reefs they had been close to hitting. It was probably the same reef that the boat that was wedged into the reef had hit. In calm weather, it was easier to discover the plateau, but Charlie had been on his guard.

Towards afternoon, the wind calmed down and they reached the target, "Lizard Island," at dusk, without any other incidents. They found a good place to anchor where Preb had been a few times before—near shore. The *Mermaid* was moored and the quartet, Charlie on slightly swaying legs, headed toward the top of the island. It was about 400 meters high and was called "Cook's Look." According to Preb, Captain Cook had gone there when, in 1770, he had sought to find a way through what he perceived to be an impenetrable wall of coral. In the twilight, you could see from the top this pearl band that stretched, from horizon to horizon.

A kind of pigeon could be heard from the Eucalyptus trees below and meter-long lizards lay resting completely unafraid on the rocky cliffs. The blue-pink twilight, with the sea and the reef below, constituted an unreal world. Charlie thought that the coral wall seemed endless.

Preb told them that the Aborigines, who came from Asia 40-60 thousand years ago, had rites for young men at this summit. He had his own rite; the Aquavit came out and was passed around the team.

The next morning, Preb was keen to dive for sponges, on the north side of the island, so they set out early. Sandy kept a lookout and the other three brought a knife and net that were fastened, with a belt of leather. If it got full, you would take the belt off and Sandy hoisted the nets aboard with a boat hook. The exercises were over.

Preb took oxygen tanks, something that was developed only seven-eight years earlier, by Jacques-Yves Cousteau, the diving pioneer from France. He had a saying that he wrote to his son, Jean-Michel: "Happiness, for the bee as well for the dolphin, is to exist. For man, to know existence, and to marvel at it."

They ended up in an *eldorado* of sponges, at about five meters depth. Preb had reminded the boys not to touch anything other than sponges, "since half of everything down there is poisonous." He moved forward calmly and methodically, while when snorkeling, they could only cut off three, four sponges, before they had to rise to the surface again.

Charlie felt that it was easy to focus on the job and eventually get used to all the fascinating creatures and colors. In just over an hour, they had brought together about a hundred sponges, something that the skipper considered unusual. The sponges were placed in a long bowl of salt water so as not to dry during the return journey.

Charlie felt chosen. A few days earlier, he was sitting in a dusty truck and had no idea what to expect. Now he was part of the sea, with a special task to perform. He decided that was what he was going to be—free! This year that took him out into the world and into adulthood was undoubtedly his most tumultuous step in life, but also significant in terms of world events. In the spring, Sir Edmund Hillary had become the first to climb the world's highest mountain, Mount Everest, the dictator of the Soviet Union, Josef Stalin, had died, the Korean War ended and the author's wife, Heléna had come into the world (although the latter, in a worldly perspective, was relatively insignificant, but from the author's point of view of somewhat greater importance).

The following Saturday evening, the quartet entered the tavern, in the harbor to celebrate the successful trip. Charlie wanted to buy a round of Fosters and saw a cute, blonde woman behind the counter he had never seen before.

He was long and slender, reddish hair that needed trimming, and with a few days of salt-stained, totally browned face. She—petite and fair. At first, he lost it a bit, but then he rattled in his home dialect:

"Hey, can I have four Fosters, please?"

"Are you so thirsty?" came a reply from the other side of the counter.

"My skipper and the others are over there," Charlie replied, and continued, "I haven't seen you before."

"That's probably because you've never been here before. I've been working here on weekends for a hundred years."

"We came here a week ago; my name is Charlie—what's yours?"

"Abigail" replied again from behind the counter, while four beers were being served on the bar, "but most people call me Abby."

"It was nice to meet Abby," Charlie concluded with a little smile, pleased with his accomplishment.

"New mate?" Ritch wondered as Charlie returned to the table.

"Buzz off" Charlie replied a little embarrassed. "I just ordered beer."

"It would have been quicker to walk to town," Preb said, and everyone laughed and toasted Charlie's success at the bar. Abby made herself available to serve the quartet and as she served Charlie, she wondered where they came from.

"California," Charlie replied.

"Where the movies come from" Abby countered.

"Yes," Ritch replied, introducing himself as he did not want to be outside Charlie's newly formed community. "We don't live far from there," he added.

"How exciting" Abby said.

"Not half as exciting as diving here," Charlie replied.

"Do you also make movies?" Abby wondered.

"Not really," Ritch replied, "but it's a good idea."

Charlie felt it was not as interesting to talk about sponges as filming why he curtly said: "we are Preb's new Partners."

"So, sponge pickers" Abby replied with a big smile and returned to the counter, with a new order for four Fosters. Since that evening, Charlie had a strong desire to visit the tavern on Saturdays.

On Monday, the parts for Sandy's engine arrived. Sandy came to the workshop in the afternoon and wondered if Ritch could start the renovation.

"Sure," he replied, and continued, "it would be good if you could get some tools and give me some help."

"Tools are already in the boat and I want to be involved in the repair," Sandy replied.

It took the rest of the day to get the engine out of the boat. There was a small crane on the deck with a chain and the engine was lifted onto a low, stable, wooden wagon, with truck wheels. The wagon was rolled behind the workshop where it was washed with acid diluted with water that Preb stored there. After the next day's diving, Ritch disassembled the entire engine and put the parts in solvent. He found that his original diagnosis, broken head gasket, was correct. After a simple renovation, it would all be reassembled.

Sandy was ordered to obtain a torque wrench to pull the bolts in the cylinder head and the next day it was done. The engine was mounted in the boat and started after a few attempts and purred like a cat.

Sandy radiated like sunshine and wondered what Ritch would charge for the work. "Nothing," he replied, and continued, "tell others if you are satisfied with my work, so maybe soon I can have an operating workshop."

"I shall do that," Sandy replied. "Tell me if I can do something to help you in the workshop."

"Maybe you can talk to others about donating tools and machines that they have lying around?"

"Good idea," Sandy replied. Already the next afternoon there was a big pile of all kinds of things in front of Preb's workshop.

"If you can organize a workshop on my premises, it's your business and your income," Preb told Ritch, who liked the developments. Preb realized that there was time left between sponge handling and, in addition, it was beneficial for him and everyone in the area, to have a real mechanic in the harbor.

Ritch painted a sign with the text "Ritch's Boat Repair" and got Preb's permission to hang it under the "Aussie Sponges" sign. A couple of months later, just before Christmas, the trio were sitting in the tavern and Preb dropped the bomb: "I've been thinking," he said. Charlie had too, of Abby, but Preb would discuss business. "You manage things nicely. When you arrived, we discussed possible partnerships. I want to offer you 25% each in the company, with a corresponding share of the company's profits. The workshop is my private property and is not included in the contract. What do you think?"

Charlie didn't know what to say, stunned by the nice offer. Ritch replied with a smile:

"Aye, aye Skip!"

"Suits me as well," Charlie replied. Preb stretched out his hand and all three shook hands simultaneously across the table.

"But I decide," he added.

Preb had done everything himself before and now the harvests had more than tripled. Charlie had been experimenting with the packing method in the cartons for some time. To prevent the fungi from sticking together, Preb had packed them loosely in the cartons. Charlie had put one layer in the bottom, newsprint, one more layer, newsprint, etc. He forced in about three times the number of sponges previously packed. Then he had sealed it and left it in a corner for four weeks. He pulled out the box and checked the contents. The sponges at once returned to their original shape.

He showed Preb, who at once appreciated what Charlie had come up with.

"Shipping costs will be halved," he said. Since sponges in the dry state were almost weightless, they paid per package.

Ritch had started to get a reputation for being a good mechanic and customers were flowing in at a rapid pace. Preb thought that Ritch could do all the after-work with the sponges and avoid diving and so it was.

CHAPTER EIGHT

One day, Charlie heard the news that America had taken 23,000 prisoners of war in Korea. North Korea had sent "persuaders" to South Korea for a period of ninety days to try and persuade them to return to the north. Only seventy prisoners of war had agreed to it.

McCarthy was probably right when he warned against communism, he thought. To those who were released and stayed in the south, he extended a thought: *Welcome to the free world.*

Charlie had taken courage and one evening he asked Abby if she would like to go scuba diving off the reef. She accepted the offer and on Sunday the two had taken the *Mermaid* on a trip to the nearest reef, which was a great mound, a half hour trip from the harbor.

She had brought them lunch from the tavern and liked the self-assured American's company. As they snorkeled, he had the opportunity to touch her naturally. Once under the surface, they stopped and caught each other's eyes, stayed still for a few moments, and Charlie took her hand and kicked them to the surface again.

Up at the surface they had taken off the goggles and quietly kicked their legs so as not to sink down again and embraced in a fierce kiss. It was the beginning of a happy time. Every Sunday they were in the water or out on other excursions. Charlie liked her natural way and she liked the wiry diver. His work was even unusual to the community.

Her friends invited them to a barbecue party in Cairns and

everyone was very curious about the American. After a while, Ritch offered to sleep in the boat or move to his own home so that the lucky ones could be for themselves, but Charlie didn't accept.

"I can't imagine suggesting to Abby that we should live together," Charlie said. "Besides, that's not what I want either," he continued.

But he liked Abby a lot. Out of a sense of duty that had become routine, inherited or of his own will, Charlie had a strong sense of duty. It was aimed primarily at Preb and the company, but other strings would remain unbound. He felt great respect for his fellow human beings. For that reason, he would not take Abby for granted. He was deeply concerned that he might end up in a situation where he was going to hurt someone. The time at school at CBS had left a deep mark on him. About with living with someone else, for example. Constantly considering others and relenting one's own interests to make life as tolerable as possible, Charlie had trained in diplomacy without even knowing it at the time. But it was evident from his actions.

Far later, a letter was sent to the company from the Japanese trading house. Mr. Otani had expressed his delight that the volumes had risen in the past year and suggested that the terms of the business should be discussed, and an agreement concluded for the business. He also wrote that there was a great need for Tuna in Japan and wanted to know if Preb had the opportunity to deliver frozen Tuna to Japan.

"Surely we have no fish to deliver?" Charlie exclaimed when Preb told them about the letter.

"Nope," Preb replied, continuing, "but others who do not have contacts in Japan have products." Finally, Mr. Otani suggested that Preb come to Tokyo to negotiate. He did not know that there were several partners and Preb suggested:

"I think you should go Charlie."

"Certainly," he replied, adding: "I can ask the shipping company if they can give me a freebee on the trip, as we are to negotiate increased exports to Japan."

Charlie received an immediate, positive message from the freight forwarder and Mr. Otani was contacted, with the suggestion that Charlie might visit him. Mr. Otani was delighted to hear that an American was a partner and that he was welcome. Charlie managed to get to Sydney early and visited Beppi, who was overwhelmed in the typical Italian way of revisiting with Charlie who was full of stories of life up north. There was a Lockheed Super Constellation plane every week from Sydney via the Philippines to Tokyo and two weeks later, Charlie boarded an airplane, for the first time in his life. He thought that the plane resembled a dolphin with wings—similarly a friendly nose, elegantly streamlined body and with what was perhaps most distinctive for the plane, three tail fins. It wasn't as dramatic as he had imagined, but the start was fantastic. The sound of the engines and the feeling of power when pressed against the backrest had been the highlight. The rest of the flight was like sailing on the sea, he thought. In addition, being looked after by hostesses in light blue uniforms did not make matters worse. The journey would take fourteen hours. Stopovers and refueling took place at Papua, New Guinea and Leyete in the Philippines, where Charlie bought a postcard and a new crew boarded. On the plane, he wrote the following to the ranch: "Dear Grandfather, Grandmother and Imelda. I live in Australia. On my way to Tokyo for business. All is well with me. Hope the same applies to you. Charlie." They flew over Okinawa, still occupied by America. The occupation of the rest of Japan had ended two years earlier, in 1952. Tokyo was largely destroyed by US bombings, causing major fires. As they flew over the coast, Charlie could see visible traces of the war.

The only thing Charlie really knew about Japan was that they had forced the United States into World War II, by attacking Pearl Harbor. Mr. Otani was waiting at Tokyo International, with a sign saying, "Charlie Long," Charlie walked up to the little man, with carbon black hair, and said, "I'm Charlie Long." The man bowed and replied, "*Masaharu Otani*. Please follow me." A car was waiting, and the driver bowed and took care of Charlie's luggage. They sat in the back seat and took off in traffic teeming with bicycles and mopeds. "We are still short of gas in Japan," Mr. Otani said, pointing to the hubbub. He took Charlie to a small hotel and when he checked in, he suggested that Charlie rest for a while and then be picked up by the driver for a late dinner if it suited. "Excellent, thank you," Charlie replied, giving a gentle bow to Mr. Otani who smiled and bowed back. "We will pick you up at 21:00."

Charlie had a hard time understanding what Mr. Otani said, because his English was like other Asians in general. They couldn't pronounce the letter "R," which is why he called Charlie something that sounded like "chaa-lii." At dinner, Mr. Otani's assistant, Mr. Noataka Kakuda, was also present. After a small bowl of the local drink, Saké, Mr. Otani suggested that he order a mixed compote of simple dishes, which suited Charlie as the texts in the menu were unreadable to him. American occupation had not apparently affected the menus. When the hosting couple had interviewed their guest about his background, they had commented that extent of space on which he had grown up were non-existent in Japan. They showed Charlie great reverence and admiration, in that his family owned a large ranch. A 100 million people lived in Japan, compared to America's 150 million, but on a fraction of the surface, comparable to the state of California where Charlie came from.

"In addition, we have people who have seen Tokyo destroyed twice, during their own lifetime," continued Mr. Kakuda. The first time in an earthquake in 1923, when the same type of fires devastated the city as during the 1944 and 1945 bombings. Despite this, Americans were popular in Japan insured the hosting couple.

They hoped that Charlie would learn as much as possible, from his stay in Japan and of the Japanese mentality, which made a deep impression on Charlie. He felt that these gentlemen were genuinely eager to cooperate, not just contract, and long-term.

"We have been allied with the United States for one hundred years, apart from the unfortunate war" said Mr. Otani and continued: "we are extremely far behind your technology and lack raw materials of all kinds that need to be imported. That is why we are very keen to extend our cooperation with you."

They conveyed the feeling of Japanese tradition by telling of the Emperor, Hirohito, who was regarded more as a spiritual being than a fellow human being. Until the end of the war, only a few had seen him at all. He lived in the imperial palace, in the middle of the city. He had been forced to flee to a bomb shelter, during the war when the palace was leveled by the bombs.

At the end of the war, he had for the first time spoken to his people publicly via radio, and with his high-pitched voice proclaimed that peace had come. It was a big event. No one was more honorable than the emperor. Trams passing the palace had staff who called out when the passengers should bow during passing.

Those who historically ranked second, after the emperor, were "Shoguns," leaders over large individual parts of Japan. There was a saying for this: "You can look at the gods, but seeing a Shogun makes you blind, and the Emperor you cannot see at all."

The first dish that came in looked like a beautiful painting and resembled an arranged coral reef. *Fishing bait*, Charlie thought. Mr.

Otani explained that it was fish called Sushi. According to legend, the dish was named after an event, during the war.

A group of soldiers who were engaged in the production of military equipment ended up after a time in hardship regarding food, and the only things available were fish and rice. Central to the Japanese were two things: soybean soup and Saké, the rice wine. A commander, with relatives in the Saké industry, managed, under the pretext of the necessity to procure raw materials for production, to arrange it so that the Saké factory sent a barrel of Soya to the military.

This happened in the village of Zushi.

For months, workers lived on dipping fish, rice and vegetables in Soy. By chance someone mixed a little "Wasabi" horseradish cream in soy and presto, "Sushi" was a concept.

Charlie was fiddling a bit with the sticks and trying to do as his hosts.

"It is against our culture to ask if anyone needs help. We do not want anyone to lose their face to anyone, but it is welcomed to ask for help," said Mr. Otani.

"I would appreciate if you wanted to show me how to do it," Charlie replied. With the support of the middle finger, the sticks were then squeezed with the thumb. Charlie did as best he could and after a while managed the bait, which he liked very much.

Mr. Otani said that while the fish is raw, it was frozen to kill all bacteria. The hosts were anxious for Charlie to understand the culture of Japan.

"We are happy to show respect," they continued. "Our natural location—we are an island kingdom, which for centuries has been largely isolated from the outside world—requires humility for this world if we are to develop."

"Isn't that required by all who seek to cooperate?" Charlie replied.

"A toast to our guest" exclaimed Mr. Otani and Charlie forced down what they called wine. "Beauty and harmony are two other things we value," the host continued. "That means we treasure things in our vicinity."

Mr. Otani had been to New York several times and could compare Japan, with the western world.

"When you see what you have achieved in your cities, you cannot help but be impressed," he continued. "We want to try to reduce our technological disadvantage and our trading house strives for cooperation internationally."

He had been employed for fifteen years in the same company.

"It is traditionally done here," Mr. Otani said. "We have an inherited loyalty that makes it shameful to quit a company for personal reasons, such as not liking your boss or the like."

"It sounds like the army," Charlie replied.

"Sure, it can be likened to coercion, but that's not the issue," replied Mr. Otani.

Typical of a dinner like this was that the most experienced at the company led the conversation while the others quietly agreed to what was being discussed. *Mr. Otani was probably in his forties and his colleague was maybe around thirty, but it was difficult to determine the age of these gentlemen,* Charlie thought.

When the next order arrived, he thought it was reminiscent of the first one, with the difference that it now seemed cooked. He washed down the remains of "Wasabi" with a glass of beer of the Kirin brand, which he liked.

"We have had a system in our country that meant that few people decide over everyone else. Four companies controlled a quarter of the country's capital before the war. They each controlled about three hundred companies, and four families owned the parent companies.

They were called "Zaibatsu" because of their position of power. One of these companies is called Mitsubishi."

"It's the same in America," Charlie politely tried to inflict.

"What I say applied before the war," Mr. Otani continued. "After the war, Japan would be "democratized" by the occupying powers. Russia simply took a few islands to the north as part of that process. They represented communism and, with "informants," tried to turn the Japanese into their belief in communism. What is characteristic of the post-war world are the incompatible contrasts of the free world and communism.

Japan has been forced by the occupying powers to resemble a middle ground between these orientations. Politically, the Zaibatsu system could not exist. It was believed that it was the rich who were responsible for the war actions and therefore the rich should no longer remain rich. A winding-up commission was set up and the assets of fifteen Zaibatsun were frozen and thereby dissolved. Eighty other holding companies and 4,500 companies were declared to be "limited groups." They were prohibited from owning shares in other companies and employees were prohibited from taking employment other than in the company they already worked. In this way, they reinforced the loyalty of the Japanese to the company they worked in, with enforced laws. It was General Douglas MacArthur who signed the peace treaty with Japan, and he led the occupation of the country. He stated:

"Christian causes will assist a defeated and suffering people and restore in the East a nation." The occupation powers taxed income heavily. The new managers would be prevented from making money, which is why the tax scale rose steeply at median wages, up to 85 per cent. This led to a new strategy for executives: they simply let the companies pay their private expenses such as cars, drivers, dinners and housing. The Japanese endured these levies, with equanimity.

The occupation forces showed no signs of being avenging victors but ruled with a gentle hand, which won favor among the Japanese who wanted to cooperate with them.

A good example of the effects of these compelling processes was Toyota Motor Company. They had created a sales branch four years earlier (1950) called "Toyota Motor Sales," which was completely independent of Toyota Motor Company.

"Can't you change things now that the occupation has ended?" Charlie wondered rightly. "The laws are still in force and it is difficult in any country to abolish or change laws—it was only two years, since the occupation ended," added Mr. Otani (it would take another thirty years before the two companies finally merged in 1984).

The dessert consisted of something similar to a banana-split but lacking chocolate. It was deep-fried banana with sweet sauce, something that Charlie asked for every day, during his visit to Japan.

"You must be tired after such a long journey, Mr. Long. We drive you to the hotel now and pick you up at ten tomorrow, so we can discuss the business," he continued.

"I look forward to it," Charlie replied.

The trading house was in an industrial part of Tokyo that survived the war relatively well. The building, since the beginning of the century, completely gray, three stories high and noticeably worn. The receptionist was a thin, little lady in a colorful, tight dress who got up and bowed as the trio entered. Charlie bowed slightly back.

Mr. Otani said something very brief and they were shown into a small but beautiful conference room, with room for six people. There was only one window. At the top of the entrance, there was something similar to milk-colored glass, but which was probably made of paper for light.

All decor was wood. *No wonder it burned*, Charlie thought. Soon, another little, beautifully dressed lady came in with tea. By this time Charlie had learned to say "yes," which he replied when she addressed him meaningfully and nodded to the teacup: "*hai,*" said Charlie.

Mr. Otani continued with his stories. The history of the trading house was from the last century. They had bought fish at the big fish market in Tokyo and sold to restaurants and fish shops and fishmongers to half of Japan. They bought silk and made fine clothes and sold to both clothing stores and tailors around Japan. They purchased soybean soup and Saké and distributed both near and far (within Japan). The company was large but had not been classified as *Zaibatsu,* but it was a limited group. After the war, Mr. Otani had visited America to seek steel imports and other basic commodities, in order to industrialize Japan.

"We have ten times as many residents as Australia but only a fraction of your commodity resources," he continued, adding: "but we have good opportunities to make money."

A few years after the end of the war, Japan had 150 percent inflation. The land reform, which meant that landowners (who with the nobility were the wealthiest), with usable land, had to relinquish the land to those who used the land, coupled with the introduction of citizens' right to strike, boosted the poor to middle class. Japan became an equal society, for the first time in history. Less productive managers and corporate executives were simply set aside, for the benefit of younger leaders who were full of ideas and renewal. These reforms favored growth in the country, although all purges were unlikely to benefit the purging company. The director of *Mitsuibank* had been deposed the year before (1953) and became chairman of the board of SONY, which presumably benefited the latter company. He was motivated by a share issue in which he urged the bank's officials to buy shares (in "their" company, i.e. SONY), which they also did and thus became quite wealthy. Companies often issued shares and still do, to raise capital for a company. Capital was then, and is presently often the case, a lacking resource in the companies. The banks were also forced to raise interest rates sharply to fight inflation, which made borrowing very expensive for the companies. A few years later, inflation had declined, despite the rapid increase in growth. Households needed everything. There was the wartime black market trading in fresh memory and the need for consumption was enormous. Double-digit growth, savings rates of twenty percent and low inflation meant that people could afford to consume.

"We are facing a period of strong economic growth," continued Mr. Otani. Encouraged by these positive messages, Charlie suggested the following:

"We should consider what resources are available, in my new home country, and find out if they may be of interest to your business."

Mr. Otani replied, "You are very forthright Mr. Long. That's what I've learned from America. In Japan, progress is slowly being made, through small hints in a desired direction, mixed with not saying anything at all. You have come to do business on our invitation. We have great respect for that. We know that you are open-minded, and we shall do our best to meet your expectations on that point. The question you are highlighting is at the heart of our discussions. We agree."

Charlie thought the introduction would lead to an admonition and felt very relieved and slightly victorious. *Good start*, he thought. After lunch in the staff dining room consisting of *sansai* soup with vegetables from the mountains and fish, they went to the plant.

"We need to increase the volume of sponges," said Mr. Otani.

"You have increased your purchases in step with our increased harvests during the past year," Charlie replied, adding: "The volumes you have received have been at current prices. We need to adjust them."

Without suggesting any reaction to Charlie's comment, Mr. Otani continued:

"It would be interesting for us to import tuna as well. Do you have any friends in that regard?"

"It will be my pleasure to ask the local fishermen about it," Charlie replied, and continued, "what volumes of sponges are we talking about?"

"I have to explain one thing before we talk about volumes, Mr. Long," replied Mr. Otani and continued: "when we sign a contract it means that we expect the supplier to fulfill it and deliver agreed volumes and during the time period stipulated in the contract. Deviations from delivery fulfillment are regarded as breach of contract. By comparison, I can say that China is a major trading partner for Japan, and it is generally accepted that promised volumes are rarely or never fulfilled as those who sign the agreements are usually politically appointed officials who pretend to make big deals to advance within the party. There we buy what we need and hope for deliveries."

"Charlie replied, "Aussie Sponges will deliver what we finally commit to deliver."

"Then that thing is settled," replied Mr. Otani. He continued: "Let's drink tea. Then we'll talk about prices and what we expect."

As they slowly sipped tea, Mr. Otani said:

"We have had monarchy for 124 generations. The dynasty has ruled for 2,000 years. It is so old that it has no name. We have a deeply rooted sense of time here. Changes are progressing slowly. We can grow a tree for generations, and it is no bigger than a cat—the so-called Bonzai tree. You have shown that you are reliable as a supplier. We want to develop our cooperation."

"I am very honored by your openness and would like to state, on behalf of our company, that we will do everything to meet your needs," Charlie replied.

"We need to increase volumes by 50 percent or more," Mr. Otani said.

"That is encouraging," Charlie replied, adding: "When we deliver today's volumes, we do so at prices that have remained unchanged for several years. Prices and volumes must be weighed against each other, and in today's situation, prices need to be adjusted north."

"It is a natural view for a supplier to state," replied Mr. Otani, and continued, "we therefore ask you to do a calculation of annual volumes and prices based on existing volumes, 25, 50, 75 and 100 percent higher volume."

Charlie was impressed of Mr. Otani's way of concealing his feelings and managed to keep his face completely unmoved when he replied, "Your needs seem to be great. We will try to meet your volume requirements, but I ask that we may do some calculations and other considerations before I present a proposal."

"Take the time needed," replied Mr. Otani.

Charlie politely thanked them and was taken to the hotel by the driver. He took a walk among the myriad of shops and people who were all very different to himself. It felt like being in another world and he thought it must have been a similar experience when Mr. Otani was in New York.

They would meet him for dinner at a restaurant very close to the hotel called Kamezaki, which means scent of plum flower. The interior was entirely of wood and had been spared from fire for 150 years. Behind the restaurant was a small garden that was trimmed in every part as a perfectly tended flower. Everything was in miniature, with a small spring, a vaulted bridge over the water, Bonzai trees, and even a small bamboo forest.

The trio gathered and the atmosphere was very positive after several glasses of Saké.

"We hope we didn't tire you out with our stories," said Mr. Otani, looking as if he meant what he said.

"On the contrary, Mr. Otani," Charlie replied, "Your hospitality honors me. It is also interesting to learn about the history of Japan which is quite fascinating."

All talk of business was put off until tomorrow. They separated from dinner as friends.

The next day was a repeat of the day before. The meeting started with the obligatory tea and some small talk.

"Have you considered our volume requirements?" wondered Mr. Otani.

"I have," Charlie replied, "and I have some concerns about the proposed volumes and have set prices, with these concerns in mind. Let me explain—today's prices need to be increased by ten percent to cover our costs and to generate acceptable profit. We can increase the volume by 25 percent without increasing staffing, by simply working more. This means that today's price level calculated at plus ten percent would be acceptable for 125 percent volume compared to today's level."

"Not entirely unreasonable," replied Mr. Otani, who thus revealed how extremely anxious he was to increase imports.

"If we are to increase by 50 percent," Charlie continued, "we must increase the price by 20 percent, to cover the acquisition of new staff. With my calculations, prices should increase by ten percent further for a 75 percent increase in volume and by another ten percent, for a 100 percent volume increase."

Mr. Otani for the first time showed signs of moderate surprise.

He gathered himself and replied, "Mr. Long, this is the first time in my career that I have seen price increases in volume increases—it is customary for the opposite to apply."

Charlie, who was prepared for the comment, continued:

"We have a small business. If we are going to manage the volumes, we must create the resources to produce these, something that we today lack.

"If the volumes are to be increased by 100 percent, in addition to acquiring a new boat, we must also acquire a capable crew, something that I see as worrying, and in addition, hire more for the after-work and obtain new premises. Initially, this expansion will cost more than revenue provides, so our prices must increase."

Mr. Otani and his colleague asked for more tea for their guest and excused themselves to confer individually. When they were away, Charlie wondered if he had spoiled the chances altogether of good business in Japan.

After a while, the gentlemen returned and Mr. Otani said, "We have respect and understanding for your approach. We propose that we sign a three-year agreement, where volumes are increased from today's by 25 percent and that prices are adjusted "north" by eight percent in year one, nine percent in year two and by ten percent in year three, calculated from today's prices."

Charlie was inclined to ask for reflection time, but when the result was much better than the conditions that currently applied, he answered, "Definitely!"

"We also want you to find out the possibilities for tuna," continued Mr. Otani, as he reached out to seal the deal.

"I will do just that," Charlie replied, taking Mr. Otani's hand.

Charlie could hardly wait to tell the news to Preb and Ritch, but it had to wait. After more soup, Charlie was given a contract which he asked to read in a private room. The agreement contained exactly what was agreed upon. After both parties had signed the agreement, a small ceremony would be held in Charlie's honor.

The trio was invited visit the company's chief executive, who had a private room with a glass wall next to a large office, with about ten employees. The only thing that separated the boss from the others was that he sat facing everyone else, face to door. As the trio stepped into the office, everyone stood up and bowed. Charlie had grown accustomed to the bow and bowed back as they walked to the boss. The manager made a hint to bow and Charlie bowed a little more, which was appreciated.

They stepped into the manager's private room where tea and a bottle of Saké were set. The manager explained that the trading house was very old and that they appreciated doing business with Americans.

"As do we with you," replied Charlie.

"We have reason to celebrate," said the manager.

"That we have," Charlie replied, adding, "I'm glad you chose us."

"Your humility is most appropriate," replied the manager, raising his little Saké glass, in a toast. They said goodbye and Charlie could look forward to the return trip the next day. First, the trio would celebrate, with a traditional theatrical performance (in Japanese) followed by dinner. The theater was beautiful in that the show went in the old style with colorful, typical clothes, but the context left much to Charlie's imagination when he could only understand one word—*Hai*.

During the dinner afterwards, Mr. Otani spoke of a word he wanted Charlie to learn. It was more mental than any other meaning. It suggests the very essence of Japan, not the material value he explained. The word fit in with life itself, and with the fact that they had jointly concluded an agreement. The word was: *Yutakasa* and means "has great value."

"Yutakasa," Charlie replied, promising to remember it.

Mr. Otani took a napkin and wrote the word in normal Western letters, and next to it in Japanese letters. Charlie was keen to keep the napkin, which he folded and stuffed into his pocket. When they dropped Charlie off at the hotel, it was as if they had known each other for a long time.

"Please visit us if you come to Australia," Charlie said.

"Of course," the two traders agreed, bowing their goodbyes.

On the return trip, Charlie felt more harmonious than ever. For the first time in his life he had the feeling of having created something—he brought a sales contract home with him!

Not only would Abby and the others be proud of him, he was proud of himself. He had decided to wait to tell the good news face to face.

In the taxi from the bus station in Cairns, he had a couple of bottles of Fosters with which he was going to toast. He first stopped at the restaurant to see if Abby was there without thinking that it was a weekday.

"She's free today Charlie" came from behind the bar when he showed up.

"Sure, of course" Charlie replied.

"All dressed up, aren't ya?" he heard someone say. "Are you going to a party?"

"I've been away," Charlie replied.

"In the city?"

"Better yet—in Japan," Charlie replied.

"Wow" came from behind the counter.

Preb and Ritch were completely overwhelmed by Charlie's achievement.

"It couldn't be better!" exclaimed Preb.

Sandy was immediately contracted to be a part-time skipper so Preb and Charlie could dive freely even in the afternoons. It was all about living up to the new volume requirements and Charlie wanted to get the volumes up quickly. During the transport trips to and from the reef, Charlie talked to Sandy about the possibility of delivering tuna. Sandy pondered the matter, and, after a while, he announced that he and some others were willing to try. One would put the tuna on ice already in the fishing boats when they were cleaned and drive the fish directly to large freezer vessels in Cairns. The problem was keeping the fish frozen, which was solved by renting a special freezer warehouse for the purpose provided by the shipping company. Charlie negotiated a one-year contract that was extended by one year at a time if neither party terminated the agreement.

CHAPTER NINE

It was the beginning of a prosperous time for both the fishermen and for Aussie Sponges, who received commissions on the sales value, from the fishermen. It was a happy time for Charlie. Too good to be true, and a year later, about the same time James Dean died in a traffic accident, Abby dumped Charlie. Maybe it wasn't that strange, he thought. After all, he had never let her close to his life, considering he was afraid of hurting her. Besides, he wasn't used to showing his feelings openly. She was in town during weekdays, and working on weekends, which is why they had only met on Sundays. They had often been out with the *Mermaid* and Charlie took the opportunity to pick sponges "since they were there." Now he had to pay the price for his sense of duty.

"I can't stay here," he said after a few days to Ritch.

"That's the stupidest thing I've heard since Studebaker put the front in back," Ritch replied, and continued, "We have a company to run. Why would you leave?"

"I do not know. I just know I have to do something different—change myself."

"We need you," Preb said.

"You need someone," Charlie replied, "not necessarily me, which is obvious to some others here."

"It's a shame if you have to leave, but if you have to, you must,"

Preb replied.

"Don't count on me," Ritch said, and continued: "The workshop is going well, the business is as well. I'll stay."

Depressed, Charlie said: "You have shown me confidence and believed in me. I'll never forget that."

"You have your stake in the company," Preb said, "and you can come back whenever you want."

"I promise to come back," Charlie replied, "but I won't promise to stay."

Charlie had been told many stories about people who had gone north from Cairns. They had not realized how hot it would be, nor how wet, for months at a time. Nor about how sparsely populated the area was except at the coasts. Nor that much of Australia's desert, one-third the size of the Sahara. It was just that all this attracted Charlie. He liked everything that was not structured or predetermined. The fact that it seemed difficult only made the prospects even greater. "Only sheep and fools venture inland," he had been told.

Charlie decided to travel to the Carpentaria—a gulf and small village on the map named Karumba. The bus trip there would go via steppe land and take two days to travel the approximately 100 miles. All the territory north of the Capricorn seems to fascinate other residents of Australia. The monsoon period is a concept. In January and February, it usually rains about 750 mm. This usually comes after months of heat and certain periods when it does not rain at all, usually in June and July. The rain is usually accompanied by heavy lightning, which seems to last indefinitely. Cairns and the regions where he had previously been down on the coast did not have the same weather phenomenon as the inland. There was only one road west and it went via Ravenshoe and Normanton. It didn't take long for the heat to rise and he could see dead kangaroos at the roadside.

It was dry and now he saw what it would be like in the bush.

Halfway to Normanton, the passengers overnighted at a gas station that operated a small motel. Arriving in Normanton the next night, he hitchhiked with a fisherman the remaining miles to Karumba. They became friends immediately when Charlie told him what he was doing.

"I have heard of pearl fishermen in the west, but never about sponge pickers," said the fisherman.

"Probably no big difference," Charlie replied. It was a sticky night in November.

"We are heading into the wet season," said the fisherman. "For months it does nothing else. The only way out of not getting cranky is to sit in 'The Animal Bar,' with everyone else or be out at sea, or preferably not be here," he continued, adding, "we are a fairly tight net collection of skippers here. Thirty fishermen, the barge driver who does transports along the coast and to the islands offshore, the mineral boat captain who ships silver, lead and zinc from the mine twenty miles south, and a lot of farmers are here, of course. What are you doing here?"

Charlie replied, "Maybe see if there is any work for me nearby?"

"If you have no reason to be here, you should probably find something else somewhere else," said the fisherman, and continued, "we can be isolated for a month, during the wet season. Karumba is found at the outlet of the Norman River, on marshlands that often get flooded and deposit crocodiles everywhere. We are the only coastal village in more than 100 miles. The closest neighbor is Normanton, and that's where you came from. The roads to and from the village are often completely submerged and cars cannot drive on them. Then comes what the Aborigines call *Banggerreng*, the culmination of the rain that means 'knock them down rains.' Sometime in April, it will get normal again."

"Seems like you're patterned here," Charlie said.

"Yes," the fisherman replied, "but there are no two seasons that are the same—the only question is how the rainstorms will ruin existence. You might be able to help on the fishing boats."

"I have good experience with marine life," Charlie said.

"There is enough to do here if you want it, but for all the world I can't understand why," the fisherman replied, and continued, "if you want to continue with marine life you can stay or continue to another village, but do you want to? An alternative that differs from what you have done is to see the heart of the country, the bush, and be on land for a while to compare."

"Would the bush be better than the coast?" Charlie wondered.

"Not necessarily, but you won't get swimming skin between the toes," the fisherman replied, and continued, "The only positive thing about the wet season is that the ants move indoors, and they keep the cockroaches out. In addition, we lift the boats at Christmas time so that the hurricanes will not sink them."

"What do you think I should do then?" Charlie wondered.

"I'm thinking about it," the fisherman replied. Then he said, "I would probably take a bus to Alice."

"Alice?" Charlie replied.

"Alice Springs," said the fisherman.

A visit to the Animal Bar was mandatory. Despite the late hour, there were plenty of people and food could still be served. The fisherman ordered Fosters with sausage and Charlie took Fosters with parrot fish and salad. That fish was rare where he came from and a delicacy. The salad was mixed with chopped avocado and papaya which was the local specialty and it was very wonderful to Charlie. He was invited by the fisherman to sleep over and take the time he needed to decide what he wanted to do. New faces were not common in Animal Bar, so most of the other local guests soon took part in Charlie's story.

The others did not give Charlie any more hope of finding something sensible to do in the village, over the wet season, and he felt that he might as well be on his way again soon.

The barge captain invited Charlie to join him on a four-day supply trip to Mornington Island and back, which Charlie accepted. His impression of the journey was the same as that of an explorer, rather than a crew member. The skipper quickly noticed that Charlie was at home on the water and was enjoying himself on board. What distinguished the environment, from what Charlie was used to, was the lack of reefs in the Gulf of Carpentaria and the sticky heat.

Cans, magazines, fruits and drinks would be unloaded in Mornington, until then it was almost uneventful on the trip. Charlie thought about what Sandy had told them about his time during the war when he was shipping goods along the Solomon Islands and wondered if he could now work out a bonus in the form of alcohol to help unload, but quickly rejected that idea. He told the captain about Sandy's story and the captain filled in that it was probably a wonder that Sandy managed to survive, as the Japanese sank everything they could.

Once back in Karumba, Charlie had another night with the fisherman—then he took the bus south. The next morning, he got his last glimpse of the ocean and hitchhiked to Normanton to catch the bus at noon, heading for Alice Springs.

In fact, he was relieved to leave this part of the country. He was looking forward to being on his way—where to mattered less. The surroundings went from dense, gnarly landscape, with poor visibility from the bus, to open grasslands where the view was unobstructed to the horizon.

He would have plenty of time to think about what he wanted to do over the next hundred and sixty miles to Alice. So far, everything that had happened, since he and Ritch decided to take the *Quantas* from San Diego, just over two years earlier, had mostly developed by chance, he thought. It would probably continue that way.

The first night was in Cloncurry where Charlie would change this bus to one that came from Townsville and was passing Alice, on the road to Perth on the west coast.

"It's getting hot after Cloncurry," the new driver told Charlie. Summer was approaching and the bus was traveling between two deserts, Tanami in the north and Simpson in the south. The road was mostly dusty, and it blew a constant warm, sandy wind. Off the road, the ground had a reddish tone and was quite grassy.

The trip passed Mount Isa, a small hilltop of about 500 meters where there was a zinc mine and a small, Irish Pub where they had lunch, via some pubs, with associated gas stations that claimed names of Oban, Urandangi and Tobermorey, and finally the next day's overnight stay in Lucy Creek.

Although the travelers were inside the bus, they had sand in their mouths and Charlie relished a public shower in the pub and a Fosters.

"Welcome to Never Never Land," said the bartender.

"I've heard that before," Charlie replied. Then the bartender filled in with what was apparently his favorite subject: the drought.

"We're in a drought now," he said. "It rains four-five times a year here, and it's been a long time now."

Charlie thought the dry feeling was better than the stickiness in Karumba and, with a cool beer in his hand, it was really comfortable.

"Alice is the only town in 100 miles," said the bartender, "and there are opportunities there. By the way, I've heard that a countryman of yours has bought large piece of useless land north of Alice, around the Tea Tree," he continued.

"What does he do with the land then?" Charlie wondered.

"Would assume he is trying to breed livestock, between the dry periods," replied the bartender. "I should look for him," Charlies said.

"When you get to their gates, you have five miles left to the house itself," replied the bartender.

"Sounds like Texas," Charlie said.

Charlie asked the bartender if he had the name, but he didn't. What he could do, however, was search by phone for a landowner near Tea Tree through an operator.

After a quarter, the bartender had the name and phone number of a farm called Hammond and an owner named Murphy. Charlie brought his beer and went to one of the short ends of the bar and called the number he had, despite the late hour.

"Murphy" replied in a rough voice.

"My name is Charlie Long, and I'm in Lucy Creek, on my way to Alice," Charlie replied.

"You don't sound like an Australian," he heard in the handset.

"I'm not either, but I live here."

"What is your request?" Murphy wondered.

"I just heard that you have a farm and I need something to do."

"Come out to us tomorrow and we can talk about it," Murphy replied. The directions were to continue with the bus towards Alice and change to another one that went towards Darwin, and then get off at "Tea Tree." He would then be picked up there.

Charlie felt he was more fortunate than likely and thanked the bartender by ordering two beers this time—one for himself and one for the bartender.

Late in the afternoon the next day Charlie got off the bus in Tea Tree. He was the only one who got off there and the stop consisted of a small parking lot and a bar with a time schedule posted on the wall.

A small truck was waiting for him in the parking lot. Charlie walked up to it and introduced himself to a dark-skinned man sitting in the driver's seat who replied, "Ernie. Get in."

On the way to the farm, Charlie tried to ask for details of the farm's activities, but all he received was a short "um-hum" with nodding when Charlie got it right. He noticed that Ernie was completely different from everyone else he had met before and realized that Ernie must be an Aborigine. He had heard that they rarely wanted eye contact, which is why Charlie tried not to look him directly in the eyes.

After a while, Ernie lightened up a bit as he interpreted Charlie's respect and told him that he was working on the farm with Bushtucker. Ernie realized that Charlie sounded like Murphy and that Charlie had no idea what Bushtucker was and continued: "food." Charlie countered with an "um-hum" and the ice was broken, Ernie confirming with a little smile.

An hour later in 40-degree heat, the truck pulled up towards a large, gray, wooden building, through a gate on which it stood "Hammond farm." Before leaving the truck, a stately man stood with his hands on his hips on the built-in patio that went around the house, staring at the visitor. Charlie threw his bag over his shoulder and walked through the dust towards the house, with a smile, shouting at some distance: "Mr. Murphy?"

"Correct" the man replied from the porch.

"Charlie?"

Charlie replied with an outstretched hand.

"Welcome to Hammond," replied Murphy and continued, "you can call me Murph. Everyone else does. Come in, it's cooler indoors, and we'll have something to drink."

"That would be fine," Charlie replied.

The house was three stories high and entirely of wood. It was probably built around the turn of the century and reminded Charlie of the farm he himself grew up on. He thought for a brief moment about grandfather, grandmother and Imelda but dismissed the thought, just as quickly.

They settled in the salon and soon a little, Aboriginal woman brought iced tea. She nodded to Charlie who said hello to her. Murph said "thank you" and nodded which apparently meant she could leave the room.

"Tell me about yourself," Murph said.

Charlie told him that he had grown up on a ranch in California and worked with pigs all the free hours, during his upbringing at different schools, that his parents had passed away, that he and Ritch had worked their way here, on a boat two years earlier, and that he had been a diver since then in Cairns.

Now he wanted to try something else and, therefore, sought the heart of Australia, which he had heard lay near Alice.

"You really ended up in a historic part of the country," Murph replied. "The area is called the 'Red Center' and should be reminiscent of parts of California," he thought, continuing, "Your growing up on a ranch suits me well—we need help with most things, but you will be missing the water."

It turned out that Murph had recently bought as much land as Sydney, with surrounding neighborhoods. Hammond had just over 5,000 head of cattle, in several paddocks, each three miles square.

"I don't know much about livestock," Charlie said in his open and honest manner.

"You'll learn," Murph replied, stretching out his hand and saying, "You start tomorrow."

Murph had settled in Australia, after the end of the war, in 1945. He was well acquainted with Australia, as he had been based here and helped the Australian Army pave the road between Darwin and Mount Isa, to facilitate ore transport in response to the threat from the Japanese.

Murph had purchased a smaller farm that sheared sheep, for surrounding sheep farmers up north in Hidden Valley. For some years, there had been a drought and he had had his eyes on Hammond. Although the land was huge on the surface, the cost in arid areas was only a fraction of the price of farms near the coast.

Drought had been the factor that finally forced the previous owner to give up. The price of borrowed capital had increased, with the general rise in interest rates. The animals had both lost weight and the price of beef was lower than in many years, which combined meant that the bank forced a sale and, as they put it, "it was best for all parties." The price Murph had received for the farm in the north was enough for half the purchase price for Hammond, and the bank was able to reduce the loan but still keep the entire estate as collateral.

Murph had reasoned that interest costs would probably go down over time and beef prices would probably rise, which would probably make for a good deal.

As Charlie had in-depth knowledge of how to run a ranch, Murph saw him as a future key figure on the farm. First, he would learn its boundaries and water holes. Water was especially important when driving cattle between these small oases when grazing. Wandering animals would roam where the grass was best, and they could venture far from water.

"Ask Ernie about water," Murph said, adding, "they find water with their eyes closed." Ernie was a hunter. This meant that he was responsible for the hunt and keeping intruders away.

The hunt was the easiest explained Ernie. Invasive animals were worse.

"It's like chasing something that is not visible," he explained when they were out with the truck on the steppe to get acquainted with the terrain.

"We have many of the country's different species here, ranging from honey ants to kangaroos. Many species have problems, with new species introduced into the country," Ernie continued. "For example, we have the sugar cane frog that was introduced from Hawaii twenty years ago, for them to eat sugar cane beetles. Their skin contains a poison and when our domestic animals see a slow dinner, they eat it up and face agonizing death. By the way, the frogs didn't eat the beetles either.

Other animals we have on the land that are dangerous to the cattle apart from toxic spiders and snakes are *Woylie*. It has been given that name by the Aborigines, but it is actually called brush-tailed *bettong*." It is like a small ball of fur when it is small. Adult, it is smaller than a rabbit, of which we have millions, but it has large claws and teeth and is not an animal you want to be near.

Another problem is "echidna," a small ant eater, with needles. It drills down into loose soil and thus forms cavities in which the livestock can get hurt. If you can live in the Aboriginal way, I can take you to a settlement on the farm, which is on a riverbank, on the border of the Tanami desert," Ernie said.

"I'm ready to try it if it's okay with Murph," Charlie replied.

"He'll approve of that—that's what he did when he bought the farm."

The next day, Ernie drove Charlie to the settlement. Ernie explained that his relatives could live wherever they wanted on the farm and that at this time they had chosen the proximity to the water pool, as it attracted many animals. The place was called Baobab. It was the name of an ancient tree that normally looked like a caricature of a tree—a wide, cone-shaped trunk that was bare, apparently without bark, with a large crown at the top.

The tree was reminiscent of a dust brush and had the same reddish color as the ground all around. The tree that the place was named after was apparently many times older than the others and had several stems and crowns and resembled a huge oak tree.

There the chief lived in the tribe. Ernie thought it was his father but that was somewhat uncertain. After the introductions, Ernie promised to come back in a week.

When Ernie had left and Charlie was alone with these seemingly totally isolated people, Charlie began to wonder what he had gotten himself into. He felt completely alien to these indigenous people. Most were completely without clothing.

The chieftain, who was an old man, had a piece of leather at the front of his body. His name was Moon Dog. It turned out that he knew how to speak English and there was only one other person who knew a little English and that was the medicine man, Melaleuca. He had become a medicine man by curing a skin condition of a child by crushing the leaves of a Melaleuca tree and regularly lubricating the skin, with the juice. It is called Tea Tree in English, after Captain Cook made tea, on dried Melaleuca leaves.

Moon Dog spoke with guttural sounds, in short bursts. Charlie thought he was pretty scary. He pointed to a place on the other side of the huge tree and Charlie understood that was where he was to sleep. Charlie had only a blanket to cover him at night.

The entire tribe consisted of just over thirty people of all ages. There were probably just as many or more dogs. Charlie put down his blanket at the place selected by the chief and tried an "um-hum" which hit home with the chief.

Soon, half a dozen hunters arrived with a giant kangaroo hanging on a long branch between them. The chieftain showed his appreciation with a smile and everyone seemed happy and pleased. The hunters greeted Charlie but did not seem to take much notice of him. A fire seemed to be continuously burning a short distance away from the chief's tree. The animal was quickly cut by a couple of hunters and the legs were thrown here and there to the dogs. The fine cuts of meat were grilled on iron skewers, probably the only modernity found among these Aborigines. Smaller pieces were rolled into pieces of skin and placed directly on the coals. The tail was grilled without removing the skin. It became an appetizer. When it was finished, the skin was like a thin crust and you simply cut thin slices of the tail and shared among the tribe. The kids apparently liked the tail. They received milk from goats in wooden bowls which were passed between them.

"Tomorrow hunting," Moon Dog said.

"Um-hum," Charlie replied, causing several little smiles.

To do your natural needs, you went a long way to a small slope where there was a log you could sit on. It was somewhat inaccessible, with thorny bushes all around, and called Spinifex. Children, men and women sat on the long log, at the same time, without distinction. When Charlie was there, a little girl came and she wanted to show him something, on the way back to the small village.

In an opening, several children had a small playground with pebbles laid out in rings drawn in the sand. It reminded Charlie of the "hop-scotch" that the girls jumped at home when he was little. She looked happy as she jumped around between the rings, with her friends, many of whom were probably her siblings.

Charlie thought about what Mr. Otani had said about time and harmony. It harmonized with the Aborigines. Here and now, nothing else seemed to worry them. Charlie tried to jump between the rings also putting his feet on top of each other in the other ring and then turning and jumping back, which caused cries of laugher from the children. They had learned something new and probably someone told Moon Dog about Charlie's feat, but there was nothing other to say when he came back than: "Good, good."

Charlie turned to what he thought was a strange moan and saw two who lay coupling completely unashamedly, a short distance away. Nobody cared about that apparently. Later, he noticed that such a thing could happen anywhere at any time and apparently also with anyone. Couple relationships or romance did not seem to exist.

It was warm even at night, but Moon Dog always had three dogs with him when he slept. They probably were his favorites and every night he said the same thing, "Three dog night." What he implied was that it was chilly, but the real reason was probably that he liked the company of dogs.

When Charlie was to sleep the first night, Moon Dog came with two, very young girls. Charlie was a little bothered by this but showed absolutely nothing. He saw it as a nice gesture from the chieftain and found himself well on the blanket between the two stoves.

He had no plans whatsoever for physical contact with the girls but was glad to hear their breathing within minutes, as they had just fallen asleep.

The moon lit up the entire landscape in a way he had never experienced before. It was not white, as it was on the sea. The glow had a yellow-brownish tone and Charlie at first couldn't understand what it could be.

He probably thought it was because the air in the steppe areas contained so many dust particles. He tried sleeping to the weak breathing from the girls and the howling, at a distance, from the dingos. He had just fallen asleep when he was awakened by the leader of the hunting patrol. He got a spear with a stone arrow in the front and then they took off.

There were half a dozen hunters going out this morning. The target was apparently on the opposite side of the small lake where they spread out. Five men stood intermittently in a crescent a bit from the beach completely silent, with Charlie somewhere in the middle. Then a hunter silently crept into the shore, until he was near the middle of the crescent.

Charlie saw no animals at all, until he heard the scream from the hunter at the beach. He had screamed and leaped forward, driving a number of kangaroos, hares and other smaller animals straight toward the hunters. Charlie didn't even react when several jumped past at lightning speed, but the others managed to hit a hare, and a wallaby, a smaller species similar to the kangaroo.

Charlie had noticed that the kangaroos he had seen had all scattered in different directions. Other animals often protect their offspring, but these animals did not appear to do so. It must be their protection mechanism, he thought.

On the way back to the village, the hunters passed a group of women who were digging up honey ants. *It will make for a good dessert*, Charlie thought. They also took the roots from the bushes they dug under. Later, Charlie saw how to boil the roots and he ate them like any vegetable.

The hunters also had traps. *The simplest methods were best*, Charlie thought. They dug a pit at a depth of one meter and put some leaves over. At a visible hole, if something had fallen in, you speared the animal, pulled it up, put back the leaves again and then you continued.

During the days, everyone often bathed in the banana-shaped lake called "Lander." It had apparently been fished out long ago because there were no fish in the lake. In the summer, there was quite a bit of water in the lake, but one could imagine that in very rainy weather, it would easily overflow.

There was a fairly, wide, desiccated riverbed that led down to the lake. It was bordered by cone-shaped mountains perhaps twenty meters high which had a lovely, orange-brown tone. There was green grass on the sides of the riverbed which should mean that there was water in the river sometimes. Whether the Aborigines wanted water or not was unknown, but one thing was certain: it was a harsh climate.

One day, they got nothing during the hunt. They had many goats and pigs which were not fenced, and Moon Dog grunted that a pig would be slaughtered. Charlie offered to take care of the matter and, in his trained manner, he repeated what he had done on Fiji and slaughtered the pig, with two incisions on each side of his neck in a single motion. This impressed the hunters. He had learned to treat the Aborigines as they had treated him. He did not take advantage of his knowledge but allowed several people to take part in the cutting. That way, Charlie blended in wherever he went.

He had learned to be responsive to his surroundings. One reason for this was probably that Charlie had been far from home all his life. Now, he had the opportunity to participate in a food chain that took only what was necessary for survival.

The Aborigines had of course influenced their environment through their presence, during the 40-60 thousand years they had inhabited Australia. One example was the burning of areas to facilitate hunting. In their context, however, the indigenous population had overall a limited impact on the country, as they were relatively few in number on a continent of America's size. The week Charlie spent with Moon Dog and his clan left a deep impression. Despite this, he was relieved when he heard the rattle from Ernie's truck. Ernie brought some gifts to Moon Dog, from Murph. There were fruits, vegetables, pineapple juice and tobacco. Aborigines never got alcohol. Charlie told Moon Dog he would come back, and he meant it.

Murph was glad that Charlie had gained an insight into what life in the bush meant.

"It is better to experience yourself than I tell you about it," he had said.

"I want you to be in control of what's going on at the farm," Murph told Charlie at dinner.

He had to know where the animals were, if they were healthy, if they were pregnant, if the grazing was good, if the paddocks were in need of repair (which they always were) and assist with whatever he could wherever needed.

Murph was raised on a farm in Montana, but, the youngest of three brothers, had been drafted, during the war and ended up in Australia. He really liked the idea that a countryman, with a similar background, and the youngster's adventurous desire would join Hammond.

Charlie thought it was a little slow to get around, on the huge farm with the old truck.

"It's the only thing that works here if you don't want to ride a camel," Murph said.

"It doesn't get into the bush," Charlie said.

"If you have any other ideas, I'd love to hear them," Murph replied.

"Motorcycle," Charlie said. "Works everywhere and uses only a fraction of the gasoline than using the truck."

"Take the truck and go to Alice and buy one," Murph said, continuing, "Our job is to breed healthy animals and sell them at the best possible price—let's try new methods."

"You sound like my grandfather," Charlie replied with a twinkle in his eye.

"Maybe it does," replied Murph, "but here you are part of the team."

Charlie had not ridden a motorcycle before, had no idea what could be good in the desert, and he had no price limit from Murph. The next day he was in Alice Springs, for the first time. He bought a newspaper and, for the first time in a long time, received news that the world had actually spun on, despite Charlie's voluntary exile into the desert.

He ate lunch and asked the waiter at the counter if there were any motorcycle dealers.

"We only have one," he replied, "and he's just down the street."

Charlie went there with his full stomach and his head full of news and felt how the idea of a motorcycle thrilled him. The dealer was a large man. He immediately showed his interest when the American was considering a motorcycle. Charlie talked about the purpose and the dealer suggested three different machines. This resulted in the choice between two used ones: a "Matchless" 500 cc and a leftover 750 cc Harley-Davidson from the war. The dealer thought it was better with the Harley because it held up better in the heat, even though the price for it was lower than for the English machine.

Charlie decided on the Harley and asked the trader to do an oil and spark plug change, before picking it up a few hours later, and with two, new tires included in the price, which the dealer accepted.

One advantage of the Harley was that there were frames to hold gasoline tanks, on each side of the rear wheel, and a rifle pouch on the front, right side. The position of the rifle on that side explained Murph, who wholeheartedly liked the idea of getting a Harley, was that, in ancient times, cavalrymen always had their sword on the right side. Thus, they always mounted a horse on the left side of the horse, something that survived when riding a motorcycle.

"We can take turns with your duties," a clearly satisfied Murph had said after his theoretical interpretation.

The Harley seemed to thrive in the heat. The dealer had included half a dozen bottles of chain oil and recommended lubricating the chain daily, after riding. Murph demanded that Charlie announce the planned itinerary every day before departure so that they could find him, if he had any problems and could not return to the house. The system was refined over time so that he would always travel clockwise. A map of the entire Hammond farm was pinned on the wall by the terrace which showed all the paddocks and an approximate number of cattle and where they were. Today's itinerary was marked with red pins. Murph soon noticed that Charlie was able to inspect four to five times the area he had previously seen in a day. In addition, he quickly returned, if there were acute problems, e.g. with calving animals that had problems. The livestock was free roaming, so it was necessary to have animals that could both calve themselves without help, and also withstand the heat.

With the swift information, it was soon possible to develop planned crops. The cattle were moved more often, so that the crops were allowed to grow freely for longer times and thus produced fatter cattle. In order for the cattle to stay healthy, it was important to breed new blood, with new breeding animals. Charlie figured that if they could breed a breed that had the desired qualities and which became a little bigger, the earnings would increase by large sums. By weight, each millimeter cow corresponded to about one kilo, which meant ten kilos a centimeter. If all could become a centimeter longer and thus weigh ten kilos more than today's livestock on average, the total weight would increase by astonishing ten kilos times 5,000 animals, or a total of fifty tons! The breed they had in the yard was "Poll Hereford" and fared well, in that environment. Murph devoted daytime to this search for breeding animals and left much of the care of the farm to Charlie. Charlie enjoyed the farm and his mission. He had a lot of thoughts on how to increase the return (you got paid per kilo) and made the farm more efficient. He recalled when they watered the pigs at home to reduce weight loss, but it was impossible on Hammond. What Charlie then introduced was to direct deliveries to the slaughterhouse in Alice for periods when it was cooler than scalding, by truck at dawn. Then he told Murph about his trip to Japan and the trading house there.

"We are already exporting to Asia, through the beef market in Darwin," said Murph.

"It costs nothing to write to the trading house," Charlie replied. Mr. Otani was willing to buy beef in unlimited quantities and he arranged the transport, with the same shipping company hired by Aussie Sponges, but in freezer ships directly from Darwin. The journey there took half the time compared to Cairns, because the distance is shorter and the road, since the war, was paved from "Elliott" north. These methods brought good profits to Hammond and Murph could not have been more pleased with Charlie. In the summer of 1957, the crew celebrated the results in Alice, with good food and drink. At the pub, a song was played over and over again on the radio called "Heartbreak Hotel," with an artist named Elvis Presley. Charlie liked the music immediately and asked the bartender who Elvis Presley was. The bartender answered that Elvis had surfaced the year before, with that particular song but that novelties usually take a year or so to reach Alice. "Shall we dance?" he heard a female voice say behind him, with American dialect. He turned and looked into the eyes of something he thought was a mirage. Wide smile, raven black hair, tan, and in a red checkered "lumberjack" shirt, she stood there waiting for an answer. "Why not?" was all Charlie could spurt out and got up from the stool.

"I can't sit still when Elvis plays," said the mirage.

"I've never heard him before," Charlie replied, "but he sounds good! My name is Charlie."

"Shannon" replied the mirage and continued, "I heard you were from the States." "California," Charlie replied. "And you?" he wondered.

"Arizona," she replied.

"Where?"

"You don't know, anyway," Shannon replied a little facetiously.

"Try me."

"Williams."

"Sure," Charlie replied, "that's where the train goes up to the Grand Canyon."

"You knew!" she exclaimed.

"What are you doing in Alice?" Charlie asked.

"I took the bus here to look at Ayers Rock."

"I've heard about it but haven't seen it," Charlie said.

"Join me tomorrow," Shannon said.

His immediate thought was "I can't," but he was completely engrossed by her.

"Why not?" he repeated himself.

Shannon stayed at one of the city's two hotels. Charlie asked if the pub had rooms for rent and there was a vacancy. He told Murph that he would take the day off and return in the evening, to the great delight of the men.

"What are you doing in Australia?" Charlie said at last.

Digging opals in Coober Pedy, a day's trip south," Shannon replied.

Charlie had an irresistible desire to dig for opals.

Charlie and Shannon were real contrasts. Similar in age, but completely different in appearance. He was tall and slender, reddish and with rather angular features. She was short, even for a woman, very light-skinned, under the tan, pitch black hair, and had soft features.

Her cheekbones were somewhat distinctive, and her chin had a definite v-shape. But what was most distinctive about Shannon was her profile. From the side, you could think she was a full-blooded Indian, if you overlooked her bright complexion. The nose was distinctive and went in a straight line down from the forehead.

After a dance with Shannon, Charlie was completely mesmerized. Eager to leave the next morning, he sought her out at the hotel where they had breakfast together. She was obviously happy with her new company and very talkative. He was told that she had come to Australia a few months earlier with her parents on a round trip of the world and chosen to stay. It was clear that she was quite independent and adventurous.

In Adelaide, she had heard of several opal mines, around Coober Pedy, and as she was obsessed with jewels in general, she liked the idea of trying to find stones on her own.

Charlie could easily imagine how this Native American creature in cowboy boots, red checkered shirt and wide-brimmed hat roamed the prairie and rinsed dust.

"Where is your horse?" Charlie teased.

She probably did not realize the teasing when she answered, "Which horse?"

"You have cowboy boots," he said.

"Everyone does in Arizona," she replied a little coolly, and continued, "they're good to have in the terrain—you've heard of snakes?"

Charlie, diplomatically enough, let Shannon have the last word.

The bus to Ayers Rock took an hour and was packed with tourists. It was the start of a full day trip where you would hike up one side on the trail. Charlie thought of Shannon's nose and that the hikers must look like ants on it in profile.

Ayers Rock looks like a giant tree stump, in terracotta color, in the middle of a huge steppe. It has stood there for millions of years and has always been surrounded by mysticism. The indigenous people worshiped whatever higher powers they now worshiped and had rituals at its peak.

When they reached the high plateau, Charlie thought of Preb's rituals when he had accomplished something and uncorked his Aquavit.

"Preb and Ritch—yes!" he thought. He quickly had something else to think about when Shannon exclaimed, "It's like being on the moon!"

Charlie had his own little ritual and opened his Fosters for both. The guide had distributed four backpacks of water and large sandwiches that they ate, in small groups at the top. Then the visitors got a little history of the mountain and its mystery before the return trip.

Charlie felt he wanted the day to never end and thought intensely about how he would play his next card. All he wanted to do was follow Shannon regardless of destination.

On the way down, Shannon told him, "My bus leaves at six o'clock tonight."

"Would you like to have company?" Charlie wondered.

"It's a free world," Shannon replied.

Charlie was split between the sense of duty to Murph and Hammond and the desire to break out again for the unknown. For some reason, it was always the unknown that took the upper hand,

and this time it reinforced the feeling of the desire to be with Shannon. The round went to Shannon.

"I have things I need to do at the farm," Charlie said, and continued, "but I'm thinking of leaving it. Do you mind if I come to Coober, in a few weeks?"

"I'll be there," Shannon replied with an inviting smile. Charlie's heart beat in loops! They took leave at the bus station in Alice with a firm handshake and "See you again!" Charlie couldn't wait.

"Murph would understand," he thought. The prospects for Hammond were good and Murph would manage anyway, he comforted himself during the bus trip back to Tea Tree.

"I had hoped you would stay on Hammond" was Murph's reaction when Charlie told of his plans to try his luck in the Opal Mines south.

"Hammond is a nice station. You have given me great confidence and liberty, which I really appreciate. I have learned a lot about life here and have great experiences from here. Now, I have to follow my instincts and try something new," Charlie said.

"You've earned your liberty here, and you've given the farm better conditions to survive, which everyone here appreciates," Murph replied, noticeably disappointed that Charlie would leave them.

One day the following week, Ernie came and asked Charlie to accompany him to his relatives.

"They want you to attend a ceremony for the good conditions of the year," he said.

It was near Christmas, an unknown concept for the Aborigines, and in the middle of summer. Normally, the drought had caused difficult times around Christmas but this year it had rained a number of times. That's why the conditions for livestock grazing and hunting were better than in many years. They had moved to a new place further from the small banana-shaped lake when it was close to flooding their small village.

Meanwhile, Charlie had visited Moon Dog and his clan once a month at Hammond, mostly to make sure they got most necessities, but also to enjoy their harmonious existence. During these visits, he always had tools such as machete, ropes, blankets, and other things that they could hardly make themselves.

He had always been careful to park the motorcycle a bit away from their camp, so as not to scare them and walk into the camp. Every visit had been something of a small feast for Charlie. It was like entering the world of dreams. He thought that the big Baobab trees, with their unlikely proportions, sparsely scattered on the reddish ground, resembled creatures with life, as if the branches could move by their own will and speak to him. The surface of the trees shifted from seemingly bare, and thus merely constituting an extension of the ground, to looking like the skin of an elephant—greyish with crevices and pits, around the entire trunk.

The Aborigines were one with nature and Charlie couldn't help but marvel at it. The only thing they seemed to be wasting was time. He had not thought much about how to say goodbye to his friends in the bush and now he had the perfect opportunity, with the planned harvest ceremony they were heading for.

How would he explain that he was going away and not coming back? Ernie promised he would explain after they left the camp.

Once at the camp, Charlie saw that there were more fires than usual and that a meal was being prepared, in front of Moon Dog's place, in an open little courtyard. All men had smeared the front of their upper body with something similar to white chalk or lime. Ernie explained that it was a white pigment used to make the ceremony solemn. They both got a small bowl of pigment and, like all the other men, smeared the front of their upper body.

Moon Dog, unlike all others, with his white hair, looked even more fearful than the others, if possible. Characteristic of the ceremony was that everyone wore colored fabrics around their hips.

The guests, Ernie and Charlie, sat down next to Moon Dog and then first one and then several started playing on their Didgeridoo's—hollow, bamboo tubes or branches hollowed out, with the help of termites and glowing charcoal, which evoked surrealistic base tones that, after a short while, felt numbing.

When the children were rowdy, a short *Yagga-yagga* was called out, which must have meant "silent, silent," for soon it became calm again.

Around the largest fire, there were kangaroo pieces and wild turkeys rolled in kangaroo skin, lying on the coals. All lay on kangaroo legs so as not to lie directly on the coals. The children got kangaroo tail in the usual order.

Ernie explained that they celebrated the heroes of heaven who created the earth's creations, with songs and dance in the same way as this evening, but that was not why they had been gathered for a ceremony.

Tonight's ceremony was for a white friend who would travel away forever. Charlie was moved and proud that the whole clan was celebrating him. Moon Dog chimed in a song in a slightly higher tone than the musicians but still in deep bass. Charlie tried to gently imitate the chieftain with questionable results. The other men agreed with a monotonous "ya-ya-ya-ye-ye-ye."

The songs, the music, the fires, the white-painted, upper body that reflected the light of the fires, the scents of the flesh, the endless steppe and the sky with its many stars made a deep impression on Charlie. Some danced in a ring and the children did the same. The girls Charlie had slept with, during the week he visited them when he first came to Hammond, picked him up and he danced with them to everyone's delight.

Later, Moon Dog said his usual "Three Dog Night" and indicated to Charlie that he should bring his two heaters, which he preferred rather than to try to find his way home, with the truck in the moonlight, whereupon the guests stayed overnight.

The next morning, Charlie said goodbye to Moon Dog. It was a brief farewell where Charlie was at the receiving end of good advice. Moon Dog looked Charlie in the eye for the first and last time and said, "My friend, take light steps."

Charlie smiled and replied, "um-hum."

Then Ernie also said goodbye to Moon Dog, and they rattled off with the truck. On the way to the house, Ernie told him that it was rare for Moon Dog to look a white straight into the eyes. It was a sign of confidence. Charlie had taken Ernie's advice to treat the Aborigines in their own way, which they obviously respected.

Ernie liked Charlie and was sorry that he was leaving. After a moment of silence, Charlie suddenly said, "A Sheila."

"Um-hum" said Ernie, with a meaningful expression.

At the farewell dinner that Murph and his wife, Lydia, hosted that evening, Murph said that Charlie was welcome back anytime. As a token of their appreciation, they wanted to give Charlie monetary proof. Murph handed Charlie an envelope with what appeared to be a wad of notes.

"We have sold five young animals to the farm next door; half the amount goes to your starting capital for the mine," said Murph.

"I'll manage it well," Charlie replied. Lydia gave Charlie a wide-brimmed, brown, felt hat to take for Shannon. Then they said goodbye, thanked each other deeply, and Ernie drove Charlie back to Tea Tree.

MICHAEL OWENS

CHAPTER TEN

The bus trip to Coober Pedy took two days. Charlie appreciated the solitude of the bus and thought of the time at Hammond and what lay ahead of him. The bus station in Coober was, as usual, a roadside post, with a petrol station and a small restaurant next door.

Charlie had a well-deserved Fosters and asked for an American Sheila. He found out that she was on a claim half an hour away, at a large mining area. He could sleep in the restaurant in a small guest room and hitchhike, with someone who was going there the next day. It was too late to do anything but accept and stay overnight. "Half an hour away" felt endless, with the knowledge that Shannon was there. He consoled himself with a few Fosters and managed to temporarily suppress his longing for Shannon.

The next day, Charlie got a lift with a truck that was going up to the mining area. Once in front, he saw a large area that looked like a single, large, gravel pit. Large piles of sandy soil and stones that were undoubtedly shaped by humans were everywhere.

Here they do noodling, the truck driver explained. Newcomers to the mines could sift through the piles, free of charge, which were already sifted by those who had the rights. The odds of finding opals in these piles were small, but it did happen every now and then. Charlie asked a noodler if he knew an American in the area.

"Sure," replied the man, "over at Lightning Ridge."

The man pointed out the direction and Charlie wandered for a while in that direction, with thoughts on how to explain his presence to Shannon.

Lightning Ridge was an area of steppes surrounded by a mountain ridge that looked like a washboard; roads dotted the mountain and machines constantly scraped the surface, in search of the valuable opals. On the steppe, there were white, crooked indentation posts everywhere.

After asking several people, he found Shannon sitting on an old car tire next to some rectangular shafts.

"I have a Christmas present for you," Charlie said.

Shannon jumped up like a shot from a cannon and screamed, "Charlie!" Gave him a baby hug and continued, "What a thrill to see you again!"

"Here," Charlie replied, handing over the felt hat he received from Lydia. "Merry Christmas," he continued.

Shannon was noticeably moved by Charlie's fine gift. She tilted her head slightly and, with a hint of embarrassment, she said, "I have nothing for you; I didn't know if you would come here."

"No need," Charlie replied, and continued, "but you might be able to help me get settled. I plan to stay for a while."

"That's exactly what I was hoping for," Shannon replied, "I have a tiny cottage included when I bought my claim—come with me!" she said, taking his hand to pull him away to the cabin.

Charlie had a backpack and an Aussie mattress; a thin cushion with canvas cover.

"I am really happy with the hat," Charlie heard from somewhere under the wide brim.

"It was thoughtful of you," she said, looking up at Charlie with her eager, dark deer eyes.

"I had some help," Charlie replied, changing the subject: "can you get food somewhere?"

"We have a small cafe that is run as a cooperative by all of us who work here," Shannon replied, and continued, "We pay a small fee for some to keep it open and it's a lifesaver here."

"I would like to see the café; can't you show me, so I can invite you to lunch?" Charlie wondered.

"Never thought you would ask," he heard from somewhere below the brim. "But I want to show you my cabin first," Shannon continued.

The cottage was a shed built with a myriad of old, building debris, it seemed, but it lay in the shade of a tree, which was more important. Shannon was happy with the cottage because was among the better in the area. There was a hall, with a bench and a table, sink without a tap, and some simple cooking utensils. Dishwashing was done in a plastic bucket. Water was outside in a barrel that was filled up by the café cooperative, from time to time. In the rain, the barrel was filled up automatically, although rain was rare. Behind the cottage was an outhouse and a small space with tables and some old, wooden chairs. Shannon disappeared into the outhouse and Charlie heard several loud thumps from inside. When she came out again, Charlie asked if she'd killed someone in there.

"There are Redback spiders here," Shannon replied, "always check under the lid and knock on the bench—so they fall, before you sit down."

"Thanks for the tip," Charlie replied, rolling his eyes as if he were a newcomer to the bush. In addition to the hall, there was a small room where Shannon slept.

"You can stay in the hall if you want," she said.

"I can live in the yard," Charlie said.

"Then at least you can come in when it rains," Shannon replied.

He left his backpack and they walked towards the cafe.

"There is a shower there," Shannon said.

"Have we got a new member?" wondered a skinny bearded man behind the counter.

"Maybe so" Charlie replied.

"Are you a Ringer?" said the man behind the counter.

"Um-hum" Charlie answered in the Aboriginal way.

"On the house" was heard from inside the beard, more friendly this time.

"I come from a station north of Tea Tree, and thank you," Charlie replied.

"Doesn't sound like it."

"Originally from California," Charlie replied.

"You Americans are like flies on a dead Guana," said the beard, smiling, "Shannon's friends are my friends."

They had a hefty miners lunch consisting of meat stew and potatoes, with bread.

"Standard mine food," Shannon said.

"But it tasted good," said Charlie.

"There is a claim office in the area staffed by a Notary on Mondays," Shannon said. "Until you decide what you want to do, you are welcome to help me, so I can teach you how to do this," she continued.

"Taken!" said a happy Charlie and he raised his beer in a toast: "To Opals!" he said.

"To opals!" replied an obviously happy opal miner in a new felt hat named Shannon.

"How long have you been in Australia?" Shannon wondered.

"About five years now," Charlie replied, continuing, "and you?"

"About five months."

"Have you managed to find any opals then?"

"Enough for it to pay off anyway, but it takes longer to sift when you're alone."

"We can probably improve the pace a bit now," Charlie said.

Shannon's rented claim was located near the base of the ridge called "Lightning Ridge." There were hundreds of different claims, on the prairie below the mountain, all of which were about the same size. Some had one or a couple and some had ten claims. Whoever rented to Shannon had about ten and rented out half. She hired one. The rent consisted of a strange combination of payment in kind. The rarest opal that very rarely anyone found was the black opal. Sometimes someone found an opal that was only partially black with other color combinations and they were also highly sought after. The rent amounted to half of all opals found, with the addition of all found black opals. The latter may seem slightly stomach-churning, but only a couple of black opals were found, in the area in a whole year. The finesse of the system was that if you did not find anything at all, you also did not have to pay. It was something that appealed to Shannon. The system was based on the fact that those who rented the claims actually reported their findings. It turned out that it was with the opal people as with fishermen: when you had found a treasure you made a speedy dash to the cafe to try to impress the others having found the greatest opals, just like with classic fishing stories. In addition, the opals would be converted into money. The notary who handled the area's legal affairs collected opals every Monday. The stones were weighed, measured, color determined and recorded, after which the stones were handed to him and you got a receipt with a so-called "Bag number."

The notary then handed these bags to a buyer in Coober who priced the stones, according to a list based on the mentioned information plus/minus quality characteristics such as luster and shape. Next Monday, the money could then be redeemed against the receipt. What would then be withheld to the owner of the claim was deducted and the rest was paid out. No one complained about the system.

Shannon's enclosure included an area that was relatively hilly and large as four tennis courts. Most claims were about the same size, but the hilly ones were considered to be the worst as they were more difficult to handle. What you dug up would be sifted on different grids and the piles were transported, so it was simply more strenuous to transport oneself and the earth around the mine shaft.

When it came to the actual likelihood of hits for opals, it did not matter where you were. The entire area yielded results and, based on experience, it was at three to ten meters depth that the stones were found, down to twenty-five meters depth, no matter how it looked on the surface.

"Do you want to see some of my stones?" Shannon wondered.

"Of course," Charlie replied.

Back in her cabin, Shannon rolled away a small box that obscured a hole in the wall. She took out an earthy cloth bag that didn't seem to weigh anything at all. The contents were poured onto the small, hall table and despite the poor light, Charlie could see that they were not ordinary stones. Although they were dull, you could see clear colors.

"You see here what we are looking for," Shannon said, and continued: "these are cleaned. When we sift the earth, they are easy to miss."

"I can hardly wait," Charlie replied.

There were six stones on the table. Everyone was small. "What do you think these are worth?" he wondered.

"Somewhere around ten dollars apiece."

"Seems good" Charlie thought.

"We should go and try 'fossicking,'" Shannon said. "That's what you usually do, before you start sifting. We scrape off the surface with a rake, scoop up dirt with a shovel and pour it over a fine grid that you have on a stand a short distance away where you have already finished digging in an old shaft."

You went back and forth in rows that resembled the shaft on a typewriter, as you rolled forward the next line. This time of year, they were better off in the shaft, because of the heat, but for once she felt it was necessary. Wearing her new hat, she picked up the equipment in a wheelbarrow and walked off towards the mountain.

"How did you get here?" Charlie wondered.

"Just like you, by bus," he heard from under the hat.

"I mean why did you just come here?"

"Coober is apparently a well-known mining area. If you must dig for opals, it is Australia that applies, and I was advised to come here."

"I thought diamonds and gold were more sought after than opals," Charlie replied.

"That may be for some, but opals are far rarer," Shannon said. "In addition, I think they are more exciting, with all possible color changes, often in the same stone."

"You have a point there," Charlie said.

The screen grid was erected over a partially filled, rectangular hole, in the ground.

"Now we're ready," Shannon said. Where the ground had previously been scraped, it was clear that the ground was a little lower there than the surrounding surface and scraped clear from stones. Charlie had to do the heavy scraping and Shannon scooped up the soil into the wheelbarrow.

They drove a full wheelbarrow to the screen grid and Shannon showed the slow process, of placing the shovel on the grid and, with a small knife, scraping down the earth over the grid. Charlie felt the thrill of the search. Just being close to Shannon outweighed the labor of working in the heat no matter what the work was about. Several wheelbarrows later, without results, Charlie had probably understood the principle.

"We have to keep going until we find something," Shannon said, and continued, "to be motivated to continue like this, you have to end a work day with a find—otherwise it will be difficult to get up the next day." A few wheelbarrows later, Charlie thought he saw something unusual on the grid.

"You found one," Shannon exclaimed.

"Is it any good?" Charlie wondered.

"We wash it off and check." Back at the house, the stone was brushed and then it got a water bath. "It's really nice," Shannon said, and continued, "the biggest one I've found, on the surface."

"Congratulations," Charlie said.

"It's your stone," Shannon replied, and continued, "your luck—stone."

"Thanks, thanks, thanks!" Charlie replied with a big smile. "We absolutely have to celebrate this!" Charlie said. After a shower over at the cafe, it was time to visit the beard again.

"The flies are back," was heard behind the bar.

"Gather on Guanas, was it?" Shannon replied.

"My turn to treat," Charlie said. "Three Fosters, please!"

"Thank you," the beard said, and asked, "Any luck today?"

"Not really, just a well-deserved salary for the effort," Shannon replied.

"One stone," Charlie commented.

"Not bad on the first day" the beard said.

During dinner, Shannon told Charlie that there were opals found in the inland sea that covered almost a third of the country that dried up 110 million years ago. Opals can be found, in clay layers in pockets of sandstone, that once formed the bottom of the sea. It is not known exactly how opals are formed. Some believe it took thousands of years under great pressure, and others believe they were formed quickly. It is reasonable to believe that bacteria collected silicon from their muddy environment, which accumulated in cavities in the stone where the silicon eventually transformed into opals. These silicon spheres reflect white light. The microscopically small spheres reflect light by spreading it in different wavelengths which are perceived as different colors. The different colors and patterns depend mostly on the size, and how these silicon spheres are composed in the stone.

With knowledge of how opals were formed, one can draw conclusions about where to find them, with the addition of the trial and error method.

"Up by the mountain you scrape the earth with bulldozers," Shannon continued. "There's a whole team of people working there. The method is to try to find a vein where opals can be found and then concentrate the excavations on that vein. We who reap only small incomes, just dig by hand."

"Requires patience," Charlie replied.

"It has to be that way. There are no other options. Usually you only find a small layer that has a small width, and then you scrape there until it is clean and then continue downwards as long as it seems stable." The beard arrived with a free round to the flies.

"You are welcome for turkey dinner on Christmas Day."

"We will come" Charlie and Shannon answered in chorus.

"Then we book the flies!"

A few days later, the flies had dug down a few feet, in the

rectangular hole that Shannon was mining. The heaviest job was not, as you might think, digging; it was raising the bucket of soil. Shannon had previously had to carry it up, sift, and then step down into the pit again. Now she had the advantage of working where it was cool while Charlie lifted the buckets and sifted in the heat.

The effect was that Shannon was able to cut three times more than before and it was easier to be two on the job. They agreed to share returns equally. Everyone preferred to have a first-hand contract, for which there was another queuing system. Shannon was third in line, Charlie fifth, as another person had signed up since Shannon arrived. She suggested that if her turn came to first-hand contracts, Charlie could share it with her. If they then got his, they could rent one.

"Sounds good," Charlie said, "we work better as a team."

On Christmas day, most people gathered at the cafe for the dinner the beard had prepared. He had flour in his beard and a Santa hat and fit perfectly in the role as Santa. When everyone had been at it for a while, the spirits were high, and the mood was good in all present. Some had had a fantastic year and bought rounds of Fosters.

"I want to read a poem for you," said Santa. "You've all heard 'Waltzing Matilda,' he barely managed to say before cheering filled the salon," but you may not know why he wrote it?"

"Who" whispered Charlie.

"Banjo Paterson" replied Shannon. "He died during the war and is a national saint with his ballads about the bush."

Santa continued: "Banjo had heard of a sheep shearer that, after a strike that the shearers had lost, drowned himself at a watering hole. He was so impressed with the struggle of the working class that he wrote a ballad. It is about a person walking in the bush with his canvas mat called Matilda. It describes how a hungry tramp who camps at a watering hole slaughters a sheep for food. He is caught red-handed, by the rich landowner and three, mounted police. Rather than being imprisoned and losing the freedom on the prairie that he values higher than life itself, he dives into the water and drowns himself. He called the poem 'Waltzing Matilda,' and here it comes:

"O! there was once a workhand camped in the bush, in the
    shade of a Coolabah tree;
And he sang when he saw his stew boil,
Who will come and waltz Matilda with me?
Who will come and waltz Matilda, my darling,
Who will come and waltz Matilda with me?
Waltzing Matilda carried a water-pouch,
Who will come and waltz Matilda with me?
Down came a tramp to drink at the water hole,
The workhand jumped up and took a firm grip;
And he said as he stuffed away the tramp in his bag,
"You will come and waltz Matilda with me!"
Down came resident on his fullblood;
Down came the police-one, two, three.
"Who is the tramp you have in your bag?
You will come and waltz Matilda with me."
But the workhand, he jumped into the water hole,
Drowned himself at the Coolabah tree;
And his ghost can be heard as it sings in the bush,
Who will come and waltz Matilda with me?"

Everyone then chipped in and sang 'Waltzing Matilda's,' until they could no longer cope. Someone thought it should be Australia's national anthem. Someone else told them that Winston Churchill knew the song by heart and that he had sung it for Charles de Gaulle, during a dinner in 1941. De Gaulle is said to have said, after the performance, that it was one of the world's best songs! "Dance with me," Shannon said. Charlie was once again in a dream world. After a shaky beginning, their noses rubbed and left them petrified for a short while before they first kissed, to a general cheer in the salon. They were too preoccupied, for the first few seconds, to notice the public interest but when they noticed it, both burst out in slightly embarrassed laughter.

"Come," Shannon said, taking his hand. They walked back to the cabin arms around each other all the way.

"I have a Christmas present for you," Shannon said, as they arrived. She held Charlie in her hand and pulled him into her little private crib. "You can stay here if you want," she continued.

"Then I don't see the stars," Charlie said a little feistily.

"You get to see other stars," Shannon countered.

"Then you will become my Matilda," Charlie said.

"If you call me Matilda, I'll hit you!" Charlie silenced her with a kiss.

The weeks that followed were the happiest in Charlie's life. He felt he was completely natural with Shannon. They were equal in their desire for adventure. They were both stubborn but flexible. Admittedly, they differed in their interests but were unanimous in terms of organization and trust in each other. The biggest difference was probably one that emerged after some time: she was completely satisfied with the life that the bush and the uncertainty of the future meant. He constantly had a nagging feeling of something unknown that he was heading for, some other achievement which needed to be realized.

Therefore, Charlie, who thought life smiled at him, was not really satisfied. There was always some dimension beyond the present, he felt. Most who worked in the mining area lived on one hope: to find the vein! Getting rich. Some made it and left.

Charlie had a permanent desire to perform, and to perform well. It was for him a driving force that took the upper hand over whatever he was actually doing. He could do anything as long as he could perform well.

Milking the earth of stone was part of something bigger, he felt. While Charlie was sifting, he pondered how to avoid much of the time-consuming scraping, with a knife. He experimented with an oil drum, which he cut holes in, and then he tied a fine mesh-type chicken net around it, whereupon he poured the soil into the barrel via a lid and then tumbled the barrel with a handle on the other side. The knife method was faster, he soon realized.

He wanted to flush with what was scarce—water. He realized that it was difficult to modernize mining. Shannon had the stubbornness of a donkey—she just kept on going. For safety reasons, she always stopped at eight meters depth. At greater depth, it was completely dark and made digging all the more difficult. Most people rarely found anything at greater depths than eight meters. On average, their tedious digging generated finds about every other day. Faithful toil rendered faithful returns.

After some time in the bush, you often lose contact with the outside world, which is why many people prefer the bush life. Charlie woke up from his hibernation one day when they heard on the radio in the cafe that a freedom fighter named Fidel Castro had taken command of Cuba, over a guerrilla warrior named Batista. This had apparently happened six months earlier, in January 1959.

By now, the United States had noticed that the freedom fighter was a communist and that he welcomed Russia. Many Cubans therefore emigrated to the US and the US would impose a blockade on Cuba.

"It's a free world," Shannon had said when Charlie suggested he come to Coober.

"One wonders if it really is," Charlie commented (no one could then imagine what was to come between Cuba and Russia and the United States, in the so-called "Cuba crisis," a few years later, in 1962, when the world was near a nuclear war). The idea of the free world gave Charlie an idea. After all, the cooperative sold quantities of opals, at a given price level locally. He told Shannon about his Japanese friend, Masaharu Otani, whom he had worked with in Tokyo.

"What if we could sell to Japan!" he said. Their trust in each other was wholehearted and Charlie decided to write to Mr. Otani. He wrote the following:

Wakita Enterprises
Attn: Mr. M. Otani
2400 Fushida
Tokyo, Japan
Coober Pedy, July 25, 1959

Dear Mr. Otani:

It is my great hope that you are well and that our cooperation runs without hindrance.

Our country has great exports to your country, and it is of great personal importance to me to have the opportunity to propose yet another business opportunity for you.

I now work with mining. It is on a small scale, for my part, but it is part of larger cooperatives. What we extract is exquisite. We mine for opals. Our partners currently supply a significant portion of what can be extracted from Australia.

What we want to suggest to your company is that you consider conveying our exquisite stones within your country.

Every opal that is delivered is polished and ready for sale. Certificates are provided with respect to quality, carats and color. Prices can be listed schematically but vary according to color.

I enclose a sample, with the associated certificate.

With the hope of your prompt response.

Yours faithfully,

Charlie Long

Claim # 7

Coober Pedy, SA

Australia

One month later, the answer came from Mr. Otani. They were more than willing to buy opals from the cooperative. Charlie had long thought about how pricing might be established and how to submit the proposal to the cooperative.

He realized that some would never be interested as the only thing that seemed to apply to them was "money now." At the same time, he did not want the sales channel that existed to fail. The solution was to submit a proposal for the cooperative, which meant that a maximum of half of everything brought to the notary would go to Japan. The price to Japan would be 25 percent higher than for the local market.

After all, the notary was paid by the cooperative and he had no objections to the proposal. Some did not want to participate, while others liked the idea of better prices. In any case, it was clear that they could easily supply the trading house, with a significant share of the outcome of the cooperative and hopefully at higher prices than before.

Charlie confirmed that it had the capacity to deliver and attached an indicative price list increased by twenty-five percent. Mr. Otani realized that quantities from mining could not be guaranteed. What he requested, however, was that the intention to deliver "a significant proportion of the mine's production" was stated, in the agreement signed by the parties.

The price agreed was at 120 percent, after Mr. Otani required "some downward adjustment." What was somewhat unexpected, but perhaps could have been foreseen, was that better-quality opals were to be sent to Japan, as they commanded a higher price, but this was not noticed in the local market. Six months later, the system rolled out and everyone seemed satisfied.

From January 1, 1960, Shannon received first-hand contracts on two claims. This was a success and now they were facing a crossroads. They could do as they had originally envisioned: renting out one claim and continuing to mine the other together. In purely financial terms, it would be good business to pursue that alternative. Another possibility would be to abandon the rented claim and rent out the new contracted claims and leave Coober. They now had small savings in NAB, National Australia Bank, and would, according to the rules of the cooperative, have the right to lease a first-hand contract, for a maximum of two years, which would generate part of the cost of living (if the tenant did not mine the ground within two years, the right to first-hand contracts was forfeited).

Shannon was anxious to mine her new parcel, until they eventually found some black opals. They had not yet found any black opal and even if they had, they would have been handed over to the holder of the first-hand contract. Charlie liked the idea of using his own land. The new lot, however, lacked housing. He was immensely popular, after the agreement with Japan, which is why he soon gathered enough building material to be able to erect a small "house" next to a tree grove in the area. There were large plants around the tree trunks that Charlie took down and wrapped around a couple of branches as a small shady resting place behind the house to Shannon's great delight. She never complained about her harsh surroundings and rough duties. It was partly her attitude that made her so good-natured, and partly that she'd fallen in love with Charlie.

Unconsciously, it was probably the hope of the great treasure that occupied Shannon's mind. Mining is something that can be likened to a gambling addiction. You are believing that the next shovel will contain the opal with a big "O."

Charlie was in many ways like Shannon. He also lived strongly on hope but was, unlike Shannon, undecided on the direction of travel. Inside him, there was less of fisherman delight than with Shannon. Of course, it was always exciting to see what the next bucket could mean for current finds. The problem was monotony. There was some dimension missing. Without even knowing that that was the case, there was something unknown that gnawed him inboard. Freedom and profitability were the great attributes with mining. Both appreciated these factors, but Charlie was still not completely satisfied.

Maybe he longed for the "free world," with Ritch and stock-car races and what life in California meant.

It had been raining for two days and you could not dig in the ground as the soil was moist and soft. In the evening, as they sat grilling the ribs they got from the beard out on the patio, with the stars as their only company, Charlie said to Shannon, "Do you never get tired of anything?"

"What would that be?"

"The bush, dig, the cottage, me, whatever?"

"This has become my life now, and you make me happy."

"You also make me happy Shannon—you're the best thing that

ever happened to me. "But I think I have to move on."

"What do you mean by that?"

"I cannot answer that. But whatever I want to do, I want you nearby."

"If you want to leave Coober, I'll follow," Shannon said.

"That was nice to hear," Charlie said. There was a bathtub by the wall that had been filled by the rain. "Let's jump in," Charlie said. The water was perfect – lukewarm, enough for a bath.

"Can you do this in California?" Shannon wondered.

"Everywhere" Charlie replied.

"Liar!" she shot back. "You just say that to attract me," she continued.

"Maybe so," Charlie said, "maybe so."

They had not yet found any black opal and Shannon was determined to have one, before leaving Coober. Since Charlie still had no concrete plans, he could just as well remain. He suggested:

"What would you say about learning to dive?"

"I really would like to," Shannon replied.

A few weeks later, Preb had replied that they would be very welcome to visit Cairns. They worked intensively for a few more weeks. On an unsuccessful day, Charlie felt more than usual disheartened towards the end of the day's sifting when he saw an unusually large opal.

"Come up!" he shouted to Shannon. She had never seen a black opal, and she saw immediately that they had something unusual. They took the stone with them to a long-time miner and showed their stone. He scratched it and said, "First class, black opal—congratulations!" Charlie and Shannon rushed to the Café and showed the beard their find. Now they could go, Shannon said.

PART FOUR

Returning Home

MICHAEL OWENS

CHAPTER ELEVEN

They first traveled by bus to Tea Tree where Murph welcomed them with pleasure. Lydia immediately became fond of Shannon and they enjoyed being with each other. Charlie asked Ernie to drive them to the Aborigines one day. There he greeted Moon Dog and Shannon was discreetly introduced to the chieftain. She brought with her a beautiful, bright opal that shimmered like a mother of pearl that she gave to Moon Dog. He gave her a wide smile and said, "um-hum." After a short feast, they went back to Hammond and on to the coast and the port at Cairns. It was a hysterical reunion! The friends had not seen each other in five years and, in addition, Charlie came back with Shannon. They had a real dinner, at the restaurant in the harbor, and Shannon felt that she was back in civilization again, something she enjoyed. Preb told them that Sandy was solely devoted to fishing tuna and that he was no longer a skipper on the *Mermaid*. Preb and Ritch ran the entire operation. The workshop was appreciated throughout the neighborhood and business went well.

"We have set aside dividends for you in a special account," said Preb.

"Then they can sit there, until I need the money—which I appreciate a lot may be added," Charlie replied.

Over the next few weeks, they were usually all four out with the *Mermaid*. It only took a few days, before Shannon learned to dive, and she was fascinated by this world.

"You voluntarily left this!" she exclaimed one day. "I follow my instincts, good and bad," Charlie replied.

"Then I'll take care of them in the future," Shannon said.

They got a lot of sponges and Shannon enjoyed working the sea. Mesmerized by the beautiful aquarium environment, she couldn't get enough.

"Surely we have no reason to rush back to Coober?" Charlie said more as a statement than a question.

"What is Coober?" Shannon wryly said.

During a dinner at the restaurant in the harbor, the happy sponge team semi-watched the news, on the TV in the bar. Shannon recognized the one presidential candidate, Senator John F. Kennedy, of Massachusetts. It was a debate between him and someone no one recognized, Richard M. Nixon. They asked the bartender to raise the volume. It was a demagogic ping-pong match that they thought Nixon scored in points, but which Kennedy won on charisma. Nixon had a darker complexion and wiped the sweat from his forehead and upper lip, while Kennedy seemed unmoved by the pressure of the situation. The issues that were debated felt strange to Charlie and Ritch. Shannon was more interested. She'd been in Australia no more than three years and felt more concerned about what was going on in America. The election was later won by Kennedy, with just under 119,000 votes out of 68.8 million votes. For the first time in history, the media seemed to have become a message unto itself.

Kennedy also had something that Nixon lacked, namely the support of the war veterans. It was common knowledge that he was a hero, since the Japanese fighter split his torpedo boat, and that his brother perished in the war. This meant that his mother was a "Gold Star Mom," which brought massive support from all other "Gold

Star Mom's."

The Democrat he was, Kennedy became America's youngest president ever who would only live for another three years, until he was shot in Dallas on November 22, 1963.

A free world, Charlie thought as he heard the news of Kennedy's death. Shannon and Charlie had given up the right to cooperate in Cooper the year before. The years in Cairn's outskirts, with the *Mermaid* on the barrier reef had borne fruit for the fungal team (they called themselves the Aussie Sponge Team). Someone who bore another fruit was Shannon. She had noticed that her period was absent and for several weeks. Before she told Charlie anything, she would find out if she was really pregnant. It was one thing, for the family back home in Arizona, that Shannon lived in a fishing village, with another American. If she was pregnant, it would be scandal at home.

The Cairns doctor concluded that she really was pregnant. Shannon was overjoyed. The same day she took Charlie on a walk to a small shaded park, on the way to the city.

"Charlie," she said. "I have something important to tell you."

Charlie had no clue. Her acquaintance was easy, and she had never been this serious before. He thought she would say she would go home again. Leave him. It became so quiet that you could only perceive a breath of wind, which reminded him of Hammond.

"I'm listening," Charlie replied.

It was quiet for a short while, as Shannon first looked down at the ground and gathered her thoughts. Then she swallowed, her happy eyes gleamed and the rest of her face lit up. She looked Charlie in the eyes and said, "Charlie, my darling, we're going to have a baby!" Charlie thought his heart stopped. Then he held her around her waist and lifted her up and they spun around several turns.

"Didn't I say that? You are the best thing that has happened to me in my entire life! Now we will celebrate," he continued, not fully comprehending it was true.

Ritch and Preb said they had already realized this a long time ago, but Charlie had not. Habitually, Preb quickly took his Aquavit and invited the team around. The doctor had told Shannon to skip alcohol, during her pregnancy, which she gladly did.

When the sponge team had celebrated a few days, Shannon came to Charlie with a thought:

"What do we do when the baby comes?"

"What to do then?" Charlie asked back.

"Do we want the baby to grow up here, in Australia?"

"What's wrong with Australia?"

"Nothing, but we should discuss where the little one will grow up."

"You're thinking of moving back to America," Charlie said.

"Exactly," Shannon said briefly.

"Where do you want to move in that case, and what do you think we should do there?"

"I don't know," Shannon replied disappointedly.

Charlie noticed it and said, "If you want to go back to America, I'll be with you." Charlie thought he wanted to be as far from the California Ranch as possible, which meant Hawaii, Alaska or the East Coast. It occurred to him that he should tell Grandpa & Co. that he was expecting, which he did with a card and the following text: "Cairns, December 10, 1963. My girlfriend, Shannon, and I are expecting a baby. Moving back to America. Undetermined location. Greetings, Charlie."

Shannon had no reason to go to Arizona.

"Let's try a completely neutral place where we can dive all year round," Shannon proposed.

"You said it" Charlie replied and continued, "Florida!"

"Florida sounds good. It's probably cheap down there in the marshes with all the alligators," she continued.

Christmas was celebrated with Ritch and Preb, with grilled turkey at the restaurant along with most of the nearby residents.

"We'll be home soon," said Shannon.

"We will," Charlie replied.

He replied with words unsupported by genuine intent. If he were to return to America, it was for Shannon's sake. He pondered this. Was it really for her sake? Of course, it was, because she wanted to return, but it was also because the baby would grow up in America. But why?

He felt free in Australia in a way he couldn't even remember from his childhood. Admittedly, there was a fixed point in existence, Grandfather's ranch, but it had been a part of Charlie's life that had not left many positive memories. Those he liked had disappeared from his life, by moving around the orphanage, in Santa Barbara and then the CBS boarding school, in Coachella.

All his life, until he left America, he had spent with strangers. It was the same in Australia, but the people he was with, he had chosen himself, in an environment he did not have to be. The thought of the expected baby's future convinced Charlie that it was better to go to America than to stay in Australia. After all, Charlie's rootlessness had characterized him even in adulthood and what he wanted more than to be free himself was that the baby should have a fixed point in existence. Perhaps, it was also in this way that Charlie realized that they were a family, in need of support, and that he had to do something lasting for his and their future, i.e. really become an adult and take responsibility for both himself and two others.

Subconsciously, Charlie had probably suppressed what would

inevitably come the day he was back in America, namely, to be confronted by grandfather. Did Grandpa's approach to Charlie really motivate Charlie's total break? Maybe it had been the teen's rebellion against his grandfather and his reaction to the parents' early demise that manifested itself in Charlie's distancing. Time, in Australia, had not made it easier to reverse the break and to make contact. Now Charlie was facing a decision of how and when to contact Grandpa. The decision to return to America also made the thought of meeting Grandpa real. It was better to do it sooner than later, Charlie thought.

"We go and visit our relatives on the way to Florida," Charlie told Shannon.

"I would like to meet your relatives and also, I want you to meet my family," Shannon replied.

What struck Charlie at that moment was that he had never been outside of California, in America.

"I'd love to meet them too," Charlie added.

He thought that having Shannon with him would make it easier to meet with Grandpa and Grandma. He had no direct desire to see them again, but thought that it might be a relief, after so long. He hadn't heard from them, since he left America, almost eleven years earlier, and he became a little curious about what had happened to them and to America in the meantime.

Ritch, on the other hand, had no thoughts of returning. He had a popular workshop and lived in a small bungalow, on a shaded hill, overlooking the Coral Sea and enjoyed his life.

"Better to be a big fish in a small pond than the other way around" was his slogan. *He had nothing better to return to*, he thought.

Charlie offered Ritch to buy his stake in Aussie Sponges when it became clear that he and Shannon were prepared to leave Australia.

"If I buy your share, you won't do any more good. With you as a partner, anything can happen, so my answer will be no thanks," Ritch said. Preb said something similar when he received the corresponding offer. Thus, Charlie would remain a sleeping partner of Aussie Sponges.

Preb announced the news of Shannon's pregnancy to Sandy, with an invitation to a farewell barbecue party, on the dock, to everyone in the area.

"Bring your own fish" was the message.

Everyone was there. Sandy and some thirty other fishermen, the restaurant staff, some regular customers to the workshop, and even the local press. Charlie was interviewed and then an article was published in the Cairns Daily News, about the man who created exports of sponges and tuna to Japan and who would now return home to America, with his fiancée.

Charlie described how he had been received with open arms wherever he had been in the country and he praised Australia's opportunities. He would carry that spirit with him, he promised. The article was a fine tribute both to Charlie and to Australia.

"You even sound like an Australian," Shannon said, after the interview.

"No worries" Charlie replied.

MICHAEL OWENS

CHAPTER TWELVE

Cairns · March 1964

"Time to travel," Charlie said one morning. Their feeling was a mixture of anticipation and doubt about definitely leaving Australia. "We will let you know where we end up," he continued.

With a thousandfold best wishes, a bag of sponges and a black opal, Charlie and Shannon left Cairns, on a propeller plane destined for Sydney. They searched for Beppi, who now had a new tavern: Beppi's, which was located in a finer part of Sydney, near the southern side of the bridge, over the bay. Beppi was delighted in Italian fashion about meeting them both and ecstatic over the news that Shannon was now pregnant, in the fourth month. It was an emotional dinner at the restaurant that Beppi treated them to.

"You've been through a lot since we first met," Beppi told Charlie.

"So have you," Charlie replied, and continued: "Your own restaurant, in the best part of the city, is fantastic!"

"More tourists are coming now, and people have other eating habits now than ten years ago," Beppi replied. He continued: "The challenge lies in always renewing the menu and making all customers feel that they are having a real experience when eating here, in which I think we succeed."

"I can attest to that" came from Shannon.

The next day, the *Caravelle* (the world's first stern-mounted jet aircraft) took off headed for Oahu, in Hawaii and then Los Angeles. When they landed in Honolulu on Oahu, it was the first time, in nearly eleven years, that Charlie set foot on American soil. He had arranged a new passport in Sydney at the consulate there and, in the passport control, the inspector said:

"Welcome home."

Charlie was anxious that they would relive what he and Ritch had done (except what happened with "V" and "D" they met at the bar) on the island; Visit the battleship "Arizona" which was at the bottom of Pearl Harbor and then stroll through the beautiful Japanese garden. Shannon had never been to Hawaii and she was strongly affected by the visit to the battleship. They spent a few days on Waikiki Beach and marveled at the feeling conveyed, by the myriad of tourists around them.

They even talked differently since Charlie had left the country. Colorful swimsuits, surfing, and a "let-go" attitude made Charlie feel like something of an alien. With his accent, he was a stranger in his home country.

He got the feeling that time had skipped a generation and that he timewise had stood still. Expressions he did not understand he had never heard before, e.g. "Sock it to me baby," (roughly means "check this out").

On TV, you could see the news that a colored twenty-two-year-old named Cassius Clay had won the World Cup title, in boxing, against Sonny Liston and to a slightly shocked audience repeated loudly: "I am the greatest, I am the greatest." He had, of course, won the title, but his statement was astonishing. He somehow radiated rebellion.

America is a young nation even today, but conservative. With the 1960s came the liberation from authority and conservatism. This was expressed in the way in which speech and visible uprisings were wired across the world, in the media, which accelerated the process. Charlie noticed the use of "we" in various descriptions of events. Automatically, when using "we," you exclude those that are not part of that particular group. In the media, and in restaurants were heard: "We" this and "we" that such as "we Negroes," "we students," "we bus-drivers" etc. America's 1787 Constitution begins with: "We, the people . . ." Had they studied it? The only thing that reminded Charlie of the time, before he left America, was when Lyndon B. Johnson made a statement. He was Vice President when President Kennedy was shot and was sworn in as President on the plane back to Washington, from Dallas. He was from Texas and spoke, with the Southern accent, and slowly. The president said that "we" assist the French people in Indochina, with "advisers" to fight the communists in northern Vietnam. *The free world*, Charlie thought. Homecoming became infinitely more tumultuous for Charlie than for Shannon. When they landed in Los Angeles, he called the ranch to tell them they were on their way. Imelda replied. When she heard his voice, she became overjoyed. She told Charlie that Grandpa was out somewhere but that she would announce that Charlie was on his way.

They rented a car at the airport that they intended to use on their trip to Arizona to greet Shannon's family as well. It was a white, Oldsmobile Vista Cruiser. A combination with roof and side windows in the rear, V-8 engine and automatic transmission. The interior was bright red vinyl. Charlie had recently driven a small pickup with manual gearbox and had never driven an automatic before. The system of the rental car was that you could leave the car at any airport that had an Avis office. The car they rented had Texas plates and was just as nice to ride in as their plane from Hawaii. A full tank cost five dollars even.

It took them a little longer than necessary to go to the ranch. It was exciting to experience how the neighborhoods around Los Angeles had changed, since he left the area in 1953 and they were in no hurry. The leisurely pace was also caused by Charlie's apprehension of meeting with grandfather and grandmother. The only thing that didn't seem to have changed, since Charlie left, was the ranch. He remained completely silent when they saw the outskirts of the farm. It was dusk and you could see lights, in the windows. When he saw the stairs, in front of the house, he relived what he had been reminded of a few days earlier when he saw pictures in *Life Magazine*, from President Kennedy's funeral. In front of the grave at Arlington Cemetery in Washington stood little John Jr. in salute. He recalled when he himself, four years old, had saluted for the uniformed guests, with the big green car, when Dad had died and that they had saluted back, in the yard below the stairs. Before they even stopped the car, Imelda came out in a rush. She had aged and become a little rounder, but it was the same, old Imelda. It was a sweet reunion. They hugged and she cried.

"This is Shannon," Charlie said. Then came Grandma first and then Grandpa out on the stairs. He had to support Imelda when they saw Charlie. Charlie ran up the stairs and hugged them both simultaneously, for a long while. Shannon waited below the stairs.

"I want you to meet Shannon," Charlie said, turning around and beckoning to her to come up the stairs.

"It's nice to have you here," said grandfather.

"Now come to dinner," Grandma said. Imelda disappeared into the kitchen and, with her arm around Grandma, the troop marched into the dimly lit living room, with dark, wooden panels where nothing had changed, since Charlie had left.

Grandfather offered his classic drink, a "Manhattan" that held the obligatory red cherry, and they toasted the reunion. Charlie had some small gifts with him. Grandmother got a "Luau," the flower wreath from Hawaii and a large washing sponge, from Aussie Sponges, and grandfather got a beautiful, shimmering opal which was accompanied, by the certificate that it should be included and become a necklace for "someone." Grandma was fascinated more than Grandpa over the fact that they had harvested both the sponge and the opal themselves. Charlie's life became a bit more understandable to them. Imelda had prepared a dish Charlie loved as a child: "Hamhocks" that Grandfather normally tried to avoid but agreed to on this occasion. It was a 19th-century dish that was common among cotton pickers, in the south. It consisted of pork cooked in broth and then they added spinach and ate the dish with mashed potatoes. Charlie said it was the best he'd eaten since he was last at the ranch.

Grandpa's impulse had been to bark at Charlie because he had left them without warning, but he calmed down, with Shannon's presence. He contented himself with quietly saying that they had grown accustomed to fact that Charlie left and that his messages were appreciated even if they were short.

It was a nice dinner, as Charlie told about his experience of working across the Pacific, with Ritch, diving at the barrier reef, Hammond and the Aborigines, mining and, of course, Shannon and that they had become a couple.

Grandfather had concerns about how they lived. Charlie had a hard time convincing them that customs were totally different in Australia, and especially in the countryside. What really pleased Grandpa and Grandma was that they were back in America.

Charlie didn't immediately want to tell them that they weren't going to stay in California; that could wait. At coffee, in the living room, after dinner, Grandpa talked about the farm and how it had developed since he left. Despite his age, Imelda's hubby was still the foreman. It was the same stock of pigs as before, about 5,000 animals.

"While in Australia, I noticed in the bush, as it's called in Australia, that it is difficult to rationalize or even change the ways of using nature," Charlie said.

"You have become many experiences richer," commented grandfather.

"My experiences from the Ranch have helped me along the way," Charlie replied.

"The situation is very different here in this country than in the early 1950s when you left. We have become more and more involved in the development of the world around us, because of the Cuba crisis. The President has a red telephone in the oval room that goes directly to the Kremlin. Now, military training, as it is called, is underway by our "advisors" in Vietnam, which today amounts to 25,000 men. We are heading into a new war."

"We heard President Johnson on TV the other day," Charlie replied.

"You must be tired," Grandma was heard saying. "Imelda has arranged our guest rooms for you."

"One room is enough," Charlie countered.

"Separate rooms, as long as you are unmarried, in my house" said grandfather with definite tone.

Grandma wanted to show Shannon her room and they left Grandpa and Charlie alone, in the living room.

"You hurt your grandmother very much when you left," said grandfather.

"I've thought about it many times," Charlie replied, "but I couldn't bring myself to more than contact by postcard or to return earlier."

"We knew thanks to your cards that you were well, but we didn't know if you would come back. That's why I donated the ranch to a foundation."

Charlie was completely unmoved.

"This means that two managers will run the farm according to my guidelines when I die, and the returns go where I have decided.

"That sounds reasonable," Charlie replied.

"The terms say that if you do not live or work at the ranch, the returns will accrue to Imelda, with her husband. It applies as long as they live. Then you inherit the ranch."

"I have no intention of running the Ranch, but I appreciate you telling me your plans," Charlie replied.

"I had hoped you wanted to take over," said Grandpa.

"There you have one of the reasons I left," Charlie continued, adding, "What I remember most clearly, from my entire upbringing, are the eternal plans for what I should do. No thanks!"

"What plans do you have then?"

"We plan to settle in Florida," Charlie replied.

"Yikes, Florida!" said grandfather, "marshland and alligators. What do you want to be there for?"

Because it's far from here, Charlie thought, but he replied, "I can't answer that. I just know that I travelled around Australia for the same unknown reason—I'm drawn to the unknown. We have worked with scuba diving for sponges, and we want to be close to the sea, because we are used to such a life."

"Considering how you have managed, for such a long time in another continent, it will probably go extremely well for you, in Florida," Grandpa admitted. "Just tell me if you need help," he continued. "By the way: what will you name the baby?"

"We haven't given much thought to that, yet," Charlie replied.

"Are you going to get married?"

"We haven't thought much about that yet, either. But if we do, it will be for ours and the child's sake."

"Of course," Grandpa replied, adding, "Shannon is a nice girl."

"Thanks, Grandpa."

The next day, Charlie and Shannon took a long walk to Lake Matthews.

"This is where I learned to swim."

"So wonderfully beautiful," said Shannon.

"That it is—but I feel nothing special about being here," Charlie said. "For me, the ranch and all that has to do with it is just one institution among every other, in my childhood," he continued. "I can leave here at any time,"

Shannon said. "We will soon,"

Charlie replied, "very soon." It soon became clear to Grandpa and Grandma that the couple would move on to visit the family in Arizona. Grandfather was seventy-five years old and age began to be noticeable in both him and grandmother.

"I wonder if I will see them again?" wondered Charlie.

A few days later, Shannon and Charlie left the ranch. Charlie had collected his collections of stamps and coins, the cash box from CBS, and a plastic model of Kennedy's torpedo boat, PT 109. That was all that was left of his childhood—grandfather had thrown the rest. They steered their rented Vista Cruiser east, on Interstate 10 past Palm Springs, through the steppes, via Indio and took in a motel, in Blythe, just off the Arizona border. It was thirty degrees when they entered the motel which had a large, illuminated pool, under tall palm trees. Charlie was noticeably relieved having completed the visit to the ranch.

"There is nothing wrong with your grandparents," Shannon said.

"Maybe not, but I prefer to have them at a distance. We have no reason to stay in California anyway," Charlie said, snuggling up against Shannon. At that moment, he knew that his future belonged to her. "Will you marry me?" he asked. "Never thought you would ask. I shall consider the matter," she answered facetiously.

"Think fast, I might regret it," he said, smiling.

"I'm done," Shannon said.

"And?"

"Sure, I want you stupid," Shannon replied, snuggling back and giving him a long kiss.

"We'll get married," Charlie shouted to those sitting around and in the bar next door, as they walked out from the pool. Everyone applauded and the bartender treated the happy couple to a beer.

"Are you from Australia?" the bartender asked.

"Both yes and no," Charlie replied. "We've been living there for quite some time."

"It sounds like it" the bartender said.

"We plan to travel around America now," Charlie continued.

"Where to then," the bartender wondered.

"Now to Arizona, and probably on to Florida."

"Arizona," the bartender said, heaving his eyes.

"Watch out," Shannon said, "I'm from there." The bartender mildly tried to infer that it was mostly scorpions and rocks that inhabited Arizona when he then added:

"There are more people living in the suburbs of Los Angeles than in all of Arizona." "Maybe so," Shannon replied, "but that's the beauty with the state."

After Blythe, the radio lost contact with the outside world. Out in the desert, on the road northeast, it became stifling hot. They were probably fifteen miles north of Phoenix, at lunchtime, and they were blessing that the car was from Texas. Everyone who had brains in the south had white cars. After some tall glasses of Coca-Cola and ice cream, the couple continued north. With newly purchased sunglasses and cheap scarves on their heads, labeled "Corona" beer—advertising which they had moistened with water, the journey continued to elevate where there were various fantastic cacti, many three meters high, all around the steppe.

At dusk, the landscape turned into a reddish color. The mountains that bordered the road had a brownish-red color similar to rust that was reinforced in the late evening sun. Just at dusk, they rolled into a small town, called Sedona. Shannon knew it was one of the finest cities in Arizona thanks to the scenery. They pulled into a small motel, along the road and then walked to a small restaurant nearby. Finally, Charlie was in an environment he recognized. The floor had black and white checkered panes, the chairs had steel frames and silver colored, vinyl seats, the bar counter was clad in aluminum and there was a jukebox, in one corner. "My kind of restaurant," Charlie blurted out.

"Welcome" said a small thin waitress and showed them to a window table.

Charlie ordered his favorite dish, consisting of T-bone steak, medium, baked potatoes, corn, and salad with blue cheese dressing. Shannon had not eaten a sensible burger for ages, so she ordered one, with bacon and deep-fried strips of baked potatoes and the peel on. It was the best dinner they could remember. But it wasn't just for the sake of good food. They were alone, on their way to the unknown, and very dear to each other. They also were expecting. Charlie attracted interest wherever he opened his mouth, as everyone thought he was from Australia. It made him interesting. When he was in Australia, he sounded different and was therefore interesting there. Now, the same thing happened in America.

"I sometimes wonder where I belong," he said.

"With me," Shannon replied. Charlie smiled.

The next morning, Shannon called her parents in Williams, telling them of her arrival. At lunchtime, they entered the small, western-like town, from the east via Route 66.

Shannon's family had not seen her in five years. Now she was approaching along with the reason for her long absence, which made Charlie wary.

As they drove toward the entrance to the single-story house, which appeared in the shade of a few large, Eucalyptus trees, Shannon's brother came out first. He was significantly younger than Shannon and you could see that they were siblings. He wore chaps and a checkered shirt and reminded Charlie of the first time he saw Shannon, in the Alice Springs restaurant. Just behind, came Dad and Mom and a big, brown dog of indeterminate breed.

They hugged for an eternity, Charlie thought, before Shannon attempted to introduce him. Charlie first greeted Mom which was the correct order, then Dad and last, brother Pete.

"Are you from Australia?" Pete wondered.

"You can say that," Charlie replied. He felt something like an idol to Pete, but not quite as popular with his parents.

"Have you had a good trip?" the father wondered.

"Hot" Charlie said.

"Come in and you'll have iced tea," said the mother. Here, too, was a dear reunion, though with a warmth that Charlie never had experienced before. A real family.

"This is how we want it," he thought.

The mother wanted to get acquainted with Charlie, while he felt that the father wanted to measure up Charlie, even measure himself against Charlie.

"It seems to have gone well for you in Australia," he said.

Charlie was tempted to answer: "No worries Mate" but replied, "It's a big country with many opportunities; it suited us well."

"What made you come back?" the father wondered.

"Shannon," Charlie replied.

He realized that the answer was difficult for the parents to accept, but he wanted to tell them about their planned marriage, and they had agreed that she would tell them. For a few seconds that felt eternal, it became quiet after which Shannon said, "We have something important to announce: We are getting married!"

The mother stood up and cheered, as she hugged both Shannon and Charlie. The father did not seem particularly surprised but congratulated the couple. Pete thought it was fantastic. The mother immediately wanted to know the details but soon realized that there were no details to tell.

"We have to celebrate this with lunch," the father declared, and the company walked away to a small, Mexican restaurant that was located on a gravel plot that served as a parking lot. They walked under a few trees to the entrance where there was an old sign that said: *Cantina* and sat down at a large wooden table.

Soon, the parents realized that the couple were not going to stay in Arizona, to their great disappointment. In any case, the mother was anxious they get married near Shannon's parents' home, which was the usual thing. Shannon promised to ponder the matter. After a while, the parents seemed to have grown accustomed to the idea that Shannon would be a married woman, something they had suspected but really didn't want to admit to themselves.

Pete was completely taken by the stories of Aborigines and the Barrier Reef. The idea of swimming where there are sharks was staggering. And Shannon had been doing it for years! After a while,

Dad's respect for Charlie increased. He realized that it was a very independent person his daughter would marry.

Charlie enjoyed their company. It was a down-to-earth family that in no way could be compared to the environment in which Charlie had grown up. They had something Charlie lacked: a real family.

The next day Charlie, Shannon and Pete took the train, with a steam locomotive from Williams north via the "Kaibab Range" to the Grand Canyon. They had to take the bus the last bit and then walk to the edge. What spread out below them was the most amazing sight Charlie had ever experienced. On the southern side, where they were, they were at 2,500 meters altitude and it was two kilometers down to the Colorado River and just as far across to the north side.

For millions of years, this huge valley had been formed by the river far below. It was a bit hazy, but you could see "Indian Mountain," fourteen miles north, in the state of Utah.

"I want to get married right here!" exclaimed Shannon.

"I can't imagine a better place than this," Charlie replied. Pete thought it was a great idea. Elated by their experiences, the trio returned to Williams to tell the happy news.

MICHAEL OWENS

CHAPTER THIRTEEN

To the day three weeks later, the wedding took place in early May 1964, and Shannon was now visibly pregnant. It was a small wedding party that boarded the train in Williams to the Grand Canyon: Charlie's grandfather and grandmother, Imelda and her husband on his side. On Shannon's side, were Dad and Mom, Pete, an aunt with husband and a couple that were childhood friends of Shannon. It was a crystal clear and an unusually cool day for May. The wedding was outside the reach of the church. The couple had chosen a "Justice of the Peace" or a peace judge, for the wedding ceremony. He was a round man in his sixties, with a beard and a big cowboy hat. Pete joked with Charlie about the place they had chosen: "remember forever that you got married on a donkey trail," he had said. "We stick to the plateau," Charlie said calmly.

He felt the place was the best imaginable, because it was in harmony with the environment where he met Shannon. Here, one could look out over the largest and most magnificent valley, in the world, formed by water for a billion years. He had a curious thought, as he looked down into the valley, with the huge abyss they had in front of them. Could there be any symbolism, before marriage? He quickly shook the thought from his head. Shannon was radiant—dark hair over a white blouse, with Native American embroidery on the front and the small lump on her stomach. Charlie was wearing dark trousers, with a white shirt and a Bolo, a small jade stone that hung in a braided leather cord around his neck that replaced the tie. His bright, red hair was a nice contrast to Shannon's dark ditto and they were, to say the least, a handsome pair. The judge turned his back on the valley, and the bride and groom could look past him, toward the valley and Utah on the other side. Both answered "yes" and repeated the oath of allegiance, after the judge: "Until death do us part."

After the wedding ceremony, they sat down at a table outside the restaurant next to the vantage point and had a mixture of various snacks and a large, roast beef steak that was bloody inside. Grandfather and grandmother thrived and Imelda with her husband did as well. After an attempt to persuade the couple to come to the ranch, Charlie said it was now time for them to continue their journey.

"We're heading for Florida this afternoon," Charlie said.

"Then we can only wish you the best of luck," said grandfather, handing an envelope to Charlie with the lettering, "Mr. & Mrs. Charlie Long."

"I guess I realize what this is," Charlie said, and continued: "It will be the down payment on our house. We are very grateful."

Shannon packed some things from her room and the couple received a silver set from her parents. When all the farewells were completed, they set south and stayed in Flagstaff at a Howard Johnson motel where Charlie asked for a wedding suite. The manager congratulated and gave Charlie the AAA discount even though he was not a member there.

After a nice, first night as real spouses, they continued south, toward New Mexico. During a refueling, they were advised to stop at the Carlsbad Caverns. It is a huge, cave system far below the surface that you reach by elevator. They have guided tours that go on narrow walking paths, in the fully lit cave area.

"Unbelievable!" Shannon said as they walked around the beautiful cave system with their hundreds of stalactites and stalagmites. These are formations formed by the water that has dripped from the ceiling of the cave, for thousands of years. When they came up from the cave it was dusk and warm.

"It looks like Coober Pedy," Charlie said.

"Home, sweet home," Shannon replied.

The journey continued through Texas. At each gas station and community, Texas' own flag "The Lone Star" waved red, white and blue, with a white star in the blue field and reflected the local patriotism.

Charlie recalled from school that America was fighting against Mexico, over the rule of Texas and that a decisive battle had been fought in San Antonio, at Fort Alamo, and the pair were now on their way to taste an important part of Texas history. When they arrived in San Antonio, it was 40 degrees and they were told to hike to the river that runs through the city.

At the Riverwalk, there was a shaded promenade, with lots of bars and cafes and the water cooled the surroundings. A hundred years earlier they could imagine how this river provided horses with water in the same place.

From there, it was a short walk to the characteristic facade of the fort, with its peak in the middle of the wall and two, large, hefty, wooden doors below. They took a guided tour, with a young woman who, in broad Texas dialect, told the tragic story of how a series of unfortunate circumstances allowed Mexico's General Antonio López de Santa Anna to defeat the fort on March 6, 1836.

In fact, Texas's struggle for independence was part of a Mexican civil war. Texas belonged to Mexico, and, in many places, Federalists in Texas, made widespread attempts to fight the Mexican Army with

Santa Anna at the head. Various groups sought to form a coalition against Santa Anna and the purpose was to declare the "Federal Constitution," of 1824. They called for rebellion against Mexico, by recruiting a real army, with Sam Houston, as commander-in-chief.

Some felt that the battle had already been won against Mexico, after liberating San Antonio six months earlier, in October 1835, and pardoned the Centralists, for the promise that they would not fight the re-introduction of the 1824 Constitution.

Others wanted to go further into Mexico, and a third view was that they would take "Matamoros," a town near the mouth of the Rio Grande, on the border with Mexico, where there was a customs house. Then, you could prevent war in Texas, they thought. This came to be called the "Matamoros Expedition."

The first, unfortunate circumstance was that volunteer armies were already in the field outside of Houston's command. The other was that disagreement among the insurgents about the approach led to a rift between two governing councils, with Henry Smith on one side and Vice Governor James W. Robinson on the other. The third unfortunate circumstance was that Lieutenant James C. Neill had orders from Sam Houston, to fortify the Fort Alamo garrison, but Messrs. Johnson and Grant had recruited just under 200 of his soldiers, including clothing and supplies, for the Matamoros expedition. This weakened the Alamo dramatically. Governor Smith asked Sam Houston to be in charge, of the expedition (January 1836), who in turn appointed James Bowie (who was then a well-known warrior with a peculiar knife which later came to bear his name) to lead the expedition. The War Council appointed Johnson to lead it. He declined and James W. Fannin was appointed. Then Johnson reconsidered. Thus, there were three expedition leaders. Sam Houston tried to stabilize the situation by ordering Bowie to San Antonio, to assess the situation there. Smith ordered Lieutenant-Colonel Travis, with thirty men to reinforce the garrison. Neill, who had been in the field since October, would get supplies and recruit new staff, but would go home to meet his family.

Without an army under his command, Sam Houston was instructed by Smith to negotiate peace, with the Cherokee Indians, so that they would not fight on the part of the Centralists. However, the Indians returned to Texas. With General Santa Anna in the lead, they noticed that the defense was fragmented. They wanted to take the San Antonio garrison and thus this important political center. A second division, led by Santa Anna's General José Urrea went towards Matamoros, entered the city and marched on toward Goliad. With these cities under his control, Santa Anna believed that panic would erupt among Federalists and that he could occupy all of Texas. On March 2, 1836, Federalist delegates announced Texas' independence from Mexico and the formation of the "Republic of Texas." Sam Houston was named commander-in-chief of all the troops in the field. On March 6, he marched toward San Antonio to reinforce the garrison. Just before dawn the same day, Santa Anna attacked Fort Alamo, in San Antonio, with 2,300 soldiers, against Travis's 150 combat soldiers—a total force of 187. These 150 soldiers fought furiously against an overpowering enemy.

The Mexicans suffered heavy losses. They climbed the walls into the fort, turned one of the cannons towards the gates that were blown up, and at sunrise the battle of the fort was over.

The Mexicans were merciless towards the defenders. Lieutenant Dickinson, who had wife and children in the fort fought valiantly. Desperately he tied the child on his back and jumped from the two-story building. Both died in the process. Jim Bowie was seriously ill and was murdered in his bed. When the fort was taken, the seven remaining soldiers gave up. All seven were assassinated, under direct orders from General Santa Anna.

One pleaded not to be shot in the head. He was shot with six shots—in the head. The others were also murdered. The bodies were put into a pile and burned.

A total of 521 Mexicans were killed, with an equal number wounded. Only on March 11 did Sam Houston arrive at Fort Alamo. The devastation was total, and he was met with by a disgusting sight. The remains of the burnt bodies remained in the yard.

He immediately went east and gathered recruits along the way. In mid-April, he and his troops were near the city that now bears his name: Houston.

He was informed that Santa Anna had advanced before his army, with a small number of the soldiers sent against Harrisburg, to punish the leaders of the uprising and that he was thus vulnerable. On April 21, Houston attacked San Jacinto. Mexico's general, as well as President, was captured the following day when he tried to reunite with his army.

Those representing the Republic of Texas drafted a treaty called the *Treaty of Velasco* in which Santa Anna promised to grant Texas her freedom. In December 1836, all Centralist forces were crushed.

The Alamo became the very symbol of Texas freedom. There, they fought heroically against an overpowering army. The soldiers were self-sacrificing in the struggle for their freedom. Therefore, the Alamo is the very foundation of Texas freedom.

The guide's story made a deep impression on Charlie. This was confirmed by a letter recovered inside the fort that David "Davy" Crockett wrote to his family, two months before he was shot, in the Alamo:

San Augustine, Texas, January 9, 1836

My dear son and daughter,

This is the first suitable opportunity to write to you. I am now blessed with excellent health and good spirits despite having many difficulties. I have managed to survive and have been well received by all with an open ceremony of friendship. I have been warmly welcomed to this landscape. A dinner and a group of ladies have honored me with an invitation to attend both Nacogdoches and this place. A cannon was fired upon my arrival and I must say that what I have seen of Texas is the world's garden. The best country and best conditions for health I have ever seen, and I believe it is a fortune for everyone who comes here. There is a world of land to occupy. It is not necessary to pay for the land. Everyone who settles is entitled to at once, 4,000 acres minus 428 hectares of land you harvest usually constitute the payment. Most likely, I will settle on the border or Chactaw Rio on the Red River which I undoubtedly consider to be the best land in the world with plenty of timber and the best water sources and mill streams—and all the prerequisites for ample access to hunting. It is located in the valley where the Buffalo passes from north to south and back twice a year and plenty of bees and honey. I have every reason to suppose that I am granted the right to the land and I would like to see all my friends settle down there. It would mean happiness for all of them. I swore to Congress and signed up as a volunteer (illegible) and will be traveling to the Rio Grande in a few days with other volunteers from America (in the belief that he would take part in the Matamoros expedition). All volunteers have the right to vote for a delegate to Congress and I have confidence that I will be elected member to shape the Constitution of this province. I have joy in my destiny. I would rather be in this situation than be elected for life to Congress. It is my hope that I can still create a fortune for myself and my family despite the hitherto weak conditions.

I have not written to William but have asked John to instruct him on what to do. I hope you show him this letter and also Brother John as it is now not possible to write to them. I hope you all do your best and I will do the same. Don't worry about me. I'm among friends. I have to finish with my respect.

Your devoted father.
Farewell.
David Crockett.

Charlie was greatly affected by the letter. He realized at once what a father was fighting for. Hope and dreams had lessor priority than the struggle for freedom, which Davy Crockett never experienced.

For him, other states were previously just names in squares on a map. Now he felt a strong affinity for America that he had never known before.

The "free world" came to mind.

"I'm really glad we came here," Charlie told Shannon.

"We got nothing for free," she replied.

Two days later, they came to the coast at Corpus Christi. They entered a hotel by the sea and swam in the warm waters of the Gulf of Mexico, with soft white sand and tall palm trees along the waterfront.

"Almost like the Barrier Reef," Charlie said.

"Although the water was not so murky," Shannon replied.

After swimming, the waitress recommended a local specialty, with the coffee—pecan-pie. It is pie made with pecan—nuts that come from the pecan tree that are only found in the south.

Shannon had an everlasting craving for sweets and now she got her fancy. Charlie liked the pie he ate with vanilla ice cream.

On the radio, tunes were heard that were radically different, from banjo and the usual murmur. It was completely different and almost shocking. Local teens listened to the music and talked about "they have to buy the record!" The song that was played was called "Satisfaction," with an English group called "The Rolling Stones." Shannon liked the song directly and Charlie likewise.

It was going to be a national plague that summer along with "She Loves Me," with the Beatles. The Pop Revolution had begun.

Charlie couldn't let go of their experiences at Fort Alamo. He would carry the impression with him, for the rest of his life. Texas had become a state, in 1845, nine years after its liberation from Mexico. He now understood why they are so patriotic in Texas. In their constitution, they have the right to become an independent state, if the majority of residents vote for such a division. If it turned out that Florida was a disappointment, it was Texas he wanted to return to.

With nearly 160 miles to New Orleans, Charlie headed north, with the radio at high volume, and open windows in the heat. At a typical Southern state café, in Louisiana, he noticed a sign on the wall at the entrance: "No coloreds allowed." It was odd not to accept someone because of his skin color. They had heard of unrest that occurred in the South, with blacks revolting against whites, who sought to deny blacks their legal rights of 1870, regardless of race or skin color. This "revolution" was led by Martin Luther King Jr., who received the Nobel Peace Prize the same year (1964).

Police and military had forcibly tried to quell this revolution, in countless cities such as Little Rock, Arkansas, Oxford, Mississippi and Tuscaloosa, Alabama. The unrest had been preceded by blacks trying to enroll students in schools that were paid for with taxes.

The lawyer who paved the way for the black's opportunities to study at universities was named John Doar, and he called this "the second American revolution." John Doar worked with civil rights and considered that the segregation of blacks, in the south resembled a caste system. He was determined to make sure that this system was eliminated. At this point, however, the situation seemed impossible to change, but he felt: "hope is not to participate in something because it is successful; hope is to participate in something that you feel is right." He was the one who walked in with James Meredith in 1962, when James became the University of Mississippi's first black student.

When Pastor King was asked what rights the blacks wanted, the answer was: "Everyone..., here..., now." He delivered a classic message in his speech at the Lincoln Memorial, in Washington, D.C. the year before: "I have a Dream."

The dream was that everyone would be treated equally. Charlie thought of the contradiction in "giving" any group equality. To do such a thing must mean that a certain group possesses something the other group needs or wants. Although the group that owns the right to "give" equality wants the same, the question is demeaning for the group that "gets" equality. To "give" equality is in itself a contradiction to the desired state.

Pastor King's "I have a Dream" had a strong impact in politics. President Johnson signed a new Civil Rights Act, in 1964, as a direct result of the "revolution." Before that, for example, interracial marriage was banned (the Supreme Court would prohibit that kind of state law, in 1967, but it took until 2000 when Alabama, as the last state, removed the ban).

The law gave the police the right to punish restaurants, employers and the like who applied segregation. It would take many more years for blacks to be treated as equals as change was slow in the south. John

Doar had succeeded (ten years later he would sit on the committee that ousted President Nixon and is considered to have materially affected the events of the 20th century in America). Charlie and Shannon went to another cafe.

With their ice cream cones, they continued, with their Texas-registered, Vista Cruiser, east in the water-crossed landscape. The surroundings differed greatly, from the occasional lakes seen in Texas. They had seen many oil-drilling towers and oil pumps in Texas, but they were literally paving the roads in Louisiana. Where you could see the sea, there were plenty of oil platforms off the coast.

At Intercoastal City, they stopped for the evening and had dinner at a restaurant on Vermillion Bay. The waiter told them that they were heading for the part of the state, with the most water. In the Mississippi, water flows from one third of America. In addition, water drenches the ground to the order of thirty-three football fields daily. This is due to the fact that "Nutria," a rodent imported from South America, by fur farmers, turned loose and ate the roots of plants, pipeline ducts that were excavated in countless numbers, and the general rise in water level.

"The coast is lost," said the waiter, and continued: "the worst is in the delta. We only have crocodiles and pipelines now. The oil is more important than anything else for Louisiana. There are about 500 oil licenses, in the sea, from which nearly 100 million barrels of oil are extracted each year, representing half the state's total revenue. We supply America with one third of all oil consumed. We raise the most fish, second only to Alaska, and our wildlife, by comparison, makes Florida's Everglades look like a small zoo."

Another local patriot, Charlie thought. The next day, they arrived in New Orleans and learned that the charming old town was largely below sea level. However, it did not seem to worry the residents there.

With its many old two-story houses, it reminded Charlie of parts of Sydney, with similar brownish buildings.

After all, they were used to fish and had dinner at a restaurant on Bourbon Street that, like most other restaurants in town, had "Jambalaya." It is a tasty, fish stew in Cajun fashion; heavily spiced and heavenly good.

Then they strolled around among the countless jazz bars and heard much of the southern blues music, in the live version. One song that was played over and over was House of the rising sun with a group called The Animals, which was about a local brothel. *Local Patriots*, Charlie thought.

They drove all next day and passed Mobile, Alabama and stopped at a motel in Pensacola, Florida. Without knowing where they really were, it felt like they had arrived. Charlie wanted to stay in Pensacola for a special reason.

His father, Charles, had been stationed at the air base there to undergo his undergraduate training. The next day, Charlie and Shannon drove up to the guard at the gate to the base and he described his case: to visit the base where his father had learned to fly twenty-six years earlier.

He was instructed to drive over to an administration building marked "G-Adm" which was along the main street and seek out a Captain Higgins. Higgins was a forty-year-old woman who belonged to the USAF. She found a folder in the archive, under the department "Annapolis '38" that stated 2nd Lt. Charles Long. His address was to the ranch in California, so there was no doubt that he was the right person. It was stated which barracks he lived in, what planes he had flown, during his time there, that he was approved and relocated to San Diego, and that he had been reported injured, during a training session north of Los Angeles, at the Santa Monica Mountains, in 1939.

The school airplane from the war was in a hangar and Capt. Higgins offered to show the plane to the visitors. There were half a dozen planes Charles had trained in, and Charlie had to climb up and try one of them, in the cockpit. His impression was that it was a wonder that the plane could fly. A sheet metal cage with lever in the middle, foot rudder pedals, flap handles and a few gauges.

Higgins talked about the training and that it was still the equivalent of basic training, for propeller flying, albeit with newer planes. Then they were dark blue, but their students now flew bright yellow trainers. Charlie had no physical remnant of his father. Captain Higgins offered to make an original copy of Dad Charles's flight certificate in large format, with a sketched image of an aircraft carrier and a plane in the air and the certificate text below.

"Nothing would be more appreciated," Charlie told the Captain.

Then she invited Charlie and Shannon to lunch at the officers' mess.

"It's the same mess that your father visited," Higgins said, and she continued: "The operations are developing here but the environment remains the same. Our location by the sea is good from a training standpoint and the climate is good for beginners, in the air. When your father was here, he belonged to a very limited number of genuine aviators. Now the crowds are large, and the world has changed. We can refuel in the air and fly all over the world, in some cases completely out of reach of any enemies."

"What do you mean by out of reach?" Charlie wondered.

"President Johnson has lifted the classified information on a spy plane called SR-71 and is called Blackbird. It flies at three times the speed of sound, Mach 3, faster than a rifle bullet. Materials for the plane are, for example, titanium screws, alloy control cables used in wristwatches, and gold-plated switches to better conduct in high temperature.

"During one of the first test flights, with the plane, the speed gauge showed the wrong speed and later, it turned out that the pilot flew at Mach 3.2. The cabling in the plane had melted and it was a wonder that the pilot managed to land. The plane gets so hot from the friction against the air that it grows 10 – 12 cm in length. We fly over 80,000 feet, just over 24,000 meters, and then you actually see that the earth is round. These days, after the Cuba crisis, we need to know what other countries are doing and then it may cost whatever it takes."

"Why do you want to fly so fast?" Charlie wondered.

"It will be much harder to shoot down at that speed, and missiles cannot reach that height," Captain Higgins explained.

"How come President Johnson announced the plane?" Charlie continued.

"He had good reasons," replied the captain, and continued: "We have had the spy plane, U-2, for almost ten years now, and it is considered vulnerable. The shooting down of Gary Powers over the Soviet Union, in 1960, and the 1962 shooting down of Major Rudolph Anderson (who perished) over Cuba, have shown that to be the case. As early as 1958, they wanted a plane that would be impossible to shoot down, and in which you could basically fly around the world without landing. A base was established in the Nevada desert and the project was called Oxcart. The CIA made sure that everyone involved was appointed official staff. This eliminated the obligation to report to the state of Nevada that they worked there. It was and is top secret. The pilots on the base have identical blue NASA uniforms, without a name, no matter what plane they fly so that no unauthorized person knows who flies the Blackbird, or the Habu that the pilots call the plane."

"Habu?" Charlie wondered curiously.

"Secret flights started on Okinawa," Higgins replied, continuing, "and when the locals saw the black plane with the cobra-like shape, they called the plane, "Habu," after a poisonous lizard-like creature, on the island called Habu."

"The president had several reasons for releasing the information on Blackbird. It began with the editor at Aviation Week, a Mr. Hotz, telling a General Carroll that he had reasons to write that a sequel to U-2 was planned. He promised silence, after pressure from the general, that "it was not in the nation's interest that possible successors were planned." This was the fall of 1963, two months before President Kennedy was assassinated.

"One week after Kennedy's assassination, Johnson briefed Secretary of Defense, Robert McNamara, if and, if so how, to inform the public about Oxcart's technological progress. It was agreed to wait until the autumn elections, in order to make a political point.

What happened next forced the enlightenment: Senator Barry Goldwater (Republican) accused the Democrats (with President Johnson in the lead) of not investing in new aircraft projects. Thus, on February 29, 1964, Johnson was forced to state: "America has successfully developed an advanced experimental plan, A-11, which has flown at speeds over 2,000 miles per hour at altitudes above 70,000 feet ... manufactured by Lockheed Corporation ... all personnel involved in the project are instructed to refrain from disclosing information, regarding the program. "In July of 1964 the existence of SR-71 was announced."

"The free world," Charlie thought.[1]

1) **An SR-71 Blackbird was intercepted over Sweden in 1982 during The Cold War (1979–1985),
a late phase of the Cold War marked by a sharp increase in hostility between the Soviet
Union and the West.**

The SR-71 Blackbird, or "HABU" was based at Mildenhall, UK, and operated in the Baltic
Sea area during the years 1977 to 1988 performing their "Baltic Express" missions. A total of
322 such missions were flown, and, in a few instances, the mission was also flown in reverse.

The SR-71's entered the area at an altitude of about 21,500 meters (70,000 feet) about 80
km south of Copenhagen, accelerated to Mach 2.98 – 3.0, continued eastwards and then
northwards along the coasts of East Germany, Poland and the Baltic states. This was followed
by a left turn westward, crossing the Baltic Sea to the Swedish side just south of Åland, then
another left turn southward and flying through the narrow corridor of international airspace
between the Swedish islands of Öland and Gotland.

Initially the Mach 3 left turn westward south of Åland was so wide that the SR-71's ended
up well inside Swedish air space, which led to a diplomatic protest. This was handled very
smartly by the SR-71's slowing down to Mach 2.54 reducing the turn radius, thus staying
outside Swedish airspace before accelerating to Mach 3 again on the southbound leg.

"During the introduction in 1980 of the Swedish fighter "JA37 Viggen" at Fighter Wing
F13 outside of Norrköping, we had very intensive air operations over the Baltic Sea. At the
time, we started to receive intel that the SR-71 operated over the Baltic Sea. Very soon, the
Swedish Air Force was getting opportunities to test the Viggen capabilities against the SR-71.
There were many Viggen – SR-71 contacts during the years leading up to the escort incident
on 29 June 1987, when four Viggen planes escorted a SR-71 with engine trouble (right engine
had exploded) to Denmark, preventing interference and possibly destruction by launched
Mig Fighters."

The following narrative is by Colonel Per-Olof Eldh, who flew the early single ship JA37
Viggen intercept from Fighter Wing F13, 1 November 1982:

"I was on patrol over the sea, alone, near Gotland, in a JA37 Viggen when I got the order
to prepare for an intercept. The AOC (Air Operator Centre) provided target info on data link
and it was presented on the radar and tactical map display. I accelerated to Mach 1.35 at about
8,000 meters (~26,000 feet) and started pointing my nose up. Full afterburner was applied
during the entire intercept.

I selected the Skyflash for a simulated missile launch. The JA37's max radar lock range
was about 60 km and the tactical display covered 80 km for situational awareness. I slaved
my radar to the AOC data link. The target info showed that the target was flying westward
at Mach 2.54 at an altitude of 21,500 meters (70,000 feet) at a far distance. The air combat
controller on the ground gave me an intercept position south of Åland and I quickly assumed
that the target could be either a MiG-25 Foxbat or a SR-71 Blackbird flying in the direction
of Stockholm. The target turned left and came south towards me. The closing velocity
increased very quickly as the intercept angle approached 180 degrees (head-on). The radar
and indicated target data provided by the AOC were on an echo at maximum range. I gave
the lock command and the PS-46 locked on immediately. The target initiated intense radar
jamming, but my radar stayed on the target.

The engagement envelope for the Skyflash was indicated on the HSD, the radar display
and the tactical display. I conducted a simulated firing in the middle of the envelope with
an aiming error close to zero. The closing speed was approaching Mach 4.5 and the target
indication was starting to point upward. I was quickly approaching my permitted ceiling of
16,000 meters (52,500 feet). My highest altitude was 60,700 feet with lowest speed Mach 1,45. I

briefly got a visual on the target, an SR-71 which appeared charcoal grey as it passed 6 – 9,000 feet above me.

I started rolling over, very carefully, in order to bring my nose down. Coming back into the envelope of 58,000 feet, I gradually reduced burner and glided with engine running at idle due to low fuel. Descending from close to 19,000 meters caused some grievances for the air traffic controllers of civilian planes.

After the mission, a phone call was waiting for me, with a colonel at the Air Force HQ on the other end. He was well aware of my intercept and I had a short talk with him in general terms. He asked me if I had successfully fulfilled the mission goals during the intercept and if the weapon system had performed as planned, and so on.

The general impression was that everything had gone as expected."

This intercept was one of several intercepts of a SR-71 Blackbird which led to locked-on missiles by the Swedish Air Force. Other nations tried, but no SR-71was ever shot down.

Intercept point at Swedish Coast over islands of Öland and Gotland

The JA37 Viggen, and the SR-71 flying above, 1 November, 1982 (Artist: Stefan Löfgren)

MICHAEL OWENS

CHAPTER FOURTEEN

"Only hip people move to Florida," said their waiter, at the restaurant outside Tallahassee.

"That's good news," Charlie replied.

"What to do in Florida, if I may ask?" the waiter wondered.

"Feel free to ask—we appreciate any tips you can give us," Charlie replied, and continued, "We will probably drive south along the coast to see if there are good diving opportunities."

"If you want to dive, you can stay here!" said the waiter. "We have the largest system of underwater caves and canals found in the whole of America, just south of us, in Leon Sinks," he continued. "It is a cave system that stretches more than 27 kilometers, sometimes at more than sixty meters depth. Spearheads from Paleo Indians, dating back 10,000 years, have been found, along with the remains of ice age animals and coal, in Wakulla Springs next to Leon. It is therefore presumed that many of these canals were dry at that time."

"We are used to diving on reefs," Shannon contended.

"At least it's an incredible world down there," the waiter continued.

He was from Fort Lauderdale and had dived for many years in the cave systems. They were almost sacred to the locals, who often had their children baptized, at one of the attributes leading to the caves.

"In Wakulla there is a cave that is as big as a church, about

13 meters wide and 25 meters high—but then you have to swim into the cave system for 1,300 meters first."

"Nothing for beginners in other words," Charlie said.

"No," the waiter replied. Many people have drowned when they haven't found their way back out again."

"Where do you think we should look for regular diving—in the sea?" Charlie wondered. "Both coasts and the Florida Keys at the bottom of the south, where Hemingway lived," came the answer. He continued: "I think the Keys will be a little small for you. A little jewel on the coast is Boca Raton, just north of Lauderdale—ports, inland waterways, charming, little town that you should look at."

"Weird name" Shannon replied. "What does it mean?" she wondered.

"The rat's mouth, in Spanish," answered the waiter.

When he left, Charlie said, "It seems good anywhere. What do you say about continuing south?"

"We can't live off swimming in caves like that, of course!" Shannon replied. As they passed a "For Sale" sign fifteen miles south the next day, they turned onto a long, dirt road lined with wooden houses, on one side down towards a stream. It was the Suwanee River, which originated, in the "Okefenokee" swamp in Georgia. The area resembled pure jungle. Big umbrella-like trees bordered the road and the forest behind was dense. They arrived at a house built with redwood and which had a terrace on the sides and towards the river. It was a bungalow but built on a meter-high foundation and you had to go up a flight of stairs to get up on the terrace. They stepped out and then a large, light brown dog with a short-trimmed coat jumped towards them. Shannon was scared at first, but the dog was kind.

"There is no one home," the neighbor shouted. He then told them that the family who owned the house lived in New York and that if they were interested, they would call the realtor.

"Can we have a look around the site?" Charlie wondered.

"Of course, but beware of the water; there are alligators that often swim among the water lilies."

"Really?" Shannon wondered.

"Yes," answered the neighbor, and continued, "a month ago I shot one that was up on the grass."

"We'll keep a look out" Charlie said.

On the gently sloping lawn down towards the river was the beginning of a long, wooden jetty that went straight out among the water lilies, for twenty to twenty-five meters. The river was perhaps 200 meters wide and completely deserted. The only sounds that could be heard were a little rustling among the water lilies that were lazily bobbing in the water and some birds screaming in the distance.

Everything was green. Even the water.

"What a jungle paradise," Shannon said.

"Why not?" Charlie replied. He continued, "It's a bit desolate here."

"Yeah," Shannon replied. The dog met them again at the car and he pounced off after a few pats from Shannon. "We might find something on the coast instead?"

"It doesn't hurt to look," Charlie replied.

They continued to the west coast south, to see as much of it as possible, before turning left and heading to Boca Raton.

Outside of Tampa, the coast looked interesting at Clearwater. There was an endless beach with white sand and Charlie and Shannon cooled off, in the calm water.

"Watch out when you walk on the beach," a lifeguard shouted.

"We're used to diving," Charlie called back.

"You have not dived around here I take it" came from the guard.

"No, in Australia," Charlie replied.

"There are small stingrays with poisonous thorns lying in the sand here."

"Thanks for the tip," Charlie called back.

After swimming, the two of them found that the water was not particularly suitable for diving. It was murky and there were no natural reefs or other good hiding places for offshore fish, so they continued south.

Just south of Clearwater, the couple stayed at John's Pass, in St. Petersburg. The area resembled a common, widespread city, on a coast, but just below, they found a small paradise. They were then in Madeira Beach. It was a taste of what they had heard about Florida being Caribbean, without being in the Caribbean.

Rows of tiny shops lined the streets and it was reminiscent of Honolulu, Shannon thought. Madeira Beach was a residential area, bordering the Gulf of Mexico and constituted a peninsula, with coast even inland and a large bay. To pass south, one crossed an old steel bridge, to the next peninsula.

On both sides of the bridge, restaurants and bars lay side by side, on large wooden decks, with pillars facing the water. Pelicans sunbathed on the pillars and people roamed among the small shops. In the water, you could sometimes see some dolphins, on the way out to the sea, and there were plenty of seagulls. It was buzzing with different kinds of boats just like Sydney.

"This is my kind of place," Charlie said.

They had dinner on the south side of the bridge, on the terrace outside one of the many restaurants. Although they had been in Australia for so long, they had never eaten alligator. Since it was on the menu, the couple tried the dish to some disappointment. They agreed that it looked like overcooked tuna—a little chewy and not quite flavorful.

The rest was better. The environment, the scents from the sea and various dishes, the birds, the sounds and the twilight made them feel in their own element. Everything was apparently good, except the diving. They pulled into a small, waterfront hotel and continued the next day past Fort Myers to South Bay at Lake Okeechobee. The name comes from the Indian words for "big water." You can see wading birds, over a mile out into the water, because it is so shallow. The lake is only seven meters deep at its deepest point. It is often called "Florida's Big Floating Heart" and is the Everglade's main source of water.

A hundred years earlier, the water flowed unobstructed to the south and provided a sea of grass, eighty kilometers wide and less than thirty centimeters deep, with water. The grass has grown there for over 4,000 years and is called "sawgrass" and can easily cut clothes and skin. As a result of modern road construction and drainage, the Everglades have steadily shrunk southward.

Visitors who want to experience the inhospitable area can travel from "Forty Mile Bend" on the "Tamiami Trail," with Seminole-Indians taking tourists, with their airboats around the park. Otherwise, you can drive on U.S. 27 and experience the Flamingo, hawks and alligators, from the car. *That could wait*, Charlie thought. They rolled past West Palm Beach and took a right on Interstate 1, toward Boca Raton.

The road bordered the Atlantic and it was a lovely sight. Deep blue water, palm trees, white sand and protected lagoons enticed the couple to see more of the area. Once in Boca Raton, the couple parked their Vista Cruiser and walked around in the small town. Time seemed to have stood still. It was a picture image of Madeira Beach, Shannon thought, and she felt that the waiter was right in that it was a small paradise.

They were advised by a police officer to drive just south of the city to Hotel Flamingo, if they were looking for a good hotel. Soon, they were at a large, pink hotel, surrounded by palm trees facing the street and which lay directly on the beach.

"We have to stay here!" exclaimed Shannon.

"No argument," Charlie replied.

After checking in, they took a swim in the ocean, which was much cooler than the Gulf of Mexico. "Refreshing," it seemed to both. As they lay on the beach, they heard a tall man talking in a New York dialect, with a younger woman, who did not seem to be connected with the man. They did not hear the conversation directly but noticed that he was asking for her name.

"Such a place," mused Shannon and smirked almost imperceptibly.

"All over," Charlie replied uninterestedly.

At dinner on the terrace, Charlie and Shannon agreed that Florida was right.

"The climate and the environment suit me," Charlie said.

"I love being by the sea," Shannon replied, continuing, "and I love you."

"Um–hum" Charlie replied in the Aboriginal way, getting him a slight kick on the leg. "And I you," he continued.

"And I you what?" teased Shannon.

"The same," Charlie replied. He had a hard time saying such things and particularly in an official environment. The practical side in him grabbed Charlie and he continued, "Tomorrow we will drive around the neighborhood and look around. Then we'll return the car and get our own."

The next day they went up and down the coast north and south of Boca. They set out on the promontory at Palm Beach and watched the long-sheltered bay where the Pelicans plunged for fish. *This is good*, he thought. Very close to Boca was "Delray Beach." Both fell in love, with the area. It was shaded, with many different types of trees, throughout the area, with many smaller white, wooden houses. But it was something else that caught their interest. They parked at a small marina and walked around the docks. It was near the center of a horseshoe-shaped bay that was lined by houses, with their own jetties and boats moored at the site.

"We can call any broker," Shannon said.

"Certainly. Let's see if we find a for sale sign" Charlie replied. On the land side of a street, they soon found a house, with a sign "For Rent."

"Perfect" Charlie said. "After all, we don't have money, for a house and we might feel like renting for a while?" he continued.

Charlie called the Delray Realty broker who asked them to come at once. The house was a white, single story, with kitchen and glass doors and separate mosquito net doors onto a small terrace, two bedrooms, a dining room and a living room, and a triangular indoor pool, with glass roof over the pool. The owner apparently had several houses that he rented out. This one had been vacant for a while, probably because it needed maintenance. The price per month was set at one hundred dollars. After the tour, the broker who liked the couple said he had the opportunity to show more from the air—they could take a helicopter ride across the coast if they were interested.

"Of course," Charlie thought. They drove to a small private airfield where there was a helicopter company that the broker used. The helicopter was four-seater and had intercom. During the trip, the broker said that there was a steady influx of people from the north due to the climate, who often wanted to spend part of the winter in Florida. In addition, many retired here. Some customers wanted to see areas from the air to simply point to a place where they wanted to live. If there was no house right there, the broker would buy land and, if possible, let a contractor build something that suited the client to live in.

"We probably want something that already exists," Charlie said.

From the air, the coast looked reasonably inhabited, with an uninterrupted chain of roads, cities and houses along the coast. What was striking was that just south of Jupiter there was strip of land off the coast, with a nice channel inside. Delray was similar. Why did the broker consider that the coast was better in these areas, rather than those located on the ocean?

"We have usually seen several hurricanes each fall, and it is good to have some protection against the sea," the broker said. After the fine flight, the broker talked through the terms of the house, with the couple.

"We take it for seventy-five dollars a month," Charlie said.

"I'll pass it on to the owner" promised the realtor, who would return with a reply. Once back at the Flamingo Hotel, reality would soon catch up with the lucky ones.

"What do we do now?" Shannon wondered.

"Swim," Charlie replied.

"I mean what should we do?"

"We can think about it tomorrow," Charlie said. They swam and took a walk in the port district of Boca and found a small, open-air restaurant facing the sea where they had dinner.

"I think about what the broker told us," Charlie said.

"Told?" Shannon replied.

"Well, people are moving down, for the sake of the climate. They only live here periodically. Some stay as retirees. Probably prices play a lesser role for this type of people than for the locals. This means an increased inflow of both people and money."

"And?"

"We should look for things that appeal to people: land, furniture, cars."

After dinner, Charlie had a beer on the terrace when Shannon had a piece of apple pie, with vanilla ice cream. They looked out at the darkening sea and started talking to another couple who also had their drinks in hand.

"Are you from here?" Charlie asked.

"Yes," replied the man who was perhaps in his '40s. "McKinley," the man said, extending his hand to Charlie—James McKinley."

"Charlie," he replied, shaking the man's hand. The ladies greeted and then the conversation was in full swing.

"You obviously don't come from here," James said.

"We come from Australia," Charlie said, "but I grew up in California. My wife comes from Arizona."

"Then you will enjoy Florida," James said. "Water everywhere." James McKinley lived with his wife and two teenage daughters in Boca and had always lived there. He said he had taken over the company, McKinley & Co. from his father, a few years earlier, and that mechanical parts were manufactured for workshops that supplied to different industries, among others, to the automotive industry.

"When will the baby come?" wondered James' wife.

"In two months," Shannon replied, "in August."

"It's the hottest time here," Darlene continued.

"Where do you live?" James wondered.

"Along Highway 1, at the Flamingo Hotel," Charlie replied.

"Ah, along the Dixie" came from James. He told them that the road was called "The Dixie," or "Dixie Highway," just because it leads to the south and thus to "Dixie."

"We're thinking of settling here and looking for houses,"

Charlie continued.

"Do you have something in mind yet?" Darlene wondered.

"Yes," replied Shannon, "in Delray Beach."

"It's a good area," James said, adding: "Boca has over three miles of beach and beautiful tropical canals within protected lagoons. Delray is the best place in the area. If you need help in any way, you are welcome to contact me," he said, giving Charlie his business card.

"Thanks, maybe we should," Charlie replied. He told them about the broker and the price of the house they were planning to rent.

"It's probably a good price if you get it under a hundred dollars a month," James said. "Why is the town called Boca Raton," Shannon wondered.

"Everyone wonders about it," James replied, adding: "Boca means mouth in Spanish. Raton literally means rat, but they meant cowardly thief. On maps of the 18th century, there was a *Boca Ratones* designation that showed a passage, in Miami's Biscayne Bay, the inlet of thieves. In the early 19th century, the designation was mistakenly used for Lake Boca Raton, whose inlet was then closed. E and S were abandoned in the 1920s, but the pronunciation remained: Rah-tone."

"Fascinating," remarked Shannon, who had a keen interest in things.

James continued: "Then there were mostly farmers here. Many of them were Japanese immigrants who grew pineapple. The city was founded in 1925, and an architect named Addison Mizner designed the well-known Cloister Hotel, now called the Country Club, and the town hall, with its typical shape similar to Fort Alamo in Texas."

"We've seen the town hall and thought it looked like the Alamo," Charlie replied.

"The city has grown rapidly since World War II," James continued. "We had 723 inhabitants in 1940 when the army established its radar school here, at what is now the airfield. Some 30,000 people worked at the school then! Later, we had a safari park, in the 1950s, and the population gradually grew to over 25,000, as it is now."

"That sounds convincing," Charlie thought.

"Well, that's good," replied Darlene, "and, in addition, we have a university, since two years ago, Florida Atlantic, which is located on the old airfield area and which attracts many young people here," she added.

"You will enjoy it here," James said, continuing: "We have been thinking about going to New York to see the world fair that has recently opened. You may want to join us?"

"It sounds really exciting; none of us have been to New York," Shannon replied.

"Then I'll arrange tickets," James said.

The next day they visited the broker again. He had not yet spoken to the owner of the house and called him, with the couple present. Charlie's proposal was presented, and the owner countered with eighty-five dollars a month.

"We'll take it," Charlie replied.

The owner said they could move in at once. A lease was signed by the broker, Charlie signed, and the broker would then mail it to the owner. After the meeting, Shannon said:

"I can hardly believe it. We have a house to live in already!"

She liked the address: 328 Melaleuca Drive, Delray Beach, Boca Raton, Florida.

When they had finished with the essentials, they were invited to a barbecue party, with James and Darlene, who had some other guests as well. They lived in a larger single-story house, with a large indoor pool that was glazed with doors that could open onto the garden. The front was facing one of Boca's canals and the only thing that separated the plot from the canal was the road and some palm trees. The other guests were delighted to meet Shannon and Charlie and warmly welcomed the new residents.

After a while, Charlie talked to James, joking with him that one of the other ladies thought that Charlie was like a red-haired Clark Gable.

"He sounded like Clark Gable," she had said. It was his way of saying "Charlie." It sounded like "Chaa-li," she thought. "I must work on that," Charlie said. "By the way," Charlie said, "we live on Melaleuca Drive. Why is a street in Florida called Melaleuca?"

"It is probably because we have imported them from Australia— they spread faster than forest fires," James replied.

"Do you use them for anything?" Charlie wondered.

"What could you use them for?" James asked back.

"The Aborigines took the leaves for wound dressing," Charlie said, and continued: "Captain James Cook learned to have the leaves boiled in water to make tea, which is why the tree is now called Tea Tree in Australia."

"We have to rename the road you live on," James said. The guests were amazed at their new inhabitants and their backgrounds, especially what had happened in Australia. None of the others had been outside of America and they couldn't get enough of stories of living, with the Aborigines in the bush. They were quick to gain confidence in the newly relocated couple and the guests were happy in their company.

James's barbecue party, from that night on, would be called "Bushtucker," and Florida was thus enriched, with a permanent expression. James noted that Charlie had a natural tendency to be curious about the nature of things. As he listened to Charlie, he heard the intrinsic analyst within him. Especially interesting was that he was a person who was constantly on his way somewhere.

The approaching baby was going to change Charlie on that point. More or less consciously, Charlie had the will to park permanently. As the seeker he was, he wanted to see the World's Fair in New York. Half a month later, there would be a new existence, he thought.

For the first time in the new house, Charlie cleaned up the house. A skylight, above the pool, leaked and had to be sealed. He was helped by a plumber in replacing all gaskets in the faucets that were dry and dripped, and then all half-rotted carpets were removed. There was an old tub in the garden.

"It's reminiscent of Coober," Shannon said. She had a thought: goldfish.

The tub was placed right at the front door where there were dense bushes that were sheltered from the sun. They bought some large, aquarium plants and a dozen goldfish and then there was something alive in the garden besides all the wild bushes and trees. Shannon's ideas were usually something Charlie liked, but he began to wonder if they had anything to do with pregnancy. They were a bit bizarre at times. While he was repairing what would become their home, Charlie pondered on what he would do for a living.

MICHAEL OWENS

PART FIVE

Dealing with Disaster

MICHAEL OWENS

CHAPTER FIFTEEN

Boca Raton, FL · June 30, 1985.

"Welcome to Long Cadillac," Charlie heard Gail responding.

"Good morning," Charlie said. He had taken his Merlin on a trip out through Boca's canals following the incidents yesterday, to be able to think in peace. The boat trip had done him good and he had gathered his thoughts into a strategy.

After the trip, he had told Shannon that it was time to put new plans in motion and that he would, by all accounts, let go of Long Cadillac. She knew better than to argue with Charlie when it came to that kind of development, and with her usual patience, she had quietly listened to the details.

"Whatever you do, you should know that you have my support," she had said during dinner at "Pelican Wharf," the restaurant at Boca Marina. "As long as you shave," she had continued, with a smile.

"You should know that you, Peter and Anna are the best thing that ever happened to me," Charlie replied.

Peter was soon twenty-one and working on oil pipeline repairs, in Canada, and Anna was seventeen and still attended high school, "Boca High."

"Do you remember the great farm that went bankrupt near Naples when we came to Florida?" Charlie wondered.

"I do. Wasn't the farm called Golden Gate Estates?" Shannon wondered.

"That's right," Charlie replied.

"Why are you asking about it?" Shannon wondered.

"You know, things change over time," Charlie replied, continuing, "when we met Jim McKinley, he supplied parts to the automotive industry. As relocation to Florida increased, he sought other markets for his manufacturing. He contributed to the manufacture of drilling equipment that helped water-lacking Jupiter find brackish water, at just over 300 meters.

When they had the water, he helped with the desalination equipment, which cleans the water to 99 percent. He then met a fellow from the Apache Corporation in Minneapolis and Jim provided them with antifreeze technology for their orange groves.

When he visited their headquarters in Minneapolis's first skyscraper, the Foshay Tower, on the 21st floor, in 1979, one could overlook Interstate 94 which bypassed a large, newly built site, with large buildings. That was then the nation's largest shopping mall, Southdale, and people flocked there. That's why we bought the land around Boca, because that type of development will come to Florida."

"And?" Shannon wondered.

"It's probably going to be difficult for the company, I think," Charlie replied.

He told her that the money was running out and that there was no basis for him to continue the business. "In some way, I sensed that this was coming and that was why we made alternative investments: the land and the commodity exchange."

"I mean, after the oil crisis in 1973, with the Arab countries' oil embargo on America for supporting Israel in the Middle East war, the market has been flooded with Japanese cars."

"I know," Shannon replied, continuing, "your sign in the office speaks clear language: help ten Americans lose their jobs—buy a foreign car."

"Sure, and then came thousands of oil drilling towers, in the Gulf, new oil fields, in Alaska and Mexico, and now prices have dropped making oil drilling in Texas unprofitable. Even banks are going belly-up there nowadays.

Our margins have been squeezed for competing with imported cars; the development has turned against the car industry. If I simply leave the company, it will probably be difficult. So that it may go bankrupt, and then our name will be published in the press when the newspapers get news of it."

"We have to prepare Anna for that," Shannon replied. "She can be harassed in school."

"We must," Charlie replied.

"And what plans do you have then?" Shannon wondered.

"Do you remember when we were at the club, where we first lived when we came here and IBM had a conference there, at the same time as Apple Computers?"

"Not directly, but what does that have to do with anything?"

"We overheard a person from Apple say something to his colleague about being discreet as IBM staff were scattered around the hotel. IBM since then has its personal computers manufactured here. I think it was 1981.

"When we were at the World's Fair, in 1964, we saw a girl wearing a Bic ballpoint pen laced to her skate, with the point against the ice. Then she twirled around, and, after a few laps, you could still write with the pen. It became a bestseller after that, and at a cheap price to boot.

"Something tells me it can come to be with personal computers like with the ballpoint pen and the calculator. When the calculator arrived, it was a luxury gadget, admittedly tremendously good, but expensive. If the personal computers have a similar development, millions of keys will be needed for all the keyboards, not to mention all the keys needed for corporate keyboards and calculators." He saw that Shannon was not particularly impressed, but he knew that she analyzed every word he uttered.

"Would you be able to manufacture them?" Shannon wondered.

"With the help of a factory that makes plastic details," Charlie replied.

Gail continued: "Oh, good thing you called: Bob Haskins has been looking for you."

"Yeah," Charlie replied, "but I don't want to talk to him right now." Gail heard in the tone of his voice that Charlie had something else on his mind. "Gail," Charlie said calmly, "I'm not coming back to the office." It was silent at the other end of the line.

"I guess yesterday's meeting did not go well," she said gloomily.

"That's right," Charlie replied, continuing: "Long Cadillac will be taken over by Laurel and Hardy—perhaps by the bank as well."

"What does that mean for me?" Gail wondered.

"That's what I was getting to," Charlie replied. "Meet me at Arby's, at noon."

"I'll be there," Gail replied.

"I owe you for the sandwich you bought yesterday," Charlie said as he saw Gail outside Arby's. She smiled and shook her head.

"Not at all," she said.

"In any case, I'm the one paying for lunch," Charlie replied. They each took their turkey and ham sandwich with extra mustard and a big coke. At a window table a little secluded, Charlie told her he had been forced out of the company by VenCap and Mr. Haskins.

She knew there had been trouble with both for a while and probably wasn't completely surprised, other than when Charlie said he wouldn't come back.

"What I've been thinking," Charlie said, "is to offer you and some of the others the opportunity to start with me in a new business."

"What would that be about?" Gail wondered.

"I can't tell you about that right now, but soon, I think. I just want you to know that I have always appreciated you and your honesty, and that you, along with some of the others at the company, would be great for me to work with," Charlie said.

She was obviously flattered by what Charlie told her and replied, "If the alternative is to stay at the company with Laurel & Hardy, you have my answer now—count on me!"

"Thanks. I was hoping for that," Charlie said. He asked her to keep the matter to herself, until he could formalize the plans. That Gail promised. Then Charlie told her that it would probably be troublesome for Long Cadillac, if the remaining owners took over, without providing the company with credit. In the event of a bankruptcy, it would be in the newspaper, so Gail should be prepared for that possibility.

"Oh my God!" exclaimed Gail.

"I trust your discretion," Charlie said gravely. Receptionists tend to be hardened and this also applied to Gail. She nodded.

After lunch Charlie visited Jim McKinley unannounced. He was immediately received.

"Hi Charlie!" Jim smiled and reached out his hand. Charlie shook Jim's hand and repeated the greeting.

"I need a piece of advice," Charlie said.

"Let's hear it," Jim said.

"The bank you visited yesterday has stopped my credit," Charlie said, dropping the bomb to Jim.

"I thought Bob's comment yesterday, on the phone, seemed baffling. Now I know it was you who called. They were more kind to me," Jim said.

"You haven't asked me for my advice, but you'll get it anyway: don't jump into bed with that gang—I did and that's why I'm sitting here now," Charlie replied.

"What do you mean?" Jim wondered.

Charlie explained the background to his expansion plans and how VenCap became a partner and drained the company's earnings, through idiotic dividends.

"It would be beneficial for me," Jim said.

"Read the agreement carefully" Charlie said.

"I'll do that," Jim replied, thanking Charlie for the advice.

"What can I do for you then?" he continued.

"You know, old loyalties that overnight can't be used?" said Charlie.

"Possibly," Jim replied.

"You visited my bank yesterday that I have used, since I came to Florida," Charlie said, continuing, "I need another bank contact, a new attorney, and you to back me up in confidence."

"The last thing is the easiest, and you have my word on that. My old bank, FNBFL, is not very credit-willing. My lawyer is also not one I would like to recommend. Let me think about it."

"I would be happy if you could think fast and give me some suggestions as soon as possible," Charlie said.

"What are you up to?" wondered Jim, who had noted Charlie's tight mouth and slightly fluttering nostrils.

"I can't tell you yet, because we're not formally ready."

"I understand," Jim replied. "Do you want to come over for a little

Bushtucker tonight?" "Certainly, on another night—it's important for me to talk to Anna tonight," Charlie replied.

"I understand," Jim said, continuing, "let me make some calls and I can come back to you."

"Call me at home; I won't go to the office anymore."

"OK," Jim said.

Anna was an alert girl who was not at all interested, in either the home or her father's business. She did pretty well at school, and she had many friends who usually visited her at the Long family's home, to stay by the pool. She was not worried about what Charlie told them, during dinner. She had noticed that his car was gone but that he himself was at home.

"It's a good change for you, Dad," was Anna's comment on Charlie's story about the company. After dinner, Charlie called Peter who just said, "they can go to hell." Charlie shared that view but was keen to highlight the positive in the new plans. Charlie promised to call soon when he knew more.

Jim called the next day. He had informed his old bank, who did not know Jim's plans to switch to FSB, that he knew of a possible FSB customer who might be interested in switching to FNBFL. The bank showed interest, and without knowing who it was, Jim was encouraged to ask Charlie to visit the bank's president.

Then Jim continued: "If I know you right, it's not a lawyer you need, but a legal representative for a business deal. Correct?"

"That's right," Charlie replied.

"I've talked to Apache Corporation. They believe it is an advantage not to have local representation in that kind of business and can recommend a person who assisted them in the procurement of orange and lemon groves in Florida. He used the soil erosion as a means of pressure to reduce prices, in a way that was favorable to the buyer."

"That sounds good. Ask him to call me," Charlie said.

"Bushtucker?" Jim wondered.

"Gladly."

"Seven o'clock," Jim said.

"OK. Jim?"

"Yes."

"Thank you," Charlie said.

"No worries," Jim replied.

"I'll buy a company," Charlie told Jim and Darlene later in the evening. "But they don't know it yet," he continued. Jim heaved his eyes.

"How do you know then that you will be able to buy the company?" he wondered.

"Car dealers know a lot about many," Charlie replied. "For example, when some entrepreneurs and their companies buy a used Cadillac, rather than a new one. Not because they prefer an old one but because the company is suffering. I want to do business before it becomes clear that Long Cadillac is in trouble, which they have."

"Interesting that you say they about your company," Darlene said.

"I've already left the company," Charlie replied.

"Don't you find it hard to jettison yourself from the company?" Darlene wondered.

"It depends on how things are going," Charlie replied, continuing: "here the greed of my partners has meant that they gaped, in my opinion, for too much. They reaped the profits and now believe that they can run the company without me, and have, therefore, given me a bid that they know I cannot accept. When the situation becomes unsustainable for me, I can't remain, and it becomes necessary to leave the company, no matter what I think."

"I suppose you don't want to talk about your new plans," Darlene said.

"Not until a deal is completed," Charlie replied.

"I see the fire in you," Darlene continued, "You're probably doing the right thing."

"Calm before the storm," Charlie replied.

He knew it was only a matter of time before Long Cadillac would run into difficulties. The ship lacked rudder. After all, Laurel & Hardy were just gophers, good at drainage, but handling a company and running it was something completely different.

Charlie had plans to offer Gail, the Marketing Manager, CFO and his assistant, the workshop's foreman and possibly several others, employment in the new business. It would be tough to handle twenty-six branches without this team, Charlie thought.

He had inherited the ranch ten years earlier and he had several pieces of land around Boca that could be mortgaged or sold. In addition, he received annual dividends from Aussie Sponges, so it could be possible to finance a bid for a company.

It was advisable to become a customer of the new bank before a transaction was carried out, in case a loan was required, he thought. That's why he sought the head of FNBFL first. That happened to be a woman named Hazel. He referred to Jim, and Hazel told him that Jim had warmly recommended Charlie. Charlie outlined his background and what happened to Long Cadillac. After all, he was recognized as a person through the company which helped a lot.

Without giving any guarantees about future financing, Hazel was clearly interested in having Charlie as a customer. Since Charlie had no personal mortgages in favor of the other bank, there were no practical barriers to switching banks. Charlie had to give an overview of his finances and the manager would present the case to the board and return with the message the following week.

The next step was to seek out the owner of the intended object of

Charlie's future plans.

As the owner of Long Cadillac, no one took special notice when he was seen in a restaurant, with what people usually perceived as customers. However, Charlie did not want to appear with this person locally.

He knew the owner of the company since both he and several people at the company had bought cars from Long Cadillac, for a long time. The last time someone had bought something was several years earlier and then used cars. "Rather a used Cadillac than a new Ford" was something that was sometimes heard in the exhibition hall. Charlie thought it was a signal that the business was idling. Private companies had no official disclosure requirements regarding their accounts, so it was not easy to find out facts about the company. In addition, he did not know where the raw materials came from, so you could not easily check with the suppliers either. Neither did he want to ask if anyone knew someone at the company who could know something about the matter as he could risk revealing his interest.

"Let's go intuition," Charlie thought.

"Genio Toys," answered a perfectly happy person when Charlie called.

"Long Cadillac here," Charlie said. "President, please."

"Who can I say is calling?" the voice wondered.

"Charlie," he replied.

"Jeffrey Keeney," Charlie heard someone say.

"Charlie Long," Charlie said.

"What can I do for you?" Keeney asked.

"I think I have something that may interest you. Can we meet?" said Charlie.

"Of course," answered Keeney, who knew who was on the line in the belief that there was some new car model he wanted to show and thus enjoy a free lunch.

"How about lunch today?" Charlie asked.

"Suits me just fine," Keeney said.

"Then I'll pick you up at noon."

"Excellent," replied Keeney, adding, "we can meet outside the entrance." At twelve, Charlie was there in Shannon's yellow 1976 Eldorado convertible.

"The gasoline crisis has not come to Long Cadillac," Jeffrey said.

"It has," Charlie replied, "that's why we drive around in old cars."

"I haven't booked a table but thought we could drive towards Lauderdale and take in a restaurant along the way, if that is ok," Charlie said.

"It'll be fine," Jeffrey said, without hiding his surprise.

"Where does the name Genio come from?" Charlie wondered.

"We make toys as you know. The name derives from Aladdin and the wishing pot, where he conjured up the woman who could fulfill everyone's wishes and who was called Genie."

"Interesting," Charlie said, but he actually didn't think so.

"You didn't invite me to lunch to talk about toys, right?" said Jeffrey.

"That's exactly why I offered you lunch," Charlie replied.

Charlie stopped at a "Red Lobster" restaurant and both took the special: steak with lobster.

"How do you like your steak?" the waitress asked Jeffrey who replied: "de-horn it, wipe it's ass and send it in."

"Will do."

Charlie thought Jeffrey was a bit crude and he wondered if it was due to the situation in the company.

"Medium," he told the waitress.

When she left them, Jeffrey asked, "Do you want to buy toys?" and continued: "We are, after all, a manufacturer and we sell to Mattel and other wholesalers."

"Better up," Charlie replied. "I intend to diversify my business. In addition to Long Cadillac, I run a ranch in California and have invested in land in Florida. The next box to tick is a manufacturing company. I want to discuss a takeover of Genio with you."

Jeffrey didn't look surprised even though he was. He was probably ten years older than Charlie and it was natural to consider the ownership issue before retirement. Charlie had no idea if there were kids in the business or if Jeffrey had any thoughts of selling.

It was silent for thirty, long seconds, then Jeffrey replied:

"What makes you think I would like to sell Genio?"

"Many things" Charlie replied drily.

"Cash is one of them, pension another, industry terms a third. What do I know but I wanted to discuss the opportunity with you."

Jeffrey liked Charlie's honesty and vague hint of foreign accent. The food was served with iced tea and Jeffrey replied:

"There is nothing new about the terms of the industry, you can always sell toys. I have not given much thought to retirement. Cash, on the other hand, I often think about."

"So, do I," Charlie said. "So much so that I am prepared to discuss a cash offer for Genio, provided everything is in order with the company."

"I want to discuss the matter with our attorney before responding to your proposal," Jeffrey said.

"I think you should do that," Charlie replied, "who is it?"

"We have BC, Broad and Cassel."

"I know them," Charlie said, "they're good. How is the toy industry in general?"

"Up and down with commodity prices," replied Jeffrey, who continued, "and in the car industry?"

"Up and down, with the oil price," Charlie countered. He talked about Japanese cars' progress in America and that Toyota now also manufactures cars in the country and that "MPG," miles per gallon, has become a concept in America. All of this had not directly helped the sale of relatively, fuel-thirsty Cadillacs.

"All industries and markets change over time," Charlie said.

"How do you adapt then?" Jeffrey wondered.

"In my industry, as you know, the manufacturer rules. Then we can attract locally with smart financing solutions such as subsidized interest and with what the customer can see, free washes and the like. That we should meet the competition with similar small cars is in my opinion not a good route to pursue for Cadillac. We have a segment of customers who would never buy a small car regardless of the gas price. Then we have not been directly assisted by the tax legislation either."

"Why?" Jeffrey wondered.

"Do you remember when we took over the government in Japan, after the war and raised taxes there to 85% of the income?"

"Not directly in that respect," Jeffrey replied, "but I remember we seized half a million of their Samurai swords."

"Maybe we did, but what I would come to realize was that, after the tax increase, it became interesting and profitable for people to let the companies pay for cars and other private things that would otherwise cost a lot in tax. After all, we have had similar effects here, with the progressive tax scale. The more tax increases, the more people let companies pay—for example, the car."

"It makes sense," Jeffrey thought.

"It has made sense for us in the car industry; the more the companies pay, the more goods people can enjoy. They bought more expensive cars than you would have ever bought if you had to pay yourself. Now the squirrel wheel has been spinning and a theoretical value should be taxed on the benefit of driving the car owned by the company."

"I didn't notice any of that," Jeffrey said.

"It may be, because so far, it has been allowed to voluntarily disclose the benefit and to state any arbitrary value in tax returns. Now it will be a pre-determined value and, of course, the taxes will be higher for those who drive more expensive cars than for those who drive a small Japanese car."

"We tax our own cars higher than Japanese?" suggested Jeffrey.

"That is how you can put it," Charlie replied, continuing, "we are fighting both against other countries and against our own."

"Nothing noticeable in private consumption," Jeffrey said. "Your industry is probably not affected now that consumption demand is high. With us, the competition is felt. It is noticed by the banks as well. Our big banks have been burned when lending large volumes at high interest rates to bankrupt countries, in the third world, that are now unable to pay interest on the loans. Now Japanese banks such as the Mitsui Trust and Mitsubishi Bank have ousted us in our home market and funded the new Mall of America in Minneapolis, with over 400 stores and an indoor playground."

"We sell an Asian version of Barbie there," Jeffrey said, "to the Japanese," and continued: "Ninety-five percent of all girls between the ages of three and eleven have a Barbie doll, or more."

"My first business was with a Japanese trading house in Tokyo," Charlie said, continuing: "We are becoming increasingly global. When you buy an American car, you import a large part of the car parts from other countries. Since I started in Tokyo over twenty years ago, world trade has doubled."

"A good thing—is it not?" Jeffrey said.

"Sure, it is. If you see this in a global perspective. What we are talking about are also changes in different industries and you obviously view it from your own operations. Where profitability existed in the past, losses may now be generated, and tactics must change. Take the banks: they lent to the third world who do not repay. They lent to land and housing in Texas and got burned, because people were forced out of oil production, due to imports and competition from Alaska. What do you do then? Well, you sacrifice loyalty to old established customers, in the hunt for quick profits in new business. I just happened to get hit by it, so I know."

"Problems have an ability to be contagious," Jeffrey said.

On their return trip they talked about local things, the club, golf, family and the hot summer. Jeffrey would revert back, with some kind of message, regarding his possible interest in discussing a transfer of the business, within a week. That was enough, Charlie thought.

When Charlie came home, he was told that Jim and Gail had called. He called Gail and found out that many had been looking for him and she wondered what message she should leave. She was instructed to say that Charlie was on vacation. Apparently, the bank had called again, and they could well continue to seek him, he thought. Then he called Jim and found out that Jim had now studied the intended plan that VenCap had presented and had rejected it. He had also shelved the plans for a bank change.

"It was a close call," Jim had said.

"I'm glad," Charlie said, adding: "It may be relevant to hire your contacts in Minneapolis—can you ask them to call me?"

"Certainly. I will ask one of their Partners to contact you."

"Good—what's the name of the company?"

"You've heard of Irwin Jacobs, I guess?"

"Well, the majority owner of ITT, right?"

"Correct. It was he who bought the accounts receivable, in the W.T. Grant bankruptcy, and recovered $100 million. He had his own table, at the Beverly Hills Hotel, when Drexel Lambert with Mike Milken, at the head, held his "Pirates Party" and Diana Ross entertained. The price was squeezed and down to $26 when Drexel presented a $3 billion cash box, for hostile bids, and, guessing, could get as much more according to other advisors such as Goldman Sachs, and it became public through the Wall Street Journal that Irwin Jacobs was openly critical of ITT's leadership."

"I read about it and that Jacobs would probably bid on ITT, but it fell on rising prices when the company sold out parts of the business."

"Just so. It's his lawyer I'm talking about. The company is called Holmes & Hewitt, called H&H, and the partner is Steve Holmes."

"Can I afford him?"

"You can't afford not to hire him."

"I hear what you're saying," Charlie said.

"I will ask him to call you," Jim replied.

The next call went to Mike Burns. If there was going to be a deal, Charlie would have to mortgage the pieces of land or sell them. Mike had been completely uninterested in the branches' land, "stone dead" was his comment, but the plots were something completely different. One location just west of Boca's outskirts was all four plots around a crossing. It was right in time for a mall there. Shops on one or more sides of the road, restaurants and gas station on the other.

"Burns," Charlie heard Mike answer.

"Charlie Long in Boca," Charlie said.

"The car dealer?"

"Correct. The situation has changed," Charlie said.

"And what can I help you with?" Mike wondered.

"What we didn't talk about last was land I own around Boca,"

Charlie replied.

"And what do you want to do with the land then?" Mike wondered.

"I think it might be good timing to build a shopping center on some of the land lots and that you might be able to convey such a deal."

"It's immediately more interesting. We are contractors for several ongoing centers, and you have purchasing power in the area."

"How do we proceed?" Charlie wondered.

"If you could start by sending drawings and maps of the area so that we can assess the location and areas, we will come back with a possible time to look for ourselves," Mike said.

"I'll see to it," Charlie replied.

"Shall we sell the land?" Shannon wondered. She was the one who always balanced her husband and made him turn to the alternatives, in order to eventually find the best solution. He could and would always vent ideas with her. In some way, he always got perspective on both himself and potential business. Cool ideas like Shannon could hatch when she was pregnant was Charlie's everyday nature when it came to business. Trends were his favorite.

"Don't go against a trend," he used to say.

"The prices of land have only gone up since we came here," Charlie said, and continued: "If I thought that trend would continue, I would of course mortgage the land to finance the purchase of Genio. Given the banks' general caution, with their lending, and that I also have problems with my bank, we should probably sell to have the lowest possible debt. Then if the business needs credit, we can take them in the company's name, if the transformation requires it.

"How then, transformation?" Shannon wondered.

"There is a lot of evidence that toys are an over-priced market. Everything must be sold through wholesalers first and then stores around the country and everyone gets their margin. We will quickly try to revamp the business. I will bring my best colleagues from the company and it is my absolute conviction that we can enter the market for keys for computers, calculators and the like."

"What makes you think you can do it?" Shannon wondered.

"Because I think it's a growing market. You know what we did, with the trading house in Tokyo. Turn the steak: we will buy the raw materials cheaply in Asia and sell the keys here, which will then be exported back to Asia again. We are the leader in computers here in the country. That trend has just begun—the global market."

"Are you sure you can do the manufacturing and get big companies to buy from you?"

"Of course not. While the pot is boiling, I should approach IBM and try to get some indication of how their purchases work and partly if I can be on the quotation page regarding keys. Then we have Texas Instruments, ITT, Honeywell, Apple and many more to approach."

"When you mention such companies, the market certainly seems big," Shannon said. "You should probably clear the situation with the company first," she continued.

"Others now have that problem in their hands—not me," Charlie replied.

"You know, it's you they will try to hang," Shannon replied emotionally.

"You are probably right, but in practice they cannot demand anything from me. Both you and I know that it is only a matter of time before the company gets urgent problems. The bank has financed the land and the business. The cars are repossessed by Cadillac if they are not paid. Laurel & Hardy will then sell the assets and they cannot. It's the bank that has problems, not me."

"It's our name," Shannon replied dejectedly.

"It gets on the front page of the newspaper, but people soon forget," Charlie said.

"It won't be fun for Anna," Shannon said.

"It certainly won't be," Charlie replied, "but who knows, they might have some idea of selling the chain to someone else who saves the situation," Charlie said.

"Let's hope so," Shannon said.

Unfortunately, Charlie answered the phone when it rang at home the following day. "Long," he replied.

"Charlie, this is Bob Haskins."

"What can I do for you?" Charlie wondered.

"I would like to rewind the tape from our last call," Bob said.

"And exactly what do you mean by that?" Charlie wondered.

"The discussion was slightly overheated" Bob said.

"By your side," Charlie replied.

"I was in a squeeze" Bob said.

"I know who you sat with, and it didn't sound like it," Charlie countered, continuing: "you're hungry for new business and sent us to the sidelines when something new came to light, right?"

"Like I said, I was clumsy."

"What do you want to do about it now?" Charlie wondered.

"What do you want me to do?" Bob wondered.

"Call the dogs off and give me some rest," Charlie replied.

"Can we meet and talk about it?" Bob wondered. After just over twenty years in the car industry, Charlie was never one to burn any bridges or close any doors, at least not if he could prevent it.

"I'm coming to your office this afternoon," Charlie said.

"I'll be there," Bob replied.

Charlie's CFO was not the one who unnecessarily disturbed Charlie when he was away from the office.

"Long" Charlie answered again when it rang.

"Chuck here" said the voice at the other end. Chuck was really named Charles, but he was called Chuck. The name suited him very well. The name was short and concise, just like the carrier. Chuck liked facts. Without a whim, he ground matters down to a few sentences, so as not to waste time on non-essentials.

He never wondered what happened to Charlie, or the family, or the weather, or anything foreign. He never wondered about such things because he simply didn't care. If anyone admitted that the situation was good, Chuck accepted it as something good. If someone had problems, it was not necessarily bad, but a matter to be solved. Someone who did not know him could think he was bone dry.

Those who knew him knew he could be like a cobra: he struck before anyone knew what had happened.

"Hi Chuck, what's on?" Charlie wondered.

"When the bank withdrew interest, at the end of June, we reached our credit limit and went into overdraft," Charlie heard the robotic voice say.

"And what do we do about it in the short term?" Charlie wondered.

"Pushing back our supplier payments," Chuck replied.

"OK," Charlie said, continuing, "I'll be visiting Bob Haskins this afternoon to try and arrange the credits."

"Do you want me to come along?" Chuck wondered.

"No, it is better that you are not present, so we do not have to answer those kinds of questions."

"Understood," Chuck said."

"I'll call you after the meeting," Charlie said.

"Long," Charlie replied slightly annoyed when the phone rang the third time.

"This is Steve Holmes in Minneapolis."

"I've been waiting for your call," Charlie replied.

"Jim McKinley referred me to you about a business deal where we might be of help to you," Steve said.

"I think it would be an advantage for us, if you could take a look at the plans," Charlie said.

"In that case, I suggest you visit us here in Minneapolis, to discuss the matter," Steve said.

The time was set for Friday the same week, which suited Charlie, because maybe the whole family could meet there, over the weekend, if Peter could fly down to them from Alberta.

"Shannon" shouted Charlie. He heard a vague "yes" from the pool. "Can you and Anna accompany me to Minneapolis this weekend?"

It was time for a trip, she thought, and she would check with Peter.

"Do it," Charlie replied, "I have to go to the bank."

Then Shannon came into the room and said, "We will on one condition—that you shave." Charlie had felt like he was in a vacuum, after meeting Laurel & Hardy and then, as something of another person, out on a new mission, with the plans about Genio.

"If you do it now, I can arrange a salad for lunch," Shannon said. Charlie woke up from his vacuum and did as he was told.

Nora Stevens kindly welcomed Charlie to the bank.

"I'll let him know you're here," she said.

"Thank you" Charlie answered politely. Soon Bob Haskins came out to meet him at the door.

"Come in," Bob said. Bob had an office on the second floor. If you walked out of his office, you could look out over the entire bank, with customers, cash registers, guards and its fancy marble floors. The office had windows with the same view but with draped, almost translucent white curtains.

That's where they sat, Charlie thought, "Laurel, Hardy, and Jim."

"Would you like something to drink?" Bob wondered.

"Some water," Charlie replied. Nora came in with bottled water without bubbles for them. "I want to discuss the future of Long Cadillac with you," Bob said, and continued, "We have certain principles to follow." Charlie thought back to the conversation when Laurel & Hardy were there and replied, "So I heard."

"The Board believes that we have been generous, in financing your expansion," Bob said.

"The financing of a magnificently organized car dealership," Charlie replied.

"They mean we shouldn't finance further expansion," Bob said.

"For every unit, we have built or purchased, we have increased our earnings by $100,000 to $200,000 a year; what is wrong with that?" Charlie wondered.

"It is well done by you. However, our view is that the loan to you as an individual customer has become too large according to our credit policy," Bob said.

"So, you said. What is the reason for the bank to boomerang on me?" Charlie wondered.

"I wouldn't call it a reverse," Bob replied, continuing, "as long as you have liquidity problems, we can't finance expansion."

"We wouldn't have liquidity problems unless you and VenCap had coerced and assured me that it was the best solution for the company," Charlie said.

"Times are changing; it was the best option then."

"I am prepared to contradict that statement," Charlie replied, continuing, "As I see it, there are two options: either the bank allows $500,000 in business credits, which does not go to expansion, and we meet our immediate needs, or I will take you on your word and ride towards the sunset."

"What happens if we take the latter option?" Bob wondered.

"We can both figure that out," Charlie replied.

"I'll take up the matter to the board and get back to you next week," Bob said.

At home, Charlie called Chuck and told him that he had asked for $500,000 in business credit and that Bob would return with a message the following week.

"Good," replied Chuck, and continued, "When are you expected to return to the office?"

"It depends on how the bank responds. I will keep in touch," replied Charlie, who did not want to admit that the bank situation was worrying for the company.

"OK," Chuck said, wishing Charlie a nice weekend.

Shannon had contacted Peter who normally worked the weekends through but who had been granted his request for a free weekend. She booked them at the newly built Hyatt Regency, at Nicollet Mall, in the middle of the City of Minneapolis and they flew up on Thursday night, from Fort Lauderdale via Atlanta. Peter would land on Friday night via Toronto.

Charlie, Shannon and Anna thought the city was a mix between the modern and the old, with many low, old buildings, in a fairly, scattered city center and with few skyscrapers in the middle.

They had been advised to dine on the 50th floor of IDS Tower, the same scraper in which Steve Holmes's office occupied floors 29-32, which the hotel arranged. It was a warm evening and the walk to Nicollet Mall, which is a pedestrian street apart from the buses, was like walking in New Orleans, Shannon thought. From the dinner table, the family had a nice view of the city, which was unusually lush, they thought.

What made the biggest impression on Charlie, however, was that the windows in the toilet where the men fulfilled their simpler needs went down to the floor right where they were standing, giving a slight feeling of vertigo. As he stood there, he felt strongly about tomorrow's meeting with Steve Holmes and even stronger about hitting Bob Haskins, and preferably Laurel & Hardy, in the nuts.

On the return walk to the hotel after dinner, Charlie, Shannon and Anna passed an unusual building that caught their interest. All other blocks were grassless concrete bastions. This was like it had been cut out of an old movie; green lawn that went, from a beautiful wrought-iron fence, by the sidewalk and a long way inward, to an old, dark brown brick house, with clinging plants on the facade. It was only three stories high, with higher windows on the ground floor than on the two upper floors. When they came to the gate they could read: Mission of the Old Saints. Charlie recalled that he had seen a similar building of the same name on the outskirts of Chinatown in San Francisco, when he was there at a vendor conference organized by GM.

"I wonder what they do," Anna said without addressing anyone in particular. Charlie was surprised that she noticed the name at all. She was more interested in arriving at the hotel as soon as possible so as not to miss any important television programs, such as Dallas or any other soap.

"It's some charity I would think," Shannon suggested.

"You mean someone who helps others?" said Anna.

"Rather both themselves and then others, in that order," Charlie replied slightly cynically. By that time Anna had exhausted her interest in the subject and continued:

"Can we go to Donaldson's tomorrow Mommy?"

"Sure, we can," Shannon replied. Charlie knew that the world's largest, or possibly the second largest, shopping mall was located near the airport.

"You can take a taxi, to the Mall of America," he said. When he told them about the 400 stores, Anna was on fire.

After breakfast, Shannon asked the taxi driver to take them the "tourist route" to the mall. He appreciated showing Floridians the outskirts of the beautiful city, with its eleven lakes and drove south toward the "Lakes of the Isles."

On the one-way promenade, along the lakes, they passed the first and largest, Lake Calhoun. Along the walkway that ran along the shoreline, there was a center line to separate cyclists and those who walked. There were many sailboats and canoes on the lake and on a large beach there were plenty of bathers.

They continued past Lake Harriet, with similar activities, and the chauffeur said: "We need to get gas" and then he turned into a "76" station called: "West Harriet Car Care."

A young guy came out and refueled the car and cleaned the window. A large champagne-colored poodle loomed around the yard, which turned out to be a service garage.

Anna looked around and thought she was in another world. The entire corner was occupied by the station. The rest was like an old, Western town. Low one or two-story houses, in different materials and colors, pharmacies, supermarkets, hairdressers, ice cream parlors, café, art gallery and trees along the sidewalks made the place idyllic.

The dog passed the taxi and Anna opened her door to greet it. "He works here," said the guy who was filling the tank.

"Is it your dog?" Anna asked.

"It's Mike's dog, he who has the station," replied the guy.

"What's his name?" Anna asked.

"Champagne."

"Well, he has a nice dog," Anna said.

"Sure," the guy replied.

The journey continued south on France Avenue, which the chauffeur said was the most charming part of the city. The area was a mix of villas, shops, low-rise apartments and restaurants. Particularly distinctive was the greenery. It was lush everywhere.

Then they came out on I 94 and drove directly toward the airport. Anna saw the big mall first and exclaimed, "Look Mom—there it is!" The building was gigantic. On each side, there were parking houses that held thousands of cars. Once inside, a great world opened up. Shops wherever you looked. Cafes, restaurants, and a large playground, with great Disney characters, jungle, slides, ball ocean and mini golf course. The day was saved, Anna thought.

Charlie took the elevator up to the 30th floor of the IDS Tower at 09:50. "Hewitt & Holmes" was behind a pair of tall, dark brown, wooden doors. Charlie introduced himself to the receptionist who announced him to Steve Holmes' secretary. Steve sat on the 32nd floor but conference rooms were also on the thirtieth. Charlie was asked to sit down, and Mr. Holmes would come down. After a while, a man came forward and introduced himself as "Holmes."

"Charlie Long," replied Charlie. Steve was about fifty, Charlie thought, which meant they were the same age. He was slightly gray and dressed in a dark blue suit and made a pretty harsh impression. He showed Charlie into a smaller conference room that was in a corner, with large windows all around. It was so bright that Charlie wished he had sunglasses on. On the table were two yellow-striped writing pads and two pens. Water was bottled. On a side table was a telephone.

Clinical, Charlie thought. Steve told him that the company was founded a hundred years earlier, in New Richmond, Wisconsin, by two, young lawyers who had moved the business to Minneapolis in the early 1900s. Now they were second on Wall Street when it came to M&A, corporate mergers and acquisitions.

"We are involved in both large and small acquisitions, mainly in eastern America," Steve said.

"You were highly recommended by Jim McKinley," Charlie said.

"Now tell us what you want to do," Steve said.

Charlie gave a brief version of Long Cadillac's expansion, how the bank recommended VenCap as a partner, to secure the financing, and that it required half of the profits in dividend income annually, and that the bank had now stripped additional credit and could possibly terminate existing credit. The money was gone despite the company generating good profits.

"I realize the problem," Steve replied, who continued: "You seem to have a well-functioning business that is out of phase, with the cash register. That's one thing. The solution is another. What do you wish to do on the buying side?"

"It's an idea I've had, for years," Charlie replied, continuing, "I've seen the changes in the car industry, since the oil crisis at the beginning of the last decade. We have large imports of small cars nowadays and everyone talks about gasoline consumption, and I realize that it is impossible for a retailer to influence the development. A few years ago, I happened to overhear someone from Apple Computers discussing that they should be discreet, because there was an IBM conference, at the hotel I visited in Boca. After all, IBM had just started manufacturing personal computers, in Boca just before. That was probably in 1981. At the time, I was no longer thinking about the matter, but, after a while, I wondered if personal computers could be products of the future, like the ink pen, calculator and other things that exploded on the market."

"Computers are a technical world outside my area of expertise," Steve said, but what were you thinking?

"My idea is to catch a trend, if it turns out to be a trend that is. What I plan on is the following: I suppose we talk in confidentiality?"

"Give me a dollar," Steve said. Judging by his expression, there was no debate, after which Charlie opened his wallet and produced a banknote which he gave to Steve.

"Thank you," Steve said. "Now I am bound by confidentiality as I have received compensation for my advice."

"Excellent," Charlie said, continuing: "So, computers are probably just at the beginning of their development. To manage these, you have to use a keyboard." Steve listened and seemed genuinely interested, in what he heard. "There are just over one hundred keys in each keyboard."

"Go on," Steve said.

"What I want to do is buy a company in Boca that makes toys."

Steve didn't know whether to laugh or cry, but he had in mind that a connection between toys and keys was somewhere over the horizon.

"Toys?" said Steve in wonder.

"It may sound strange, but they cast all kinds of plastic, in every imaginable color. The machines should be able to switch to other tools, and cast keys," Charlie said.

"If so," said Steve, "are there opportunities to take the market?"

"We won't know if we don't try," Charlie replied, continuing: "many people need the product besides IBM. I will ask some other companies about their needs."

"So, you want to take over a company that today manufactures toys and completely change its direction to manufacture keys, is that correctly understood?" Steve wondered.

"That's right," Charlie replied. He thought it sounded twisted when he heard someone else express the matter in clear text.

"I like the idea," Steve said.

"I have met the owner and expressed my interest, in buying the company. He would revert with some sort of message next week after talking to his lawyer."

"Good," Steve said drily.

"I have no idea about the price, but I suppose they are not very profitable. They haven't bought any cars from me, in a couple of years and then they bought used."

"It's a good sign, if you're a buyer," Steve said.

"When it comes to financing, I have several options," Charlie said.

"If you've been following the press, you have probably heard of Kohlberg & Kravis and other company pirates?" said Steve.

"It was they who coined the proverb similar to a well-known brand from your home state: Flipper."

"The dolphin?" Charlie wondered.

"Sure," Steve said, "you know those who make burgers at McDonalds are called Hamburger flippers."

"Yes?"

"Kravis has coined the motto "quick flips," with which he intends the following: go in, with capital, and sell quickly, with profit. What is doubly ironic about his line is that nowadays you do not even need money to buy a company. Certain transactions are done without the money even leaving the bank; they spin around within the same bank. Your credit that the bank threatens to plug can be extended immediately, if someone else provides guarantees for them. Both banks then become winners: the person who provides a guarantee collects a commission on the guarantees and your bank can continue to charge high interest rates, despite more collateral. Neither in your car company, nor in the toy shop do we need any money. I have booked a table and now I suggest we go for lunch."

Charlie was running on all cylinders. Last week he had believed that Long Cadillac was threatened with bankruptcy, which was the natural result if the money ran out and it was futile to arrange new capital. Here was a large dose of hope and a security in dealing with problems that he lacked at home.

"You can't afford not to hire Steve Holmes," Jim had said.

They walked a few blocks to "Murray's," the best steakhouse in Minneapolis assured Steve. The founder was named Murray and he was long gone. The restaurant was basically unchanged since the 1930s. Wooden trimmings, chandeliers hung from the ceiling, all round tables with white tablecloths, and waiters and waitresses in white jackets. It projected class, all the way.

"Your table is waiting," said the tuxedoed head waiter.

When they had ordered the "classic," a piece of beef fillet that was chosen by weight, Charlie said, "What kind of costs does your commitment to a project entail?"

"It depends" Steve replied. "Normally, we usually agree on a commission on the size of the transaction. Here, financing can become part of our agreement and then we can make our commission available from the bank; it can be a combination."

"And if we do not conduct any transaction?" Charlie wondered.

"Of course, this is one of the possible alternatives, and, in that case, we will invoice for time spent."

"And what is that?" Charlie wondered.

"Fair costs" Steve replied.

"Do you see opportunities in the alternatives I have highlighted today?" Charlie wondered.

"Doubtless I do," Steve replied, in a first hint of joyous expression, "doubtless." When they ate, Steve told him that he lived outside the city, just west on a large lake called "Lake Minnetonka." Right off the road there was a good restaurant overlooking the lake where you could get a fantastic "brunch" on the weekends which he recommended, because Charlie told him that his family was in town with him.

"It's cold in the winter here," Steve said on the way back to IDS

Tower, "that's why we've linked the houses, with the corridors you see everywhere," he continued, pointing to the glass corridors a few floors up so that you could walk from building to building."

"That makes it easier to understand" Charlie replied.

"Sometimes you need skis to get around in the streets in the winter," Steve continued. "That was the way Irwin Jacobs started."

"Did he ski on the streets?" Charlie wondered. For the first time, Charlie heard Steve laugh. "No, he sold used skis from a booth at Nicollet Mall," Steve replied.

"I've heard of him," Charlie said.

"He's going to go a long way," Steve said, not knowing how right he was.

"We will too," countered Charlie, who was now in his best fighting mood.

"Maybe so" Steve said, "maybe so."

Back at Steve Holme's office, Steve said: "The walk probably did us both good. Now we have a lot to do. First, we will cut ties between the bank and Long Cadillac. If I understood the matter correctly, we had a seemingly hopeless situation. Is that true?"

"I have no liquid funds, and the bank will announce next week, if we can get new credit, or if they even terminate the ones we have," Charlie replied.

"Right," Steve said. "What is the sustainable profit of the company per year?" he continued.

"We generate about two million dollars a year," Charlie replied.

"This means that the company can pay for today's loan volume at today's interest rates plus take on interest costs of one million dollars a year and still be quite profitable," Steve stated, and complained over the sickness of the deal, where VenCap thus demanded half the profit in cash, one million dollars, the state tax of 40 percent of the profit, or

$0.8 million, which means that all profits are diluted from the company.

"It's like milking a stone," Charlie said.

"We are going to do a rescue operation," Steve said, adding: "What I want to do is make sure that the company becomes independent from the bank and that VenCap disappears, without any creditors suffering any loss," Steve said.

"I can live with that," Charlie replied, "but remember that where I come from, we stand by agreements that are sealed with a handshake."

"As the situation is now, everyone can be distressed, including those I just talked about. Those who have tried to reap short quick results at your company's expense today are at risk of losing their investment and what I do not want to do is neither to improve nor worsen their situation."

"Go on," Charlie said.

"If the company collapses, which, despite profits, it risks doing, because the money is running out, you will probably lose all money involved, and one person will lose face, namely you."

Charlie nodded and said, "uh-hum."

"What I want to advise you to do is the following: we will immediately form a new company in Delaware. We form it there because they have lower taxes there for operations conducted outside of Delaware and if you are sued by VenCap, which is possible, it is more difficult to gain access to the company than if it is registered in Florida.

"Do you not need permission to conduct business and own land, in other states?" Charlie wondered.

"Yes, but that is just a formality. Then the new company buys all the assets and operations of Long Cadillac, at a correct market valuation."

"The new company has no money," Charlie countered.

"Were you not here this morning; companies don't need money to buy things," Steve replied. "We are issuing a note payable—a 100-year debt note."

"Can you do that?" Charlie wondered.

"As long as no one who has claims on the company suffers financial damage, you can," Steve replied, and continued: "but it may be that VenCap has entered into your agreement with you that you are not allowed to divest assets from the company, over a certain amount, and in that case, we risk a lawsuit, but we can counter that by claiming that they have already made a large part of the profits through an unfair agreement and a battery of other objections. Their prospects of winning a large sum, I think, are small, even if you would have formally violated a contractual term, which we are in fact only discussing hypothetically now, since we do not know if there is such a condition.

"I'll check it out," Charlie said.

"Send a copy of the contract to me," Steve asked, who continued: we also need a market valuation of land and buildings."

"I will arrange that," Charlie replied, thinking of Mike Burns.

"Can you call now so we'll save time?" Steve wondered more like a demand. Charlie called Mike Burns and he was unavailable.

"Ask him to call me at this number or the Hyatt in Minneapolis this weekend. It's urgent," Charlie said.

"The next point is to evaluate are the operations. We can do that calculation. Send me your latest annual report as soon as possible."

Charlie called Chuck who said Bob Haskins had been looking for him and promised to fax the latest annual report to Steve right away. Then Charlie called the bank. Steve listened in on the call:

"The board has dealt with your case" they heard from the handset.

"And?" Charlie replied.

"Unfortunately, I must announce that we cannot grant any increased credit to Long Cadillac."

"For what reason?" Charlie wondered. "The main reason is that we have to reduce some individual commitments, because they are relatively large," Bob replied.

"That must mean that Long Cadillac and some others account for a large portion of the bank's income," Charlie said.

Bob realized the irony of the words and replied, "It's the bank's policy, and we need to increase the repayment rate, on existing credits as well."

"Is it negotiable?" Charlie wondered.

"I'm afraid it's not," Bob said.

"You know we can't do it without selling units," Charlie said.

"My hands are tied," Bob replied.

"Send me your decision in writing," Charlie said.

"I'll see what I can do," Bob said, and the call ended. Steve just shook his head.

"I can't pay interest, with a note payable," Charlie said.

"Not as it seems right now, with the bank's attitude. Otherwise, they agree to lend to cover interest costs. They raise interest rates, lend to cover them, and thus increase their earnings," said Steve and continued: "once we have transferred all the assets, it will be up to us to finance the payment to the bank and others. This will be the one part of one or two bond loans that we will ensure that Drexel issues. The type of bonds I am talking about have poor ratings and we have to pay three to five percent more a year than to the bank, which is worth it. In order for them to issue the bonds, they will request five percent of the amount as commission."

Blood suckers, Charlie thought.

"If we figure it, we can probably increase the loan considerably, as we will not share the profits with VenCap, in the new company. That means we can take costs up to a million dollars and still pay less than what VenCap charged, right?"

"Correct" Charlie replied.

"This means that we can increase the cost of existing loans and also borrow more, which we can use for step two, namely, to buy the toy factory."

"It sounds elegant," Charlie said, "but what happens to the old company?"

"First, we rename it, to something meaningless like "Bob's Fast Foods" or the like. Then, when the debts have been paid, we can either simply ignore the company or liquidate it, in practice it doesn't matter."

"Then VenCap sits there with an agreement, in an empty company."

"Exactly" Steve replied and continued: "I will ask one of my colleagues to organize the new company, to set up transfer agreements and note payable and to brief Drexel, as soon as we have the valuations on land and buildings. Then we courier the documents down to you, you sign and courier back. In the meantime, I figure out what remains on the bond issue and then we have the payment for the new company financed—at least in part."

"I'll visit a new bank next week to try to change banks as soon as possible," Charlie filled in.

"The conditions should be pretty good now—you hardly ask for any credits."

"Now to the toy factory: what do we know?" Steve wondered.

Charlie told him what he knew, which wasn't much. Steve got the name of Genio's law firm, Broad & Cassel, and said that they would probably come back, with an opinion in principle, if they were prepared to discuss a sale the following week.

The phone in the corner rang.

"It's a Mike Burns," Steve said. After a moment's explanation, it turned out that Mike had people around Florida who could certainly make valuations, which could be part of the supposed private land deal, which is why he accepted the assignment.

"Good," Steve said. "Back to the new company. If we are told by Genio to proceed, we shall, as soon as possible, sign a letter that both parties sign, which is a statement of intent. It does not bind the parties to execute a transaction, but it prevents the seller from entering into an agreement with another buyer, during the period of validity, normally three months."

"I can mention that to the owner when we talk," Charlie said.

"OK," Steve thought. "Then, if we think we can complete the deal, we will review the company's accounts; and perform a so-called due diligence, to see if everything is in order with the company."

"My CFO can do that," Charlie said.

"He probably can," Steve replied, "but it's better with someone from the outside. I suggest you hire one of the major accounting firms in, for example, Miami, to do a deep dive into the company's books."

"I understand," Charlie replied, noting this on his yellow pad.

"A little roughly, we should be able to issue bonds that are financed by the old company's operations by up to five million dollars, in addition to what is required to buy the business. If Genio is worth more, we can set up a holding company that issues its own bonds. The nice thing is that the toy company can then pay the interest itself, by paying group contributions to the parent company."

"Elegant," Charlie said again.

"Next week we will have a lot to do," Steve said.

"I hope so," Charlie replied.

When they agreed that they couldn't do much more, Steve told them about nice things to do, with the family, over the weekend in Minneapolis. Charlie thanked Steve for his advice and then he went down to the huge courtyard at IDS, a glass-covered courtyard with shops around and a café in the middle. He needed a moment's reflection. He was glad he took Jim's advice to hire a lawyer from outside. What looked on the border of hopelessness had been transformed into brilliant opportunities and Charlie was in a good mood. He knew that Shannon and Anna would be happy after mega-shopping and it was soon time for Peter to land. The whole family had not been together since Christmas and Charlie wanted to take advantage of the weekend. He bought a cup of coffee at a stand and settled down, at a small round white table. After looking at the surroundings and the multitude of people passing by, tourists with cameras, businessmen in dark suits and all sorts of other people, it struck him suddenly—it was the first time he could remember that he was alone, among people.

He had devoted his life, since coming back from Australia, to set up the company and had been constantly surrounded by people. The only time he could be solo was in the boat. Now he was sitting in a cafe and relaxing alone, something he had never done before. The thought that struck him was that he had a jewel in Shannon who constantly took care of both the children and their home. He was fully aware that he had devoted himself to what he thought was fun, the business, and that he had largely neglected Anna and Peter. When he should have been with them, he had never "had time."

The truth was that he had prioritized something else. Peter, though Charlie had managed to bring him up in the same town, even in the same house they had bought when Charlie worked at Ford, had become like his father.

He was independent, restless and went where his nose pointed.

After high school, he had seen an ad about pipeline work, in Canada, and there was no stopping him from going. Charlie didn't want to either, since he didn't want to force Peter into something he wasn't meant for, or apt to do.

Anna was more like Shannon—confident, and happy in her personal socializing. She had better access to her role model, mother, than Peter ever had with his father.

Charlie's thoughts gave him some perspective on what he had accomplished so far in his life. He also wondered what it was he was getting himself into with recent developments. One thing was clear, anyway: the kids were all right and he would set aside work this weekend. *Better to concentrate on them*, he thought.

After a rewarding cup of coffee, he walked past a terracotta-colored house, with a sea of antennae on the roof. The facade, and thus the roof's shape, was completely irregular, similar to large-format building blocks that suddenly came to an end. On the entrance door which lay in the diagonally cut corner was: "WCCO, channel 4."

Of course, every big city, with self-esteem, had its own TV station, and this was apparently the local station. "Tours daily at 3 p.m." it said on a sign. Charlie had never been to a TV studio before and he had the time, which is why he stepped in and was met by an empty hall and a staircase up to the first floor. The show cost ten dollars, and he asked why?

"Otherwise we'd have a lot of kids here" was the answer.

The studio itself was quite obscure. The part that was illuminated was the airing section, with a large table and a large wall behind for weather maps. Around the studio, there were lots of stands for lighting and half a dozen, large TV cameras, on fixed racks and some on moving rails.

Mike Walcher was the anchor and he always sat in place, during the guided tours. He was probably thirty-five and always looked happy said the guide.

The floor below the studio was custom built, with 2.5 meters of concrete underneath to be completely vibration free. He was told that they had their own production of mostly investigative reporting, e.g. how public officials managed public funds, and that they naturally bought what were considered good programs. The channel was the one that had the most viewers, in the entire Twin Cities region, Minneapolis-Saint Paul.

The company's chief executive, Tom Doar Jr., had led the company for two decades, the guide explained, adding that he was the nephew of famed Civil Rights lawyer, John Doar, who was on the commission that ousted President Nixon. Excited by the tour, he then went out into the summer heat again.

The next block was below street level—an open area with trees where people sat on benches and steps and ate ice cream and strolled. A poster on a bar announced a music festival that night in the square, with groups Charlie had never heard of. *We're going here tonight*, Charlie thought.

He lay down on the bed, in the hotel room, and to quench his curiosity, he turned on channel 4. During an advertisement for the evening's event, it was announced that "Prince" stood as sponsor for tonight's festival and that he would guest play, during the evening. Charlie had heard of him. It was he who was obsessed with the purple color. There are many stories in the car industry, and one was just about Prince. He liked BMW. It was rumored that when he bought new cars, they were immediately repainted, in a favorite, special, dark purple color. He was from Minneapolis and had been named the most accomplished artist in the industry, by sponsoring young talent—they could even borrow his own recording studio. Anna would love to see him live!

Charlie had met Frank Malone, at Malone Cadillac in Saint Paul, at many sales conferences and he realized they needed a car. He called him and told him he was in town.

"I will send a car over with a staffer. He lives in Minneapolis and can take the bus home," Frank said.

When Shannon and Anna had buried the bed, under a mountain of bags, Charlie told them that the day had been better than expected, which they also thought. Peter arrived at the hotel, just in time for dinner, which would be at the "children's" favorite place, namely TGIF, Thank God It's Friday's, which was along the highway west of the city.

Peter was in a brilliant mood and told the waitress that it was a birthday dinner for Anna. Of course, it wasn't, and she was ashamed when the waitress strapped half a dozen gas balloons on her. It didn't get better either. In the middle of the dinner, four waiters gathered around her and loudly sang "happy birthday." Everyone had fun during the evening. The ladies had no idea about the outdoor concert either which was a nice surprise. Prince played his Purple Rain and the crowd was ecstatic.

The next day was Saturday and Charlie had another little surprise for the family. They packed swimsuits and went for half an hour to Wisconsin to a large parking lot in a field where there was a sign: "Apple River Inner tubing."

The car was emptied of swimsuits and they changed and rented large, inner tubes for tractor tires and other necessary accessories, such as a small tube for the cooler box, cooler box, soft drinks and beer, and then walked with the tube around the stomach over to the river. Then they sat down in the water with their buttocks in the water and their legs hung over the tube and coasted lazily down the Apple River.

If you collided with someone, you bounced off lightly and exchanged some kind words. At bends in the river, there were large nets, under the bulletin boards, with the text Beer Target, where you could toss empty beer cans. Three hours later, a small waterfall of about 1 1/2 meters indicated the end of the journey.

Peter took his tube and went back a bit to run the waterfall again. Then they took their gear, threw the tubes on a cage mounted on the roof of a bus, and were driven back to the starting point.

Charlie felt the same joy and freedom he had felt while diving with Shannon at the Barrier Reef. Here the family came close. As usual, Charlie didn't know what he was looking for, but whatever it was, he wanted his family's support. Now, it was his job to make sure everyone was happy, and he had decided to do just that. During dinner in the evening, or rather at the brunch the next day, he would talk about the developments with the company and about the plans for the new business.

MICHAEL OWENS

CHAPTER SIXTEEN

Boca Raton, FL · July 6, 1985

A week had passed since Charlie had had the unfortunate encounter, with Laurel & Hardy.

"I'm back!" he shouted happily when he saw Gail at the reception. She was happy to see her boss it seemed.

"Has the vacation been nice?" she wondered, so that others would hear and confirm that Charlie had been off.

"Just fine, thank you," Charlie replied, "and how are you?" he continued.

"Fine," replied Gail, who continued: "there are plenty of messages on your desk—I have put them bundled from each person."

"Thank you" Charlie replied and walked away to his suite. He felt invincible, which was a stark contrast to the feeling he had when he left the same building a week earlier.

"I'll go through it" he said.

Gail didn't know that Charlie would be coming back to the office but had put the messages on his desk anyway. *She handled my reappearance well*, he thought as he looked at his desk. Half the surface was covered by the yellow Post-its. It used to be so, but it had been a long time since Charlie had been away for a whole week.

Jeepers he thought, and he was struck by the fact that the little, yellow carriers of duties also came from Minneapolis. A few years earlier, a chemist at the Minnesota Mining & Manufacturing Corporation, popularly known as "3M," in Saint Paul, had been working on making a glue similar to what is on their tape. He tried on paper and thought he had failed when it wouldn't stick. When he showed it to a colleague, the colleague put the piece of paper on his computer screen, noting that the paper could be removed without breaking it, and there was no trace of the sticker on the glass. There, the idea of doing things was born—reminder notes. With this paste, notes could be set up anywhere and they did not blow away when secretaries ran past either. They were given different colors (although yellow won) and were made in small blocks. They became a global success!

Now there were six rows, with the yellow notes on the desk and he put his leather-covered writing pad, which he called his "Matilda" over the whole lot. *There* he thought. In fact, it was he who was in command now.

A knock on the door and Gail stuck her head inside the heavy wooden door.

"Can I come in?" she wondered.

"Sure," Charlie answered, which was his standard answer to that question.

"I didn't think you would come here again," she said.

"I didn't think so either, Gail, but we've been drawing up a new map this weekend," Charlie replied.

"That sounds good," Gail thought. "Do you want coffee?"

"Yes, thank you, and then I'd rather not talk to anyone except Chuck," Charlie replied. "By the way, bring two cups and ask him to come here."

"Will do," Gail said, closing the door behind her.

Soon it knocked again, and Chuck stepped in with two cups.

"Good morning" an unusually happy Chuck exclaimed.

"The same" Charlie replied. "Come in and sit down," he continued.

"How was your vacation?" Chuck wondered.

"It has been productive," Charlie replied, adding: "In addition, the whole family gathered in Minneapolis over the weekend. We went floating inner tubes on the Apple River which was really fun."

"That sounds good," Chuck replied.

"And what about the company?" Charlie wondered.

"The cash situation is bad. We have to do something about the situation as soon as possible," Chuck said.

"That's exactly what we're going to do," Charlie said. "I need to get some peace from Bob Haskins for the moment. Tell Gail that you will take his call, if he is looking for me."

"OK," Chuck replied.

"I have a solution to our liquidity problems pending," Charlie said. He didn't want to talk about the toy factory yet. Chuck looked noticeably interested in the sequel. "Have you heard of Drexel Lambert and Michael Milken?" Charlie wondered.

Chuck read everything there was about finance and Charlie thought he knew the answer.

"Um-hum" came from Chuck, something he had picked up from Charlie. "Well, then I don't have to draw the whole background. When did you plan for vacation?"

"I was going to take three weeks, as usual. in July," Chuck replied without conviction that this would be the case.

"Can you put it off?" Charlie wondered. Chuck knew how to read the manager. Charlie's tone and demeanor described the issue as an established fact. Chuck had previously been forced to postpone needed leave, just to end up in an even worse position when he was in the Bahamas or some other place, with constant phone calls and faxes. He felt that the pattern was about to be repeated when he answered, "Of course."

"Good," said Charlie, "because we have a lot to do and we have to do it now if we are to succeed." Now Chuck became seriously interested. He liked it when things heated up and he felt Charlie had important things going on.

"What are we going to do?" Chuck wondered, as he read one of Charlie's signs saying, "If it's not broken, we'll fix it until it is."

"I have hired a new lawyer in Minneapolis who has presented a proposal on how to arrange future financing for the company and at the same time get rid of Laurel & Hardy and Bob Haskins. The plan is to have Drexel Lambert issue a bond loan to the market that will finance a purchase of the business of the company." Charlie let it sink in, with Chuck.

"Um-hum" came again from Chuck who saw parts of his career fast-forward, with the duties related to what he had just heard.

"We will make sure that the loan far exceeds the bank's debts and we will get rid of Bob Haskins. We also change banks."

"What do we do with the old company?" Chuck wondered.

"Ideally, we want to liquidate it, in orderly form. We rename it for security, if it goes bankrupt."

"It should work," Chuck said.

"The lawyer is arranging a new company based in Delaware, to begin with. I already have contact with FNBFL and will manage this issue, for the time being. Mike Burns will evaluate land and buildings and the law firm will evaluate the business. They establish transfer agreements and arrange financing through Drexel. Then you change the names of the companies simultaneously."

"Laurel & Hardy will be sitting here with an empty company," said Chuck, "and that could mean trouble."

"Quite right, but it is something we may deal with later. Right now, this is what goes and what we must do, if the business of the company is not to suffer. When the new company is ready, you must transfer all agreements that the company has to the new company."

Chuck sighed inside and replied, "OK." He realized that the situation of the company forced Charlie into a corner. Then he knew there was going to be action and it was always a reason to escape from ongoing daily matters that others in his department could just as well handle.

When Chuck left the room, Charlie called Mike Burns. They needed a week to make the assessments, if they worked under time constraints. He knew that the attorneys were evaluating the business itself and that Charlie could leave them at it for the moment.

Adding to the development of the weekend, the new bank, FNBFL, had come to a different position, where no credit in the company would be needed. What was most important, after all, was the transfer of the operations to a new company, and then it was unnecessary for the bank to consider a credit request that Charlie would not need. That's why Charlie called the bank and explained the matter.

"It does change the situation significantly" came the reply. Charlie heard disappointment in the tone and wondered if they would be hesitant to accept the company without credit, with associated profits for the bank not materializing. Charlie then said that one could start the relationship in that way, and then finance the business through the bank and use bond loans for expansion. The bank would revert back. When he had applied, Charlie thought that the bank might be less interested, if you were not a sole financier and thus had control of the debt burden in the company, with the possibility to influence and control repayments to themselves. *A hypothetical problem*, Charlie thought.

Genio would give word this week so he could wait for the moment. *It's best to keep that proposition to himself for the time being,* he thought.

After lunch consisting of a sandwich, in the staff room with the staff, Steve Holmes called.

"Did the family appreciate our city?" he wondered.

"Very much" Charlie replied.

"We have an indicative acceptance from Drexel to issue bonds to the firm," Steve said.

"Then we proceed" Charlie replied.

"Good," said Steve, who continued: "if everyone does what they are supposed to, we should be ready with a new parent company, new bank, values and prospectus in a week."

"We form a new company and buy the assets against the note payable while we wait for the bond money—is that correctly understood?" Charlie wondered.

"That's right," Steve replied.

"Then we move on according to plan," Charlie said.

"We will," Steve said.

Charlie had a strong desire to call Genio when the phone rang. It was Gail who said that Laurel was on the line.

"Let him through," Charlie said.

"How was the holiday?" Laurel wondered.

"What did you do at the bank?" Charlie countered. It got quiet in the handset. "I know you were there with Jim McKinley and that has certainly not helped my position with the bank."

"I cannot discuss other activities," replied Laurel apologetically.

"You cut the branch you are sitting on yourself" Charlie said, noticeably annoyed. "What are you calling about?" he continued.

"We want to know about your position on our bid." Charlie hadn't thought of their ultimatum in the last few days and of when he was in a different position, but he became even more annoyed when he thought about the bid to stay with the nine percent in the company towards increased funding from VenCap.

"I can't give you my position now because I haven't decided yet," Charlie replied.

"We want your message by Friday," Laurel said.

"You will be notified," Charlie said and continued, "what options do we have to what you offered?"

"None" said Laurel just as expected.

"And what will you do if I turn it down?"

"Time will tell," Laurel replied.

"You've probably got that right for once," Charlie said, asking for postponement of the deadline for the week after, which was definitely the longest Laurel could accept.

When Gail saw on her display that Charlie had hung up, she called him. "Coffee?" she wondered.

"Gladly" Charlie replied. When she came in, Charlie had looked through the notes under the Matilda and selected just over half that others could take care of. He had two small bundles.

"Give these to the sales department and the others to Chuck," he asked. It was about delegating matters, if he was to finish the rescue operation.

The next day Jeffrey Keeney from Genio called. "I've had discussions with our lawyer," Charlie heard over the phone.

"Have you come up with anything?" Charlie asked.

"We have decided that we are willing to start negotiations with you on a takeover," Jeffrey said.

"It's the best I've heard this week" Charlie exclaimed genuinely happy with the message.

"May I invite you to lunch?" Charlie wondered.

"Yes, yes" Jeffrey replied, and it was decided that they would repeat the procedure from their previous lunch at Red Lobster. During lunch, Charlie wondered if they wanted to present any price level they had in mind.

"Rather, we would like to hear an offer from you," was the reply when Jeffrey ate his bloody steak.

"Of course, we can do that, but first we have to see the accounts," Charlie contended. "No problem," Jeffrey said, and promised to arrange the matter immediately.

"Then we want to make a statement of intent, if we move on," Charlie said.

"It'll be fine," Jeffrey said.

"My lawyer suggests we bring in a Miami accounting firm to do due diligence, Charlie said.

"That will be just fine," replied Jeffrey.

It was about not spreading the message to Genio's staff.

"We call the case Red Lobster," suggested Charlie.

Jeffrey agreed and ate in silence. Charlie had a hard time putting his finger on Jeffrey. Was he stupid or just an unpolished engineer? Jeffrey's attitude on the surface was simple: look and bid. Could it really be that simple? The problems lay probably in the sawgrass somewhere and Charlie was convinced that some obstacles would appear, during the attempt.

They exchanged the attorneys' respective names and phone numbers and Jeffrey promised to mail current figures, as soon as possible. Charlie felt that it was good to act quickly, because it would make it difficult to cook the books, before a possible sale. Of course, a company that is aware that it could be sold can take steps to increase profits in the short term, such as stripping advertising measures, investing in the future, etc. Even worse would be if the company stopped issuing credit notes for faulty deliveries, concealed litigation, or the owners stopped paying salaries, etc. Here it was about acting quickly, Charlie thought. He was not directly suspicious of Jeffrey, but he would plan some things for the takeover, if it did take place.

One such thing was to make sure Jeffrey was evicted from the company post haste. If Charlie's plans for a quick transformation from making toys to making keys worked, Jeffrey would probably be a hindrance. *How do you do that?* Charlie thought. First, he would make sure that he immediately became the CEO, in connection with the takeover of the shares. *When do you take over?* he thought. Well, if you do it on a Friday, you can make sure that a locksmith is alerted and that early Saturday morning, when everyone is still off, all locks to the company would be changed. Charlie didn't want Jeffrey in his shadow, if he was sitting in Jeffrey's office.

It's best to change the lock to the office door as well, he thought.

"What will the old company be called?" Chuck wondered when Charlie came back to the office. Charlie immediately connected and replied, "Bob's Fast Foods."

"OK, and the new one?"

"Long Cadillac," Charlie replied.

"I just wanted to check," Chuck said.

Steve Holmes had a new company ready in Delaware and he would arrange business permits for the company in Florida.

"I really like the idea," Chuck admitted in an unusual display of emotion.

"So, do I," Charlie said with a smile, and continued: "if you need help with the transfer of all our agreements to the new company, you can ask Steve for help with that also." Chuck was such that he'd rather do that sort of thing himself, because then he had control. Charlie liked that feature in Chuck, because he always wanted the ball in his field, another expression of control, and that Chuck's responsibility automatically meant that Charlie had control. Charlie realized that he always managed to reward himself, with the inspiring and pleasant tasks. Others could manage the more boring, which could be interesting, but could also require structure and therefore become monotonous.

A by-product of the phenomenon was that Charlie rarely soiled his fingers. That was what others in his vicinity, or hired advisers, could do. If things got sour, or a hot potato, you could always refer to the aides giving him advice. That is how he would probably handle Jeffrey, if it went that far.

The same thing, if the operations were transferred and Laurel & VenCap sat with an empty company and wanted to sue him. Steve Holmes was the advisor and Charlie could lean on him beautifully. In addition, the advisor would be responsible for the defense, or countermeasures, or whatever might come up.

He smiled when he thought about it later. First, the lawyers create a situation that you were not in before the lawyer was approached. They charge for that. Then they have to fix the problem, and then they get paid again.

He wondered if he was paranoid about Jeffrey. *Who knows if there will ever be a deal, with Jeffrey's business, and maybe he's the one laughing all the way to the bank,* Charlie thought.

Rather safe than risk problems, he thought. Grandfather had a saying that Charlie lived by: "If you are to cross a one-way street you have to look both ways to be on the safe side."

"If he sells, he'll have to accept he's gone," Charlie concluded.

CHAPTER SEVENTEEN

Boca Raton, FL · July 13, 1985

"Good morning Steve," Charlie replied as Gail switched the call through.

"The same. We have received Mike Burn's valuation of the land parcels and we are ready, with our own valuation of the operations."

"Good," replied Charlie and continued: "there is a technical error in the valuation of the land."

"Why?" Steve wondered.

"Two branches are not owned by the company, but by me, privately," Charlie replied.

"Are the company's credits linked to each branch in any way?" Steve wondered.

"No," Charlie replied.

"Then we simply deduct the two private land lots from the valuation," Steve said.

"These are two major units, the one in Tampa and the one in St. Petersburg. When we applied for legal title, through the local agent, we applied for these two jointly, and their secretary had missed "Cadillac" from the application and just wrote "Long," after which the registration ended up in my name and we never had reason to change to the company."

"I understand," Steve replied, "we count them out."

"What we have then, in round numbers, is five million dollars for the land according to the valuations, minus one million for the two, large pieces of land, i.e. a total of about four million dollars," Charlie said.

"OK," Steve replied, and continued: "our analysis of the financial statements shows that the operations in round numbers net two million dollars annually which is a little over a million, after tax. Private companies that do not have alternative operations and are exposed to competition, as in our case, can be paid anywhere from five to ten times the annual profit if you ignore the company's debts. In our case, there are assets, in addition to the loan liabilities, so you should add them. If we use the lowest multiple, with reference to the absence of alternatives regarding the operations, and that price pressure prevails in the market, and add surplus value in land and other assets, we end up with six million for the operations and five million for the surplus value, minus one for the land you own privately, i.e. a total of ten million dollars."

"It's not much more than the total loans amounting to nine million," Charlie replied.

"It's on the right side of the horizon," Steve said, adding: "there is no reason to pay more for the business than its loan debt—other debts, for example to suppliers, are taken over by the new company. We count on an average of surplus value and the value of the operation instead so that we end up at nine, so VenCap gets nothing."

"Will that work?" Charlie wondered.

"At least it will be difficult for them to show that we have paid a sub-price," Steve replied.

"And how much can the bond loan amount to?" Charlie wondered.

"As I have estimated, we could finance loans of five million, in addition to the current level and still make money in the company. With nine to the old company plus five, the total will be fourteen, which we round up to fifteen for commissions and some air in the system, which is definitely possible according to what Drexel has said."

"Then we have five for the toy company," Charlie noted.

"Do you think that's enough?" Steve wondered.

"After reading their numbers, I think so," Charlie replied. "They're heading up to you by mail," he continued.

"Fine. Then we can fill in the missing parts of our draft prospectus and send to Drexel during the day," Steve said.

"How are the transfers of all agreements and staff?"

"Everything is done by transporting existing agreements, and all that is needed is that we choose dates and that I sign for both companies, then we can make the transfers," Charlie replied.

"We have the note payable ready but for the amount, which we can now fill in—do we agree on nine million even?"

"We agree," Charlie replied.

"Then we courier the note down to you" Steve said, adding: "The permit we are waiting for to operate in Florida is a formality and will be granted. We date the transfer when the permit has been obtained to avoid anyone using it against us, and then we will make the transfers, note payable and contract the first of next month, which will be August 1."

"Good," Charlie said.

"Then we know where we stand. I'll notify Drexel of the amounts when we have hung up," Steve said.

A large part, if not all the financing of Genio, seemed to be within reach. Charlie considered the effects of allowing new Long Cadillac to pay interest on a bond loan that financed the purchase of Genio, and concluded that, in practice, it is the same as forming a new company to buy Genio, with a separate bond loan, with one exception: If Long Cadillac is sued, you risk both companies. A practical question about whether to form a new holding company to buy Genio was a five million bond loan, which would probably be too small to interest Drexel. The next thought was to dismiss the problem.

What was urgent was the change of bank. He booked another meeting with FNBFL the next day. Then Charlie called IBM in Boca and asked for the purchasing manager.

"I have something that might interest you," he said with a little extra pause. The buyer immediately put together a scenario in his head about a car salesman with colorful brochures under his arm and said they were not in need of any cars at the moment. Charlie was expecting that answer and said that the matter was about something completely different and that it was important to meet in person. He had extensive sales experience and managed to set up a meeting as early as Wednesday. Now he had so much clarity in the intended deal, with Genio, that he could engage accountants from Miami. He knew that Genio had a local accounting firm. Thus, there was no disagreement when it came to any of the major accounting firms. He had Price Waterhouse himself and therefore did not want to ask them.

He did not know any other auditors, so he called the operator and asked the respondent to start in alphabetical order. She came to "Arthur Andersen & Co." and Charlie asked for the number to their Miami office. Charlie asked to speak to the office manager and was immediately put through.

"We do due diligence on request" was the comment from the office manager. *He probably hoped for continued assignments, if a deal materialized,* Charlie thought, and told him what business it was about. Charlie was asked to send the letter of intent, which did not yet exist, and a certificate from Genio that they were welcome to review the accounts. In the meantime, a team would be prepared consisting of four people, all experts on different things: accounts, taxes, agreements and personnel matters.

Charlie called Jeffrey Keeney and thanked him for the accounts he claimed were on their way to Minneapolis.

"We should draw up a document that shows our intent," Charlie said.

"I don't mind if you think it is necessary," Jeffrey replied. "Call me Jeff, by the way," he said.

"OK, Jeff; we need to plan how to proceed with our due diligence, "Charlie continued. "How, then, plan?" Jeff wondered.

"The staff will probably wonder, if there are four auditors going through the accounts and asking questions," Charlie said a little drily.

"I'll think about how to handle that matter and get back to you," Jeff replied.

"Good. Meanwhile, I will arrange the statement of intent," Charlie said, ending the conversation.

When he hung up, Gail called: "Hardy has searched you and he asks you to call—it sounded urgent."

"Might as well get that over with," Charlie thought. "Thanks. Something else?"

"No, if you don't want coffee?"

"Gladly" Charlie replied and hung up.

When he had received the cup and was alone again, he looked out over the parking lot, through his tall smoke-colored windows, and smelled the scent of victory. The person he would call next was deprived of the goodies. Admittedly he might cause problems, but Charlie had his safety net in Steve & Co. "Some people don't realize that you can't have both the cake and eat it," he thought of Laurel.

"Gary."

"Charlie," he said briefly.

"We've been looking for you," Gary said.

"That's why we're talking to each other now," Charlie said.

"I hope you have a message for us now," Gary continued.

"I have, and it's probably not what you expect," Charlie replied.

"And?" Gary wondered.

"Before you get my message, I wonder if you are in the habit of acting this way?"

"What do you mean?"

"You play Monopoly with the business and with me for that matter too," Charlie replied.

"Our contract terms are clear," Gary thought.

"Maybe they are, but they should be changed," Charlie contended.

"We won't."

"Remember this conversation," Charlie said.

"Is that a threat?" Gary wondered.

"You can take it any way you want," Charlie said.

"And your answer?" Gary wondered.

"No, thank you," Charlie replied.

"Do you have an alternative? "Gary wondered.

"We'll see," Charlie replied.

Charlie called Steve again.

"It's clear with Jeffrey Keeney, at Genio, that we can make a statement of intent now," Charlie said.

"We are writing a proposal we can fax to you tomorrow," Steve replied. "How did Keeney sound on the phone?" he continued.

"As I described when we met—difficult to grasp. Either he is completely untouched as a person or sly and plays a game, "Charlie said.

"We'll soon find that out," Steve said.

The next day, Charlie started by going straight to the bank. He hoped that there would be a better dialogue with FNBFL and that they would be more businesslike than bankers. He thought of the language Bob Haskins used. *It's as if they all are cast in the same mold,* he thought. It was unlike any others he knew. Probably, the same was true for car salesmen; you develop your own jargon. Whole industries get their own labels. Car dealers are sometimes called horse dealers, which originated from the infancy of the car industry when farmers wanted to exchange horses for cars.

"The board has dealt with your request and asked me some additional questions," said Hazel Goldberg. Charlie thought her last name was suitable for a banker and probably therefore a name taken.

"Do you see any issues?" Charlie wondered.

"Not at all, but we want to confirm certain things," she said. "We would like to see your future plans and if the bank has the opportunity, to participate in the financing, before we proceed," Hazel said.

Charlie outlined his idea to transfer operations to a new, debt free company and finance this buyout with a bond issue.

"We then would have all collateral unpledged and can use them for credit if needed for business expansion."

Bankers sometimes can see around the corner and Hazel wondered, if there would be any problems, with transferring the business to a new company.

"We do it on market terms, and the bank is fully repaid, so I hardly think so," Charlie said.

"Then I see the risks to the bank as non-existent in that the company has no credit, and therefore FNBFL welcomes Long Cadillac and your family as customers," Hazel said happily. Charlie thanked her for the kindness and accepted with a handshake.

"I shall ask our corporate department to prepare accounts and other things," Hazel continued.

"We can coordinate that on our side through Chuck, our CFO. Let's plan for a shift the first week in August," Charlie said.

"It will probably be possible," Hazel replied.

"Okay, let's work toward that," Charlie said, thanking Hazel. He briefed Chuck when he returned to the office.

"We'll keep this to ourselves for as long as possible," Charlie said.

"I understand," Chuck said.

"We have just over two weeks to arrange this transfer between the companies, and then we change the bank a couple of days afterwards: let me know if you see any obstacles, in the meantime," Charlie said. The fax from Steve had arrived and was on his Matilda. "Confidential" was at the top of what was typically stamp text.

"Letter of intent" was the heading. *Now we have another person in the office who knows this, if she has read it,* Charlie thought, not wanting to worry about that predicament at the moment.

The draft agreement stated that the parties intended to discuss the acquisition of the company Genio, with any associated properties such as real estate and other things that could possibly house the factory and that due diligence would be carried out as soon as possible. The parties would strive for a price agreement to be finalized by October last, giving three and a half months to complete the acquisition. Thereafter, the statement of intent would not be valid, and the seller would be free to negotiate with others.

Charlie liked the proposal and called Jeff.

"Can we meet for lunch?" he wondered.

"You can pick me up as usual at twelve" was the reply.

Charlie had two copies with him, and Jeff signed the deal without a wink, and Charlie did the same. They took one copy each and both seemed satisfied.

"What I need from you is now a statement, provided to Arthur Andersen & Co. in Miami that they have the right to conduct a due diligence on the company."

"I'll arrange that this afternoon and mail it to you," Jeff replied. The next day, the letter arrived, and Charlie mailed a copy to AA & Co. in Miami. Then he went to IBM's office in Boca.

"My name is Charlie Long and I'm looking for the purchasing manager," Charlie said as he met the receptionist at IBM.

"You're expected," she replied, asking Charlie to sit down. The purchasing manager was young, Charlie thought, and he had a hard-edged face that Charlie thought resembled the face of a soldier. It turned out that he was a second-generation immigrant from Cuba, and his name was Anthony Caturano. Anthony was more than a little fascinated by Charlie's accent and by Charlie's background. Charlie had actually lived outside the country for eleven years while Anthony had never been outside the country. He said that they had been manufacturing personal computers for four years in Boca with success. They shipped to the whole country and exported to mainly Europe and Asia.

"I intend to work with you in a way that can be interesting for both parties," Charlie said, in his slightly polished manner. All company cars at IBM, in Boca, were Ford, which Charlie knew, and Anthony was waiting for the opening to come from Charlie.

"I suppose IBM doesn't produce all the components on its own," Charlie said.

"That's right," Anthony replied; "Many components come from outside and are also found in other companies' computers."

"My ambition is to diversify my business into a manufacturing industry," Charlie continued.

"Are you going to make computers?" Anthony wondered with

surprise.

"What I am going to produce gives me great opportunities to collaborate with you, not compete," Charlie replied, thereby attracting interest from Anthony. "Both of us are here in Boca, and I see great advantages with the logistics," Charlie said.

"Given" Anthony answered, waiting for the continuation.

"How would your interest be in working with a local company that can provide first-class keys to your keyboards?"

"It could be interesting. However, we have high demands on age resistance when it comes to the material as it relates to products that are to be used intensively and for a long time.

"Do you have top quality?" asked Anthony.

"What we have is extensive experience in that kind of manufacturing, and the quality is unparalleled," replied Charlie, well aware that he would have to live up to his words, if and when there would be business with IBM and others.

"In that case, we want to discuss a future with you," Anthony said, noticeably interested, and continued: "volumes are rising across the category and we would like to have more suppliers."

"What I need are specifications, in order to be able to offer— plastic type/quality, dimensions, colors, product series size and delivery times," Charlie replied.

"We will produce documentation and provide you with that shortly," Anthony said. "Good, send it to me personally at the company address," Charlie said.

"I was expecting a call about cars," Anthony said with a smile.

"We can also talk about that, if it may be relevant to you," Charlie replied.

"We have a company policy that stipulates Ford" was the short answer.

"I understand," Charlie said, thanking Anthony for the meeting. Excited by the outcome of the meeting, Charlie returned to his office. Chuck had announced that Charlie was to call him.

"Chuck," he replied when Charlie called.

"Charlie—what's on?"

"We have a tough situation with the checkout. Can we arrange the summer sale?"

"Absolutely" Charlie replied without hesitation. "All used—prices are reduced by ten percent now on Saturday," Charlie continued.

"Good. I will inform sales," Chuck replied.

"Announce that they can give fifteen percent off, if they don't have a trade-in," Charlie continued.

"OK," Chuck said, and that thing was done.

Charlie continued: "Tell the branches to speed up cash deliveries here too, with immediate effect."

"OK," Chuck said, pleased.

Charlie was determined to cope with the cash problems, in the weeks that remained, until the bond loan became a reality and then he would no longer have to worry about it.

Charlie called Shannon to tell the good news from IBM and he was told that Jim and his wife would come over for a little Bushtucker that evening.

"Good," Charlie thought, "we have something to celebrate. Tell them to bring swimsuits."

Charlie came home and was in a brilliant mood. He was looking forward to a barbecue evening, with friends Jim and Darlene and most of all a swim in the pool. It was hot and sticky, as it can only be an evening in July, in Florida, before a thunderstorm.

He noticed that Shannon was in an equally, brilliant mood and that Anna was gigglier than usual. He was not allowed to enter her room, which was not unusual, but what was strange was that both she and Shannon were giggling at the same time.

"What on earth is it with you today?" Charlie wondered without addressing the question to anyone.

"Dad, have a beer and sit by the pool; we have a surprise for you."

He did as he was told and felt satisfied with the task he was given.

"Close your eyes" said Anna and Charlie promised to obey. Soon he felt something warm moving intensely on his stomach.

"Now you can look," Anna said. Charlie had already realized what he saw when he opened his eyes. In his arms, he had a little, lively something that alternated between dark and light brown with white patches all over a small body that seemed to have far too much skin with nice, little, curls over his neck.

"What on earth is this?" exclaimed Charlie.

"It's Morris," Anna replied with a smile that could melt ice. Charlie wasn't the first to lose his speech, but now he was stunned. When he recovered, he said, "Is it a Boxer?"

"Yes, honey," replied Shannon, "what do you think of him?"

"He's the cutest thing I've ever seen since Anna was born," Charlie said.

"I'll take care of him! He can be with me when I do my homework," Anna said.

"Then we have something else to celebrate today," Charlie said, patting Morris. Charlie realized that he was facing fait accompli. Jim and Darlene were completely taken by Morris and thought it was great having a dog in the family.

The ladies were playing with the dog when Charlie suggested that he and Jim bring some cold beer and have a swim. As they swam for a couple of lengths, they sat down on the pool edge and Charlie talked about their plans.

"I have been close to losing the car company, because of the bank and VenCap and my own ignorance. Thanks to the contact with Steve Holmes that you recommended, I now have a solution that means the company is saved, but what I have today is mortgaged up to the chimney."

"And thanks to your information, I emerged from those two hyenas without losing my skin," Jim countered.

"But I have other plans, too," Charlie continued, telling him that he had begun negotiations to buy "Genio." When he was done with his brief tale of account, Jim tuned in:

"Then you need precision tools to punch the keys, which we could produce," Jim said.

"I hadn't thought of that," Charlie replied.

"We have been supplying precision tools to Wood Newspaper Machinery Company, in New Jersey, for twenty-five years and your needs are probably similar to the tools we supply to them!" said Jim.

They laughed and hoisted their beers to celebrate the unlikely development.

"It's getting better and better," Charlie thought. "If that deal comes to fruition, I will have two companies to work for. Even though I was distancing myself from what was expected of me, by my grandfather, I would like Peter's help with the marketing of the new company's products."

"Have you asked him about it?" Jim wondered.

"No, but in time I will think about doing it if the deal works," Charlie replied, and continued: "for the next two weeks we will have a lot to do to close the deal: the first of August we will transfer the entire business of the car company, land and everything to a newly formed Delaware company. The printing presses are getting pretty hot right now at Drexel to get out the prospectus and attract interested investors, to sign up for the bonds, we switch banks, while I leave VenCap, in the dust, and we are negotiating with "Genio," on the purchase of the company."

"You probably need a drink," Jim said, suggesting that they go inside to Morris and the ladies, just as the first raindrops began to hit the water in the pool.

"You know who's going to have a dog in the office soon," Charlie said as they walked through the patio's large sliding glass doors.

"Mr. Long, I suppose," Jim replied.

Charlie nodded and replied, "ten-four."

The next morning, Chuck entered Charlie's office with several documents to be signed, regarding the new company.

"Have you considered the ownership issue?" Chuck wondered.

"Yes, of course," replied Charlie, "were there any doubts?"

"No, but that is one thing that should be considered, before we sign the documents. After all, you've owned Long Cadillac alone. You should consider letting other family members, and maybe some key people in the firm, become owners of the new company," Chuck said.

Charlie's immediate reaction was that, with such a distribution, the children would become part-owners of a company, with debts of $15 million and that it would be a burden on them, even if the prospects were good. In addition, the new company risked a lawsuit from VenCap, because they bought the properties from the old company, at market price, but the lawsuit risk still existed there.

"As the conditions are now, with these companies' finances, I think it is inappropriate to take on other owners," Charlie replied.

"OK," replied Chuck, who rarely sought a debate, after submitting a point of view or proposal. Charlie, while signing the corporate documents considered the fact that if he had spread ownership to multiple individuals, VenCap could get fuel for the fire, thus arguing that the purpose of the property transfer was to enrich their children at VenCap's expense, which could be cause in itself for legal action.

Then Charlie called Steve Holmes to check the status of the prospectus.

"It will be ready by tomorrow," Steve replied, "and it became really appealing, even to you."

"Why?" Charlie wondered.

"I got the impression of what your new bank wanted, namely to be involved in financing in the future, and we wrote that the bonds, which run for five years, would allow early redemption without any special fees at any time, after two years have passed."

"Excellent" Charlie replied.

"Furthermore, without asking you, we have added a disclaimer to the terms of the agreement, namely that part of the issue may be used to diversify the business."

"That's right," Charlie replied.

"I know," Steve replied, explaining that investors cannot then oppose how the loan is used, nor criticize investments in "Genio." Steve explained that the subscription period would be two weeks, so the amount, if given full subscription, could be available to the new company two weeks after the end of the subscription period, or at the middle of August.

"I'm going to have a furious Bob Haskins on my tail for a few weeks then," Charlie said, thanking Steve.

Charlie asked Gail for two cups of coffee, and that she should ask Chuck to come back. When Chuck sat down, Charlie said, "As you know, we have problems with the cashier. In addition, I have those blood hounds Laurel & Hardy poking me in the neck. What we are doing, new company, transfer of property there, contract transport etc. may not, under any conditions, come to anyone else's knowledge.

"Um-hum," replied Chuck, who told no more than necessary to anyone no matter what he was doing.

"I want you to have all these company documents in a special folder in your own briefcase, and that you bring it home daily."

Most often, Chuck brought the briefcase with him daily which was why no one would react to that matter, and Chuck promised to do as he was asked.

"I want you to keep the documents, in your briefcase even in daytime," Charlie continued. After the brief coffee meeting, Charlie called Jeff to see how he planned to organize the small invasion of four AA & Co. men wearing suits.

"I informed the staff that I had hired the agency to do a "strength and weaknesses" analysis of the company, and no one said they were bothered by that. They may think they can vent their complaints, what do I know?" Jeff replied. He had talked to the office manager at AA & Co. who announced that their team would be there the last week of the month. Charlie was very pleased with the message he received and put then phone back in the receiver.

He had a revelation: *Imagine if I were to take over the crown jewels of the company, Tampa and St. Petersburg, the land I own, and skip the rest?* He shook off the idea, which was suddenly molded into a new one: *The Tampa branch manager has increased sales the fastest of all branches, including Boca. Tampa is admittedly a metropolis and the purchasing power in the area grew rapidly, but so did Miami, Palm Beach and Fort Lauderdale, all around Boca.*

If I promote him to the President of the new company, I can be chairman of the board and oversee the business, and also take the helm with full force in Genio, Charlie thought. He thought further, *What a ridiculous name! Here, we have to come up with something better."*

He wanted something that had to do with the new focus on keys and wondered what was really happening in the production.

Ford's car company was named Ford because the founder was named Ford. *I don't like calling the company Long*, he thought. After all, the manufacturing process transformed plastic grains into punches by heating the plastic, which in molten form was pressed into punching tools. In the final phase, when you have a female and a male, you combine them, the female, which is black, with the male, (which formed the very letter of the key) into a finished key.

The machines were powered and heated with electricity. Plastics that soften when heated are called thermoplastics. *Long Thermoplastics*, he thought and at the same time he dismissed the name. *That didn't sound scientific enough*, he thought, and thought about mechanical engineering. If the company were to be a subsidiary of the new Long Cadillac, the company could in any case be called "Long—something. *Tech, tech, tech*, he thought. "Long Tech?" "Thermo-tech?" *There we have it!* he thought: "Long Thermotech." He tasted the name and it sounded entrusting.

Now, life began as a dog handler. Not that Charlie was against Morris at all, but Anna was at school and couldn't go home to be with Morris at lunch, and even less in daytime, if she didn't have an hour off. Shannon hoped to see Charlie far more often for lunch, in the future. At least it was a nice break from what was going on in the office and Charlie liked to toss ideas with her, especially with the recent events unfolding.

"If you like your shoes, put them in the closet," he heard Shannon say from inside the kitchen. Charlie had the habit of taking off his shoes as soon as he could—even in the office—if he was out of sight. Little Morris didn't have many teeth, but they could tear most anything apart. It didn't take more than a few days for Charlie to get used to the new routine and he appreciated both Morris and being home with Shannon at lunchtime.

CHAPTER EIGHTEEN

The following Monday, July 20, 1985

Laurel's Lincoln was parked in a designated parking space outside the office when Charlie arrived. *Was it only three weeks since they were here, on Fateful Monday?* he thought, while wondering how there could be so many anomalies in business.

Since his time at the orphanage in Santa Barbara and Coachella Boarding School, he had an aversion to institutions of all kinds, and he felt a distrust of everything that could be likened to any form of authority or supremacy. His feeling was that regardless of their intentions, good or bad, the overall purpose was to make money off others.

He judged ordinary business differently. There, unlike the state and other institutions, it was a matter of survival.

Now probably two representatives from a form of supremacy sat waiting for him, unannounced in the usual order, and Charlie then became, consciously or not, the reactionary variant of himself. The patient diplomat stood back in favor of the steel warrior.

Hell, he thought as he parked the car in front of the entrance.

"You have visitors waiting," Gail said with a little acid in her voice. "They are in the conference room," she continued.

Charlie had come up with new procedures this past week. His

office was always locked if he was absent. Visitors had to wait at the reception. Today's visit was no exception: they had to sit in the conference room and wait.

"I saw their car," Charlie replied just as sourly. Gail had sympathy for her boss. She could read through his whole being when something was troubling Charlie, otherwise, it was never noticeable. She wondered if he had a natural reflex that always elicited a little smile regardless of whom he met, and the little quick greeting. Maybe it was his way of slightly going up a key when greeting that made the ever-happy impression regardless of circumstance. Maybe it was because he always wanted to help create positive vibrations in his surroundings. Maybe it was because he was always happy inside.

Anyway, she was happy with her boss and was careful not to trouble him unnecessarily. In addition, she had perfected this idea in practice by constantly consulting Chuck on approaching problems. An estimated half of all the boring cases that did not necessarily have to pass by Charlie could be left to Chuck. He had the same ambitions when it came to freeing Charlie from unnecessary matters.

The two gentlemen who were now waiting for Charlie never wanted to talk to anyone but Charlie. Charlie unlocked his office and entered the conference room through his own office.

"Gail said we had to wait here and not in your office," Hardy said noticeably annoyed.

"Good morning yourself," Charlie replied briefly.

"And the door was locked," Laurel continued. Charlie thought that here is the delaying tactic that applies and to respond directly to questions was out of question.

"What are you doing here?" Charlie wondered.

"We have some practical issues," Laurel continued.

"And that affects me?" Charlie wondered.

"To the highest degree," Hardy replied supremely and Laurel continued: "and how is the business going?"

"You get the monthly reports—read them!" Charlie replied.

"We wonder how things are really going," Hardy said.

Now the driver wants to be important also, Charlie thought.

"There is nothing wrong with the business," Charlie replied.

"How come the dividend that was due for payment June last has not been paid?" Hardy wondered.

"I have to check with the finance department," Charlie said.

"You can do so immediately," Hardy growled. Charlie thought it was pointless as they were barely able to pay suppliers, which is why he continued: "You are aware of our liquid situation and the situation has not improved since you were here three weeks ago with your pathetic attempt to take over the company."

"We were going to raise that issue as well," Laurel said, and continued, "as you know, VenCap has deciding vote on significant board issues." He let it sink in for ten seconds to create some drama and continued: "A CEO who is unable to control the ship can no longer have the confidence of the board."

Charlie couldn't believe his ears, but in his back of the head was the fact that eleven days into the future, VenCap would lead an empty company which would then be called "Bob's Fast Foods."

"If you mean what I think you mean, you might as well crawl back under the stones you came from," Charlie hissed.

"What we mean," Hardy said, "is that you apparently failed to fulfill the company's legal obligations, and that the board must then take action, unless improvement is made as soon as possible."

Charlie needed oxygen. He succeeded in collecting energy to remain calm and replied:

"As you probably recall, I asked you to remember our last call as I wanted to know if there was an opportunity to renegotiate the agreement." The words did not elicit any visible reaction. "What you have done to both me and the company seems to have other objectives," he continued, quite emotionally. "My picture of the situation is that you, through a coup aimed at me, strangled the supply of money to take over my shares. If you did not have such intentions, which are certainly linked to a bonus on execution, any party with good intentions would agree to a renegotiation of the agreement. Therefore, I now ask again: can we renegotiate the agreement?"

Charlie saw that his little speech had the desired effect on the two bloodsuckers; It was a very correct conclusion, which they had a hard time denying before him. Of course, Charlie never expected them to admit in any way to what he had said. The situation was beyond sense and reason. Here it was about playing their cards like in poker.

Why? The correct answer is prestige. For them to back down now would be the same as admitting evil intent and losing face. As there was no answer for many seconds, Charlie continued: "I see myself as a victim, of your short-term profit maximization. That you do not answer, I interpret as a no. If you will excuse me, I don't have time to play office with you anymore. You can see yourselves out."

"There were a few more things," Hardy said, seemingly unmoved but with a little less conviction in his voice. "The board has decided that your salary should be reduced by one third." "I have not been present at any board meeting," Charlie countered. "When we assumed that such a proposal would be voted down by you, we used our casting vote on the issue," Hardy said emotionally. Charlie thought he had experienced most everything, but he continued without commenting further:

"And what was the other?"

"We have an invoice for consulting fees, for the first half of the year," Hardy said.

"We haven't asked you to perform any services!" Charlie groaned.

"We have the right to invoice the time we have been here," replied Hardy. He handed over the invoice to Charlie, who moaned as he read the content.

"Thirty-eight thousand dollars!" he exclaimed.

"By agreement," Hardy said. The only thing Charlie knew for certain was that he would never pay that bill.

"If that's all, I ask you to leave me in peace now," Charlie said with a capitulating tone. Hardy thought they had salted a lot in Charlie's seemingly open wounds and said, "We'll be back."

Charlie didn't respond when they left the conference room.

Eleven days left with this kind of crap, he thought, smiling to himself, as he walked into his own room. His Matilda had a fresh, weekly report, from the sales manager at the surface. The campaign had started well overall and the figures were better than the year before, which was natural, since there had been no campaign that week.

Charlie was generally skeptical of all kinds of statistics. Figures were always presented to benefit a certain party, e.g. unemployment that could be reduced to fit the government's ambitions to demonstrate low unemployment, for its own political purposes when excluding adults who were in various educational programs and similar labor market policy measures.

Numbers were numbers, with the problem that what they aimed to describe was influenced by the subjective nature of the person who assembled them. Figures, that at first glance, looked positive, as in the weekly report, were often worthless due to completely unknown factors omitted in the presentation.

The report now before him had a completely different purpose. It was used to compete among the branches. What Charlie first saw was a complete compilation of all the branches. He wanted it that way. The next page showed the sales figures per branch and the change versus prior year and forecast as a percentage. The report was distributed to all branches every Monday and as usual Tampa and St. Petersburg were at the top. Of course, all branch managers wanted to be at the top and Charlie believed in man's vanity and need for recognition.

This fact, he believed, meant that everyone strived to sell the most, with retained margins, and then get some of the colleagues 'and managers' envy, with the subsequent padding of the pay envelope. Right or wrong, this was the intention.

Charlie called the sales manager, thanked him for the report, with just enough praise, and told him that the campaign would last, until the end of the month. It was a little doubtful to have a campaign for three weeks, but Charlie felt that the risks were limited by the fact that it was the holiday month.

Many left Florida, in July, because of the sticky heat, and if vacationers were home after all, they could always be tempted to buy a new car. Among the letters on the desk, lay one from Genio. It was from Jeff and held a copy of the letter to AA & Co. They were welcomed the last week, in July, to do their due diligence. Jeff had planned their attendance ahead and would inform the office staff that he was considering switching auditors and, as part of the new company's routines, to do a full audit for a week. It sounded like a good alternative to Charlie and thus, the Genio issue was resolved on his part, until the auditors were able to send their report, a week into August, he guessed.

The idea of offering Peter the sales manager position if the deal progressed, rattled him. How much should one, as a parent, control the life of their children? Could he do the right thing? Who did he have the most in mind for the future: himself or Peter? Once asked, that specific question was easiest to answer. Charlie could take over Tampa himself, he already owned the land, and do well with it. So, it was not mostly for his own sake, but because Peter would then not have to work six days a week at permafrost in Canada, preparing pipelines and drive oil, with long-haulers. Charlie liked selling, and the idea of being a coach in the context of just Peter would be instructive for Peter. Was it not then to do him a favor? Charlie, who was generally a positive person, realized that he could certainly be doing Peter a favor. But only on one condition: that Peter wanted it himself. He had been in Canada for two years and maybe he was ready for something new? Charlie hoped so and made his next call.

It was to the head of the office at AA & Co., in Miami. He confirmed that he had received a clearance from Jeff and that the audit would take place the last week of the month. What Charlie was particularly keen to know was Genio's purchase prices and plastic qualities. He was told that this information was the company's own business secret and that no such information was disclosed to the client, if the transaction was not completed.

Charlie was advised turn to an independent consulting firm, McKinsey & Co., to get general information about a particular industry. *It can wait*, he thought. He thanked them for the advice and the conversation ended.

The more he thought about the advice he received, the more he thought he could reap, if he followed the advice. They could inform him regarding possible manufacturers of personal computers and, in addition, what volumes they produced. He got the number for them, in Miami, and got a "Senior Consultant," which probably meant "multi-year experience," *two or more*, he thought.

The consultant replied that it was possible to identify who manufactured personal computers, where they manufactured them, volumes, qualities, prospects and other things of interest for an estimated sum of twenty-five thousand dollars, approximately. Charlie thought that they probably had the information available already and that some "Senior Consultant" then let some assistant write a report that the senior then signed.

Nuts, Charlie thought and asked them to make the report and then post it to his home address. Charlie felt like he was at an auction and coughed and thereby bought something very fragile, with low value and at an exorbitant price.

He had no computer monitor in his office. It struck him as a flash of lightning when he considered that if he was going to make something of it, it would be in his best interests to know what it was used for and put the car keys in his pocket.

"I go to lunch, if you have no business for me," he told Gail, revived by his newly acquired tactics and left the office. There was a mall in Boca and he parked in front of Computerworld. Once inside the door, he felt liberated and he was immediately alerted by an eager, young man who had a small pin on his shirt that read "Yes, I can!" Charlie asked to look at the personal computers that were in the store. When asked what it would be used for, he did not want to show his total ignorance and referred to his daughter's schoolwork.

There were a few different ones to choose from and he was shown three different computers. One was a proven model, which was slightly simpler than the others and was called "PET Commodore." It had poorer "performance" than the IBM PC and Macintosh, which came the year before. Charlie didn't want to be too interested in IBM, which he was obviously most interested in, but pretended to be interested in Macintosh. After spending half his lunch, with the salesman, he stepped out in the heat again with brochures in his hand.

Shannon waited with a salad at home and she was asked to look at the brochures and think about which machine might appeal to her. "Your personal secretary," he told her. As usual, Shannon was clear-sighted. After looking through the brochures and only reading about what functions were available and completely skipping the sections on performance, the verdict was dropped:

"PET and Macintosh are ugly and cream-colored and do not fit in your study. I like IBM best."

Charlie was actually more interested in what the appliances could be used for than what they looked like. Shannon's decision in favor of IBM was apparently dependent on appearance. *That detail might be important*, Charlie thought. He had been informed by the dedicated salesman that Macintosh was the latest in the line of newcomers, in the personal computer world, and that it had arrived, just a year earlier, in 1984.

They would probably adapt the design of the machines, he thought. As he read through the brochures, he soon realized that he was not knowledgeable enough to decide which one was the best. Various accessories such as "Disc Drive," memory cassettes, cables that cost ten dollars (!) each, and different performance meant absolutely nothing to Charlie. However, like Shannon, he thought IBM was the most appealing.

After lunch and another walk with Morris, he returned to the office and called McKinsey again. He asked them to include a competitor analysis to their investigation, which at Charlie's request could be included at no additional cost.

Then he called up the person in the company who dealt with data communication and asked him to give his opinion regarding the three machines, in the brochures on the Matilda. He himself had an IBM machine at home and thought it was probably the PC that would appeal to most buyers. He added that for the novice user, IBM would probably be more suitable to handle compared to the Macintosh. In addition, IBM was cheaper. He was somewhat surprised by Charlie's newly awakened interest in personal computers and Charlie defended himself that it could be good for Anna, for schoolwork which sounded quite truthful.

In fact, he was also thinking about letting her be the test pilot for the computer, to ask her about her impression of the machine. He thanked the tech for the advice and the computer manager could return to the statistics, or whatever it was he did, during his days. Charlie realized that people were necessary in the company, but he was only remotely versed in the actual work behind the routines of the company.

He had decided to buy an IBM and then called Peter. He was out on the Tundra as usual and a clerk promised to deliver Charlie's message. It was high time that he planted a small seed, with Peter, about an upcoming salesman job. Then he called Steve Holmes in Minneapolis. He was told that their impression of Genio's accounts that had arrived the day before showed signs of a weak company. They did not have very good profits and they had not increased from the year before, either. It was typical of a privately-owned company that some things just rolled on out of old habit. A general tendency also was that there was no reason to strive to generate maximum profit, as the tax cost was in proportion to the profit. Therefore, it was not entirely clear whether Jeff intentionally held back the results or whether the company simply had mediocre profitability. However, what one could read from the annual report was that wage costs were unusually high in relation to turnover, and that the balance sheet was unnecessarily bloated.

The latter could be due to the fact that stocks had been built up unnecessarily and that customers were used to paying slowly, because the accounts receivable routines were poor. The former could be due to Jeff taking the results as salary, to himself, to wife, to children, and, somewhat absurdly, the dog might also be paid. It was better to pay salaries to people, with lower incomes, to avoid the progressive tax increase associated with higher salaries. All this and much more would come to light, during the due diligence, by AA & Co.

However, the preliminary analysis, based on the material obtained and which could not have been cooked since Jeff was not aware of Charlie's or hopefully any other party's interest in acquiring the company at the time of the release of the annual report, was that the company was not very valuable. After all, it is quite difficult for an owner of a company to try to sell a company on results that do not exist, and which have not existed.

On the way home, Charlie bought an IBM machine with what the seller said had outstanding performance and an accessory kit for the incredible price of $2,999.00. He managed to negotiate for a technician to come to the house and install the machine the next day.

Charlie had a notion that it could really be that this particular thing could fall in price like TV sets, ballpoint pens, calculator and other things had done before. *The benefits of the machine would probably be decisive*, he thought. One thing he was convinced of: Anna would probably be the only student in the class, with a personal computer at home. *She would have to spend many more years in school, for this machine to pay off*, he thought. Shannon gave her husband a cold beer as he emerged from the pool and said, "I've been thinking about Genio."

"How so?" Charlie wondered.

"Well, toys are always sought after, and now you plan to jettison them and produce keys?"

"That's exactly what I want to do," Charlie replied, continuing: "We have looked at Genio's development and they have parked the business at some level. I imagine there are reasons for their current situation. One reason may be that they must deal with quantities of different types of plastic and that they have high tool costs, as they manufacture everything from building blocks to toy cars. What I want to do is literally produce millions of keys, with a small number of tools. It also seems to be enough, with two different types of plastic."

"Wouldn't you keep some of the toys?" Shannon wondered.

"It may take time but it's probably easier to streamline the business for one thing," Charlie replied, while Morris knocked Charlie's beer into the pool.

The phone rang and Charlie heard how Shannon was delighted to hear Peter's voice. Charlie put on a bathrobe and went in to talk to him. *He had to take it a little cautiously*, he thought. Being used to diplomacy is one thing—dealing with your son is something entirely different. Charlie really wanted to confide in Peter about his desire to get his help, in the new company, and at the same time, he did not want to place too much demands on him. It was his life anyway and the proposal meant a drastic change for Peter.

"I heard you were on the line," Charlie said in a third receiver, so Shannon could join the conversation.

"Hi" said Peter, who seemed to be in a good mood.

"Morris just knocked my beer into the pool," Charlie said.

"You have serious problems, I hear," Peter replied, laughing.

"There's one thing I wanted to ask you," Charlie said.

"Shoot," Peter replied.

"As you know, I have plans to buy a toy company."

"Well, you mentioned that at the brunch at Lake Minnetonka. How are you doing by the way?"

"That's exactly what I wanted to talk to you about," Charlie said. "We are negotiating and there are probably good chances that we can take over the company."

"That's good then," Peter replied.

"Sure, but we don't know until about a month from now I would think," Charlie said.

"Good luck," Peter said.

"Now, here is what I wanted to mention to you Peter," Charlie said.

"OK," Peter said.

"Have you thought about doing anything other than what you do now?" Charlie wondered, cautiously.

"Dad, I'm thrilled up here. Good friends, good money. I can't ask for more," Peter replied.

"Peter, if I take over this company, I will need help from someone I can fully trust,"

Charlie said without making it sound as a request, "and it would be a real pleasure for me to do so with your help."

"What would that be?" Peter wondered.

"I have no experience in the plastics industry, but I have long experience in sales, and I like it," Charlie said, and continued: "together we could change the company's direction and if you want to manage the marketing of the products with me as coach it might grow into something big over time and then you become directly involved, in both the responsibility and the results."

"I know nothing about sales and even less about plastic things," countered Peter.

"Peter, nobody who starts with anything knows everything. You didn't know anything about pipelines when you came to Canada?"

"You are quite right in that," Peter replied.

"But you learned," Shannon chimed in.

"Listen, I think I realize what you're thinking, and I appreciate your confidence. What I do now I do as an independent, on my own, and for myself. I have heard, since I was little that I was the boss's son and I don't like it. The last thing I want is to be considered a Dandy, someone who just rides on someone else's wave."

"Peter, I know how you think, believe me. The reason I left the ranch and went to sea, with my old friend Ritch, was due to the exact same relationship—and one more thing: my grandfather expected me to take over the ranch.

My maternal grandfather hoped I would take over his newspaper, the Whittier Daily News. The mere thought of appeasing them at will was disgusting to me when I was seventeen. I did exactly what I wanted at the time I left the country and I never regretted my decision. Actually, I have never engaged in anything I have not wanted to do. In this way, I am a happy, fortunate person.

You should know that I have thought a lot about my experiences while wrestling with the idea of suggesting as a father exactly what I revolted against. I don't expect you to do this at all. But I think we would be a strong team and together we can do something good, with this new company."

"Um-hum" they heard in the receiver.

"Then, to your thought of being a "dandy;" no such thing here. If we do this, you will not have any easy position. On the contrary. You get a difficult position. Everything you do must be better than any other employee's effort, just because you are my son and because their job will depend on the fact that what you do holds high class. If it were easy, I could and would ask someone else."

"I hear what you say," Peter replied emphatically.

"Is it OK, if I think about it?" he continued.

"That's what I was hoping you would say," Charlie replied.

"We miss you," Shannon said.

"The same" answered Peter.

MICHAEL OWENS

CHAPTER NINETEEN

The next morning, Charlie asked Gail to come in, with two cups of coffee.

"We talked about changes at lunch a few weeks ago," said Charlie, who had a bad conscience for having told her plans to transfer staff to a new company, without following up with her for three weeks.

"Well, I've wondered," Gail said cautiously.

"The situation has changed since then and, fortunately, I have something concrete to announce," Charlie said.

"Was it because of the visit yesterday?" wondered Gail, who had a feeling for the events, even though she was not present.

"Their presence is like having a boil you know where, but they will get the short end of the straw, if we manage to make the changes I am planning," Charlie replied.

"You know you can count on me," Gail said.

"I know Gail, otherwise I wouldn't talk to you now. What we say doesn't leave this room—OK?"

"OK," Gail replied.

"Here's how it goes: in the company, things happen that make Laurel & Hardy history. We will probably buy another company, and, in that case, I will want to offer you a job as a first receptionist. You have shown that you have integrity and you are an exemplary face externally. These are important factors as we will have contact, with

341

very large companies. Probably no one else here will be offered any position in the new company."

"I'm glad you want me there, but may I ask how you will work yourself?"

"Of course, I have a plan for that, too, but I want to keep that to myself for the time being," Charlie said.

"Before I take the job at another company, I want to know who my boss will be," Gail said.

"Of course," Charlie replied.

Charlie wrestled with another problem. Every season during the summer campaign he had always traveled around to the branches to support the campaign and to meet the staff. After all, the campaign had been launched early for known reasons and extended to last the rest of the month.

The crux was that the bond issue, the company change, due diligence and the bank change were going on simultaneously. Being unavailable or difficult to reach was not a good alternative. He decided to have the branch manager in Tampa make the visits for "educational purposes."

One Saturday remained before the end of the month and Charlie would personally visit the branches closest to Boca. Charlie presented the task to the Tampa branch manager so that "you can share your experience as winners in sales growth, with the other branches."

The message seemed to have a stimulating effect on the branch manager, and he was taking the bait, without a second thought. Charlie asked Gail to inform the branches via a new tool called group fax. One document was faxed once to many recipients at one time.

Brilliant, Charlie thought: *another potential market for keys.*

Charlie thought about the conversation he had, with the purchasing manager at IBM. He had said that "the market is endless," which sounded persistently in Charlie's head. No market but possibly the universe could be infinite. Still, he was attracted by the purchasing manager's optimism for the future and was eager to believe him.

The reason why IBM had chosen Boca for the production of personal computers had been confidentiality. It was thought that a small town, in swampy Florida, could avoid competitors' natural source of information, because it was inaccessible there. After all, everyone else in the industry was in California.

No one at IBM, except the very select staff, had been aware of what was going on in Boca. In September 1980, five years earlier, a dozen technicians called The Dirty Dozen, with design as a specialty, had been formed in Boca.

These technicians had called the project, Acorn, which would be symbolic of the huge tree's growth, from the small acorn. In addition, they inferred something hard and durable—oak.

A year later, the first IBM personal computer was delivered in Boca Raton, Florida, for the price $3,000. Now, he had a later version of the computer at home for the same price, though posting better performance and a range of accessories. *It was likely that the market could grow in line with availability and that prices would fall over time, volumes increase,* and so on Charlie thought. But how could Jeff, with his manufacturing in the same small town, not come up with the idea of making keys for computers? He would probably never know why, but a logical answer could simply be that he had enough on his hands with toy manufacturing.

Then it often becomes difficult to have a periscope view and be able to see "around the corner." He thought that development in general, perhaps even regularly, was a result of chance. That had been the case his whole life, and therefore it was Charlie's natural conclusion.

He still hadn't figured out what to do with a personal computer, but he knew that you could write with the machine in a program called "Writing Assistant." Then there was a registry program called "Filing Assistant." In the office, he had both in the form of flesh and blood and why one would want to use and rely on these machines was a mystery to Charlie. But apparently, people were generally prepared to pay $3,000 for the pleasure of owning their own PC and why would Charlie doubt the market? It was not relevant to doubt anything now that so many events were going on at the same time. If everything fell into place, he would within a month lead a brand, new business, at the same time, he planned to take Long Cadillac to the next level, with a new manager.

He would be chairman of the board but not directly active, in daily matters. Mentally, he was focusing on the new company and he had been helped to get rid of his old company, through VenCap's greed. That VenCap behaved in such a way was no coincidence. However, their actions, or rather, the result thereof, were a coincidence. The plan to take over the company, at Charlie's expense, was now dangerously close to robbing them of their ownership, and the irony was that they had no idea what to expect.

If they had played their cards better, they could have been half owners, of the entire Long Cadillac group, with its subsidiary, Long Thermotech. Within a week, they would have half of Bob's Fast Foods, which would be debt free (except for an unpaid invoice at $38,000 from them) but totally worthless. What they themselves intended to take part in, namely the game that was called hostile takeovers, in financial jargon, would backfire and become a real meltdown. *Whoever gets in the game*, thought Charlie.

He decided to have an early lunch.

"The issue was immediately fully subscribed," Steve Holmes said when Charlie answered the phone.

"That was the best news I've heard in a while," Charlie said.

"That means we can look forward to receiving the cash any day in the last week of the month," Steve continued.

"I call that timing," said a very relieved Charlie, adding: "there was another thing, my wife said something the other day that has led to an idea."

"Let's hear it," Steve replied.

"It may well be that only a few of the machines at Genio can be transformed, for the new product—keys—and that you could then continue with some toys."

"Of course, you can have two products in the same factory," Steve replied.

"My idea is to allow Genio to continue as usual and to launch its own stores, for example, in the Mall of America, and build a network of stores and then spin out that business, if key manufacturing goes well, "Charlie said.

"It's an appealing thought," Steve said, "then we get back some of the loan money and Drexel can finance the same business again."

"You see money in everything," Charlie said positively.

"If we don't make money from what we do, we might as well not do anything—or as Ivan Boesky, Michael Milken's companion, has said: "greed is good.""

"At just the right dosage, it's probably motivating," Charlie countered.

"You're right," Steve replied, continuing: "capitalism has its conditions, and we're dancing with the wolves now."

When they ended the conversation, he thought of the last thing Steven had said: "We are dancing with the wolves now." Was he about to become one himself?

A twenty-year career, as a successful car dealer, he was as late as three weeks earlier prepared to completely hand over his business, without a fight, due to opportunists like VenCap. Now, with the help of Wall Street's most successful finance group, Drexel Burnham Lambert, and Steve Holmes, he had reversed the roles and Charlie was soon able to jettison both VenCap and Bob Haskins. Had he then succeeded in something? The debts of the new Long Cadillac even exceeded the market value of the company, as he would borrow 100 percent of the purchase price and fees, but after Drexel retained their five percent commission, he would only actually receive 95 percent cash. "*Eat or be eaten*," Charlie thought. Now a car dealer would become a venture capitalist and, with borrowed funds, buy a toy company. Where was the logic in this? Survival? Revenge? Take command?

Probably all three.

CHAPTER TWENTY

That anyone could buy anything, and besides having no money, was the melody of the time. Car dealers, toy factory, keys; *Why not throw in a tomato crop too*? Charlie thought.

Strange constellations were common. After all, Apache Corporation in Minneapolis had combined oil drilling with orange groves in California, Harley-Davidson merged with American Machine and Foundry (AMF), in 1969, which had bowling balls and sports equipment on its manufacturing list (a merger that was successfully disbanded in 1981 by the management buying out Harley-Davidson, which at market value at the time of writing is larger than General Motors-March 2005) and, for example, tobacco company, Philip Morris, which owns Kraft and other food companies. So-called "conglomerates" were everywhere.

One reason for the conglomerate phenomenon was that the companies managed cash in droves, on their balance sheets. The natural thing for a company that has more money than is needed in the operation of its business is to simply return cash to its shareholders, in the form of a dividend.

However, dividend distributions do not usually result in the management of the company receiving a pat on the back or monetary reward such as, bonus. Besides, it's not fun, for the management. Fun for the management is often what is important outside the company's ordinary so-called core business.

What women do at the micro level is what men do at the macro level: buy things. It is more macho to introduce to its Board of Directors how, through an acquisition, it is likely that the return on dormant capital can be increased and in this way emphasize their own greatness and with the delusion that it would also benefit the shareholders.

The phenomenon had its own special fashion word, for this kind acquisition: "diversification." In fact, what may well be good for all three parties, management, the company and shareholders, can often result in disaster for the buying company.

The acquisition itself had become a popular sport in America. It even had its own special name: corporate finance. The largest player, in the corporate finance branch was Drexel Burnham Lambert. They appeared daily in the mass media, in some context that was associated with acquisitions, mergers and so-called LBO's, loan financed purchases.

Most controversial of all was Michael Milken. He was Trading Manager at the Bond Department. The company had been founded twelve years earlier, in 1973, as a result of a merger between Drexel Firestone, an investment bank, with its best years behind it, and Burnham & Co.

The Belgian company, Bruxells Lambert, bought in, in 1976, and they sought to create a niche in the market by assisting medium-sized companies that had limited opportunities for raising capital. Milken regularly traded bonds that had weak collateral, which were divided into three security grades, popularly called below investment level (lower than BBB), speculative level, and high return level.

The market for these was limited when Drexel began, in 1973, and Milken traded with so-called fallen angels, bonds that were downgraded, due to the companies that issued the bonds getting into hardship. His idea of such bonds was that they had significant trading value, for the simple reason that the market did not want them.

He went out and found buyers of these bonds, by telling insurance companies and other fund managers this theory, which he was not the first to put forward, but he was the first to create a market for them. The bonds that an investor had bought which were later upgraded by the issuer's recovery made huge profits. In this way, Milken's network grew.

In 1977, Lehman Brothers issued bonds, under investment status totaling $263 million, for, among others, Pan American Airlines. Issuing new bonds with such low status was new. Milken felt that he could do the same—he had buyers. That same year, he managed to make seven bond issues totaling $154 million.

His office was located in Manhattan where the company's management resided and who controlled the trades. The following year, he alone accounted for most of the company's earnings, and because he refused to be under management's control, he asked to move the business to Los Angeles. The management could not say no to his request and Milken, along with thirty colleagues, moved. The business flourished and acquisition artists such as T. Boone Pickens and Carl Icahn literally flocked to his office in Beverly Hills.

A small specialty was launched by Milken: bond issues were regularly increased to more than needed. This way money was left over, which could be used to buy new bonds.

Over a ten-year period, Milken financed over a thousand companies. Among these were CNN with Ted Turner, Chrysler, MCI, Warner Communications and McGaw Cellular.

Others also issued bonds, but Milken was the king of so-called junk bonds. No one else could organize capital in such a short time.

And now, in practice, the issue money was ready. *It would certainly be fun to kick out VenCap and Bob Haskins*, Charlie thought. The sales campaign went well, so money also rolled in, with good speed into the company. AA & Co. was doing their due diligence, the bank change was underway, and in a perfect world he would also be seizing Genio soon.

Did all this depend on greed? Surely not. That's how the chips fell. With good advisors, Charlie was on his way to riding out the storm.

Luck, talent and timing, he thought.

CHAPTER TWENTY-ONE

Boca Raton, FL · July 30, 1985

Drexel paid out the bond loan minus their seven hundred and fifty-thousand-dollar commission, as planned, on July 30. The money was deposited into a newly opened account in the "new" Long Cadillac's bank, FNBFL, and arrived the following day, July 31, a total of fourteen million two hundred and fifty thousand dollars.

Hazel notified Charlie over the phone and suggested lunch, which he declined.

"I would love to come another time; we have a hectic month-end now," he said. She had already taken a liking to Charlie, not love, but someone that attracted her curiosity. He was brief, and what he had said occurred.

He asked her to transfer exactly nine million dollars to FSB at once.

"Have you sold the company" Bob Haskins said.

"Why?" Charlie wondered and triumphed inside.

"Nine million dollars have been deposited into your checking account!" Bob spurted out. "Excellent. Thanks for the information," Charlie said calmly.

"What is going on?" Bob continued.

Charlie didn't owe Bob any answers. On the contrary.

"The amount should cover the loans we have, including the interest that is due today. Pay off the loans," he said.

"Have you changed banks?" Bob wondered. Charlie knew that Bob could see that the money had been paid from FNBFL and he could therefore confirm that part.

"Does VenCap know about this?" Bob wondered.

"You should ask them that," Charlie countered.

"What's going on?" Bob insisted.

"I don't owe you any explanations," Charlie replied.

"It would make it easier for me to explain the matter to the board of the bank," Bob tried.

"Bob, you mean VenCap, right?" Charlie continued calmly. Bob was disarmed.

"It would help me to understand," he replied sadly.

"Bob, you've been playing under the table behind my back. You blame your board. I do not owe you or the bank anything, so you may continue to wonder. Thanks for twenty years of cooperation," Charlie said, quietly putting the handset in its receiver.

The sweetness of victory, he thought as he called Shannon and told her that everything was ready with the new bank and with the loan.

CHAPTER TWENTY-TWO

Boca Raton, FL · August 1, 1985

Charlie had arranged a meeting, with the judge in the municipal building—the one that looked like the Alamo, already at nine. The situation with "new" Long Cadillac's purchase of the business from Long Cadillac, at market value and the former partners VenCap, was explained in simple terms to the judge who did not have to ask Charlie to clarify.

"What I want is a visitor ban from any VenCap representative," Charlie said. He did not want to let the Laurel & Hardy inside in the future, and it would be possible to call a police officer to evict them if the judge issued a visitor ban. The judge issued the ban, signed the document and Charlie was back in the office at ten o'clock.

He asked Gail to copy the document, lock the original in the safe and keep the copy herself. It was only a matter of time before the blood suckers would visit again. Gail was ordered to show them the document and that if they did not voluntarily leave the building, she should call the police.

"You've got a package," she said, handing a FEDEX envelope to Charlie. It was from AA & Co. in Miami. The envelope contained a memorandum and the title was "Red Lobster—due diligence, July 1985."

The document began with a summary, which was all Charlie needed to know at this stage. It stated that the company had zero growth in the last five years, that profitability was weak, during the same period, that the company had been used for private expenses, admittedly modest, and so the kicker: since Jeff had not been able to cook the figures, before the unplanned sale, he and his attorney claimed that profitability was deliberately kept down, by an unnecessarily high rent paid to himself, as Jeff owned the factory building privately.

When reviewing the returns, it was found that the company could hardly afford to pay the necessary rent to cover interest and amortization. Their little scam had easily been revealed. Jeff had thus tried to claim that the company was more profitable than it really was, for the purpose of pumping up the purchase price.

Charlie asked Gail to copy the document and send it, with FEDEX, to Steve Holmes, in Minneapolis, without showing anyone else what she was doing.

He then called Mike Burns to ask him to value another property in Boca, namely the Genio plant. Then, with Steve's calculations on Genio's value, he could make a bid. One thing was certain: Genio was hardly worth more than the excess from the bond issue.

When Charlie lifted the handset, he heard Gail warn him that Hardy was calling for him.

"Let him through," Charlie said.

"Have you changed your bank?" wondered a friendly voice.

"That's right," Charlie replied, in a matter of fact way.

"Why?" Laurel wondered.

"Business reasons, which you ought to be able to figure out yourself," Charlie replied.

"Then you can pay the dividend now," Laurel said.

"The company has no more money now than it had when you

were here last week," Charlie said, without clarifying the matter.

"Your place on the board has been questioned," Laurel said sourly.

"Welcome to the club. I've long questioned your role on the board, "Charlie replied, continuing:" if you will excuse me, I have a lot to do."

It was clear that Bob Haskins had a hot line to VenCap. Once they realized what had happened, VenCap would probably come up with some sort of lawsuit, but it was not relevant, on this lovely day. Charlie was the master of the plot in his own company and VenCap was half owner of an admittedly debt-free but otherwise completely worthless company now called "Bob's Fast Foods."

McKinsey's report was an interesting read for Charlie. They presented a very diverse group of small suppliers of plastic parts to the manufacturers of computers and similar machines. Some were on the west coast and one was in Minneapolis, which was a subsidiary of ITT (which Irwin Jacobs tried to take over with Drexel's financial assistance without success). Charlie laughed out loud as he read what the Minneapolis-based company was called: ITT Thermotech.

Long Thermotech was better, he thought. The picture that emerged of this diverse group of suppliers showed one important thing: they just seemed to deliver locally. Of course, having a local supplier would be an advantage for IBM in Boca.

Charlie was completely convinced to buy the company and play on several keys at once. The valuations came in a few days later. Genio had bank loans and there were loans on the factory as well, although the latter only concerned the seller. The bid would refer to market value, seen from the buyer's perspective, and was thus independent of any liabilities relating to the property. Mike Burns had valued the old building at a million dollars. Steve Holmes valued the company at about double, about $2 million. The modest valuation was because the company had bank loans of about five million dollars and that both growth and profitability growth were equal to zero. Steve suggested that a total bid of two and a half million dollars be put forward. That may make Jeff negotiable.

Charlie invited Jeff to the usual place, Red Lobster, on Dixie Highway, and presented his bid while Jeff took a bite of raw meat. In normal order, Jeff seemed unmoved, by what he had just been told. He mumbled something, with food in his mouth, that he expected more.

"It's a hell of a lot of money," Charlie said.

"Sure, but it's been years of labor for it too," Jeff replied.

"Which you have let the company pay for in the process," Charlie complained.

"I can continue with that," Jeff replied.

"Sure, but you have an attractive bid on the table that I suggest you carefully consider," Charlie said.

"Can you spike it with something?" Jeff wondered.

"What do you mean?" Charlie asked.

"Can we agree that I remain on the board and receive fees for it, salary, or the like?" said Jeff.

"Jeff, it's like this: if I am to buy Genio, it will be a clean deal. It is the purchase price that we agree on that applies. Nothing else."

Jeff promised to discuss the matter with his lawyer and the discussion would resume the next day. Charlie reported the development to Steve.

"We have him on the hook," he replied. "Tomorrow you try to get him to accept, preferably without his lawyer present," Steve continued.

The next day, Charlie invited Jeff to his office. The idea had been suggested by Steve to try to impress Jeff and sense the taste of money.

"Your offer was at the low end," Jeff said.

"Maybe so, but that's what I can manage. Nothing more," Charlie replied.

"No fringes?" wondered Jeff, who didn't really have much room to negotiate.

"One thing I can do: you can get a new Cadillac, at my purchase price," Charlie replied. If Jeff did snap at that, it wouldn't cost Charlie anything, but there was something about the Cadillac car brand. Jeff would probably feel richer, with such a car than he was going to be, and with an impression, you come a long way. Charlie saw that the proposal had some effect on Jeff, who countered: "two-point-six."

"Agreed" Charlie answered, and the agreement was consummated in the conference room.

"What color do you want on the car?" Charlie wondered.

"Green," Jeff replied.

"Why green?" Charlie wondered.

"The color of money" Jeff answered more than a little satisfied with the deal.

"The deal is done," Charlie told Steve Holmes.

"That was quick," Steve replied.

"It's hard to put a finger on him but he accepted anyway and that's why I want to ask you to draft a purchase contract between the new Long Cadillac and Jeff," Charlie said.

"Now that Jeff thinks the deal is done and has lowered his guard, he is ripe for a little price massage," Steve said.

"How?" Charlie wondered.

"In a few days we, will announce that we have problems with the loans, but that for 2-300,000 lower price, we have a deal," Steve replied.

"You probably didn't really listen to me at our first meeting in Minneapolis," Charlie said calmly.

"Didn't miss a word," Steve countered.

"Steve, I told you then and I'll say it again; where I come from a handshake seals a deal. I want to continue to be able to look Jeff in the eyes long after the deal is closed, and I want to sell cars to him in the future as well. That's how it is."

"It's understood," Steve replied. He would draw up the three necessary documents to execute the transaction—Share Transfer Agreement, the Seller's Guarantees and the Settlement Note for the transfer of the shares themselves. The date of closing would be September 1st.

The staff would be informed on the last Friday of August, with Charlie as new owner and CEO present. On Saturday, September 1, the locks would be replaced. Whether Charlie distrusted Jeff or not didn't matter. His grandfather had said that if you want to be safe when crossing a street, you have to look in both directions, even if it is one-way. It was a mere precaution, nothing else. He would kindly inform Jeff about the matter, referring to the fact that anyone could have keys to the factory.

"We buy Genio the first of September," Charlie said as he reached Peter.

"Well, I'll be a son of a gun" the son countered happily.

"It is my hope that you want to help me with the marketing," Charlie said encouragingly.

"I've been thinking a lot about it since you mentioned the opportunity," Peter replied.

"I really need your help, and I think it would be exciting to run the company with you," Charlie continued.

"Hell, why not," Peter replied happily, "but I'll probably need to polish my language a bit."

"Welcome home kid!" said Charlie, very happy for the first time in a long time.

He considered his situation: the company he had built up and admittedly lived off well for twenty years was now again his but mortgaged at its market value. The new company that was about to become his might be worth, at best, $400,000 more than he would pay. His debts exceeded what he received in cash by $750,000. So, at the moment, he was at a net minus $350,000 at best.

Soon fifty, a likely lawsuit under way, two companies, and net debt. Ironically, it was the properties in Tampa and St. Petersburg and the land around the four-way intersection in Boca that had value.

Then, of course, he had the ranch. From a financial point of view, it was far from bad, but his business accomplishments had no added value, which tormented Charlie. The hope was that Florida's population growth would enhance the car company and that the personal computer industry would flourish.

The idea that Peter would be on board inspired Charlie immensely. He had one month's notice and would drive all the way to Florida, from the Tundra north of Calgary, so by mid-September he would probably be in Boca.

"I have good and bad news," Charlie told the Tampa branch manager. "Come here as soon as you can," he continued. The same evening, Charlie took out branch manager, a Mr. Bill Hart to dinner in Boca.

Bill was first informed, perhaps slightly teasing, that Charlie noticed good development for the branches. Particularly Tampa and St. Petersburg which is why Bill was needed for other branches in general, and for Boca headquarters.

"Your numbers are good too," contended Bill, who did not seem to be interested in being closer to the head office.

"Sure, we have good numbers thanks to the large move into Fort Lauderdale and Miami, and to some extent Jupiter and Palm Beach, but we need your knowledge on another level," Charlie continued. Bill looked confused. "Can you imagine moving here, if I make an offer?" Charlie wondered.

"What kind of offer would it be?" Bill wondered.

"President of Long Cadillac," Charlie said emphatically, without losing Bill's eyes with his own.

"When do I start !?" exclaimed Bill, noticeably delighted.

"September first," Charlie replied. They shook hands in Charlie's way. "Your first task is to appoint your successor in Tampa—you do that yourself as CEO. I will be chairman of the board. What you consider to be essential, I want to be informed about. Otherwise, you have free hands."

"I am flattered by the offer and gladly accept. But, if I may ask, why would you want to hand over the helm to someone else?" Bill wondered.

"That's a legitimate question," Charlie replied, continuing, "the first reason is that I've seen what you've accomplished in Tampa. Of course, I think your ability to develop Long Cadillac's business is better than my own. The second reason is that we will diversify the business and that I will take over the CEO responsibility in the subsidiary."

"I guess that was the bad news," Bill replied.

CHAPTER TWENTY-THREE

The next day, Laurel & Hardy came to the office. Gail beeped her boss and he sensed tightness in her tone.

"You have visitors," she said, "and it's probably best that you come out."

"What's going on here?" Hardy wondered.

"Get into the conference room," Charlie told the guests. "The copy, please," he said to Gail, who immediately handed over a document. Inside the conference room, Charlie handed over the copy to Laurel who couldn't believe his eyes.

"Restraining orders?" he exclaimed. Hardy didn't seem to understand what was going on.

"So, we have a court order that you may not be here at the company," Charlie said sharply.

"And what would be the reason for that decision?" wondered a noticeably, jittered Laurel.

"You can ask the judge about that," Charlie countered, and continued, "please remove yourself now."

"Not until we get an explanation," Hardy growled.

"I do not need to give you any explanation other than what appears in the document you have in your hand; we can get police over here if you want."

"You will hear from us," Laurel exclaimed sourly, got up and walked to the door with Hardy behind like a sluggish dog, and then marched out the door without closing it behind him.

"That's it," Charlie said, handing back the copy to Gail.

He did not know if he would let the old company live for a while or if he would liquidate it. Bankruptcy was excluded now that the debts to the bank were paid and the new Long Cadillac had taken over all other assets and liabilities, except of course the invoice that Hardy had presented regarding consulting fees, for work that had never been performed. Following a bankruptcy, that invoice would be last in payment terms, but it was a hindrance to liquidation. Chuck had struggled hard with all the transfers between old and new Long Cadillac and also postponed his vacation. It was best not to raise the issue of liquidation, until after his now much needed vacation. It was at least now time to inform Chuck that Genio and he would get new bosses.

"I have good news and I have good news," Charlie said as Chuck came in with two cups of coffee.

"No bad ones?" Chuck wondered a little cautiously. He was pale noted Charlie.

"On the contrary," Charlie said, "we'll take the most fun first." Chuck sat down in the chair and sipped the hot coffee.

"You've done a fantastic job with the company change and I want to thank you especially for that," Charlie said. "It was an interesting task," replied Chuck, who was not particularly impressed with his achievement.

"You take your wife to any place of your choice in the Bahamas— at the company's expense for two weeks." Rarely did you see a big smile on Chuck. Charlie was now allowed to experience such a rare smile. Then Charlie talked about the subsidiary Genio. Chuck was genuinely excited about the fact that he himself would become the financial officer of a group, albeit a small group. However, it was noticeable that he was less pleased that a marketing manager from Tampa would become the Group's new CEO. But he could accept the matter. Charlie told him they would have a reception, in the conference room on Friday, August 31, with the signing of the purchase contract with Jeff, Steve Holmes and Bill Hart present, as well as Jeff's attorney.

"Will you be back by then?" Charlie wondered.

"Wouldn't miss it for anything in the world," Chuck replied smiling.

Chuck returned with a nice tan, just before the closing, on the last day of August. Steve Holmes had had the opportunity to get acquainted with Charlie and Shannon, Anna and Morris the day before, after the final contract review between the parties. They had had Bushtucker, by the pool, with Jim and Darlene as other guests. The signing would take place at 11 a.m., so Chuck could notify Hazel, to pay Jeff before lunch. It was a happy event which ended with catering sandwiches from Boca Raton Country Club. At two o'clock, the company left the conference room and Charlie was left alone. He called the prepared locksmith and announced that the purchase was now completed and that he could get a copy of the last page of the agreement, which was accepted as a basis. The locks would be replaced throughout the factory the following day. Jeff was to be informed on Sunday over the phone.

At three o'clock there was an information meeting at Genio. Steve Holmes had taken the rest of the day off to go to Palm Springs and play golf over the weekend. Chuck and Charlie came to Genio, just before three o'clock and were met by a noticeably happy, former owner named Jeff.

The information to the thirty employees would be in the dining room. Jeff talked briefly about how he had founded the company as a small manufacturer of plastic toys, in the 1960s, and that the company would now be "taken to the next level" by transferring the family business to another family business, namely Long Cadillac.

Charlie was then invited to speak, and he said that he appreciated the opportunity to collaborate with new employees and that he would take on the challenge of trying to create solid growth in the company.

A roughneck machine worker, who was involved from the beginning, asked how a new owner would manage what the former had not previously succeeded in, which Charlie said was a legitimate question.

"First, we will add resources, in the form of new management. Then, new resources in the form of new machines and tools. Then we will probably set up our own stores and partially broaden the range, and with joint forces we will make Genio grow."

This struck home with the staff.

"Good sales work," said Jeff, who apparently hadn't spent much time on so-called pep talks with his staff.

"I meant every word," Charlie said.

"It was noticeable," Jeff replied.

After the meeting, Charlie told Jeff in order to keep him away from the factory on Saturday that he had a new, green Cadillac Sedan de Ville that was "loaded" with every conceivable accessory in the exhibit hall, and that he was welcome at ten the following day for a demo. Jeff was immediately interested and thanked Charlie for the kindness and accepted.

"It's so nice that I would take it myself, if I didn't have free access to demos," said Charlie, pleased with his small plan.

Jeff arrived as planned exactly at ten o'clock. After a brief tour of the hall he got also greet the new CEO, Bill Hart. Bill had been inaugurated on the plan and would keep Jeff busy with showing the car and test driving, until after lunch, and being reasonably convincing, so that Jeff would really buy the car as well.

Charlie went over to Genio to check that the lock change went as planned and there were four locksmiths who were doing the work. He was given a set of keys for his own part and a special key for a special lock, for his own office.

Back at the company, Bill, Jeff and Charlie met in Bill's office, formerly belonging to Charlie.

"We have sold a very nice car today," Bill told his chairman of the board. Jeff was clearly pleased. The documents and the preparation of the car would take a while, but who was in a hurry?

"We can probably accept a check," Charlie joked. *Best to take him on now when he's in a good mood, and Bill can be a mediator if need be*, Charlie thought. Charlie asked Gail to order sandwiches from Arby's and to bring them into the conference room. When the papers were signed and the sandwiches were in place, Charlie warmed Jeff up again by thanking him for the deal that had been made the day before, in the same room.

Jeff was rather ferocious and chewed frantically when Charlie dropped the bomb:

"For security reasons, we changed locks, in the factory today," he said calmly.

Jeff stopped chewing, but it was obviously hard to come up with something sensible, with his mouth full of food. During a brief but strained silence, he managed to park what he had in his mouth in the designated place and wondered offended: "Don't you trust me?"

"Of course, we do," Charlie replied, "but that's how we want it— no surprises."

As if on cue, a knock on the door and the workshop manager stuck in his head. "One green de Ville ready for departure," he said.

Bill thanked him and his head disappeared.

Jeff had calmed down and seemed to accept that his key chain was now useless. Bill handed over two new bundles of car keys to Jeff. Shiny keys in black leather cases with "Cadillac" in gold imprinted in the leather. If Jeff was disappointed, it wasn't possible to judge by his surface. Charlie and Bill followed him out to the new car parked outside the service shop.

"Nice to do business with you," Charlie told Jeff.

"The same" Jeff answered in a somewhat mysterious way. When he left, Charlie said, "I will never understand him."

"I'll write to him in a few weeks, just to thank him for the deal and ask if he's happy with his new car," Bill said.

"It's a good idea," Charlie said.

"Salespeople and I always do in Tampa," added Bill.

"No wonder you are successful," Charlie said, relieved that all went well with Jeff.

On Monday, Charlie started at Genio at seven. He wanted to check that the keys worked and get to know the factory. The staff who dropped in just before eight o'clock were clearly impressed, with the new manager's early presence. It was appreciated Charlie noticed.

He took a cup of coffee, in the dining room that was empty of staff, until the machine attendant who had asked him a question, during Friday's meeting came in.

"Sit down and have a cup of coffee with me," Charlie asked.

"How did you think my little song of praise sounded last Friday?" Charlie wondered, used to talking to people in their own way.

"You know," replied the man, "we never got any information before."

"Information is important," Charlie said.

"You should know that they have run this company like a fucking whorehouse," the man said.

"What do you mean?" Charlie wondered.

"We'll take care of machines, right?"

"Um-hum," Charlie replied.

"We have so many products that we spend half the time changing tools."

"There will be a change to that," Charlie replied, and continued, "we will go from short series with high conversion costs to long series with high margins and low conversion costs."

"Sounds good in my ears," the operator answered and excused himself.

Charlie spent the day in the factory. Talked to everyone and recorded the flows and processes. His first impression was about dirt. A cleaning company would spend a weekend cleaning up the factory floor, dining room, toilets, in short everywhere.

He noted that the machines were heavy and that you did not move them around unnecessarily. What he wanted to do was to divide the factory into three departments: toys, key manufacturing and overtime. The latter he had seen while visiting a car customer a few years earlier. If machines were to be taken from toy manufacturing, overtime would be needed for those who remained for the same production volume. In addition, there were only a few machines available initially for keys, so they could probably work shifts. If you divided certain machines for overtime and shifts, you likely got an easy overview of the raw material flows and it indirectly stimulated the others who did not work overtime. *Psychology contributed in many ways*, Charlie thought.

He asked the chief financial officer, a thirty-year-old football fanatic, for a list of suppliers of plastic pellets, with associated prices and qualities. He had to ask twice as the volume on the radio was lowered, after the first round of questions. Looking at the list, Charlie noted that nothing was manufactured in Florida.

Then I might as well buy the goods in Tokyo, he thought.

After a long meeting with the chief foreman, Charlie had enough documentation, for a letter to the Tokyo commercial building. Mr. Otani was obviously retired, if he was still alive, but Charlie referred to him as well as Aussie Sponges and The Opal Association in the letter, which was a tender request. *First, lower purchase prices, then test run production*, Charlie thought. He invited Jim to have a look at the machines and to judge if any of these were suitable for key conversion.

Another problem, he quickly wanted to fix was the heat in the factory. Fans were available, but cooling systems were necessary as the machines generated a lot of heat, especially in September when it was thirty-five degrees C. outside.

Two weeks later, Peter came. He had matured, during his more than two years in Canada, and radiated Charlie's confidence. He had Shannon's colors—dark hair and fair complexion. The first thing he did was jump in the pool and play with Morris.

"If you sleep out, you can come to Genio tomorrow," Charlie said.

"Well, I have to admit that I'm curious about my new job," Peter replied.

Jim had already done a test tool and the rough-cut machine operator had tried punching, with some plastics that were hard in their cold state, with mixed results. At the Genio lunch, the next day, the new marketing manager was introduced to the staff. It was clear that his responsibility would be the new product line, Keys. His mere presence was reason enough for the existing marketing manager, now sales manager for toys, to shape up his actions, so as not to risk being outmaneuvered by Peter.

Charlie had experienced a rare inertia, with the CFO, and he would soon be replaced. He ran some club life associated with football, during company time and it would be the machine shop next for him as soon as any replacement was available. Chuck was told to search and Peter as well.

Peter had already concluded that he counted better than the CFO when it came to product calculations and that you could hardly trust the man. Peter had many friends in Boca, and one of them had advised of a public accountant at the age of thirty who he knew had a good reputation among the companies and whom Peter could contact. He asked his friend to arrange a lunch where the three could meet, which happened a few days later.

Peter told in colorful terms about the newly formed group whose future was written in the stars. The accountant was named Michael Kelley and had Irish descent. He liked what he heard Peter say and was attracted by the unwritten future of the group. Michael himself perceived Peter as a true optimist, typical of a salesman and perhaps also typical, for a son of a car dealer.

He said he was generally interested, and Peter invited Michael to Genio the following Saturday, to meet Charlie and Chuck. What Michael saw in the future was, of course, the opportunity to replace Chuck and that it could be good, with a few years of experience, in a manufacturing company. On Saturday morning, Michael came to Genio and saw two Cadillac's parked outside.

Of course, he thought, stepping into the office. After about two hours, it was quite clear that Charlie and Michael fit together like a glove.

"I can present report cards if you wish," he said.

"Your word is enough," Charlie replied.

"What are your requirements of me?" Michael wondered.

"What I ask, and demand, is that you take full responsibility for the finance function of the company," Charlie replied in plain text, adding, "and what are you requesting?"

"I demand full responsibility, for the finance function of the company," Michael replied. Charlie smiled and reached out his hand. Michael took it and thus became Genio's new chief financial officer. Only then was the salary discussion started and a draft employment contract was written by Chuck. Michael had one month's notice and the parties agreed that he would begin on November 1st.

Two weeks after meeting Michael, just before Charlie's 50th birthday on October 4, 1985, a pizza delivery came to the door.

"We haven't ordered any pizza," Peter told the delivery boy.

"Special delivery to Charlie Long—is that you?" wondered the boy.

"No, I'll get Dad," Peter replied. Charlie came to the door and then the messenger handed out an envelope.

"You are hereby served notice," said the messenger, pushing the envelope into Charlie's hand and left.

"What was that about?" Shannon wondered.

"Probably, it is VenCap who wants to sue me for the purchase of the company but let me read it first."

Charlie's fears were confirmed. The lawsuit stated that "the owner emptied the company of its assets to the detriment of the applicant."

"Well," Charlie said, "they have a hard time proving it because we've done everything at current market values based on external valuations—we can fight them with loaded guns."

"Idiots" growled Peter.

"I'm faxing this to Steve tomorrow and letting him represent me in court," Charlie continued.

The next day, Steve called a few minutes after Charlie faxed the letter.

"Of course, I accept your case," he said, and continued: "I do not need to attend the first court appearance. It is a so-called oral preparation in which the plaintiff puts forward the very issue and the grounds, and the defendant, yourself, disputes whatever the plaintiff has demanded."

Oral preparation was set for the fourth of October.

"Ask to get it postponed," Shannon asked.

"After all, it's not reasonable to have to show up on your 50th birthday," Peter said.

"Asking for a postponement would be a sign of unclean flour in the bag. The case, itself, may take no more than a few minutes," assured Charlie, who was going to attend. Shannon had planned a garden party on Charlie's birthday, with a reserve booking at the Boca Raton Country Club in case of bad weather. Anyway, Charlie was unaware of the planned party.

MICHAEL OWENS

CHAPTER TWENTY-FOUR

The hearing was to be held at 09:30 in the town hall, with its Alamo form. Charlie met a VenCap representative, in the corridor and the parties were invited before a judge. A secretary took notes. The parties presented themselves and the judge asked the plaintiff to submit the contents of the lawsuit. The short version was precisely that Charlie was considered to have acted with calculated negligence when he purchased the assets from Long Cadillac and that the plaintiff could show that this was the case by having had external valuations prepared of the assets and the business itself.

"And how does the defendant claim?" the judge asked. "The defendant is contesting the suit in its entirety," Charlie said.

The judge asked the secretary to note that the main hearing would take place at the same time two weeks later, provided the parties had nothing to object to, which they did not. They had to wait outside under tense silence for a few minutes, until the secretary had finished printing. Charlie was convinced that Steve had given him correct advice in connection with the transfer and therefore felt calm.

The rest of the day was a complete pleasure for Charlie. When he got home, brunch was waiting on the terrace, with only family members and little Morris who was now half grown. In the afternoon, several catering cars arrived, and they set up long tables on the lawn. During the day, there were couriered flowers, and many who could not attend in the evening came by to congratulate Charlie. In the evening, everyone he could wish for attended, and Shannon had a special surprise for Charlie.

"G'day, Mate!" a familiar voice from the patio door shouted loudly, so it was heard all over the garden. Ritch stood on the terrace, with a big smile on his tanned face, with outstretched arms. Charlie was totally surprised and screamed:

"Ritch!" and ran forward and gave him a real bear hug. He was told that Preb greeted and that Preb was now satisfied with his life in retirement. The other guests had to cope without Charlie's attention and realized that this was a true friend from ancient times. Ritch had visited his family in California and would now be in Boca for a few days to greet Charlie and Shannon.

"Nothing could have been more fun!" exclaimed Charlie.

The party was a nice event and when all the other guests had gone, it was swimming and small talk with Ritch, until they almost fell asleep. The next day was a beautiful late summer day and everyone took time off. Charlie took the whole family, Ritch and Morris on a day trip, with their Merlin, and Anna and Peter found out how things were in Australia, in Dad's time. It was an exciting story. Now, Ritch was alone in running Aussie Sponges, with half a dozen employees. His own business was thriving and consisted mostly of servicing recreational boats and taking tourists on charter trips, with a larger boat than the one Preb owned.

Sandy had died a few years earlier, but Preb entertained himself and tourists on the docks as a true original, from a bygone era, always with his Aquavit within easy reach. Ritch had no plans to return to America. He had married a girl from Cairns and they had two teenage daughters, he told them. He had been lucky, he said and found just the right things in life.

"I can't be happier than that, though I miss you two," he said to Mr. and Mrs. Long, with a little smile. He asked Anna a little curiously why she was named Anna. She told them that Grandma had been called Anna and that she was proud of her name. "Peter then?" Ritch wondered.

"After my brother, Pete," Shannon replied.

"Your children then?" Anna wondered.

"I wondered if you would ask," Ritch replied. "The oldest's name is Shannon, after you know who, and the youngest is Margaret, but is called Margi."

"Dad, can we visit them? We want to see how you lived then!" said Anna.

"You are always more than welcome," Ritch said.

"We are happy to come to Australia. It's summer at your end soon," Charlie said. "Definitely," Ritch said.

Two weeks later, at the same time, at 09:30, the hearing began. The court consisted of a judge, a notary and a secretary. VenCap was represented by a lawyer who looked like he came from a '40s movie, too big a suit and fluffy, brown hair. Laurel was also there. Charlie was present and Steve as well. The judge read out the grounds of the lawsuit and asked if VenCap sustained the charges. The lawyer answered the question with a short "yes."

Then, the defendant was asked about his response to the charges, to which Steve replied briefly: "Disputed in its entirety."

The judge asked the plaintiff to state the reasons for his dissatisfaction, and the lawyer began with the following: "You have done everything wrong." *Shotgun tactics* were something that *liquor* attorneys were devoted to, Steve thought, and calmly replied, "Can you develop the allegation?" The lawyer continued: "To the detriment of my client, the defendant has emptied Long Cadillac of its assets at underpricing."

The judge asked the lawyer to substantiate the claim. The lawyer continued: "We have let a property appraiser value the properties and McKinsey value the business and we have come to the conclusion that the price you paid was below fair value by at least a million dollars."

The judge asked the lawyer to present the two documents, which the lawyer handed to the judge. The judge continued: "What is the defendant's opinion regarding the values?" Steve replied: "We have not been given the opportunity to review the evidence why we can neither dispute nor substantiate the case."

The judge continued: "You testify that you have acted according to the plaintiff's accusations that you have, in fact, purchased the operations from Long Cadillac, and then renamed the company to" Bob's Fast Foods," is that correct?"

Steve replied briefly, "That's right."

The judge continued: "What did you base the purchase price on?"

Steve: "Market value according to external valuation of the real estate, and the same with respect to the business."

The judge: "Are the documents in the courtroom?"

Steve: "Yes."

The judge: "Hand them to me."

Steve: "Your Honor, permission to speak?"

Judge: "Granted."

Steve: "We can probably save time, if the plaintiff's property valuation could be read out in court, one property at a time, for comparison with our own."

Judge: "Granted." The judge asked the notary to read the values according to the list. Just as expected, the Tampa and St, Petersburg branches were included at a total of one million dollars.

"Your honor," said Steve, "it seems that the plaintiff made a mistake in the valuation." The judge asked Steve to continue.

Steve: "Two of the branches, the one in Tampa and the one in St. Petersburg were not owned by the company, but by Charlie Long personally, and therefore should not be included in the company's total value." Laurel became high red in the face but managed to keep his anger to himself.

The judge replied that the court thus had reason to question the plaintiff's evidence and asked Charlie to certify what Steve had stated.

"I hereby certify that I am the owner of the properties in Tampa and St. Petersburg," Charlie said.

"You certify under oath," said the judge.

"I stand by my affidavit," Charlie said.

The judge: "We thus have a defect in the plaintiff's valuation data, which amounts to the corresponding amount that the plaintiff claims that the defendant's actions caused harm to the plaintiff, which is why I will dismiss the action, unless the plaintiff has otherwise to allege."

Laurel was now white as a sheet. The lawyer representing VenCap asked for five minutes of individual consultation with his client, which was granted. When they returned to the courtroom, the judge asked, "Do you stand by your case or do you have something else to add?"

The lawyer replied: "We have nothing to say regarding the valuations, but the company had an unpaid dividend with the same amount as the omission of valuation, which should benefit my client."

The judge briefly conferred with the notary and said: "A dividend is a capital issue that is separate from market value and therefore cannot be a liability of a buyer who has paid market value. Furthermore, it is not customary to invoke set-offs in a courtroom when the damages issue does not bear fruit. Does the plaintiff have anything to add?"

"The plaintiff has nothing to add," the lawyer replied, annoyed.

"The court rejects the case against Charlie Long," the judge said, striking his mallet.

"Amateurs," Steve said quietly to Charlie, as they smiled and shook hands.

CHAPTER TWENTY-FIVE

Boca Raton, FL · November 1, 1985

"Welcome" said Charlie and Peter in chorus when Michael Kelley came into the office. Charlie noticed that Michael was the only one wearing a tie and he liked that.

We will have professional style at Long Thermotech, he thought. After a brief introduction in Charlie's office, Peter was to direct Michael to his office. On arriving, Michael saw that someone was sitting at the desk in what would be Michael's office.

"This is your office," Peter said to Michael, who thought it was a little strange to just barge in on someone. "What is he doing in my office?" Michael wondered.

"This was his office until you arrived," Peter replied. "Charlie wants to talk to you," Peter told the CFO.

"Come in," Charlie told the CFO. "You have shown that you can hardly handle the role you have had here, at Genio," Charlie said, and continued: "You have two options: one is to run a machine out in production. The second is to leave the company today, with a full month's salary and good grades."

"I probably knew the job was a little more than I could handle," was the reply. He accepted the latter tender, retrieved his personal belongings and left the firm.

"We go our own way and we go in a line straight as an arrow," Charlie told Michael.

"The first thing we will do is create a division for the toys that we will continue to call Genio, he continued. "We are going to run in parallel with keys and if the new department with keys is successful, we might discontinue the toy division."

"Understood," replied Michael, who liked when someone pointed with their whole hand. "Then we will figure out how we can take the key market. We will bring down the purchase price, buy good value tools, and we will calculate a good margin. Then we will offer our products at the price we can live with, which then hopefully will make a clean sweep of other suppliers," Charlie said.

Michael started his new job by getting to know what the staff at the office were doing, and soon noted that there was a lot of internal analyses per product. This was eliminated in favor of better accounts receivable routines and better utilization of staff. Gail got Michael's attention when she read a newspaper at the front desk. She at once became responsible for letter writing and mail handling.

"If we are to grow, we must all do more work than we have done before," he had told her. Most people appreciated increased responsibility, and nobody protested. Michael and Peter were both driven in their respective fields but were completely different in general. They went well together as colleagues but were sometimes like cat and dog, although it could, as it usually did, lead to a good result for the company.

"That's what matters," Michael was often heard uttering.

Charlie came back after a meeting with Jim about the tools. Charlie heard Reggae music from inside Michael's room. *Another one,* Charlie thought and went in to see him. Michael lowered the sound and greeted Charlie who realized his misjudgment.

"Do you like music?" Charlie wondered.

"Yes," replied Michael, "and yourself?" he wondered.

"Very, albeit in moderate doses," Charlie replied. "We'll buy the tools for the machines on installment," Charlie told Michael. "If you can figure out what we can afford per manufactured key, we can submit a suggestion to Jim."

The calculation was phenomenal. The two types of plastic that had been bought from the Tokyo trading house were at the Yen rate that prevailed at half the purchase price versus other suppliers in America. LTT was able to punch out keys for about five cents each, including one cent to Jim. A price of ten cents would give 100 percent in margin, which surprised even Charlie. LTT could offer keys to a complete keyboard for a personal computer for just over ten dollars and it was assumed that others needed twice that price. Peter was given the challenge of offering complete keyboard keys at the price of fifteen dollars, at which he could discount on large volumes. Not too much discount, because that would be unprofessional, but a little.

Peter received a test order from IBM on 1,000 sets of keys. It became the prelude to Charlie's entry into the personal computer business and of the growth company LTT in Boca Raton, Florida. The industry for these machines grew at an avalanche rate, during the rest of the 1980s and into the '90s. In the first years, after the acquisition of Genio, the group had shown red numbers, but after breakeven results in 1988, profits had steadily increased. LTT in Boca gradually gained market share and the machines went hot in the factory, which produced millions of manufactured units per month, in 1990.

That same year, the US economy went into a recession, which was not noticed by LTT but significantly by the parent company, Long Cadillac, and others. Drexel Burnham Lambert went bankrupt in April 1990, because of insider deals and Michael Milken was jailed and fined $600 million (in 2020, Michael Milken was pardoned by President Trump, after being a thirty-year felon).

That same fall, Long Cadillac repaid the entire bond loan, partly with the help of new financing in its own bank, at lower interest rates. Anna studied literature at Berkeley University, in San Francisco and Peter was now the marketing manager at LTT, including the Genio division, which also went well. Genio had its own stores in the Mall of America in Minneapolis, Miami and a few other locations in Florida and Charlie was approached by "Toys R Us" about a possible sale.

However, Charlie had some concerns about selling one of his "three legs." Cars, keys and toys in combination had a counter-cyclical effect and balanced the Group. If and when the keys became the major part of the business, he could consider selling the Genio part. Five years later, in 1995, personal computer manufacturing was in astronomical growth, with new customers such as "Dell," "Compaq" and "Hewlett Packard" on the computer side and with Honeywell and Texas Instruments on the calculator side.

Turnover had doubled in the last five years and LTT was well known in the market. Steve was commissioned by Charlie to sell the Genio part, as a separate unit, and in September 1995, the manufacturing of the stores was bought out by Toys R Us, for a staggering $12 million. (The company that then bought out Genio had a wobbly time as a listed company, until March 2005, when a consortium, among others, consisting of Kohlberg, Kravis and Roberts, popularly called "KKR" and others bought it for the order of five billion dollars!). The time after the spin out was the best of all time for LTT. The last years of the '90's had a boom without parallel in world history and LTT punched out profits of one million dollars a month!

Steve had through his contacts in Minneapolis found out that ITT would be interested in taking over LTT. Public companies have a good memory, and Steve's participation was excluded because of his previous involvement when Irwin Jacobs tried to take over ITT in the mid-1980s.

Charlie, of course, knew he would be happy no matter who he sold to, but one ambition he had was to make sure the business remained in Boca. Steve recommended a partner in his industry who had become a major player in the corporate brokerage world on Wall Street and also in Washington on permit issues, namely Oppenheimer, based in Minneapolis. Their lead team was a couple of colleagues named Pierce Fonseca (popularly called "Fonzie" after the TV series) and Tom McNally.

Just in time for Charlie's 65th birthday, October 4, 2000, as markets were about to peak, Long Cadillac spun out LTT to another conglomerate for one hundred million dollars even.

Peter became Marketing Manager for Long Cadillac and Michael became CFO of the same company. Charlie was happy with Shannon and wanted to celebrate his life's triumph, with her in their own way—a trip with the Merlin boat, just the two of them and with a little Champagne.

"It's time to hand over the helm now," Charlie said as he toasted with the love of his life.

"To me?" Shannon wondered with a smile.

"Not the rudder. The firm!" Charlie replied. "You know?" he continued: "We have seen a continent on the other side of the earth closer than America. Now I think we should see our own."

Shannon agreed in her graceful manner, raised her glass and said, "Charlie, you're the best thing that ever happened to me," and then Charlie steered his Merlin toward the sunset.

The End

EPILOGUE

In the spring of 2001, six months after Charlie succeeded in selling his subsidiary, LTT, at a full ten times the annual profit, the world markets collapsed in a recession. The value of LTT was halved. However, it did not matter to the buyer, as the acquisition was profitable in that it acquired significant market shares in a profitable industry, in which they were already a very large player.

Sales in most industries slowed down considerably, in the early years of the new millennium, but the personal computer industry would recover. By 2003, the staggering number of one billion personal computers had been manufactured, and development only continued.

Charlie had two trump cards to play.

The land he owned outside of Boca was still undeveloped, and was located close to the land which was now in the city itself. Land values in Florida had not been affected by the business cycle, but on the contrary had increased in value, and Charlie sold the land at a tremendous price.

The land in Tampa and St. Petersburg was sold to Long Cadillac at market value, which was equivalent to twenty-five times what he had paid, just as many years earlier.

Anna had married a schoolmate, moved to the ranch, and led a good life in California on the open lands, with their three sons.

Charlie and Shannon bought a Winnebago camper van and spent a couple of years experiencing their own continent. The sea still attracted them. From the ranch they drove to the southern tip of the California peninsula, "Cabo San Lucas," in Mexico, and then north along the coast to Vancouver, Canada. From Vancouver Island, they followed the whale's migration from a tourist ship.

"My life has been a long journey," Charlie told Shannon, as he saw the whales.

"You followed the same direction your nose had, and you marveled at what you found—and fortunately you did it with me," Shannon replied tenderly.

"Ten-four."

The Author's thanks.

The catalyst for this book is partly my own experiences and partly gathered from friends and various written sources. The ambition has been to reproduce these as truthfully as possible with the hope of having done both individuals, landscapes and the mentioned nations justice. The contributions to the story from Charlie Gunnarsson and Bengt Karlsson have been invaluable. Charlie provided the name of the main character and the depictions at sea. Bengt contributed, with the depictions from Australia. Both of these stories were self-experienced. In no certain order, you, my friends, have all contributed, consciously or not: Heléna Owens, my constant companion who put up with me during my work with this book, Colonel Fredrik Hedén, who through stories from actual events and through joint flights, has enriched and maintained my interest in flight. "Red" Scritsmyer, who let me feed his pigs from his old Ford at the ranch in Pomona, just outside of Los Angeles.

Attorney Jim Pedersen, Minneapolis, who has informed me of his experiences, since the 1980s.

Tim Owens, my cousin in Madeira Beach, FL, who was my host there and on the Suwanee River.

Nils Källmark, who gave me insights on personal computer production in Boca Raton.

Sten Caap, who patiently told me about computers.

Magdalena Sundbrandt, who shared with me her experiences

from Opal-mining work in Coober Pedy.

Björn Axelsson, who gave me detailed insight about Sydney.

Elizabeth Sandberg and Annika Lobelius, who patiently read the parts of the book after which it progressed, inspired commentary on the content, and encouraged me to continue.

Bengt Lundström, whose confidence and genuine experience contributed significantly to the book's overall content.

William "Bill" M. Owens, my late father, pilot colleague, and brother of James J. Owens (who died in a rescue mission near Santa Monica during World War II) who took me to El Toro Air Base, CA, Carlsbad Caverns, NM., Fort Alamo, TX., Corpus Christi, TX., The Harlingen, TX Air Museum, and countless other places.

Robyne Thorley, who helped me with Australian expressions.

Colonel Per-Olof Eldh, who shared with me his experiences at the meeting with a "Habu," or Blackbird.

Last, but not least, all of you who not mentioned above who have shown interest in and encouraged this book.

My warmest thanks to you all.
Michael Owens
In June 2005.

www.ingramcontent.com/pod-product-compliance
Lightning Source LLC
Chambersburg PA
CBHW072320280626
47159CB00027B/111